best
sports
stories
1979

best sports stories 1979

**A PANORAMA OF THE 1978 SPORTS WORLD
INCLUDING THE 1978 CHAMPIONS OF ALL SPORTS
WITH THE YEAR'S TOP PHOTOGRAPHS**

Edited by Irving T. Marsh and Edward Ehre

E. P. DUTTON / NEW YORK

Marsh having dedicated one volume to his numerous grandchildren, Ehre dedicates this one to his two sons, Steven and Paul.

For information contact: E.P. Dutton, 2 Park Avenue,
New York, N.Y. 10016

Library of Congress Catalog Card Number: 45-35124
ISBN: 0-525-06625-X

Published simultaneously in Canada by Clarke, Irwin & Company
Limited, Toronto and Vancouver

10 9 8 7 6 5 4 3 2 1

First Edition

CONTENTS

ILLUSTRATIONS

PREFACE

After 35 years of competition, we have something new to announce:

For the first time in the *Best Sports Stories* series, which began in 1944, a tie for the top and the $250 award has been voted by our three judges—John Chamberlain, John Hutchens, and Jerry Nason—in *all* three divisions of our annual competition. We've had ties in one and even two classifications in the past, but never in all three in one year.

Of the six co-winners, however, only one is a repeater. That would be Dave Klein of the *Newark Star-Ledger* who won the news-feature award outright a year ago for his fine story "Wells Twombly, 41, the Laughter Still Echoes." This year, to show his virtuosity, he took half of the *news-coverage* award for his story on the Larry Holmes-Ken Norton fight in Las Vegas, "The Boxer Unseats the Puncher." And Steve Jacobson of Long Island's *Newsday*, often a contributor but never a winner, gained the other half with his fine piece on the final game of the World Series, "The Yankees Finally Can Say It."

Two first-time winners although previous contributors—Betty Cuniberti of *The Washington Post* and Tony Kornheiser of the *New York Times*—split the news-feature prize: Ms. Cuniberti for her story on Nancy Lopez "Her Hands Were Meant For Golf" and Kornheiser for his thoughtful piece on the New York Yankees outfielder, "Reggie Jackson's Lonely World." The magazine story co-winners were writers making their debuts in *Best Sports Stories*—Phil Berger for his word portrait of Leon Spinks in *Playboy* and Colin Campbell for his exciting article, "The Sharkers," that ran in *Sports Afield*.

There's one other interesting little tidbit: Among the magazine pieces "Thriller on the River" by Paul (Tex) Chandler is reprinted from *The Angolite*, the publication of Louisiana State Penitentiary of Angolite, La.

As has been the custom throughout this series, the stories were submitted to the judges blind, each identified by a one- or two-word "slug," newspaperese for an identifying label. Hence you will note that each story was so called by the judges in the box score and their comments, which follow:

THE BOX SCORE
(Winners in Caps)

News-Coverage Stories	Chamber-lain	Hutchens	Nason	*Total Points
Series Final [The Yankees Finally Can Say It by Steve Jacobson]	–	1	3	4
Holmes [The Boxer Unseats the Puncher by Dave Klein]	–	2	2	4
Indy [The 500 Seems to Last Forever by Edwin Pope]	–	3	–	3
3d Series [The Incredible Graig Nettles by Hal Bodley]	3	–	–	3
Masters [Man on a Crusade by Jon Roe]	2	–	–	2
Wimbledon [Martina Is Proud by Barry Lorge]	1	–	1	2

News-Feature Stories				
Nancy [Her Hands Were Meant for Golf by Betty Cuniberti]	3	–	1	4
Reggie [Reggie Jackson's Lonely World by Tony Kornheiser]	1	–	3	4
Derby [The Irish Haberdasher's Dream by Jim Murray]	–	3	–	3
Joe [And Still Champion by John Schulian]	–	1	2	3
Woody [Love Him or Hate Him by Joe Lapointe]	2	–	–	2
Team [They'd Win in Any Game by Leigh Montville]	–	–	2	2

Magazine Stories				
Spinks [Spinks by Phil Berger]	3	–	2	5
Shark [The Sharkers by Colin Campbell]	2	–	3	5
Red [Sports Writing's Poet Laureate by Harry Stein]	–	3	1	4
Stadium [Behind the Scenes at Baltimore's Big Bowl by Michael Nelson]	–	2	–	2
Triple Crown [Diary of a Triple Crown Winner by Jim Bolus]	1	1	–	2

*Based on 3 points for a first-place vote, 2 for a second, 1 for a third

JUDGES' COMMENTS

John Chamberlain

News-Coverage Stories

1. 3rd Series [The Incredible Graig Nettles by Hal Bodley]
2. Masters [Man on a Crusade by Jon Roe]
3. Wimbledon [Martina Is Proud by Barry Lorge]

1. One man's skill is another man's luck. Guidry didn't have it in that Series game that might have put Los Angeles three ahead of the Yankees. But Nettles did have it for four incredible vacuum cleaner plays at third base. The reporter couldn't miss on this story if he had stuck to simple descriptions, but he makes it a superlative news story by adding good interview bits.

2. There is subtlety in this story of Gary Player's Masters win. I like particularly the touches about Player's use of knowledge of Masters difficulties that he had gained in other years.

3. In beating Chris Evert by a comeback from a 2–4 deficit in a final set Martina Navratilova did not unravel nor does this news-coverage of her victory go to pieces. Good, straight dramatic reporting here.

News-Feature Stories

1. Nancy [Her Hands Were Meant for Golf by Betty Cuniberti]
2. Woody [Love Him or Hate Him by Joe Lapointe]
3. Reggie [Reggie Jackson's Lonely World by Tony Kornheiser]

1. The story of Nancy Lopez's rise to the top in women's golf is all warmhearted appeal. It is a family story about a nice girl who finishes first. The father's part in the story is touchingly handled. What a pair!

2. This story of Woody Hayes' refusal ever to mellow was written before his final disgrace. It explains much in advance about a come-uppance that could hardly have surprised the author.

3. This is a great story of a paradox. How, you ask as the author takes you through Florida's Alligator Alley with Reggie Jackson, can you expect a man to be paranoid while driving an $80,000 Rolls, which he has bought with his spare cash? The curious thing is that the author does explain Reggie, a man who is too easily hurt.

Magazine Stories

1. Spinks [Spinks by Phil Berger]
2. Shark [The Sharkers by Colin Campbell]
3. Triple Crown [Diary of a Triple Crown Winner by Jim Bolus]

1. When Spinks beat Ali, it was more than a mixed-up kid from a ghetto could handle. It is the inexorable piling up of foreboding detail that makes this a memorable magazine story. The sudden remembrance of what happened to battling Siki, the Senegalese who died in a barroom brawl in New York in 1925, makes an ominous close. The story was written before Spinks lost in a rematch with Ali. Maybe he was lucky to lose—that could wake him up.

2. When you bring a 1,039-pound mako shark home after playing it for 12 hours, you've got a story that would appeal to Ernest Hemingway. Whether you could write it in an appropriate Hemingway fashion is something else. The author has succeeded in a complex task. Where Hemingway had only a single psychology to explain in *The Old Man and the Sea*, in this story there were four men and a boy engaged in bringing the mako back to Montauk. They are all made real in a dramatic running account of a most scary day.

3. Triple Crown has much of the density of Spinks. It also has a great deal of excitement.

John Hutchens

News-Coverage Stories

1. Indy [The 500 Seems to Last Forever by Edwin Pope]
2. Holmes [The Boxer Unseats the Puncher by Dave Klein]
3. Series Final [The Yankees Finally Can Say It by Steve Jacobson]

1. What's the Indianapolis 500 really like? I had thought I knew a little something about it, but this piece fills me in on the reality. For instance, the author argues that the crowd of 350,000—as obscene and disgusting as a great part of it really is—does not come primarily to see accidents and death. Arguable still, perhaps, but interesting, along with "wonder at the madness of 32 men and one woman driving grenades on wheels, wearing helmets as potential death masks, knowing there can be only one winner." (The woman is Janet Guthrie, in herself a story, an eighth-place finisher here in an awesome field.) TV never can really give you the full picture, the author suggests, but it will tell you more after you have read this eyewitness report, so rich in background and incidental detail.

2. To read this account of an incredibly close heavyweight fight is to return to the age of all-out battle in which odds change throughout the melee, a single round is the determining factor between boxer and slugger, and, even so, the result is in doubt until the last second and winds up as a split decision. You *are* at the ringside here, which is what a fight story in its best tradition sets as its goal.

3. One of the fine baseball pieces of recent memory, capturing as it does the climax of the New York Yankees' unprecedented come-from-

behind saga, the championship of the world after a 14-game deficit in mid-July. Even lifelong Yankee-haters saluted them, and here is the reason why.

News-Feature Stories

1. Derby [The Irish Haberdasher's Dream by Jim Murray]
2. Team [They'd Win in Any Game by Leigh Montville]
3. Joe [And Still Champion by John Schulian]

1. A lot of us have been waiting a long time for a jocular jape like this one about the great first-Saturday-in-May con game known as the Kentucky Derby. Doubtless there have been others, but if so I have missed them, and in any case here is a fine, sardonic, highly entertaining look at all the nonsense, outright larceny, etc. that gives "Ripoffsville, U.S.A." its annual shot at mythlore.

2. Another fetching work, this one an enticing screwball item that, if you read it late at night, will find you waking up some hours later with various odd visions. What's this team? Somehow it includes Billie Jean King, Vida Blue, Ted Williams, Willie Shoemaker, Dallas Cowboy cheerleaders, Luis Tiant, Roberto Duran, plenty of chewers, spitters, and cursers but no figure skaters or swimmers. Quite a team indeed. Send for your ticket now.

3. A sad, effective portrait, this one, of one of the titanic stalwarts of his time, now fast running out. It is Joe Louis at the dinner given for him by his friends last winter at Las Vegas, and I venture to guess that no one who recalls him in his prime as fearless boxer, soldier, trail-blazer for his fellow blacks, later betrayed and neglected by many who should have revered him, can read this without profound emotion.

Magazine Stories

1. Red [Sports Writing's Poet Laureate by Harry Stein]
2. Stadium [Behind the Scenes at Baltimore's Big Bowl by Michael Nelson]
3. Triple Crown [Diary of a Triple Crown Winner by Jim Bolus]

1. A warm, admiring portrait of the best-known current sports writer, and how he came to be what he is, and how he works and still achieves at an age when a good many of his sometime colleagues and contemporaries have turned it in.

2. Even old baseball fans may never have been aware that a night game starts, after a fashion, at 6:30 in the morning. Here is a remarkable chronicle of all that went on, beginning at that hour, on a day and evening in September 1977 at Memorial Stadium in Baltimore whose Orioles were struggling to close in on the league-leading Yankees—how the early morning seat-sweepers work, what the umpires do during the day, the

tarp crew praying for no rain, the radio and television announcers fishing around for lines they will use tonight if the rain goes on and on. A regular day game must seem like a holiday.

3. An absorbing diligent narrative of the second and third acts of the Triple Crown drama, the Preakness and the Belmont—owners, trainers, jockeys, above all the two wonderful contending horses, Affirmed and Alydar, and the subtle strategies formulated for them. And, of course, moment-by-moment descriptions of the two races that were to determine whether the wonder-boy Kentuckian Steve Cauthen would become the youngest Triple Crown winner in American horse racing history.

Jerry Nason

News-Coverage Stories

1. Series Finals [The Yankees Finally Can Say It by Steve Jacobson]
2. Holmes [The Boxer Unseats the Puncher by Dave Klein]
3. Masters [Man on a Crusade by Jon Roe]

1. The Yankees winning a playoff, a pennant, and a Series may occur to you as being about as newsy as the proverbial journalistic dog biting a man, right? Wrong! The 1978 Yankees who climbed over a 14-game deficit, tied for their pennant, won the playoff, and then spotted the Dodgers the first two games of the World Series . . . Well, there you have it: a spot-news report that the writer took beyond the perimeters of his story on the sixth and final Series game. It was good judgment, and made under the gun, so to speak. It was also baseball reporting at its very best.

2. Next, I rated the vivacious report of the wild Holmes-Norton bout, a difficult deadline story to do and done extremely well.

3. Right on its heels, in my judgment, came the piece on Gary Player's winning of the Masters, a golf classic that was written with rare understanding of both the man and the situation he was in.

News-Feature Stories

1. Reggie [Reggie Jackson's Lonely World by Tony Kornheiser]
2. Joe [And Still Champion by John Schulian]
3. Nancy [Her Hands Were Meant for Golf by Betty Cuniberti]

1. The contributions made in this category are a treasure trove of good writing based on strong subject material. The piece on Cuban *beisbol* . . . the cynical view of Louisville and the Kentucky Derby . . . a typewriter tintype of Howard Cosell . . . a sports writer's cocktail-induced journey behind a trotting horse—all these and more. But this judge kept coming back, and back again, to "Reggie." A three-hour car ride on which the writer accompanied the controversial ball player to an exhibition game in Florida put the writer, and the reader, in closer communication with Jackson and provided a better understanding of this seeming extrovert

than anything this judge had previously encountered. It was a rare opportunity to come up with a good story, and here's a writer who made the most of it.

2. The Joe Louis piece was a heart wringer and 3, the piece labeled "Nancy" was superbly done—answering all your silent questions invoked by the appearance of a new and charming, and lethal, young woman in the ranks of professional golf.

Magazine Stories

1. Shark [The Sharkers by Colin Campbell]
2. Spinks [Spinks by Phil Berger]
3. Red [Sports Writing's Poet Laureate by Harry Stein]

1. "Shark" shapes up as the most exciting piece in the book—an almost terrifying report of an encounter with a giant mako in the deep waters of the North Atlantic, and of the four men and a boy who subdued it. Presumably the writer wasn't there, but created his reenactment of the event only after an enormous amount of interrogation of those who were. His task is so superbly accomplished that, even after two readings, you can smell the blood, sweat, chum, and terror; your arms ache from a prolonged struggle with this killer from the deep.

2. "Spinks" was obviously turned out by a real pro who adjusted the pace of his story to that of his subject—erratic. Pinning Spinks down for interview purposes was like attempting the capture of a cricket in a thimble, but between jumps this writer managed, somehow, to come up with a fascinating character study and, at the same time, a sensing of the confused world of Leon Spinks.

3. "Red" was excellent reading—a writer writing of another writer, but wisely electing to place his subject against the background of any day's assignments—sports.

* * * *

As for the photographs: We hope you look carefully at the winner of the action photo prize of $250, "Uneasy Rider's Nightmare" by Melissa Farlow of *The Courier-Journal* of Louisville, Ky. You will have to agree it's a tremendous shot. And the feature photo winner, "A Novel Student," by J. Don Cook of the *Daily Oklahoman*, is, shall we say, as cute as a feature photo should be.

So, here's our No. 35. Hopefully, you'll find it as intriguing as the previous 34.

IRVING T. MARSH
EDWARD EHRE

THE PRIZE-WINNING STORIES

Best News-Coverage (Co-Winner)

WORLD SERIES (Final Game)

THE YANKEES FINALLY CAN SAY IT

By Steve Jacobson

From Newsday
Copyright, ©, 1978, Newsday Inc.

In the beginning, it seemed that what the Yankees were trying to do was impossible. Certainly, for the longest time it was improbable. And then in the end they made it seem inevitable. Inexorable.

They did what they had to do. If they couldn't do enough, then they would lose, and looking back, they thought they were never afraid to lose. That, they thought, was why they couldn't lose.

The Yankees finished the World Series last night, beating the Dodgers 7–2, and winning the championship by four games to two. Even in the final game, they were betting underdogs as they had been in five of the six games and in the World Series as a whole. Then again, even gentlemen's bets gave the Yankees little chance of doing what they did.

They did what no team ever did. They won the showdown with Boston for the division championship, the scheduled playoff for the American League pennant, and the World Series. No team ever did all three. The Yankees lost the first two games of the World Series and then swept the next four. No team ever did that. And they came from 14 games behind in mid-July just to survive the summer.

Then they drank champagne to themselves. "It's the best thing that ever happened to baseball," shortstop Bucky Dent said in the euphoria of the clubhouse. "After this, other clubs will get behind and say, 'Look at the 1978 Yankees.' "

It was the Yankees' twenty-second World Series championship, culminating a season that was in many ways the most memorable.

Even in the consummate game, they came from behind. The first Dodgers batter of the night, Davey Lopes, hit a home run off Catfish Hunter. The thought was that maybe the Dodgers had been able to throw off the spell they found for themselves in New York. Then the Yankees put themselves in order in the top of the second inning with Brian Doyle doubling for the first run and Dent driving in two more with a single.

Right then, a peanut vendor in Aisle 3 of the seats painted Dodger blue expressed the feeling the Yankees had but would never have been brazen enough to say. "It's over," the vendor said. "The team that comes from behind is ahead."

And so it was. "When you're the defending champions, you have to have that inner confidence," Lou Piniella said. "We're not scared to lose. We played very loose. When we fell behind tonight, or when we lost the first two games, it didn't mean a damn thing. It was just a matter of time."

Perhaps that was all afterthought, but it was the way they made everything come out all season—at least once they began to make anything come out right. Last night, the big guys didn't do much until the game was in hand. Then Reggie Jackson hit a Jacksonian blast for the last two runs of the night. Piniella contributed one single. But the little guys did the job. Dent and Brian Doyle, the remarkable emergency second baseman, each had three hits. Doyle batted in two runs and won the praise of his teammates. Dent batted in three runs and won the car as the Most Valuable Player in the Series.

The Yankees played without Willie Randolph at second base, with Chris Chambliss sidelined or useless, and with Mickey Rivers a part-timer. Still they did things right. The Dodgers, riding the mystique of National League superiority, made the mistakes or came up short.

Lopes, the second baseman, had a chance to get Dent's single up the middle with runners on second and third in the second inning. "I was surprised he didn't knock the ball down," Dent said as gently as possible. "If he does, we only get one run. If he knocks it down, maybe he can throw me out." Lopes did not.

With one out in the Yankee sixth, the Yankee lead 3–2, and Piniella on first base, Jim Spencer struck out on a pitch in the dirt that Dodger catcher Joe Ferguson blocked. Ferguson forgot that with a runner on, the third strike is an automatic out and threw to first. Piniella advanced to second on the throw and scored on Doyle's hit. Dent singled and it was 5–2.

"You got to hit the ball to beat us," Piniella said. "We're not going to beat ourselves. We don't make mistakes. We're not afraid to lose. Maybe that's what makes us good. If somebody beats us, OK, then we have no destiny. But we're not going to be afraid."

The Yankees had come through the crucible of New York and they thought that had hardened them, made them immune to the kind of things that distracted the Dodgers. The cream of the National League was disturbed by the ambience at Yankee Stadium—the people and the place.

Rick Gossage, who relieved the gallant Hunter in the eighth inning and produced the last six outs, recalled that he was jolted by his first exposure to New York. He came from Pittsburgh with a fat contract and twice gave up home runs that cost games before the Yankees ever opened the season at home and he was booed. "I was never booed in my life," Gossage said. "Those are the toughest fans in the world there, the most demanding. They stay on your tail and make you produce. The Dodgers are a little spoiled here. It's Hollywood. They went into New York and couldn't handle it. It took me a while to handle it.

"If you can play in New York, you can play anywhere in the world. It helps you in games like this."

They had all come from somewhere else with fat contracts to learn to play in New York, where Jackson said, "The fans throw you notes with an address and say they'll give you $10 cab fare to kick your butt." Hyperbole, but New York does provide its challenge. And the unique Yankee circumstances of the constant scrutiny by the press and the player-manager-front office chemistry of the last two years make greater demands.

"They say this is the greatest team money can buy," Dent continued, "but you can't buy what's inside. You can't buy their hearts."

The Yankees were very full of themselves. They had their third straight pennant and second straight World Series. They had done so much. "This game tonight means as much to me as any game I've pitched in my life," said Hunter, who was with Oakland for its three straight World Series championships. He won 12 games this season after being virtually written off, and the Yankees needed each of them. "This game," he said, "I contributed to a club that came back like this all year. This club never gives up; it keeps coming back, coming back. I think it's the greatest team I've ever been on. I can't believe we won it all."

He was very taken by it all. "It is the greatest thing that ever happened to me," agreed Bob Lemon, the first manager ever to pick up a team at midseason and win a World Series. "If you don't get taken by this, then sex would probably be tough on you."

He laughed deeply as they all laughed. "We have the momentum now," the manager said. "I hope we can carry it over to opening day."

Best News-Coverage Story (Co-Winner)

BOXING

THE BOXER UNSEATS THE PUNCHER

By Dave Klein

From the Newark Star-Ledger
Copyright, ©, 1978, The Star-Ledger, Newark, N.J.

In a magnificent battle of searing intensity, in a heavyweight championship as good as any since Muhammad Ali and Joe Frazier tore each other apart in Manila, Larry Holmes unseated WBC champ Ken Norton last night in a split decision 15-round war at Las Vegas.

It was billed as a classic confrontation, the puncher (Norton) against the boxer (Holmes), but neither man stopped to consider roles. Each slammed into the other with unbridled fury, making good on the week-long statements indicating genuine dislike.

The round that killed Norton, the 32-year-old who inherited the crown when the WBC stripped it from Leon Spinks, was the bloody thirteenth.

Had it gone a few more seconds, Norton would have dropped. He was on his way, woozy and befuddled, victimized by a sudden change in Holmes's tactics that turned him from a dancer-and-jabber to a flat-footed, relentless pursuer and puncher.

It was close until then, Holmes taking much of the early rounds and Norton rebounding with strength in the middle frames.

And then the thirteenth. They traded left jabs, and Norton came bulling in, looking to end it. Holmes flicked a left jab, and it stopped Norton. He followed with a crashing right, came back with another left . . . twice . . . left . . . right.

Norton reeled. The ground came up and his knees turned to cement. Arms dropped, shoulders sagged, and he was unable to escape the left-and-right pummeling administered by Holmes. He tried one overhand right and missed, and Holmes, confident now, sure of it all, stepped inside the miss and pounded away.

Now he was tattooing Norton with vicious combinations, and the knees started to buckle. Norton was hurt, badly hurt, bewildered, arms leaden, legs immobile. Holmes was hitting at will, landing eight, 10, a dozen combinations.

And the bell rang.

As if possessed by inhuman endurance, Norton came out for the fourteenth and was strong again; stronger, at any rate. He landed a left and right, then two good lefts when he trapped Holmes in the corner. Now it was Holmes who suddenly looked tired, exhausted. He stopped jabbing. It was as if he knew he had had his chance, and failed to come in quickly enough for the kill.

And into the fifteenth they went, each man bone-weary, each knowing the championship was on the line, each wanting it more than anything else.

Norton landed a solid right, then another. It could have happened. It could have ended. But somewhere, somehow, Holmes found a left and a right. And they landed. And another set also hit home. And now Norton was stopped again, upright as a left jab sizzled through his careless guard, as a right followed, a terrible, vicious overhand to the jaw.

Once more Norton tried to stop what he could not stop any longer, as he threw and landed a booming right cross.

But Holmes recovered quickly, stepped up and wrapped it up with a left, and a right, and then a thundering left uppercut. And he repeated the lethal three-punch salvo.

Norton stumbled. Waved a glove, feebly.

And the bell sounded.

The ring filled with people. Holmes collapsed into the arms of his manager, Richie Giachetti. Norton sat on his stool, motionless.

They read the judges' verdicts. Joe Swessel scored it 143–142, Holmes. Lou Talbot had it 143–142, but for Norton.

And then Harold Buck's card was read. When the man said "new champion," the crowd of 5,200 exploded. Buck had given it to Holmes, again by that impossibly thin 143–142 margin.

The victory represented a valiant comeback by Holmes, too, for he had faded badly in the middle rounds. After taking four of the first five, because of his darting jabs and dancing defense, Norton came out in the sixth and started pounding.

He took the sixth, seventh, and eighth, and Holmes went to his corner after the eighth with a bloodied mouth and a split lip. Norton, his left eye rapidly puffing, won the tenth, too, looking to end it, hitting hard and often and with telling power. Indeed, one more solid smash could have ended it all in that tenth round—the round Holmes had predicted for his victory.

The eleventh was verily even, Holmes backing off now, Norton chasing him on legs that were giving out. Norton moved Holmes into the corner and hammered at the body, four and five crashing rib and stomach punches. But Holmes slipped out and the round ended.

Now the twelfth, with Holmes looking like the loser, and after Norton landed a solid right lead to the side of his head, he might have fallen. But he began to run again, to bounce and dance and his jabs began to land again. It was back to the game plan, and it forestalled disaster. Then he landed a hard right cross to Norton's chin, and the round became his.

And then came the bloody, snarling, viscerally terrifying thirteenth round. It was what beat Norton, and it was what made Holmes the champion and still undefeated after 28 bouts.

Norton collected $2.5 million for his night's work, while Holmes drew one fifth of that, $500,000.

And the WBA better be happy with its champion, because the rival WBC now has a dandy.

The 28-year-old Holmes heard the verdict while seated in the middle of the ring suffering from near exhaustion. He was helped from the arena and taken to a hotel room, where he was examined by two doctors. He was placed in a hot tub, but he was suffering from no more than an old-fashioned beating.

"I hit him with my best shots and it wasn't good enough," said Norton, who was bitter over the decision in which two judges picked Holmes by a point each, while a third preferred Norton, also by a point.

Asked what he might have done differently if he had it to do all over again, Norton said, "I'd try to win."

There was much bad feeling between the two heavyweights in the weeks leading up to the fight, but Norton said he held no grudges against Holmes—who had done most of the prefight popping off.

"I congratulated him as I'm supposed to, didn't I?" Norton said.

Bob Biron, Norton's manager, said he thought his boxer fought the best fight of his career against an improving younger man.

"Let's give credit to both of them," said Biron.

Best News-Feature Story (Co-Winner)

GOLF

HER HANDS WERE MEANT FOR GOLF

By Betty Cuniberti

From The Washington Post
Copyright, ©, 1978, The Washington Post

As a youngster, she was forbidden to wash dishes.

"I told my wife, 'Our Nancy will not do any dishes. Her hands are meant for golf.'"

Domingo Lopez always detected something special in his younger daughter, a greatness that has burst into bloom in the last 10 months on the Ladies Professional Golf Association tour. With six victories, Nancy Lopez is establishing herself as the most dominant rookie—male or female— who ever swung a golf club for pay.

The exciting thing about Lopez, however, is not her bankbook but the backdrop of her drama. She has never taken a golf lesson. Tutored only by an adoring father who could afford to rent only one bucket of balls at a time for her, Lopez has surpassed her contemporaries and joined the list of names that included Arnold Palmer, Billie Jean King, Babe Ruth—athletes who used equal parts skill, courage, and charisma to endear the public to their sport.

There has been an almost embarrassing need for such a heroine on the LPGA tour. While the women's tennis tour punctured the ozone level with provocative supertalents like King, Chris Evert, Evonne Goolagong, and Martina Navratilova, the golf tour puttered around with a group of fine but aging veterans and sexy newcomers who excelled in toothpaste commercials. The richest woman golfer ever, counting endorsements, is Laura Baugh, who has never won a tournament.

Along comes Lopez, with a swing as sweet as her smile. At last, women's golf has a superstar.

The golf world is giddy over this 21-year-old woman with puppy dog eyes and something her caddy calls "ruthless concentration." Her galleries are swelling, and the more people who watch, the better she plays.

"I feel the vibrations from a crowd. I feel them pulling for me," said Lopez. "I can't believe it's all happening to me. I can't believe people are running after me for autographs. I love it, though."

More than any other sport, golf hacks away at the mind, and here is where Lopez dominates her profession. There are many excellent drivers, chippers, and putters on the tour, but no one else does it all so well, as consistently, as easily as Lopez. She says this is partly because she has never taken a lesson. Terms like angle, path, and follow-through don't clutter her mind when she steps to a tee.

"I've never learned what it is you do when you hook or slice. I just swing to get it where I want it to go," said Lopez. "Right now, it seems like an easy game to me. I feel I can hit any shot."

Her caddy, Kim (Roscoe) Jones, has seen the Lopez confidence do its wonders. "If she makes a bogey, she doesn't get rattled because she knows she can make five straight birdies. It scares me," said Jones. "I didn't know anyone could be that perfect. She's not afraid of anything because she knows her own ability."

Jones has caddied for several years for both men and women. But never for anyone like Lopez.

"I think the ladies have a little tougher time concentrating. Chemistry or something," said Jones. "The ladies tend to play 15 or 16 holes, not the whole 18. Nancy plays all of them. And she plays the devil out of the last four."

In her two years of college at the University of Tulsa, Lopez dated a baseball player named Ron Benedetti. He says there is no separating the person from the golfer, that it all works together.

"I knew her first as a person and there was something special about her then," said Benedetti. "I don't know what it is. But it goes from her life to her golf. She has the power, the will to be the best woman golfer ever, and by a long shot. I really mean that.

"I've watched her play a lot of golf in two years, and every round she does something that amazes me, that makes me wonder, 'What is this girl made of?'

"Later she'll say to me, 'What do you like about me?' I say, 'Nancy, it's everything. Everything you do, you do with style, poise, and maturity.'

"I think her maturity has been the key to her success. She played so much amateur golf, and she knew when she was ready. She had it in the back of her mind to gradually become a superstar. She wasn't awed by the other golfers or the whole professional scene. And finishing second in her first three tournaments sure helped.

"She's always known she was good, and now that she's on the pro tour, something has come out of her that couldn't come before. It's not that she's playing out of her head. She's just finally getting the chance to play up to her potential."

Although it seems that Lopez has sprung unannounced onto the nation's golf courses, her game actually has been on a slow, steady climb since her childhood in Roswell, N.M. Domingo Lopez, now 63, and the widowed owner of the East Second Street Body Shop, imbued his family with the hard work ethic. Born in Texas, he left school after the third grade to help his father in the fields. At age 15, he tried to go back to school, but was told the lowest they would place him was the eighth grade. He wanted to start over in third grade, and when he couldn't win his argument he left, never to return.

He was a talented baseball player, but when a semipro team offered him a contract, he refused.

"A married man has no business in baseball," said Lopez, who was then 28. "They offered me $90 a month, but I could make $250 in a shipyard."

Soon he would bring love and pride to the thankless job of straightening bent fenders, and through hard work he would attain his own body shop, even though he still reads and writes very little.

When he was 40, his boss at the body shop gave him a set of golf clubs. That is very late in life to take up so intricate a game. But within a year he was a three-handicapper, and the imagination can't resist wondering what might have happened had the hours spent toiling in fields, shipyards, and body-shops been spent instead on golf courses.

In the younger of his two daughters, Domingo saw a glimpse of his own spirit, an abundance of intelligence, and the opportunities he never had.

"I remember when she was five and her six-year-old friends went to school," said Domingo. "I told her she was too young to go to school, and she said, 'But Daddy, I'm smarter than they are.'"

Even more than her intelligence, though, made the gentle man's heart pound one day when he spotted his six-year-old in the driveway, skillfully removing the training wheels from her bike with a pair of his pliers. Her special gift, like his, was in her hands.

And Nancy, in every way, emulated her father. He remembers that she liked "baby dolls and singing," but every time her mother asked to help around the house, she said, "No. I have to help Daddy."

She shadowed him everywhere, and when she was eight and plodding along the nine-hole Cahoon Park municipal course, she insisted her father let her play golf. He handed her a 4-wood, which is something like handing a jackhammer to a debutante. She wielded the heavy club and taught herself to hit the ball. Today, her slow, sweeping swing nets an average of 240 yards off the tee, even though it is, as golfer Carol Mann puts it, "a combination of offsetting mistakes" learned as a little girl with a big club.

By age 12, Lopez was beating her father. Suddenly their lives changed. All priorities were centered around her golf game. The family saved money and spent it on her golf rather than buying a dishwasher or a bigger house. In sixth grade, Domingo Lopez went to her school and told her teachers that he would not allow his daughter to play softball because it was ruining her golf swing. She has had, in her entire life, only one other form of employment—a one-month job in a clothing store, earning her $110. Every other minute has been spent on golf.

In her early adolescence, she was not the ice-cool pro of today. Between the ages of 12 and 15, when she swept through amateur tournaments, "I would throw up all the way there," she recalled.

But her father and mother were always at her side, prodding but not pushing. Domingo Lopez remembers one day, "I heard her crying in her room. She was in high school and her boyfriend told her, 'You either play golf or be with me. Not both.' My wife told her, 'You take golf and you'll be the happiest girl in the world. You can always get a boy.'"

In 1975 after her graduation from high school, Lopez entered the U.S.

Open and finished second. There was immediate talk of her turning professional, but she had a $10,000 scholarship and wanted badly to go to college.

"I told her," said her father, " 'You go to college and see what it's like. But don't ever give up golf, not even if you make F, F, F.' "

College golf was little more than a waiting room for Lopez. She won 14 of 18 tournaments she played. She refined her game, by instinct.

"The strongest part of Nancy's game is that she plays by feel," said Mann, considered the LPGA's top analyst and student of the game. "All her senses come into play. That's when golf is an art.

"We know how we feel, when we're strong, when we're weak. Pace and strength are the keys. She has a sense of self, and that's all you need, really.

"The beautiful thing is, I don't think she's conscious of any of this. I saw her play at 17, and she's so much smoother, so much better now. It's just come from practice. She's probably the best putter on the tour. I don't think she's missed enough putts to make mental problems for herself. Leave her here for 10 years. It will happen. It happens to everyone."

Undoubtedly there is jealousy on the tour. But Lopez is such a likable, down-to-earth woman. Mann confirms that any jealousy is directed toward the performance, not the performer.

"Nancy is a delightful girl," said Mann. "She is respectful of the tour and its players, and they know that."

Lopez genuinely enjoys the demands of fans and the press, even though she wept when she read one magazine article that said she sunbathes topless, which she says is untrue. She has had her lonely moments. Her mother died shortly after she started playing on the tour, and she broke her engagement to Benedetti.

Her life is a whirlwind of change. Mark McCormack, who handles Arnold Palmer's financial affairs, has recently added Lopez to his collection. Lopez invested in a gas well in Ohio and it came in. She has bought her sister a rabbit-fur jacket, herself a diamond ring, and taken her father to Australia and Japan. In between, she gave her old clothes to needy neighbors in Roswell.

She has won tournaments in every conceivable way. She has been tied for the lead on the last day, she has come from five strokes behind, has held onto a four-stroke lead, and has won in sudden death.

She has been distracted on a golf course only two times. In the LPGA Championship, which she won, she missed a putt after she spotted a woman in the gallery who looked like her mother. Later, she hit a spectator in the head and knocked him out with one of her tee shots. She cried through the rest of the hole, took a double bogey, and cried through the next hole— making a birdie.

The spectator told her after the round he was all right, but she still was shaken several hours later.

"It's the first time in my life I didn't want to play golf," Lopez said that night. "Today was awful. Everything came on top of me—the pressure to win the fifth straight tournament, the press, the fans. I just wanted to run."

Today, a little shakily, she stands on the precipice of more records and glory, and she wants it.

"That's what I want to do—break records. Make it so people will always remember me," said Lopez. "I love the people who come out to watch me. They're so much a part of me.

"I can feel them thinking that one day they want to say, 'We saw it. She was real.'

"It's kind of neat."

Best News-Feature Story (Co-Winner)

BASEBALL

REGGIE JACKSON'S LONELY WORLD

By Tony Kornheiser

From The New York Times
Copyright, © 1978, The New York Times Company
Reprinted by permission

"What was it that Pasternak said? 'Once in every generation there's a fool who tells the truth exactly as he sees it.' That's Reggie."

Reggie Jackson is holding a cup of coffee in his right hand and a doughnut in his left hand. The first two fingers of his left hand are on the steering wheel of his silver and blue Rolls-Royce. He is backing the $80,000 Rolls—"six different positions on the seat; it's like sitting in your living room"—between a bus and a metal fence, working with a six-inch margin for error. He is doing this casually, the way a man might pour a glass of ice tea from a pitcher. With confidence, with don't-you-just-know-it confidence.

Jackson is on his way to Fort Myers, Fla., for a game against the Kansas City Royals, a three-hour drive from the Yankee camp at Fort Lauderdale. He has permission not to ride the team bus, not so special a privilege inasmuch as Billy Martin has given Thurman Munson, Graig Nettles, Sparky Lyle, and Dick Tidrow, among others, the day off. Jackson never gets a day off. He is the Yankee who packs the house. He makes all spring-training trips, plays in every spring-training game, so the manager doesn't quibble with how he gets there. Anyway, the manager is also not on the bus; he is driving to the game with his pitching coach, Art Fowler.

"Needs gas," Jackson says, pulling into a service station.

The attendant's eyes dilate. It isn't often he sees an $80,000 Corniche. He fills the tank and begins washing the windshield.

"Sir, none of that soapy water, please. It's bad for the finish; it streaks." Jackson knows what's good and what's bad for this car. He washes it clean and wipes it down every day and waxes it every month. Himself. This car says just about everything about Reggie Jackson. It's big. It's expensive. It performs. And it has to have tender, loving care.

"Yes, sir," says the attendant. "This is purified water. Don't use the soapy stuff." He wipes a windshield blade. "I believe I'm about as good in my profession as you are in yours, if I can judge by your car here."

Jackson smiles. "Yes," he says, looking out through a window now so clean as to suggest no window at all. "Yes, I'll bet you are."

In minutes, he is heading west on State Road 84—Alligator Alley—cutting through a 75-mile stretch of Big Cypress Swamp. His eyes are scanning the trees for eagles and hawks. Suddenly he fixes on a patch of gray, hulking birds.

"See them?" he asks. "Vultures."

He rolls down the window on the driver's side and stares.

These are not pretty birds. They sit and wait for misfortune to happen. Jackson thinks about vultures. In the last seven seasons he has played for six division winners and four world champions. In the last 10 seasons he has averaged .270 in batting, 28 home runs, and 84 runs batted in; last season the numbers were .286, 32, and 110. Maybe not automatic Hall of Fame, but at the very least, impressive. The record shows that the man wins. "You'd think once in a while they might say it," Jackson says. "After 10 years some of it ought to come back to you."

Jackson is easily hurt—too easily, most people suggest. But he had never felt quite the hurt he felt last season, his first in New York. Most of his teammates—and his manager—had a dislike for him, and they showed it by leaving him virtually alone on one side of the clubhouse. They had won a pennant without him, and they treated his coming and all the attention he received from the news media like an invasion. The press quickly got on him for his terrible defensive play and his mediocre offensive play early in the season. The fans gave him a booing unheard of in New York since the days of Roger Maris. Until the final game of the World Series, Jackson was the villain.

"Is 'hell' the right word?" he is asked.

"Double it," he answered.

The Rolls moves on, eating up road.

"They look at the money I make, and they say, 'The nigger don't deserve it; he never hit .300,' " Jackson says, beginning a monologue that lasts three miles, his voice rising and falling like that of a tent-city evangelist. "They see me working hard on my defense, and they say, 'The nigger's a showboat.' They see me sign autographs for two or three hours, and they say, 'The nigger just wants his name in the papers.'

"Do they ever say, 'The nigger can play'? That he wins? That he performs under pressure? Do they look at what I withstood and say, 'That nigger has fiber'? Just once I'd like to hear that; I'd like to hear someone say, 'Thanks, thanks for playing your butt off.' No, it's always, 'What's wrong with Reggie? He's a phony, a fake, not real, a glory hound, a man-ip-u-la-tor.' Why doesn't anybody say, 'The man can do it; he goes out and does it'?"

Jackson's reputation throughout the league baffles him.

"The worst in baseball," says Claudell Washington, a teammate on the Oakland championship squad of 1974. "Guys who don't even know him don't like him. They don't like his style. Most players are quiet; Reggie is always talking. The press goes to him for comments about players before going to the players themselves. And some of the things Reggie says. In my first year at Oakland, Reggie told the papers that I played outfield like I was trying to catch grenades. I don't think he means to hurt people, but he talks so much that he can't help it."

The consensus is that Jackson has the biggest ego, the biggest mouth, and the most impeachable credentials of any superstar in baseball. For all his money, you can find few players who say they would trade places with him. What's more damaging, they don't think he cares.

"There's Reggie Jackson lovers and Reggie Jackson haters," says Billy Hunter, the Texas manager, who coached him in Baltimore. "I don't think he cares which way they go as long as they shout, 'Reggie!' "

Jackson listens. This is not making him happy. Vultures. He's hearing words and seeing vultures. He is surprised at the extent of his reputation. He doesn't want to acknowledge it.

"I'd like to say it isn't true," he says, conceding how it may well be. "Because I know I'm a good fella. I'm a good, clean, honest guy trying to be a good human being. If someone would take the time, he'd see it. But I'm resented, and apparently my way is abrasive. They doubt my motives. They don't believe me anymore."

His teammates—those who'll talk about him—say he has only himself to blame. They also say they respect the way he plays the game.

Munson, Nettles, Lyle, and Tidrow refused to talk about him, but Chris Chambliss suggested that what had probably happened to Jackson was that, in his desire to be unique, he created a monster that alienated his peers. Mickey Rivers said that last season "everything Reggie did was all right with everyone but the players." And Bucky Dent's observation was that Reggie put himself in a position where he was damned if he did and damned if he didn't. But Dent also said:

"I was really happy for him when he hit the three homers in the last game of the Series. It was a real nice ending for him, especially after what he went through. I was new here myself, and as quiet as I am, I even felt like cracking up last season."

For the first time in 30 miles, Jackson is smiling.

"Thank you," he says, as if Dent were in the back seat. "I'm very appreciative that someone else saw it like that."

Jackson will talk about last season, but he must walk into it very slowly. The words are chosen carefully. They must be correct.

"Honest to God in heaven, I didn't think it would be like that," he says. "You think I'd have gone to the Yankees if I knew? Think a person wants to be disliked? I thought guys would say: 'Here's a man who played in the Series. He can help us. Let's go along with his program, because he's been there.'

"I missed it by 180 degrees. But it would've been easy to lay down and die, and I didn't. Those homers, they told me there's a God in heaven. They told me more about my character than my talent. You can't believe the pressure. You can't believe what it's like putting on that 44 and hearing them say, 'Go.' "

The easiest question in baseball is, What do you think of Reggie? Outside the Yankees, almost everyone has an opinion. Almost everyone prefaces his answer with this disclaimer: "I've always gotten along with him. When you get to know him, he's not a bad guy."

"The chocolate hot dog?" says Dock Ellis, briefly Jackson's teammate last season with the Yankees. "It's fashionable to knock Reggie, but down deep most guys are jealous of him."

"When it gets down to the nitty-gritty," says Paul Lindblad, a teammate at Oakland, "he comes to the top. There isn't a better pressure player in baseball."

"He can carry a team on his back," says Billy Hunter, "for a week to 10 days all by himself. The thing is, he doesn't adapt to a team; the team has to adapt to him."

"R.J., R.J.," says Claudell Washington, shaking his head, "he only cares about distance. Reggie never talks about the homers that just clear the fence; he's got to hit the longest ball ever. Got to be airport with Reggie, got to be out there on the airport runway. All he wants is for people to tell him, 'Buck, you're the strongest man that ever was.' Tell him that, and there's nothing he won't do for you. When he's going good, he's the best there is."

Jackson alternates between calling these critiques compliments and knocking the men who speak evil of him. He begs to be understood for his complexities, yet he seems to need to put others into tidy boxes. The criticism that bothers him most is Washington's—that he cares only for distance, that he could be a more nearly complete player if his ego weren't so invested in going downtown. Washington is not alone in this feeling; Billy Hunter, Ken Holtzman, Jim Palmer, and Catfish Hunter say the same thing.

"It's hard for me to grasp," Jackson says, turning the Rolls off Alligator Alley onto Route 29 North, to Fort Myers. "I think it's my job to hit the long ball; whether I want to hit it 500 feet instead of 350, I struggle with. I'll take 40 or 50 homers that just clear a fence. But I can't hit .350 with 17 homers and 75 RBIs and be the asset I can be at .285 with 35 homers and 110 RBIs. That's me, what I want to do.

"But I'll tell you this: For me to play nine innings a game and play every day for a manager like Billy Martin, I have be a more complete player; he demands that. I've been working my butt off this spring to show him that I know I'm not too big to work on my defense and bunting. He makes me a better player."

Billy Martin, the magic name. The manager who almost fought with Jackson on national television in a dugout in Boston.

"Compared to last year, this year is heaven," says Martin.

"Amen," says Jackson. All he wants to do is play ball.

This year his relationship with Martin is better. His relationship with Munson is better, by so much that they talk now; they could even go to dinner together should either care to. His relationship with all the Yankees is better. They've had a full season to realize who he is and how he acts and to get used to him.

What most of them learned in one season, Holtzman and Hunter had known for years. Holtzman and Hunter like him.

"Last year the players didn't understand how Reggie could have the kind of first half he had and still keep talking," says Hunter. "It was the same at Oakland."

"At Oakland, and at Baltimore," says Holtzman, who has spent the last six seasons as Jackson's teammate.

"You've got to disregard two thirds of what you read in print that Reggie said," Hunter finds. "If you don't he can really play with your head. Only about one third matters anyway. The rest is just Reggie talking. What I think is that he tries too hard to be liked, and somewhere along the line it comes out wrong."

Jackson hears the words and seems to go into a trance.

"Yeah," he says. "Yeah, Cat's right."

This year, he says, it won't happen.

"I don't want turmoil," he says. "I'm going to do all I can to avoid turmoil, even if it means not standing up for my rights." He pauses for emphasis, in a sort of Jesse Jackson style. "First and foremost, I'm looking to stay out of trouble. Don't want nothing to do with it."

"But it'll find you, won't it?" he is asked.

"Always does," he says, exhaling ever so slightly as the Rolls pulls into the stadium lot at Fort Myers.

The uniform is tight and tapered, and he is into it in 15 minutes, ready to go. But the ride and the conversation have done his insides dirty. Too much past dredged up. He needs something to keep his stomach down.

"There's the man," calls Dave Nelson, the Royal infielder, coming over to Jackson. "Congratulations, congratulations on a helluva World Series. You deserve it."

Behind Nelson comes John Mayberry, the Royal slugger.

"Reggie!" Mayberry shouts.

"Rope, what's up?" Jackson says.

"You, man. You, with your bad self."

It is curious, but he seems most comfortable with members of other teams. With the Yankees, he is at his most comfortable at the batting cage, before games, when the other team's players are close. You sense that he is searching for vocal respect that only opposing players are willing to give him. It seems likely that still, even after his Ruthian World Series, some of his teammates are either too jealous or too stubborn to admit that they were wrong about his ability as a player.

In the clubhouse Jackson is hesitant. Even now there is a tenseness between him and many other Yankees. Yet, it may well be that he infers more hostility than actually exists.

"In the locker room I don't feel like I'm one of the guys," he says. "It's hard for me to say this. I'd like to fit in, but I don't. I don't know if I'll ever really be allowed to fit in. I need to be appreciated, even praised. I like to hear: 'Nice going. Great going. You're a helluva ball player.' But I walk in feeling disliked. Maybe I'm overdoing it. Like I never get on anybody in the clubhouse unless it's a situation where it's obvious that it's OK for me to say something. I stay in the background. I never talk to too many people, except maybe Fran Healy or Ray, the clubhouse attendant, or the press.

"I never small-talk with anyone; I don't feel that anyone cares to talk to me. So I kind of shut up. I'm always the one who has to initiate the conversation. Sometimes I hear my voice in the locker room, and I want to take it back. I don't want anyone to look at me or feel uncomfortable around me."

These words are hard to hear and harder, perhaps, to say.

And then there is a game to play. He is at peace playing baseball. He starts in right field and plays five innings, going to bat three times. Two outs and one RBI single. The people who react to him as they react to no other Yankee—loud boos, even louder cheers—are satisfied. He has been held down, but not out.

With permission to leave early, Jackson showers, dresses, and goes to his car for the drive home. There is a crowd, as usual. He signs autographs and discusses the car, its paint job and the reason he likes to park it in the shade instead of the sun. Before leaving he takes a towel and wipes it down, wiping even the inside carpeting, making sure it is perfectly clean.

Forty miles outside Fort Myers he is playing his tape deck, and the chorus of the song repeats, "We're all in this together." Jackson is singing along. "All my life," he says, "I wanted a car like this. I know it's a rich man's car; I'm proud I can afford it."

"He should be happy," says Chris Chambliss. "He has everything he could want."

"Are you happy?" Jackson is asked.

"For print?" he answers as the car moves almost silently past the swamps on Alligator Alley.

Best Magazine Story (Co-Winner)

BOXING

SPINKS

By Phil Berger

From Playboy
Copyright, ©, 1978, by Playboy

New Orleans, April 8, 1978: Leon Spinks was foot-loose again. It was not on The Leon Spinks Calendar, the increasingly speculative chart of the new heavyweight champion's day-to-day appearances that his lawyers had plotted for him, but Spinks was gone.

Bulletins followed. Spinks, it was reliably reported, was in the Jacksonville, N.C., area, his precise whereabouts unknown. There was a woman involved.

Spinks's fight presented a problem. An agreement had just been reached in the negotiations with a group of New Orleans financiers. The Spinks-Ali rematch was set for September 15 in the Superdome. The problem was that Top Rank chairman Bob Arum did not want rival promoter Don King to steal his thunder.

King had scheduled a press conference in Las Vegas for that Wednesday, April 12, to announce his World Boxing Council title fight between Larry Holmes and Ken Norton. Arum wanted to stage his press conference the day before. That required Leon Spinks, Jr., to be there. The phone lines hummed.

On Monday, April 10, the day before Arum's press conference, there was no change. Nobody had a fix on Spinks. With time running out, Arum made an unusual move. He asked Butch Lewis, Spinks's Svengali during the climb to the championship, who had recently been exiled from the Spinks camp for leaning on the champ a little too heavily, to send for Leon.

Dispatched to Jacksonville, Lewis located Spinks and transported him to New Orleans, apparently persuading him en route to let bygones be bygones.

On April 11, 20 minutes before the scheduled start of Arum's press conference, a Top Rank official discovered that room 1543 of the New Orleans Hilton was empty.

Since that was Spinks's room and since Spinks's wayfaring was by then a pattern, there was cause for alarm. But Leon, it turned out, was only tardy.

An hour late, he finally arrived. As Leon entered, Muhammad Ali ducked under the table at which he was sitting, in a comic show of fear. Lured back out, he remarked on Spinks's tardiness.

"I'm important now, brother," Spinks rasped, his bloodshot eyes twinkling.

Ali inspected the champion's brown suit and the smartly knotted tie, turned to Lewis and said, "You done fixed his tie and everything, ain't you?" Then to Spinks, he said, "You used to be quiet and didn't dress up." Ali's voice took on an exaggerated tremolo, "You . . . done . . . chaaanged, man."

"You gave me my gusto, brother," Spinks quipped.

The crowd roared.

"You don't act the same no more," said Ali, pretending to be perplexed. "You used to be early. Now you late. Making everybody wait."

"Well, that the way it supposed to be. You got to let the smell come before you come."

"You crazy," Ali told him. "I ain't going to fight you."

In New Orleans, Ali adapted his wit to Spinks's rough-edged humor. The mood was cordial. The Ali ego did not rankle Spinks as it had some of his other opponents. Leon liked him. (After he'd beaten Muhammad, Spinks went to Ali's dressing room, kissed him on the cheek, and said, "Good fight.") Ali, in turn, was not bent on unnerving Spinks. His reference to Spinks as crazy was meant as praise. He had not been able to psych Spinks during their Las Vegas title fight, a fact that colored the comic material Ali fashioned from his defeat. At one point during the New Orleans press conference, he interrupted Leon, saying, "I'll do the talking now"—a smile on his lips.

"Now, wait a minute. Shut up," Spinks said, acting cross.

"You tell me to shut up?" Ali shook his head and looked out at the audience with an aggrieved expression, "I got to take all this?"

"That's right," Spinks told him. "I'm champ now."

"Yassa, boss."

It was perfect timing that had Leon writhing in laughter, his curled tongue poking through his teeth. He reached for the microphone and said, "Ali is a wonderful person. He's a beautiful man. I love him. I love him with all my heart. Plus, he give me respect . . . can't get that nowhere."

If Spinks was feeling that he couldn't get any respect except from Ali, he was probably just reflecting on some of the events that had taken place in the past few months.

Within six weeks of defeating Muhammad Ali, Spinks had been sued by a motel for unpaid bills; had been sued for back rent by his landlord in Philadelphia; had been arrested and then photographed in handcuffs for driving the wrong way on a one-way street and for operating a motor vehicle without a license in his hometown of St. Louis; and had been discarded as heavyweight champion by the World Boxing Council in favor of the number-one challenger, Ken Norton. By then, the reeling Spinks could only say, "I haven't done anything for anyone to take my belt. I ain't disrespect no one."

And as if to add insult to injury, a look-alike of the new champion had turned up in Philadelphia. The dead ringer was, in Leon's term, "imposturing" him—signing autographs in public and encouraging local merchants to lavish complimentary goods on him.

For a couple of weeks, the man sampled the high times that Spinks calls his gusto. Then he prudently faded away.

The man may have known something. For by then, the pleasure of being the real Leon Spinks, Jr., was paling.

Nowhere was the pleasure more diminished than in Spinks's dealings with Butch Lewis of Top Rank, Inc., the champion's exclusive promoter. On the morning of March 2—two weeks after he beat Ali—Spinks arrived at Top Rank's New York office to confer with Lewis, who had told him there was business to discuss at 10:00 sharp.

When Spinks arrived, the Top Rank office was undergoing a paint job, which left its quarters cramped for seating space. Leon settled himself on top of a packing crate and waited for Lewis to appear. He was still waiting by early afternoon, when a Top Rank aide wondered if Spinks was hungry. Leon conceded that he was and let the man buy him a ham and cheese on white.

Lewis appeared shortly afterward, saying he'd been trying to track down Spinks's accountant. That Spinks had been waiting half the day did not appear to trouble Butch. It disturbed the champion though, who was beginning to reassess Lewis's role in his life.

Throughout Spinks's brief but tumultuous pro career, Lewis had been in the midst of the struggle for control over Spinks. The earliest infighting had involved Lewis and Millard "Mitt" Barnes, a white Teamsters organizer from St. Louis who was Spinks's manager of record. Although Barnes would retain his 30 percent managerial cut of Spinks's purses, he quickly lost the influence he'd had when Leon was an amateur and Barnes was his benefactor, investing time and money in Spinks's boxing future.

It was through Lewis that Barnes first learned that his past contributions (according to Mitt, he gave Spinks more spending money than strictly permitted by Olympic regulations) had been devalued. After Spinks's first pro fight, Lewis told Barnes that Leon's wife, Nova, was consulting with attorneys about canceling Mitt's contract as manager—she wanted to be the manager.

Barnes began to feel a chill in Leon's attitude toward him.

Spinks's disaffection for Barnes apparently was not so deep-rooted that he had qualms about asking him for more money. On August 8, 1977, shortly after Leon suffered an eye injury in training, he phoned Mitt for $500. According to his Western Union receipt, Barnes wired the money at 4:35 P.M. that day. An hour later, Spinks phoned back and asked for $1,500 more.

"I just wired you the $500," Barnes told him. "I got to come to Philadelphia—we've got a few things to discuss. So I'll just bring the $1,500 with me." When Barnes went to Philadelphia, Spinks had already received the $500 and split.

In Barnes's place, Lewis had taken charge of Spinks, involving himself in every facet of Leon's career, even tracking the fighter down when he went A.W.O.L. from training.

Lewis, a 31-year-old former car salesman who had become a vice-president of Top Rank, had the animated style of his former calling and an inclination for the ornate gesture. In the Manhattan phone directory, he was listed as "Lewis, P.A.," the initials referring to the nickname he'd taken for himself—Park Avenue Butch—an allusion to Top Rank's prestigious address.

It was a flair that Barnes, a slow-moving, plain-talking man, distrusted. He suspected Lewis of promoting himself with Spinks at his expense. After several "incidents" with Lewis, Barnes began to think of consulting an attorney for the problems he anticipated.

Spinks's trainer Sam Solomon had a wary eye on Lewis, too; he did not take to Butch's idea of bringing in another trainer, George Benton, to assist him.

Solomon, a short, rotund man, 63 years of age, had fought in tent shows and social clubs as a semipro boxer, and also had been a catcher in Negro baseball. Solomon is usually an affable individual, but on this occasion he became angry at having his authority as trainer undercut. Lewis thought it was a justifiable move.

"Solomon did a good job," Lewis recalled, "of being with Leon and his brother Michael. (Michael Spinks had turned pro with Top Rank in February 1977.) He'd pick 'em up all the time, get them to the gym. I'd tell him they needed this or that—and he'd get it done. Never a problem. And it wasn't until early summer that I started to see that they really weren't progressing. Sam was just great for my overseer, but he wasn't great in training them. In fact, Mike and Leon were complaining that he wasn't teaching 'em anything.

"What happened is that one day in the gym, Leon went over to George Benton, who worked in Joe Frazier's gym. He saw George showing fighters things that he thought he should know. He went to Benton and asked him, 'Man, would you show me how to do that?' Later, Leon called me and asked, 'Can't we get Benton to work with us?' "

Benton was a former middleweight contender who was training Frazier's stable of fighters, which included Frazier's own son Marvis, a promising amateur. As a fighter, Benton had been a clever operator, with a knack for avoiding punches. A classic stylist.

"George himself came to me," said Lewis, "and said, 'Look man, I don't want to start no trouble. I want you to know your fighter came over to me and asked me to show him a couple of tricks he saw me showing to some other fighters. I don't want to start no problems.' See, Solomon noticed what was going on . . . and got a little pissed."

To avoid problems, Lewis held back on hiring Benton for the time being.

By September 1977, the in-house politics occupied too much of Leon's attention. There were Barnes's calls to reestablish old ties and the warnings from others to ignore him. There was Solomon's resentment to balance against the advanced techniques that Benton probably could provide. There was hard-sell Lewis, pulling and tugging and telling Spinks so many things that it was hard to keep them all straight. In the ghetto of St. Louis, Spinks hadn't had to worry about receipts for documenting expenses or about being on time.

The worst of it was Spinks's gnawing concern that he was being manipulated against his better interest. Two other Olympic boxing gold medalists, Howard Davis and Sugar Ray Leonard, had landed exorbitant guaranteed-income deals with the TV networks. By contrast, Top Rank's guarantee to Spinks of only $30,000 for eight bouts was a pittance.

If those elements were not sufficient to cloud Spinks's thoughts, Arum provided another twist. Although Spinks had fought only five professional fights (all won by knockouts), Arum signed him to box Ali for the heavyweight championship.

The original plan called for Spinks to qualify for the title fight—he was required to defeat at least one ranking boxer, against Alfio Righetti of Italy, on September 13. Spinks's eye injury caused the fight to be rescheduled for November 18. As a tune-up for that bout, Top Rank matched Spinks against a journeyman heavyweight named Scott LeDoux in October.

The LeDoux bout was what prompted me to begin looking into the Spinks story. It was not the fight telecast from Las Vegas or the news accounts that piqued my interest. It was what a deep-throated source I'll name Whisper reported. Whisper is a nondescript individual, given to the sort of tinted glasses Spinks himself wears. On Leon, it is for effect, a kind of flair. For Whisper, it deepens his seedy anonymity, his gray slouch of a figure. He is a boxing aficionado, though, with a computerlike memory for names, dates, and the curious facts of the sweet science. He is also privy to all the intrigues and bent turns of the game.

"The thing about the LeDoux fight," Whisper said, "was what occurred outside the ring, not inside it. There was a craziness at ringside in the Spinks camp, particularly with this Butch Lewis fellow.

"Lewis sat down in the press row . . . maybe 20 feet from LeDoux's corner . . . middle of the ring. Into the ring comes Michael Spinks to fight in a prelim. And Butch stands up in the press row . . . on the floor . . . Michael is in completely the opposite corner . . . and Butch hollers, 'Hey, Sliiiiim'—Slim—that's his nickname for him. The kid turns around. Butch hollers, 'Give me fiiiiive!' The kid dutifully walks across the ring and . . . you know that give-me-five thing. Two gloves, palms down. And Butch gets his jollies. Same thing with Leon when he comes into the ring. 'Give me fiiiive, big man.'

"Then the LeDoux fight starts. And LeDoux, of course, pulled every trick in the book—the elbows, the thumb in the eye, the head butts. Meantime, though, he's managing to bang home some legitimate punches, too.

"OK. Leon was under a little pressure. And here's where Lewis began shouting instructions from press row. I couldn't believe my eyes: Leon would turn toward *this guy* for advice instead of to his corner!

"Butch's screaming and ranting led a couple of people to start heckling him. And he's done this before . . . at other fights, I've been told. 'You got faith in that white man up there? Bet $500!'

"The morning of the fight, I'd run into Joe Daszkiewicz, the trainer of LeDoux. He tells me, 'Whisper, you should have heard what went on yesterday. LeDoux is staying on the same floor as Leon. We're going past the door to his room, we hear Butch Lewis inside, carrying on. Trying to psych Leon. "If you don't win the fight, you're going back to the ghetto. You've got to win or you're through." Really laid it on!'

"Toward the end of the fight, Leon is dragging. It's his first 10-rounder. The word was that he'd been partying pretty good a few weeks before. At this point, it's a close fight. The shot at Ali is on the line. All of Spinks's people are going crazy. And here comes Lewis, running up to the ring ropes and yelling at Leon: 'Remember the ghetto! Remember the ghetto!' Really weird stuff, but I'll give him this: Maybe it helped. Because Leon sparked up at the end.

"The fight ended in a draw. Afterward, Johnny Mag, of the Nevada Athletic Commission wrote Top Rank a letter of reprimand . . . that this will not be countenanced anymore . . . that Butch Lewis is to be kept out of press row. All that sort of stuff. A very stiff letter."

The unsettling atmosphere continued for the Righetti fight. Benton was in camp. Sensing Solomon's antagonism, though, he bowed out after Spinks beat the Italian, telling Lewis he wanted to avoid further hard feelings. Lewis, though, felt that George's expertise could help against Ali. He kept after Benton and eventually persuaded him to work with Spinks. It produced a triangular training approach that involved Benton, Spinks, and Lewis's brother, Nelson Brison, who was an assistant trainer of Spinks.

"George," said Lewis, "would phone Nelson and tell him things that he should be showing Leon. And Nelson would then repeat to Spinks what George had told him. This is how it was done! OK? This is how fucked up it was. And then, as the championship fight approached, I said, 'Look, George, we coming down to the wire. I need you down here . . . if nothing else, to work the last week or so. To do whatever you can do. And if you have to do it, continue doing it through Nelson. 'Cause we can't afford to have any confrontations at this point.' "

In Las Vegas for the title fight, Benton had to continue to funnel his ideas through Brison. He showed him tactics for defensing Ali and explained a strategy he had. The key to the Benton strategy was for Spinks to pound away at Ali's left shoulder during the fight and tire the muscles that controlled Muhammad's jab, a weapon that had been crucial to Ali late in past fights. Benton also found a way to exploit Ali's energy-saving rope-a-dope tactic: When Muhammad covered up, bang away at the shoulder. When he opened up, throw the uppercut through his gloves to the chin.

"Then," said Benton, "the few times I'd seen Leon alone, I never talked loud to him. Always talked soft to him. You can take a person who's excitable and talk him down by your tone of voice. I'd tell him, 'You're going to be champ. All you got to do is do the right things. Small things. Goddamn it, you'll be riding around in a Rolls-Royce. I can see you with the pretty clothes on.' And right behind that, I'd say something that would pertain to boxing."

But the dominant figure in training camp for the Ali fight was, of course, Lewis. He used his position like a gong: He was loud and insistent and sometimes got on people's nerves.

A sparring partner of Spinks quit camp after telling Lewis that he ought to learn to respect people. Eventually, Solomon, whom Lewis berated in public on more than one occasion, got to feeling similarly. One night, he told Lewis, "You acting like you want to fight, nigger. Treating people like they're nothing. I'm not afraid of you. I may be an old man. But I'll punch you right in the mouth." A similar threat was made by Top Rank PR man Chet Cummings when Lewis kicked at his hotel door to get his attention.

After Spinks won the heavyweight crown, Lewis was not overly modest about his role in the title coup. "What you all taking Bob Arum's picture for?" he'd ask photographers. "What you all doing that for? I'm the guy that brought Leon Spinks in." In Top Rank's office, Lewis continued to berate aides, sometimes in front of Spinks. And he could be just as pushy with the champion himself.

On the evening of March 2, Lewis told Spinks he wanted him to attend the Mike Rossman vs. Alvaro "Yaqui" Lopez light heavyweight fight at Madison Square Garden. This followed Leon's nearly day-long wait for Lewis in Top Rank's office. When Spinks declined to see the fight, Lewis insisted. He said that as champion, Leon owed his public such appearances. Later, Spinks would complain about being badgered yet one more time. On that night, however, what made it more galling was that, with Nova back home, Leon had been looking forward to spending the evening with a lady he'd flown up from North Carolina. That was personal turf. And it made it one push too many.

By then, he'd suffered Lewis's dervish style too long. One sticky situation after another. Never a moment's peace. Now, as heavyweight king, he thought he'd earned the right to an orderly reign. And if his old mahatma, Lewis, was not built for that, then Spinks was prepared to go elsewhere.

The morning after the Rossman-Lopez match, Leon met with a 49-year-old former Wayne County, Mich., circuit court judge named Edward F. Bell. Bell, a tall, thin man of dignified mien, was now a practicing attorney in Detroit.

Spinks told Bell that his affairs were chaotic and needed changing.

Bell impressed Spinks. The attorney had a cool, understated manner that contrasted sharply with the klaxon style of Lewis.

Indeed, later on the same day that Spinks met with Bell, Lewis again showed the champ surprising contempt—and disrespect. Fearing he'd miss an airplane flight, Butch hurried into a limousine on Park Avenue that had been hired for Leon's use. "Grab yourself a cab," Lewis told Spinks, as he commandeered the limousine and sped to the airport.

A few days later, in Detroit, Spinks announced that Bell now represented him. With Bell, he hoped, would come a semblance of order.

March 30, 1978: In suite 840 of Detroit's Buhl Building, where the law firm of Bell and Hudson maintains its office, the Spinks watch was on its third day.

Spinks's attorneys, Bell, and Bell's colleague Lester Hudson, had sent a former Detroit police officer, who also tracked down bail jumpers, out to St. Louis to find the heavyweight champion.

The ex-cop, who had just hired on as a Spinks bodyguard, had left Detroit, saying, "If the m . . . .rf . . . .r is there, I'll find him."

Bell and Hudson hoped so. They had Arum on the phone daily, talking to him about a deal with a group of Africans (who were later replaced by the New Orleans people) on the Spinks-Ali rematch. The negotiations soon would require their flying to New York in the company of Spinks.

Bell and Hudson were not the only people who wanted Spinks in Detroit. Richard J. Smit did, too. Smit was a car salesman who had driven up three days before from the Johnny Kool Oldsmobile agency in Indianapolis, Ind., in a 1977 custom-built white Lincoln Continental limousine that he meant to sell to Spinks for $35,000—$5,000 down, a 10-month lease, and a final "balloon" pay out.

The vehicle went with the new image that Bell and Hudson were insisting soon would fit their client Spinks as snugly as the three size-42 tailor-made suits that had been hand-delivered three days earlier by a clothier from across the border in Windsor, Ont.

For those three days, Bell and Hudson had been talking persuasively into my tape recorder of the mechanisms that they had set up to ensure that Spinks's career would run smoothly and that he would rise up as a Palooka-ville do-gooder, a shining example to the youth of America. It was the image Leon talked up too: "He'p the kids, gotta he'p the kids," he'd say—an ambition that somehow always was being waylaid.

The mechanisms were supposed to change that. Like G.M. and Howard Hughes, Leon was now incorporated in Delaware, so he could enjoy that state's liberal corporate advantages. Spinks, Jr., Organization Inc.: At that date, Spinks was its only officer. The setup provided him tax relief, as well as a sense of his own future. He had, it turned out, taken to carrying an attaché case, prompting a gag:

Q: What's that you got in your hand?

SPINKS: That's my office.

In fact, though, a real office, carpeted and with a view of Detroit's Congress Street, had been cleared for Spinks in suite 840.

Downstairs, in the National Bank of Detroit, an account for Spinks was set up. What remained of his cash was transferred from New York banks. Temporary checks were issued. Spinks's taxes were brought up to date. In 1977, his first year as a professional boxer, he had twice missed making quarterly tax payments on his fight earnings. When Top Rank sent him to a New York accounting firm, Leon showed up with a shopping bag full of cash receipts. But Spinks was now supposed to be catching on to fiscal complexities. When Bell and Hudson's tax specialist had asked the high school dropout if he understood why he had to document expenses more carefully, Spinks had answered, "You're talking 'bout my business partner [Uncle

Sam] . . . looking over my shoulder . . . comin' in, saying, 'I'm not gonna let you get away with this.' "

Arrangements were made for Spinks to pursue a general-education degree. To improve his speech, he'd bought a tape recorder ("Not a little bitty box," he'd say, "a big box . . . made by Pioneer . . . that I know I can get the whole sound of my voice into it"), so that he could hear himself and learn from it. And then there was The Leon Spinks Calendar.

On white cardboard the size of fight posters, Spinks's monthly itinerary was recorded on The Leon Spinks Calendar. In Bell's office, and Hudson's, a calendar was prominently displayed. At a glance, either lawyer knew what the champ was doing.

Spinks's future engagements were marked in red and black inks—red for tentative and black for solidly booked dates. In the month ahead, Spinks was to receive the Ring Magazine championship belt (4/4) in New York, lay over a night at the Hilton and travel to Philadelphia, where he would be honored by the city of Philadelphia and would tape "The Mike Douglas Show" (4/6). Then:

April 10–15 Miami, Fla., training
April 16–22 Carribean (*sic*) exhibition tour
April 23–29 Carribean (*sic*) exhibition tour

It was an impressive-looking document, except for one thing: its efficacy. Leon Spinks, who had only to catch a plane to Detroit, hadn't been up to it for three days running, a fact that jibed less with the blue-skies future that Bell and Hudson foresaw for Spinks than with events of the past weeks.

Then there was the information from my Spinks source, Whisper, that had the jagged feel of self-destruct:

"Leon is still Leon. That's the amazing thing. Still irresponsible. Wants to do exactly what he wants to do. He's got . . . something a little loose there, I think.

"Like, he doesn't have a driver's license and yet he continues to drive. A couple of days after he was arrested for driving without a license, he drove a guy I know to the airport. Like, it didn't faze him at all. With Leon, these things just happen. Very spontaneously. And he goes with it.

"Then last week, his bodyguard was expecting his wife to fly in to St. Louis from Des Moines. Since the wife was staying with Nova, Leon says there's a possibility that Nova might be on the same flight. If Nova's on the plane, Spinks says, the guy is to call up. It's like a little game with Nova and Leon. OK? Leon flies out of town. She follows him. She never see him. Leon flies out of town again. She follows him. Like Marlene Dietrich in *Morocco*.

"Sure enough, Nova's on the plane. The guy calls up to find out what to do. The problem here is that Spinks has a broad staying with him. So? What's the answer? Take the broad and stash her in another hotel? No. Too easy. They put Nova in the room Leon had stayed in. And Leon gets another suite, two flights up. Same hotel. Nova thinks he's not even in the building. The way it went, Nova's downstairs. The girl friend is upstairs. And the news guy is trying to get Leon to sit still for an interview.

"Spinks, my friend, is going to drive you crazy."

That same afternoon, waiting in Bell and Hudson's office with car salesman Smit and others, I wondered if I would go crazy, as Whisper had prophesied. What I did know for sure was that I had a bad case of the fidgets. Three days of waiting to talk with the heavyweight champion.

The hoped-for vision of order was clearly down the tubes. Where was the artful dodger? Late that afternoon, a *St. Louis Post-Dispatch* reporter heard that Spinks was signing autographs in the ghetto and phoned Leon's bodyguard with the address. At that point, Nova and the bodyguard slipped away from the ex-cop from Detroit and went looking for Leon.

Spinks was where he was said to be. The bodyguard saw the silver Chrysler New Yorker that Leon drove when he was in St. Louis and told Nova that he'd retrieve Leon. Instead, he told Spinks, "Your wife is here, man," which gave Spinks and his St. Louis woman the chance to drive away. Back at the hotel, Nova knocked on the door of the ex-cop's room and told him that the bodyguard had screwed up.

At the time this was occurring, Smit was emerging from attorney Hudson's office in Detroit to say, "They're contacting a guy with the St. Louis police who knows Spinks. To see if he can dig him up. The word is: Be discreet."

A smile flickered across Smit's lips. Each screwy twist of waiting for Leon was a perverse entertainment for him. But that was ending. Smit left Detroit that afternoon, regretting he hadn't had a chance to try his pitch on the heavyweight champion.

" 'Cause I know Spinks is a buyer," Smit said. "All I got to do is stick his ass in the seat. Boom! Thirty-five G's. Cashier's check, if you please. All I need is five minutes."

On the chance that Spinks would slip into Detroit in the near future, Smit left the limousine with a relative of a fellow employee and made arrangements to have it driven back to Indianapolis if it turned out that Leon was on a sabbatical.

As for me, I thought of catching a flight to St. Louis but had the paranoiac vision of Spinks's plane passing mine in the night, with Leon flashing me a demonic jack-o'-lantern grin.

I took an evening flight to New York.

On his own, Spinks flew to Detroit the next day.

He hadn't much to say, except about the limousine. On that item, he did not appear to need Smit. Never mind the informed spiel on gear ratios or rear-axle options. Spinks saw the white Lincoln Continental limousine with the gold striping. He saw the AM/FM stereo casette player, the small-screen color TV, the digital clock, the bar, the sun roof, the phones for incar communications, and the two back rows of facing seats in crushed velour. He saw all that and knew what he knew. As Leon put it:

"That my m . . . .rf . . . .g car. I'm buyin."

From St. Louis, Nova phoned Detroit later that day.

"You tell Leon," she said, "that I'm going to sue him for divorce. I'm going to take all his money. And you tell him if he wants to discuss it, I'm going to my parents in Des Moines."

As she hung up, though, Nova, a woman of more than 200 pounds, winked at the photographer from the *Post-Dispatch* and said, "I'm going right to Detroit. Just said that about Des Moines to throw him off my tracks."

When Spinks won the championship, the press wrote traditional copy about the ghetto fighter's transcending deprivation. A few unkind reporters carped about the slurred speech and fractured syntax and the dearth of feeling the new champion had for the press. Ali backlash, so to speak. But by and large, Spinks was warmly depicted.

The fact was, though, he was not O.J. black, not the establishment's kind of colored. He had the discomforting sound of the back-alley, muscatel-swigging black man, and a hard-edged look to go with it. So when incidents began to occur, the press was not disposed to go easy on him.

That did not surprise Spinks. From the start, he'd met resistance as champion. In some quarters, he was still regarded as a man whose triumph over Ali was a freak of timing, a fortuitous conjunction of fate and Muhammad's middle age. In dreams before the title match, Spinks had conjured up the image of his arms raised in triumph, but he never imagined the thorny times that would follow.

"Like, I remember," he said later, when we finally connected, "the first time I went back to St. Louis after I won the championship. I was in a club. I was supposed to meet the manager of the place. I was waiting there when a guy ran up to me, point a finger in my face, say, 'You ain't shiiit. You ain't nothing.' And, like, I almost went at him. You understand? 'Cause somebody say that . . . that's just like saying, 'Let's get it on, let's fight.' I got a heating sensation in my body. A burning sensation in my chest and neck. Like what I used to get when I'm out on the street. But I thought, No, man that ain't you. Look at you now. I mean, even though he's hollering about how much he hates you . . . and whatever . . . a lot of people around here do love you. Like the people in the club—they said to the guy, 'Who in the hell is you, nigger, to come to our champ like that?' "

The encounter in St. Louis was the first of several instances in which strangers accosted Spinks and bad-mouthed him to his face. His correspondence contained a percentage of hate mail, too, mostly provoked, it seemed, by his victory over Ali, of whom he was genuinely fond. "What a joyful man Ali is," Spinks had said before the fight.

Compared with Ali, Spinks lacked the easy grace in public. At times, he could be a sunny soul, breaking into a grin that looked nearly equine in the close-ups that photographers snapped. At other times, he was perplexed by the people he encountered, particularly those who stared dead in his face without speaking. For those cases, Spinks had acquired a line—"What's wrong with you, you ill or something?"—that had proved helpful. "When I say it, then everybody start laughing. Whatever." Whatever. It was not easy being the heavyweight champion.

For Spinks, the problem was compounded by a lack of education that had been exploited before. Barnes said that when Spinks joined the Marines, he was under the impression that it was for a two-year hitch rather than the four-year term stated in his papers.

Once, to clarify whether or not Spinks's brother Evan had an *s* at the end of his name, I asked Leon to spell it. He took two faltering stabs at the spelling and gave up with an exclamation of "Oh, wow!"

Spinks's ingenuousness invited an atmosphere of conniving and intrigue and produced the internal confusion that was built into the heavyweight champion's operation. Even friends tried to take advantage.

"Some of them," Spinks said later, "try to hit me up for money. I tell 'em, 'Well, I fought hard and I worked hard to get where I got. Don't take away my gusto, 'cause you ain't got none. All you got to do is to make it for yourself and then you have some gusto. And then you ain't gotta ask nobody for anything.'"

Spinks is a creature of contradictory pieces, eluding easy labels. Although he hasn't the glibness of Ali—his sentences often lurch and sputter—he sometimes strikes a rough poetic note with his words. "I broke out in a thousand tears," or "Nobody really finds hisself, 'cause if he finds hisself, he knows the future." Similarly, though he takes his image with what sometimes seems undue sobriety ("I don't want nobody to see me just like a Tom, Dick, and Harry. I want to always keep an image as a nice neat man"), he reacted with boyish hilarity when TV had a laugh at his expense.

"What's that man," he asked, "that tells jokes . . . on 'The Gong Show' . . . has a bag on his face? Yeah. Unknown Comic. He made a joke on me one night. Said, 'I'm going to do an image of Leon Spinks.' Turns around, took the first bag off, put another bag on his face. Had the whole front of the bag black, with two teeth missing. And he turned back around, changed his face mask back, said, "You didn't know I was two-faced, either, did you?' That gassed me, man. I die laughing. I went in and holler out to my wife. Said, 'This fool is doing an image of me.'"

One moment Spinks would yank a cork from a bottle of champagne with his teeth. The next, he'd clutch a pillow to his chest or suck his thumb as he sat for an interview. The word *man-child* has been applied to him. Even Nova has been quoted as using it. It is a good word, evoking the contradictory forces within Spinks that make him difficult to pin down.

The odd angles at which Spinks sometimes carries his hands—reminiscent sometimes of the singer Joe Cocker—are part of a repertoire of body quirks signaling his moods. A bounce to his step indicates that he is in good humor. At those times, his erect carriage has a dancer's lithe quality. In foul moods, he draws in his neck and cocks his head to the side, which has an ominous effect.

But he can be sweetly attentive, too. "You know what I like?" he asked. "Meeting the mommas. All the mommas are big and fat. They get excited when they see me. They be grabbing on me"—Spinks twists his shoulders from side to side in recollection—"la de la, la de la la la."

Flying to Detroit from Boston, Leon met a little girl, about seven years of age, who had had a series of operations on her throat that left her unable to speak at the time of the flight. "Her parents," Spinks said, "had just picked her up from the hospital. And her birthday were coming up. So I sung Happy Birthday to her. Yeah, I sung it to her. And I gave her my autograph. And then we sit back there and . . . we writing notes. We was talking to each other . . . through notes. We just talked about anything and everything. Anything that she asked me about. I would tell her. She asked about boxing. She asked how a guy could get hit on the face like that. I said, 'Well, baby, it's all in the job.'"

Spinks is a visceral person who is not afraid to express himself. To the anonymous benefactor who'd flown his mother to the Montreal Olympics, Leon said, "You know, it's the nicest thing that's ever happened to us. We just love you for it." When confronted by LeDoux's dirty tactics, Spinks had asked in the ring, "Why you cheat?" a remark that had struck LeDoux by its ingenuous inflections.

The most striking instance of man-child expressiveness occurred the night Spinks talked to me of his ghetto upbringing, the anguish and humiliation of which apparently were vividly felt. At one point, as he paced his room in the Las Vegas Hilton, growing more agitated, he stopped and, with a stricken expression, said, "Get me out of here, get me out of St. Louis," which really only meant he wanted to change the subject.

Spinks has what seems an obsessive tie to his past. His very speech reflects it. His words do not falter or get jammed up at the beginning of sentences when the subject is ghetto travail. It's as though he's had the same thoughts many times before. "I was the type of person who was quiet," Spinks said. "People could do different things to me and I'd come by and make my momma think everything was all right. I would lock everything inside myself. Because the hurt I felt, I always kept it to myself. I never did try to explain to people what hurt I had went through."

His father is at the core of his pained memories. Leon, Sr., separated from the family when the boy was young. What contacts Spinks had with him afterward were mostly disappointing—he remembers being ridiculed and whupped—and filled him with a desire "to be the man my daddy wasn't."

There is a darker side to Spinks that possession of the heavyweight title seemed to provoke. Whisper had a story in that regard:

"I knew George Foreman before he knocked out Joe Frazier. A real gung-ho nice kind of kid. Now, the morning after he knocked out Joe Frazier, he walked in to the press conference . . . and like this: 'Hey, get the hell off that couch, man . . . You, I don't want you sitting there.' He's rearranging the room. How to sit. How to take pictures. And you know who did the same thing the day after he won? I swear. Leon Spinks. 'Get off the couch,' he told news guys. He's barking commands as to who sits where. 'Clear that couch. Get out of the way.' Uncanny. Absolutely uncanny. Almost to the T."

The title conferred an elaborate celebrity of a peculiarly American kind, with its mix of grand and tawdry attentions—headlines and hotel suites and the *National Enquirer* asking Leon to by-line "Why I Love America."

Being the heavyweight champion mattered. People simply did not worry about the "image" of champions in other weight divisions. The almighty shazam belonged to the heavyweight king. And with it went the recognition, concern, and gaudy fanfares inherent. Snubbed at the door of Manhattan's chic Studio 54 when he was a challenger, Spinks was "Olee olee in free" as the champion.

For Spinks, though, some measure of his newly acquired fame was the motion and commotion he could trigger. Bodies snapped to. That could be exhilarating for a young man whose background was filled with mockery and rejection. Spinks's whirlwind days, especially the ones he lived when he bolted, had people dashing about, worry and wondering about him. That might appear selfish from close up. By the long view, though, it was a payback on a hard, cold past. As Spinks once said, "See, my dad said I'd amount to nothing. He would tell people that. And it hurt me to hear him say it. It stayed in my mind. Why'd he say that? What for? Call me a fool out of the blue. Not to my face but to people who'd tell it to me. And that became my thing—to be somebody."

Underlying all contradictions, it sometimes seemed, was a mad pleasure in the inappropriate moment, the attraction to which brought unanticipated twists: Spinks would experience seizures of laughter in the midst of a sober account of one of his St. Louis driving busts or while he analyzed his impromptu disappearances. They were great gurgling sounds—laughter shot through with an unhinged quality.

At those times, the phrase "inappropriate response" had flashed in my mind like the tilt light on a pinball machine, the laughter suggesting a self-destructive impulse of the kind that made tragic heroes.

Was Spinks's gusto just a bit bent? "He's got . . . something a little loose there, I think," Whisper had said of him. The words applied, though, to the whole shebang—the Spinks High Times and Soul Aplenty Caravan. It was a hard scene to get a fix on. There was the continuing sense of the whole works' being slightly out of whack, bent in a way no orderly vision could possibly straighten.

WELCOME LEON SPINKS
HEAVYWEIGHT CHAMPION
OF THE WORLD

read the marquee outside the DiLido Hotel in Miami Beach. It was April 11, the day of the news conference with Ali. I had accompanied Spinks from New Orleans to Miami.

Situated on the ocean, with its front entrance on Collins Avenue, the DiLido is a high-rise hotel with a spacious L-shaped lobby and walls covered with pastel murals of boats and trees and monkeys and birds. The aura is art-deco draft—a movie set out of a thirties comedy. It appeared to possess the right cockeyed charm for the Spinks entourage. The mood was high on arrival.

During the press conference in New Orleans, Leon had had this exchange:

NEWSMAN: At the airport, you said you'd have something to say after you signed the contract. What do you have to say now?

SPINKS: Santa Claus.

He growled the words with a loving Satchmo sound, grinning as he did. Santa Claus: shorthand that meant the getting had been good—Spinks's signature assured that millions of dollars would be made. The pleasure remained. At the airport in Miami, when a TV sportscaster asked Spinks to describe how it felt to whip Ali, he smiled and did a soft-shoe routine, at the finish of which he extended his hand and said, "Like that."

Later, in Miami Beach, he walked Lincoln Road Mall, where he signed autographs, mugged for cameras, kissed women, and shopped.

"How much those shoes?" he asked, pointing to a pair of size-12 Pierre Cardin loafers.

"Not too much," the salesman said.

"Then I'll take them."

From a thick wad of currency, Leon peeled off a $100 bill for the salesman.

"And what are these?" Spinks asked.

"Money clips."

"Will they hold a lot of money?"

"Yes, Mr. Spinks."

"OK. Gimme one."

Spinks tried to insert his roll of bills, but it was too thick to fit inside the clip.

Spinks spent a sunny day in Miami Beach, grinning, dancing across streets, quipping to young women ("Whaddaya say, momma?"). That night, Spinks, a welterweight named Roger Stafford, and I stood by a low stone wall at the end of Lincoln Road, watching the ocean break against the shore just below. Spinks was in a form-fitting maroon shirt and cream-colored slacks. He and Stafford were drinking California pink champagne. A gentle breeze blew.

"It gonna be good to hit some m . . . .rf . . . .r again," said Spinks, putting his glass on the wall and inhaling a smoke.

"Yeahhhh, I know," said Stafford, settling back, drink down, too.

Spinks struck a fighting pose, bent at the knees, and let his hands go.

"Whap! Whap!" Stafford was moving punches through the air, emitting small grunting sounds as he did. "That's the way I did it to that dude," he said, referring to a preliminary bout he'd fought that weekend on national TV. "All over the m . . . .rf . . . .r."

"Yeahhhh," said Spinks.

"I whupped that dude good——"

"Hey. My man," Spinks interrupted, addressing me. "Hey, you ain't gonna put in the ar-ti-cle that I smoke, is you?"

"Heyyyy," I said, with an elaborate shrug that was not quite an answer.

"'Count of my image," Spinks said.

Spinks thought about it and then forgot about it and began to move sinuously, reducing his shadow punches to a stoned dance.

"Women," said Stafford. "Got to get women."

"Women," answered Spinks.

"Got to."

"Sweet nothings?" I asked.

"No. Lies," said Stafford. "Tell 'em lies."

"Liiiiees," crooned Spinks, his body rocking as he grinned. "Tell 'em liieees."

Stafford swayed in answer. "Liiieeees."

"Tell 'em liieeees."

They doubled over in laughter, Spinks making plashing sounds with his mouth.

"Liiieees."

"Tell 'em liieees."

Minutes later, Spinks was gliding through the DiLido lobby, still sipping champagne, when a team of women bowlers from Terre Haute, Ind., recognized him. Out came the cameras. Spinks obliged by posing for snapshots, drinking champagne refills as he did.

"Get outa my pitcher," a pretty young black woman said. "Just me 'n' the man."

A bowler in pin curlers arrived. "We was dressed for bed and they come up and said Leon Spinks."

"Leon," a heavyset woman said, "let me show you a picture of my grandchildren. They triplets."

"Where's the champagne?" another bowler wondered.

"It's on me," Spinks said, moving toward the hotel restaurant, waving his arm when the women hesitated. "Come on, ladies."

Soon after, the Spinks caravan was on the move. Up the road it went to Place Pigalle, a Miami Beach Club whose all-girl revue and X-rated comedienne, Pearl Williams, were the attractions. Tuesdays, though, Williams was off. So, for this night, the strippers would do.

The Leon Spinks Calendar had called for Spinks to spend this second week in April training for his Caribbean tour. But the good times would roll instead. The sun was coming up when the heavyweight champ made it back to the DiLido.

A few days later, there was another incident that still lives in my mind. Spinks was standing in the DiLido penthouse number one, his $100-a-day lodgings, idling for a moment before plunging into another day. The sun streamed through a space in the drapes. His step had a loose, easy swing. Then suddenly he was holding up the index finger of each hand, and with a rumbalike motion of the hips, he began to move, chanting in a comically falsetto voice, "Penthouse number one, penthouse number one"—and smiling. The style was Carmen Miranda's, but the pleasure was all Spinks's. Penthouse number one: top of the world, momma.

But with Spinks, the pleasure of being up there was never far removed from the trick impulses that could bring him down. And as the week progressed in Miami Beach, there were troubling notes. Complications caused the Caribbean tour to be pushed back a week, creating a gap in The Spinks Calendar that left Leon susceptible to demon whispers. A call from Lewis also augured problems. As he hung up, Spinks muttered, "One thing after another. Shit. Shit. Shit."

And a few days later, as Nova arrived in Miami Beach, Leon was on the run again, headed for St. Louis. There were problems there with Barnes. Barnes had agreed to take less than his customary 30 percent of the purse for the Spinks-Ali rematch, but he had grievances that could threaten the bout.

Lewis was to meet Spinks in St. Louis. Before Lewis left, he phoned the DiLido to check on Spinks's whereabouts. In penthouse number one, Nova picked up the phone, heard Lewis's voice, and hung up. She figured he was to blame for Spinks's latest abrupt departure.

Lewis found Spinks and told him that a meeting in New York was planned to straighten out details of the Spinks-Ali rematch. The various interests—Barnes, Bell, Arum—would be there. Spinks agreed to the trip but kept delaying.

On Wednesday, April 19, Lewis urged him to leave St. Louis. Spinks seemed inclined to but asked, "Can I take my baby with me to New York?"—a reference to his St. Louis woman. Lewis told him he could do what he wanted—just be on the flight to New York. Spinks's woman said she had to get her clothes. Lewis waited at the airport. When Spinks did not appear, he gave up and flew back to New York. That was on Thursday.

On Friday, April 21, he heard on the radio that Spinks was busted again.

"Has been released on a $3,700 bond. Spinks was taken into custody on charges involving suspected drug violations ... and failure to produce a driver's license. He was booked on suspicion of two counts of violating the Missouri controlled-substance law by possession of marijuana and cocaine. Police say warrants will be sought later today. Arrested with Spinks was a 26-year-old woman companion."

A later report stated that torn $10, $20, and $50 bills were found in the trunk of Spinks's car.

With the heavyweight champion involved, guilty or innocent hardly mattered. Wheels would turn, deals could be made. In fact, the drug charges were later dropped. But ...

Whisper called the next day.

"Battling Siki," he said.

"Who?"

"Battling Siki, my friend. Real name Louis Phal. A Senegalese Negro. Won the light-heavyweight championship in 1922. Knocked out Georges Carpentier in six rounds. Paris, France. Siki was called the Singular Senegalese. And he came here a raw fucking African. We're going back over 50 years. Loved his wine, women, and song. And belting guys in the chops. And wearing the grass-skirt-and-top-hat kind of thing. He's buried here in New York. Out in Flushing, Long Island. A couple of years ago, a boxers' association put a tombstone up ... Died in a fucking bar brawl in New York City. December 15, anno Domini 1925. Look it up."

And he clicked off.

Best Magazine Story (Co-Winner)
OUTDOORS

THE SHARKERS

By Colin Campbell

From Sports Afield
Copyright, ©, 1978, Sports Afield Magazine

On Sunday, July 19,1977, about 45 miles southeast of Montauk, Long Island, four men and a boy, all from around Paterson, N.J., caught a 1,039-pound mako shark. It was one of the biggest makos ever captured. Their 27-foot boat was too small and simple a craft from which to hunt huge dangerous fish so far at sea. And they did not know, or even care about, the rules by which one of them might have gained an official record for the second largest mako ever caught on a rod and reel—and the largest ever in the Atlantic, a terrifying creature almost 12 feet long. This is their story from 7 o'clock that Sunday morning until about 7 o'clock at night.

The boat was almost asleep. Only Rich Manos was awake. He was half-sitting, half-reclining in the helmsman's seat on the flying bridge, with his long legs pressed awkwardly against the rail to keep himself from tipping over, for the drifting boat was rocking and pitching. The sea wasn't much rougher than it had been, but the waves were at least six feet tall, and choppy. The wind was blowing at about 15 miles an hour.

Rich had climbed up on the flying bridge to get away from the cockpit, where for about an hour he had been ladling out chum and tossing sliced chunks of mossbunker and mackerel into the chum slick that stretched by now for miles away from the boat. They had been drifting on the open ocean since midnight. The open cans and buckets of chum and blood kept sliding back and forth in the stern and sloshing onto the deck, and the cockpit was slippery and a little sickening. He had fallen down several times as the boat lurched in the early-morning mist, and he had gone to the flying bridge to get away from it all.

It was chilly up there. His hands, clothes, and hair were sticky with mist and salt water and there was a bad taste in his mouth. Rich had been awake all night fishing for blue sharks and catching some, and he had been sharpening the points and edges of hooks with the file and stone he always took fishing with him. He had rigged the leaders and done dozens of other small chores. Rich was the man aboard who could do almost anything with his hands. He was part plumber, mechanic, carpenter, electrician; he even had a business as a mason on the side. And he was an experienced fisherman, although not on the ocean, and he had never fished for sharks.

One of the reels ticked. It lasted only a second and a half, but he had learned the difference between the ticking that a wave caused as it broke against the line and the ticking that a shark caused. "There's a fish," he said in a loud voice, almost a yell. Something had taken one of the three whole mackerel baits that were drifting at various distances and depths in the chum slick. The fish was on the rod in the starboard rod holder closest to the stern.

Jimmy Kooz woke up in the cramped bow. It seemed to him that a lurch had woken him—an especially big wave that had turned the boat almost on its side. Kooz walked back through the cabin. Rich was jumping down from the flying bridge just as Kooz reached the deck.

The reel clicked and then stopped clicking. The two men, both 26 years old, looked at each other. Rich picked the rod out of the holder. It was the old black rod that their 25-year-old captain, Jimmy George, had bought just the day before from the mate of one of the charterboats, back at Montauk: a solid fiberglass rod whose gold windings were new but whose tipmost roller was immobilized by corrosion or rust. Yet the line still slid smoothly in the roller's groove. Jimmy George had bought the reel with the rod: a used 10/0 Penn reel, a big heavy tool for heavy fish, and almost identical to the 10/0 reels on the other two rods. Jimmy had paid $110 for rod and reel.

Rich and Kooz were looking out over the gray waves at their farthest balloon, a yellow party balloon about 100 yards out. It bobbed on the surface. The line from the rod that Rich was holding went into the water and out to the balloon, which was tied to the line with a slip knot; and then the line dropped exactly 35 feet, including the 12-foot piano-wire leader. Toward the end of the leader the wire entered the mouth of a pound-and-a-half dead mackerel, and from the mackerel's vent dangled a big 12/0 hook.

There was a fish on that hook, a blue shark, perhaps, like the three blues they had hooked and boated during the night. Or perhaps it was a mako. At five o'clock that morning there had been a violent bite and something had torn off 300 yards of line before the line went slack. That had no doubt been a mako, according to Jimmy, who had been awake in the cockpit with Rich. But this was probably a blue.

Then the line started out again, not fast but steadily. The yellow balloon jumped about three feet to the right and stopped. It was a peculiar little motion. A few seconds later the fish started moving away fast.

Rich switched the click off the free-running spool, thinking that the click might somehow warn the fish. He was about to throw on the drag and set the hook when Kooz said, "No, no, wait a second. A little longer." Kooz had fished for sharks before with Jimmy, and they had caught blue and brown sharks up to 275 pounds. Kooz's timing was generally shrewd. So Rich waited, letting the fish swallow the bait.

The line was picking up speed, moving straight away from the starboard side of the boat, straight down the long chum line. It moved fast for another five seconds; another 10 seconds.

Kooz said, "Click it and set the hook. Now!" Rich flipped the clutch forward and braced his legs, ready to set the hook with a great upward yank.

But the tug on the line that he expected once the drag was on did not happen. Rich thought for a moment that the fish had spit the bait. Then he felt and saw the line tightening (evidently there had been some slack in it) and he pulled back hard on the rod, as hard as he could, once.

He never got to pull back twice, as he might have with a blue shark. He did not stop the fish, either, as he might have stopped a blue. Instead, the line took off straight away from the boat and the rod pitched forward with such force that he had to struggle to hold it as he backed into the starboard fighting chair. The line kept tearing off the spool. He wrestled the rod butt toward the gimbaled socket attached to the seat between his legs. He tried to jab it into the socket and he jabbed himself painfully in the left thigh. He tried again and secured the rod.

Kooz was shouting for everybody to wake up. The taut line was beginning to belly to the left, and it hit a wave and then snapped free and slapped the next wave. Rich was watching a spot on the water where he thought the fish was, and then out of the corner of his eye, much farther to the left than he was looking and about 150 yards from the boat, he saw some huge thing come out of the water.

Kooz saw it too, or at least he saw it once the fish had left the water. And Jimmy George, their friend and captain who had been sleeping in a blanket on the forward deck, he saw it too, but not until it had reached its zenith and started to flatten out and fall. And 15-year-old Bobby, Jimmy's nephew, who had been curled on the deckhouse floor, saw the patch of suds as big as the boat itself that the fish left behind once it had hit the waves and disappeared.

It was a shark, the biggest shark that any of them had ever seen, and it came shooting out of the water as if from a considerable depth, as straight as a bottle standing on a table. It looked dark gray against the brightening haze and the gray sea around it, and it kept rising. It shook its head. It turned as if on an axis and they could see its white belly. The seawater poured from its gills; the water gushed and shot down toward the sea as if from hoses. To Rich, staring at it with his long neck tilted back and his Adam's apple jumping, the fish looked 18 or 20 feet long and a yard and a half wide— although of course it couldn't be that big. Sleek and muscular, it seemed to rise three times its own height, or even four times, or five times. He could see its pointed snout and the white teeth in its mouth, and the mouth did not move. This fish seemed to Rich to be moving in slow motion. To Kooz, the shark looked as if it weighed 800 pounds, and water shot out of its gills like the exhaust from a dragster's manifold when the driver punches the accelerator and the car rises off its front wheels with the smoke shooting and billowing out of the pipes on each side.

The shark struck the water on its belly and it made the kind of splash that a boat would make if it were dropped into the water from a height. A wave went out on all sides. The sea crashed into the hole the fish had made and a fountain of water rose where the hole had been. And then foam.

Jimmy knew that he would have to get the boat moving if they wanted to catch the fish, which he felt sure they would never do. He was already on the flying bridge, having first jumped down into the cockpit and started the engine from the deckhouse because the ignition on the bridge had a loose wire and didn't work. The shark had sped off and stripped hundreds of yards of line from the reel. They would have to chase the fish if they were going to catch him before the reel lost all of its 600 yards of line. Or perhaps the reel held 700 yards. They did not know. Rich, in the fighting chair, had no more than 100 yards left on the narrowing spool, and the fish was headed far to the left now and even across the bow, and the line had a huge belly in it before it disappeared in the waves. Rich screamed hoarsely at Jimmy to get the boat moving. He was also shouting more mindless profanity than the boat had heard for many hours, and so was everybody else.

"We've got a monster!" Rich screamed. "It's gotta be a great white!"

"It jumped like a mako," Jimmy shouted back over the sound of the engine. He had assumed it was a mako as soon as it jumped, for the mako was the famous leaping shark, the supreme game fish among sharks.

"It's too big to be a mako," Rich shouted back. "I swear it's a great white. It's gotta be!"

Jimmy had caught a lot more sharks than anyone else aboard and he thought it was a mako, but he didn't know. So maybe Rich was right. Rich had fished in Maine, Michigan, Florida, New York, Pennsylvania. He had been a fisherman since he was five years old and at least he read about sharks. He had bought the magazines and watched the shark programs on television, and studied A.J. McClane's *Fishing Encyclopedia* for fun. So maybe the fish was a great white.

The Silverton was moving steadily now, its 225-horsepower gasoline engine roaring, its single screw pushing the 27-foot white fiberglass hull over the big waves. The shark was headed northeast, Jimmy noticed on the compass. They were headed more or less toward Block Island and more or less out to sea. Kooz and Bobby reeled in the other two lines and tossed the rods into the deckhouse, and they pulled up the two plastic chum buckets that were dangling and bouncing from the stern and tried to shove them out of the way in the crowded cockpit.

Kooz stayed near Rich to help whenever he could, and after about 10 minutes Rich needed his leather gloves. His left thumb was burning. As the boat moved closer to the shark and as Rich reeled in yard after yard of the 100-pound-test Ande line, he used the thumb to guide the line back and forth across the spool. Kooz gave him the gloves and Rich managed to put the left one on.

The reel warmed in his hands as the shark kept stripping line against the drag. Rich lightened the drag whenever the shark made a run. In fact the drag seemed useless, but he left it on. The reel stayed warm. Rich could feel the warm stainless steel and plastic against his right hand when he was not turning the crank. So Kooz found some rags that he dipped in seawater and then tried to hold over the sides of the reel to keep it cool. It might blow up in Rich's hands for all they knew.

Then Kooz got Rich a small can of pineapple juice from the icebox in the deckhouse cabin. Rich's voice was a wreck and he needed the juice badly.

There were two guns aboard, and Kooz rushed off again and got one of them from the cabin. It was Rich's single shot 20-gauge shotgun, a Harrington and Richardson. Rich had broken it down late the previous night after using it to dispatch the first blue shark they caught. Kooz found it on the counter next to the sink and he assembled it. The other gun, a .22 Browning autoloader that belonged to Jimmy, was ready to use any time. It too had killed sharks.

Kooz felt they might need the guns, for this fish was frightening. He had seen the movie *Jaws* and he kept thinking about it. Maybe the great white shark in the movie was just a model, but this shark of theirs moved much faster and seemed to be able to turn at right angles, instantly.

They chased the fish around the ocean for the next three hours. It was always moving, never stopping. Most of the time it stayed near the surface. It never sounded. It would run 300 yards or 400 yards underwater in a minute or even half a minute, and then there would be a splash way out there, and the boat would press toward the splash through the waves. There was much shouting and confusion. Rich struggled to hold the rod and his arms developed knots. He kept saying, "We're gonna have to fight this fish for six hours. For 10 hours. We can't land it," he said. "We'll never get it." Jimmy agreed, but it never entered their minds to cut the line. When they approached it they could see as much as six inches of its dorsal fin standing in the waves, and sometimes its whole back.

After two hours Rich gave the rod to Jimmy. Rich could have fought the fish longer, but what difference did it make? If the fish were a great white it could not have been a record. Besides, this was hardly a formal angling expedition, with sporting light tackle and nobody so much as touching the man on the rod. This was a sharking trip, a hunt, a lark; and the mood of the boat was casual. This was a democratic boat and they were after a democratic gamefish, a shark, the poor man's marlin, and everybody got a chance to fish.

It was like a club. It was like a family, Jimmy felt. His father had acquired this adventuresome little boat, or had won the price of it, anyway, on a roll of the dice—hence the boat's name, *Craps Two Sixes*—and he had bought it more for his sons Jimmy and Doug than for himself.

So now Jimmy was on the rod, and although he had fought sharks before, they were nothing compared to this one. He gritted his teeth and strained his back, burned dark by the summer's sun, and he swore at the fish, which would tear off in a straight line against the drag until the boat started to catch up again. Rich was steering now, and he could still feel the cramps in his arms. Jimmy would reel in line as the boat approached the fish, hidden under the waves, and then the fish would take off again. The strain never stopped.

Jimmy stayed with the fish for about 45 minutes—it was impossible to keep time on this ride.

At least once while Jimmy was fighting the fish, and as the boat was running up on it to gain line, he had to move from one chair to the other; for the line would suddenly move far over to one side of the boat. The single engine could not maneuver them fast enough to keep the line from threatening to pass under the keel and breaking unless the fisherman changed chairs, extracting the rod from its gimbaled socket between his legs and hotfooting it over into the next seat.

Then Kooz took the rod and Jimmy took the wheel again. Kooz wasn't a large man, neither as tall and lanky as Rich nor as chunky as Jimmy, but he had muscles and fast reflexes. In a way this was as much Kooz's fish as it was Rich's, who had hooked it, or Jimmy's, who was the captain. It was his in part because Kooz was the doctor of the chum.

Kooz had definite ideas about the way chum should look and feel. It wasn't the simple ground bunker or mackerel that most sharkers around Montauk used for chum. That was just the basis.

He had mixed the chum the night before, as they were headed out to sea. They had bought eight five-gallon cans of frozen ground bunker, far more than any thrifty or even sensible angler would think of buying.

Kooz mixed the ground bunker with seawater in a 10-gallon bucket—pretty much the way other sharkers mixed it. Then he added tropical fish food. Jimmy's uncle had found a deal someplace on two whole cases of Hartz fish food. Kooz poured box after box of the powdery fish food into his mixing bucket.

Then there was the calf's blood. Rich had procured five gallons of it in a plastic bucket from a farmer friend in New York and Kooz poured some of that in. He poured the mixture into two plastic chum buckets, which he covered and tied with clothesline to the two rear cleats, port and starboard, so that the buckets dangled over the sides just above the water. The chum buckets had holes in them so that whenever the rocking boat would sink down into the water a wave would slosh past at least one of the buckets and bits and pieces of the stew would escape into the sea.

Once he had dangled the two buckets of chum over the side he made a third batch of the same chum in his mixing pail. But to this he added still another ingredient: chunks of beef fat cut from six large slabs that he had bought a few days earlier from two butchers. He ladled out small portions of this third, fatty mixture straight over the side.

Kooz also sliced up chunks of mackerel and whole bunker and tossed them periodically into the ocean, which was standard sharking practice; and every now and then he would open up another dozen boxes of Hartz fish food and sow the waters with them. And finally, adding the perfect touch to Kooz's stew, he poured some of the calf's blood into a plastic gallon milk jug and suspended it from the side. The blood would tend to coagulate but as the seawater sloshed against the plastic bottle and ran into the holes that they had poked near the top of it, the red-brown jelly kept dissolving and trickling out.

This was their trail.

Kooz's chum had lured that enormous shark to the bait, or perhaps it had lured the fish that had lured the shark. No matter. It had found them, and now it was trying to rip the rod and line right out of Kooz's aching arms.

It may have been then that Doug George emerged from the cabin like a specter. He was seasick. His skin was gray and his light brown hair mixed with gray stood up on his head in tufts. Doug had spent some rough time in his 35 years. He had been in the Marine Corps and tougher places than that, but there could be no remembered pain like the presence of seasickness. He could fight it for hours if he stayed awake, but once he went to sleep and woke up sick he could not stop it. He was sick now and needed air. He climbed up the ladder to the flying bridge, to a ledge about two feet wide behind the padded seat where the helmsman sat. Doug tied himself to that white fiberglass ledge with half-inch nylon rope. And there he lay overlooking the cockpit, trying to sleep.

Doug felt deathly ill as he sat on his perch. The world was spinning, and as he looked down with his pale gray eyes at the cockpit below him, he saw the same whirling confusion that was going on inside him: twisted ropes, overturned buckets, mops, gaffs, knives, men running around crazily; the sounds of grunting and shouting, engine throbbing, waves tossed aside as the boat rocked forward and in circles; the smells of dead fish, blood, salt water, exhaust; and the hazy bright light of day. Doug shut his eyes.

Kooz was still on the rod and there were signs that maybe the shark was tiring. It had left the water several more times, like a porpoise, but its runs against the drag and against the line in the water seemed weaker and shorter. Kooz offered the rod to Bobby. "Come on," Kooz told him, and Jimmy and Rich encouraged him too; but the youngster thought: What if I lose the fish? I'll never live it down. He said no.

Bobby had been trying to stay out of the way. Periodically his uncle Jimmy would yell at him to go below. Jimmy was afraid he might get hurt. Bobby would hear him and disappear into the deckhouse for a minute. But he would always come back. He wasn't going to miss this monster.

Besides, Bobby was useful. It was Bobby, after all, who had spent $84 of his own money, money he had worked at a refreshment stand for $2.20 an hour to earn, to buy a beautiful flying gaff for the boat. It had a detachable stainless-steel hook on the end, barbless and extremely sharp, and a long gold anodized aluminum shaft. It was a beauty. Bobby knew you could not simply gaff a big shark with the kind of short barbed gaff the boat also carried. You might need to gaff him and then let the hook of the gaff fly off the shaft at the end of a line. You would have the shark on a line then instead of at the end of a short stick where he could twist free, or even bite your arm off.

The fish was getting closer. Kooz was on the rod and Jimmy was handling the boat. Rich got his shotgun.

As Kooz reeled in line, the shark came closer, its tail to them. The fish hovered there enormously, finning the water with his dark pectorals, his dorsal fin rigid as a piling in the waves.

Anyone could have shot the fish, and Rich was a good shot. He had hunted deer for years and had even killed several deer with a bow and arrow. So had Kooz and Jimmy—they were all hunters—but Rich hunted more than any of them and was the best shot on the boat. And he did not need to be a good shot. The fish was next to him.

Rich leaned over the gunwale slightly, aimed at a point above the eyes of the shark's massive head, and, as the head rose out of the water for a second, he fired. The shark could not have been more than six feet from the muzzle of the gun.

But the shark did not die or bleed. It thrashed and swam off in a straight line as powerfully as ever. The single slug from the 20-gauge shotgun had apparently done nothing.

Kooz gave the rod to Jimmy, and Rich climbed up on the flying bridge to steer. Meanwhile Kooz prepared Bobby's flying gaff.

They moved up on the fish again. Kooz held the flying gaff and leaned out toward it with the long gold pole, but the fish spooked and surged away.

So Kooz sat down with the rod and Jimmy got his .22 rifle. They decided the fish was too strong to gaff.

The shark was nearing the boat on the port side, coming closer. Jimmy balanced himself on the six-inch walkway that ran fore and aft beside the deckhouse. There was a short useless rail beside his left foot, and below that was the water.

He needed to aim the rifle as the boat overtook the shark, so he crossed his left arm over his chest and with his left hand grabbed the handhold on the flying bridge just to the right of his neck. Then he rested the foregrip of the little rifle over his left arm and pointed it generally at the approaching shark.

"Doug," he said to his brother, who was tied to the same handhold to the right of Jimmy's head, "Doug, open your eyes, you've got to see this. You'll never see anything like this fish as long as you live."

Doug lifted his head and looked. The shark swam in the water below him. It was a massive creature. He could hardly believe that these people had been so crazy and stupid as to try to catch this fish.

"You guys are nuts," he said to Jimmy. "You guys are outta your minds!" he yelled. "Cut him loose! Cut that line and get him outta here!"

Jimmy aimed at the shark's head. Now the blue-gray skin broke the water; now it was an inch beneath the surface. He fired. He shot the shark again and again as rapidly as he could pull the trigger of the autoloader. It sounded like a string of firecrackers. He must have shot the shark 10 times in a row, in the head and in front of the dorsal fin, an area of about 12 square feet.

But there wasn't a sign of blood and the fish moved violently—and not away from the boat but toward it and under it. There was a banging and a crashing and the shark struck the boat, or perhaps attacked it. Jimmy clutched the rail in disbelief. The shark has gone berserk, he thought; he feared the fish might kill them.

Doug said, "I'm never coming fishing with you guys again."

Then Jimmy got on the rod again, and he screamed at Bobby to go below. Bobby went. Later he returned quietly as always.

Rich sat at the helm; Kooz and Jimmy shouted a new directive now; not to get too close to the shark.

Rich did not need to be told. He was feeling an odd sensation. He was shaking. He had become scared now. He kept thinking: What if the shark jumps into the boat? It could kill somebody, thrashing his tail, lunging at people with his teeth. He could jump into the boat and land with such a smash that he sank it. They had been out of radio contact for hours. And where were they anyway, Rich wondered. They had been chasing the shark for hours and it seemed to be leading them farther out to sea. Rich could see its eye as the shark surfaced near them. He had never seen such a black circular eye. This shark's eyes weren't at all like the catlike eyes of blue sharks. They were round and black and they seemed to be looking at the boat. What was it thinking? For a short while Rich actually trembled with fear.

The others were also worried, and Jimmy was thinking about the gasoline. The boat held 120 gallons and had been full when they left Montauk, but they had traveled a long way since then. If they chased the shark for another few hours they would never make it home.

So they discussed all this, shouting back and forth over the engine, and they decided they must do everything possible to shorten the fight. They would stay away from it so that it wouldn't jump in the cockpit. But they would creep up toward it too so that it never got a chance to rest. And as soon as possible they would try to kill it from the bow with the harpoon.

This harpoon was another item designed especially for this trip, and it was a fine piece of work. Doug had bought the dart and 18-inch dart holder and attached them to a 10-foot aluminum pipe. He had whittled a piece of wooden dowel until it fit snugly into both the barb-holder below and the pipe above. And that was it. Kooz had supplied the pipe and had also bought an extra dart.

They had a beer keg for a buoy. Doug had welded an eye to the two-foot-high keg and painted the keg white.

So the three-inch brass dart or barb at the tip of the assembled harpoon would stick into the fish; and then the fish would run, they hoped, carrying the dart with him, and tied to the dart would be a quarter-inch nylon line, 50 feet long; and at the other end of the line would be the buoy. No shark could put up with that for long—bleeding from the deep wound and dragging around a heavy steel beer keg.

But who would handle the barrel? It would have to be thrown into the water together with the 50 feet of line precisely as Kooz harpooned the shark, or else the barrel and the line could get caught up on something or wrap around someone's foot and carry him off. They had no special tub in which to coil the line.

Bobby would handle the barrel. "Go up the bridge next to Rich," Jimmy told his nephew, "and hold that barrel away from you, and throw it over the side as soon as Kooz sticks the fish. Do you hear me? Keep that barrel away from you and don't you touch that rope."

Jimmy could not believe what he had just said. After protecting his nephew all day he had given him the most treacherous job of all, where soft coils of shiny nylon rope could do almost anything to a man. But there was no more time to think. The boat was moving closer to the shark.

It was out there on the port side, the side where Bobby held the barrel and where Jimmy sat in the fighting chair. The boat was moving toward it, and the boat and the shark seemed to be on a slow collision course. Everyone was shouting at each other, and Kooz and Jimmy were both shouting at Rich at the wheel. They would have to get the shark precisely at the bow where Kooz could hit it.

Kooz stood with his legs pressed against the bow rail. It was too low to hold on to. He was thinking: I hope I don't fall over. The bow flew up against a wave and then sank down, and Kooz thought that standing up would have been difficult even without the harpoon in his hands. He had never used a harpoon. A gaff, yes, but never a harpoon.

Jimmy was peering up the port side and screaming at Rich, "Cut the boat to the right! Cut the boat to the right! He's running under the boat!"

But Rich could see the shark. It was moving toward the point of the bow. Kooz could see the shark too, and it looked brown in the water and about 10 feet wide (The water must be magnifying it, he thought) and he was terrified of falling. And then the bow fell into a trough and Kooz put both arms and all his strength into a downward thrust of the harpoon. The instant the barb had penetrated the skin—toward the rear of the dorsal fin, and just to the right of it—Kooz threw himself into another big shove down into the flesh of the shark, and he could feel it cutting into gristle.

Before he had pulled up with the shaft, leaving the barb deep in the shark, he could see how the heavy steel beer barrel exploded out of Bobby's hands, how it shot straight away from the bridge and then shot down into the waves and disappeared. Bobby never got a chance to throw it. They heard and felt a series of hard bumps against the bottom of the boat, as startling and as frightening as if someone had suddenly pounded on your door late at night, and Jimmy felt the rod loosen. He reeled in his line and it was broken. The water had turned reddish with blood, but they saw neither shark nor barrel. They looked at each other blankly.

After a minute Kooz saw the barrel surface about 100 feet in front of the boat. It was moving away from them fast. Then the barrel stopped and floated. And then after an instant it was coming toward the boat, skipping across the waves. He yelled to Rich to throw the boat into reverse, but the shark missed the boat, and the can went under.

For the next half hour they chased the shark and the barrel, and sometimes they could see the barrel and sometimes not. But at least it was secure.

They rigged another dart, for they had decided to stick the shark again. Their gasoline was getting low.

Kooz rigged the dart in about five minutes. For a float he used two air-filled plastic bumpers, the kind that cushioned the side of the boat against docks and pilings. The bumpers had been Jimmy's idea.

Soon they were on top of the shark again, and from the bow, Jimmy, who had never used a harpoon either, drove the dart into the shark's flesh on the other side of the dorsal fin from where Kooz had struck. Kooz saw a big cloud of blood, and then a red stream.

Still later, they picked up the bumpers with the short gaff, and wearing gloves, they started to pull the fish in. The bumpers were at the end of a 100-foot line, twice as long as the line that held the barrel. And then they picked up the barrel and pulled in that line too. They quickly realized that they weren't pulling the shark to the boat; they were pulling the boat to the shark, which hovered near the surface, finning.

The fish took off again, and the lines and buoys that they had thrown into the boat banged past them and out to sea.

Doug was watching them. He called down from his lashed-in sickbed on the bridge and said, "Put the line into a bucket. Do it right. Coil it around so it can get out."

So as they pulled the boat up to the shark again, a job that made their arms and back cry out, they coiled the lines neatly in buckets. Bobby helped them haul in the fish.

And at last they had the shark up to the transom, right there, and it was beautiful. The waves had dropped to about three feet and they could look at it as they strained on the lines. They had never seen such a beautiful fish, a gleaming dark blue gray. It seemed to Rich that this was a free thing of the ocean and had never before been in contact with man, and later he regretted taking it from the water. But of course, this was their prize, and no one would have believed them if they had let it go.

They avoided its head, leaving the head and jaws where they could not see them in the water. They wanted to throw a loop of line around its tail. Doug had made a noose in the half-inch anchor line, and Jimmy tried to loop it around the shark's hard tail.

The shark thrashed, and the harpoon lines that Kooz was trying to wrap around the stern rail pressed his right hand against the rail so hard that it broke the large knuckle on his index finger. Kooz was out of action with that hand.

But Jimmy had the tail rope and he did not want to lose this fish. He leaned over the transom on his belly, with his legs in the air over the cockpit deck behind him and his head and arms struggling out over the water, and he grabbed the shark's sandpapery tail with his right hand, and with his left hand he looped the line around it.

The fish was theirs. They tied him to the starboard cleat. It was 11:45 in the morning.

It took them five hours to reach Montauk; the shark drowned along the way.

Jimmy established his homeward course in his normal way, in his head. His homing instinct had always worked before and it worked again that Sunday afternoon. They were joking now, and they felt very good. They saw other boats and then the Montauk light and the Great Eastern Buoy, and they heard its bell and they felt very good. Once they had rounded the tip of Long Island, other boats started noticing the huge shape and the gray dorsal that they were dragging behind them. It was Sunday and there were plenty of boats on the water.

They had acquired an escort by the time they rounded the bend into the harbor, two sportfishermen in front and three behind, and the people on the other boats were pointing at them.

And finally they arrived at the Westlake Marina, where Jimmy had docked his boat for the past two summers. They chugged straight for the scale in front of the restaurant.

A big blond young fellow at the dock—Jimmy Sweetman, an old friend of Jimmy George—looked down and asked what it was they had there. He could not really see the fish.

"We've got a thousand-pound shark, a mako, I think," Jimmy said. "A thousand pounds."

"Ahh, you're fulla it," Sweetman said amiably. "What have you got, a basking shark?"

They said no, it was no basking shark, they had a fighter, a killer; and once Sweetman had taken a better look at it in the water he said, "It is a mako! Look at the size of that mako!"

After that, people poured out of the marina's restaurant, about 100 people in all.

Children were laughing and shrieking, and girls in bikinis (it's true, there are shark groupies) were gathering with the fishermen and the tourists as the shark was hoisted out of the water. The owner of the Westlake Marina was saying, "What a fish. What a fish. For as long as I've been here I've never seen a fish like that."

There was a sharp cracking sound and as people shouted and scattered the shark crashed down onto the dock and slid into the water. It had broken the scale.

Everybody was shouting then and disagreeing about what to do. Then the young captain of one of the charterboats suggested that they take the fish to the Montauk Marine Basin to be weighed. The man phoned there first and described the fish, and they said fine, bring it over, although the marina was in the middle of a ceremony and they were handing out awards for a shark-fishing tournament that had just ended; and their mako, by the way, was too late to enter. So the sharkers tied the fish to the boat again and putted across the busy harbor.

They could not believe their eyes when they rounded the corner and drove up to the scales at Montauk Marine Basin. At least a thousand people were standing on the dock. The PA system was telling the crowd that another big shark was headed their way but have no fear, it was too late to enter the contest. Carl Darenberg had built his marina over the past 30 years on publicity as much as on hard work, and he was waiting for them as they reached the overhead scale. Someone had told him the fish weighed 1,000 pounds. He thought to himself, baloney. But he was cordial and helpful at the scale, and as the electric hoist pulled the fish out of the water, Darenberg was amazed. He too thought it was the biggest mako he had ever seen.

The tournament's presentation ceremony had disintegrated and people were crowding around the fish and trying to touch it as it rose. Children shrieked again as the teeth appeared—and no shark has the awl-like teeth of the mako. They were long and sharp and they protruded crookedly from his mouth like the teeth of some nightmare demon.

It weighed 1,039 pounds, and when the crowd heard that they clapped for a good 15 seconds. Several observers knew sharks and said that the world-record mako caught on a rod and reel had weighed 1,061 pounds and had been caught off New Zealand. And someone else said that Ernest Hemingway himself had once held the Atlantic record for a mako, and his had weighed just 786 pounds. He caught it off Bimini in the Bahamas in 1936.

Two fishery biologists, specialists in sharks, were there, and one of them, Jack Casey of the National Marine Fisheries Service in Narragansett, R.I., abandoned his examination of the tournament's sharks and asked the sharkers to let him cut open the mako and examine her ovaries, for the reproductive lives of mature pelagic sharks were little known.

It was a female, the sharkers repeated. Amazing.

The fish was indeed the common mako of the Atlantic, *Isurus oxyrinchus* Raffinesque, 1810. She had borne pups recently, within a month or two. Some of the old marks on her skin were from the teeth of males; they were mating scars. The shotgun blast had left nothing but a small round dent within a circle. The slug had not penetrated. The .22s had left no marks whatsoever.

Someone stuck a microphone in Jimmy's face, since Jimmy was the captain, and said, "I want to speak to the man who caught the shark."

Jimmy waved a hand at his friends and said, "*Five* guys caught the fish. We all caught it. All five of us worked as a team."

Darenberg seemed pained to hear Jimmy say this. Record fish were not caught by "teams."

They were in a kind of ecstasy and when Carl Darenberg told them there was a man who would mount the fish, all 11 feet 9 inches of it, for nothing, they pretty much agreed. Rich, who was an accomplished amateur taxidermist in addition to all his other skills, had planned to mount only the head; whereas Darenberg, who was an agent for the Pfluger taxidermists, would get it stuffed from nose to tail.

So 11 men, as the announcer counted them over the PA system, moved the shark from the dock to a refrigerator truck on the parking lot. One of Darenberg's 22,000-pound forklifts picked it up, and three or four men pulled it into the truck.

Rich worked inside the truck for a long time as the light faded. They had propped open the shark's jaws with a tire iron, and he was extracting teeth. He got them out with a wood chisel and he took them from the rows of spares rather than from the outer row. They each got a tooth, and some of them got more than one. Rich noticed that the fish smelled very clean. It didn't smell fishy like a blue shark. And the mako's body was hard as a brick.

That evening they returned to the Westlake Marina in the *Craps Two Sixes*, which looked as if a hurricane or a bomb had hit it. But they left it a mess that night. Most of them had slept very little in three days. Most of them could not remember going to bed that night or where they slept—only that they were very tired and happy.

The next weekend a couple of fishermen off Montauk harpooned a mako that weighed 1,250 pounds, and with an entire swordfish in her stomach, according to news reports. The news disappointed them vaguely. And they became irritated when people kept saying that they hadn't caught the fish according to regulations and that their fish didn't count. They knew it counted. The mate of a fishing boat told them he wouldn't have gone near the fish with anything less than a hand grenade, and that was the kind of thing that counted.

Other Stories

GENERAL

SPORTS WRITING'S POET LAUREATE

By Harry Stein

From Sport Magazine
Copyright, ©, 1978, M.V. Sports, Inc.

It is three quarters of an hour till the start of the 1977 World Series. Scores of millions of minds focus simultaneously on The Event. The time for reflection is past; loyalties are set, wagers cemented. Now there is only the competition itself—the Yankees versus the Dodgers, two resurgent dynasties in what is being billed as a classic pairing. Across this vast continent, around the globe, the sense of anticipation is palpable. . . .

In the press hospitality room, deep in the bowels of Yankee Stadium, the conversation among the men who will report The Event to the world is, as usual, about food.

"I was rooting for Kansas City to win in the playoffs," says one New York writer, who has covered the Yankees all season. "You shoulda seen the spread [Royals owner] Ewing Kauffmann put out!"

"It's true," agrees a guy across the table. "Steaks for breakfast!"

"And for lunch," adds the first, "even *bigger* steaks."

"Yeah," mumbles another guy, "and look what [Yankee owner] George Steinbrenner offers the press." He indicates the box dinner—cellophane-wrapped sandwiches, a cup of potato salad, and a dish of artificial chocolate pudding—that has been given each reporter. "He must've spent so much dough on free agents that he's got nothing left for us."

At the adjoining table, Red Smith of the *New York Times*, probably the most respected sports writer in the country, picks up the drift of the conversation. He leans back in his chair and smiles. "You know," he says, "one publicity man for this club said to me, 'How can you guys write such nasty things about our ball club when we feed you off the fat of the land?' " Smith holds up a half-eaten roast beef sandwich, a hunk of gristle dangling from it. "Behold, the fat of the land."

"Hey, Red," someone calls out, "who are you going for in this Series?"

Smith grins. "I'm rooting for my comfort. When Los Angeles won the National League, I was rooting for Kansas City in the American League, to shorten the flying time. Now I'm going to root for the winner of the first game to take it in five, to eliminate the need to travel an extra time." Four or five heads bob in agreement.

Make no mistake about it, any resemblance between sports writers and fans—the word, remember, comes from "fanatics"—is coincidental. Some young sports writers, fresh from stints on the sports page of their college papers, may start out as rooters, but after covering a team day after day and learning that meeting the deadline is a lot more important than who wins, after developing personal relationships with the players and coming to realize that even heroes are sometimes unpleasant human beings, it is difficult to maintain a fan's naïve enthusiasm. More than a few sports writers become bored, or cynical, and allow their prejudices to find their way into their copy. I happened to be in the Yankee pressbox the evening last spring when Reggie Jackson—then estranged from his teammates and a daily target of the New York press corps—refused to shake the other Yankees' hands after hitting a home run; the joy among certain reporters, who anticipated yet another field day at the temperamental Jackson's expense, was unbounded.

But the very best of the sports writers are beyond all that. They see themselves as reporters, journalists with a responsibility to cover the business of game-playing every bit as seriously as other journalists cover politics or finance. Their role as sports writers is not to impassion or to shill, but to inform.

Walter "Red" Smith, a man of spectacular modesty, would probably object to the loftiness of that description, but most of his colleagues—and three generations of newspaper readers—would agree that it fits no one better than him. At 72, with 43 World Series behind him, Smith may privately be pulling for his comfort, but his prose retains the same honesty, the same hard-edged insight and gentle wisdom it had 30 years ago, when he first began doing a column for the now-defunct New York *Herald Tribune*. Five years after that paper folded in 1966, he signed on with the *Times*, which not only prints his column, but syndicates it to several hundred papers around the world. Red Smith readers can count upon his 900 words to provide not only the best sports writing in their newspaper, but very likely the best *writing*.

Public recognition of that fact came in 1976, when Smith was awarded a Pulitzer Prize, the ultimate award for journalistic excellence, but his admirers have been legion for decades. Among them was Ernest Hemingway, who made mention of Smith in his own writing.

Smith dismisses the mention with a wave of his hand. "It was just a little thing," he says. He takes a bite of his Yankee roast beef sandwich. "In *Across the River and into the Trees*, Hemingway had a character 'who was reading Red Smith in the john and he liked it very much.' End of paragraph." Smith grins. "I met Hemingway once. We did not get fighting drunk together."

But, then, Smith never could take a compliment. When he won the Pulitzer, he told every interviewer who asked—and a few who didn't— that he doesn't see himself as anything special, that "I'm just a newspaper stiff trying to write better than I can." Smith even insists that he has no particular affinity for sports writing. "I was pushed into it," he says. "In 1927 I was on the copy desk of the Milwaukee *Sentinel*—I'm from Green Bay—when everyone in the sports department was fired. All I knew about sports was what the average fan knew, but I was the most dispensable copy reader." Smith finishes off his sandwich and peels the tinfoil off his Yankee chocolate pudding. "The managing editor wanted to know if I was honest. If a fight manager offered me five dollars, he asked, would I accept it? I said, 'Five dollars is a lot of money.' He said, 'Report to the sports desk.' "

From Milwaukee, Smith went to St. Louis, then to Philadelphia, then to New York with the *Herald Tribune*, and finally to the *Times*. "Most of the papers I've worked for have died," says Smith wryly. "There's nothing but whitening bones lining my tread. Only the *Times* is left—and I'm working on it."

The *Times* is willing to take its chances. Smith is a superstar among sports writers, and even so august a journal as the *Times* welcomes that kind of prestige. But, then, how many reporters can bring to the job not only Smith's considerable writing skills, but a half century of perspective as well? For, though Smith's hand is not as steady as in the past and his once-fiery hair is now snowy white, he can write with as much authority about Pepper Martin and Primo Carnera as about Pete Rose and Muhammad Ali. Indeed, in some areas of sports history—the game-by-game exploits of the 1931 St. Louis Cardinals is a prime example—Smith's recall is virtually total. The man savors the minutiae of sports the way naval historians relish the details of long-forgotten struggles on the seas.

Not surprisingly, Smith welcomes the World Series—as he welcomes the Kentucky Derby and major championship fights—as a time of reunion with those whose memories are almost as long. Now, in the Yankee hospitality room, with 20 minutes till game time, he spots a pair of other veterans and heads for their table. It seems that James T. Farrell, the author of the classic *Studs Lonigan*, and Sam Taub, who used to be a local sports editor and fight referee, have been discussing the Jack Johnson-Jim Jeffries fight which transpired in 1910.

"Oh yeah," says Taub, a pugnacious little man in an oversized blue suit and pink bow tie, "I refereed a tune-up fight for that bout, between Jeffries and Tom Sharkey. Bat Masterson hired me to do it." Yes, the reference is to *the* Bat Masterson, the former cohort of Wyatt Earp. Around the turn of the century, when Masterson left the old West, he became a sports writer and fight promoter. "Anyway," Taub says, "Jeffries won the fight I refereed and he went on to fight Johnson. The honest truth is, he was sure he was gonna beat Johnson, because he'd been assured Johnson was gonna throw the fight. But at the last minute, Johnson changed his mind. In the ring he said to Jeffries"—Taub goes into a flawless imitation of rural black speech— " 'White boy, the agreemen' don' hold good. You better know how't fight, 'cause ah'm gonna knock you out.' "

There is a pause. "Now lemme ask you," demands Taub, "where you gonna get stories like that today?"

Farrell smiles. "You know who I always found the most original of prizefighters? Battling Nelson."

Smith nods and chuckles. "Remember that story about Nelson at the Dempsey-Willard fight? It was a stifling hot Fourth of July in 1919, and

Philadelphia Billy McCarney had the lemonade concession. McCarney was just about to open for business, with this great vat of the stuff, when Battling Nelson appeared, dove into the lemonade, and took a swim in it."

Farrell laughs but Taub, who at 91 is even older than the others, cocks his head toward Red. "The Dempsey-Willard fight? In the lemonade?"

Smith nods.

"That's a true story!" says Taub triumphantly. He shakes his head.

"Those were fighters. Can you talk about these bums today, including Caly, in the same breath?"

"Oh, I don't know," says Smith. "I still think fighters are pretty colorful today. That's why, for writing purposes, boxing, along with horse racing, is my favorite game."

"Did you know Damon Runyon?" asks a listener. The reference is to the noted chronicler of ring and track characters.

"What're you doin', insultin' the man?" demands Taub.

"Yes, I knew him," says Smith.

"Who didn't know Damon Runyon," Taub insists. "He's the guy that went out lookin' for heavyweights to exploit."

And so the conversation turns to old friends, the legendary sports writers and columnists of the twenties and thirties, men who for the rest of us are the stuff of newspaper lore but who for this trio remain as vivid as last year's pennant race. They talk of Runyon and Ring Lardner and Heywood Broun.

"You know the guy I miss, Red?" asks Taub. "Frank Graham."

Smith nods. Graham was his best friend. "So do I." He pauses. "You know, Sam, the luckiest thing that ever happened to me—and I've been very lucky—was to have the chance to go around with Frank and Granny Rice as a threesome."

Farrell chimes in. "I covered the first Louis-Schmeling fight for *The Nation*, and Grantland Rice—who I hardly knew and who was the biggest sports writer in the country then—sent me a lovely note about it."

"Yep," says Smith softly, "he was the nicest man I ever knew."

The table falls silent, in something between reflection and sorrow.

"And a great newspaperman!" adds Taub spiritedly. "Not like these bums today!" He scans his friends' faces. "There are only a few great ones left, and a couple of 'em are sittin' right here at this table!"

Smith cannot help but laugh. "I guess this really is the old crocks' table, isn't it?"

It is three minutes to game time and so Smith excuses himself and heads from the room. Instantly his bittersweet mood passes. There is, after all, a game to cover.

"I'd dearly love to write a good piece today," he says, moving briskly through Yankee Stadium's subterranean passages. "You don't want to be lousy during the World Series. If you've got to be lousy, let it be in June."

He turns a corner and heads for the elevator that goes to the press level.

"And, believe me, I was very lousy yesterday." He smiles. "I had nothing to say and, by God, I said it."

"Do you know what you're going to write about tonight?" he is asked.

Smith shakes his head. "If God is good, I'll get smart around the fifth inning and start writing." The elevator doors part and he steps inside. But God is very erratic.

God is again good to Red Smith. His column, built around a postgame interview with New York's Graig Nettles, adds yet another chapter to the Yankee soap opera: Smith confirms that the gifted third baseman, like several of his teammates, is anxious to be traded—in Nettles's case, to the San Diego Padres.

But the morning the column appears, the morning after Smith's arrival in Los Angeles for the continuation of the Series, the talk among the sporting press is not about Nettles, or about Thurman Munson—who has expressed a desire to go to Cleveland—or even about Billy Martin—whose head is still rumored to be on the block. The talk is, as usual, about Reggie Jackson. The Yankee right fielder has blasted his manager for starting a rusty Catfish Hunter in the previous game and now, in an apparent fit of pique, has let it be known that he has no intention of appearing in game three, the Dodger Stadium opener, unless his allotted seats in the stands are improved.

Prior to the game, 150 reporters mill around the dugouts, trying to dig up something on the Jackson situation—anything—that their editors might take to be original. A score of writers besiege Ron Guidry, the scheduled Yankee starter in game four, soliciting his views on the brouhaha; the rookie pitcher looks at them as if they are crazy. Ten yards away, Henry Hecht of the New York *Post* complains bitterly to Phil Pepe of the New York *Daily News* that no one had called to notify him of Gabe Paul's morning press conference in which the Yankee general manager had backed Martin.

"Maybe you were asleep," Pepe says sarcastically.

"I wasn't asleep," snaps Hecht. He shakes his head. "This is the most monumental screw-up I've ever seen."

"What the hell do you want me to do about it?" demands Pepe.

Across the way, Howard Cosell—resplendent in his yellow ABC blazer—summons over a Yankee batboy and commands him to fetch Reggie Jackson for the cameras. When the batboy returns with word that Jackson has chosen not to make an appearance, Cosell turns on his heel and stalks away.

From his position behind the batting cage, Red Smith takes it all in and smiles. He's seen this kind of nonsense before. "I wonder if Reggie's waiting in the clubhouse for Bowie Kuhn to deliver his tickets," he muses. "That would make good copy for someone."

"Do you think that some members of the press are going after Jackson too hard?" he is asked.

Smith furrows his brow. "Oh, sure, some guys manage to misconstrue things he says. They don't like to let a fact get in the way of a good story." He smiles. "I don't like to admit it, but there are as many incompetents and pricks among sports writers as among doctors and grocers and shoe salesmen. A lot of them are childish, think the world is bounded by the outfield fences. Well obviously anyone who thinks that way is not only a knothead with a serious case of arrested development, but he's gonna be a lousy sports writer, too."

Al Horowitz, a Los Angeles sports writer, comes over and slaps Smith on the back. "Say, Red," he says, indicating Smith's undistinguished red sports jacket, "don't you wish you had a pretty jacket like Howard?"

Smith laughs. "God, am I glad I don't have to wear a *New York Times* blazer." He glances at Cosell, now standing by the Dodger dugout. "You know, I'm on Howard's enemies list now."

"You made it, huh?" says Horowitz.

"Why?"

"During the Kentucky Derby I took issue with the Cosell-Arcaro argument that Seattle Slew was 'the best of a very poor lot of horses,' because I happened to think that there were some awfully good horses in that field. I wrote, 'Howard Cosell has left off shilling for ABC's discredited boxing tournament to speak as a turf expert.' " Like a veteran comic, he pauses a beat. "We have not spoken since."

Horowitz laughs. "You got lucky."

"Well," says Red, "I had to live a long time before I did—and go on Howard's various shows at least 50 times without getting paid for it."

Horowitz nods. "And what do you, Mr. Smith, make of all this Reggie Jackson business?"

"Oh," replies Red, "I think there's a lot less to the Reggie Jackson flap than meets the eye. I like Reggie, but the guys that travel with the team find him a pain in the ass. He's full of bull, so they get irritated with each other. But it's nothing new—guys who traveled with the Red Sox always had the same kinds of problems with Ted Williams."

That triggers something in Horowitz's memory. "Yeah, I know all about those kinds of problems. Rube Walberg—remember him?—once came up to me on a train and grabbed me by the neck. 'You son of a bitch,' he said, 'look what you wrote about me!' I said, 'How about what you said about *me* in the clubhouse?' He said, 'But when I said it, five people heard me. When you wrote it, a million people saw it.' " Horowitz grins. "I said, 'Well, Rube, let that be a lesson to you.' "

Smith laughs uproariously. "Rube Walberg. What a character." He shakes his head, thinking back on the Athletics' and Red Sox' pitcher of the twenties and thirties. "He got mad pretty easily, all right. I heard that one time he was getting hit pretty hard, so Mickey Cochrane, his manager, went out to speak to him. Suddenly Walberg started really firing the ball, and he breezed through the rest of the game. Afterward someone asked Cochrane what he'd said to Walberg. 'I told him,' replied Mickey, 'that he looked more like a f——ed-out old whore than any f——ed-out old whore I'd ever seen.' "

Horowitz laughs. "Say, Red, did you ever have any ball player mad at you?"

"Just once," Smith says. "Bill Werber, who was a pretty good third baseman with the Athletics when I was working in Philadelphia. I don't like Werber. He was a graduate of Duke and very smug about his formal schooling. When other infielders would shout, 'I got it' on pop flies, he would instruct them to say, 'I have it.' I just didn't think the guy had any class at all, and when he was traded, I said as much in the paper." Smith pauses. "Well, I didn't see Werber again until the following fall, when he was in the World Series. The instant he saw me he grabbed me and bodily ejected me from the dugout. I was deeply tempted to let him have it with my typewriter, but that didn't seem appropriate to the occasion."

Smith squints out toward the outfield where a trio of Dodgers are shagging flies. "But over all the years, he's the only ball player who——" He hesitates. "Well, sure, occasionally there are guys I don't hit it off with personally. Like Jackie Robinson, he was one of those. I had tremendous respect for the man, but any time I wrote anything even slightly critical of him, he took me for a racist. I resented it. Hell, I'd been known as 'the nigger lover' by the Athletics for years."

Smith was indeed one of the first reporters to speak out against baseball's color line, but rarely used his column as his forum. It is only in comparatively recent years that he has been outspoken in print, inveighing, for example, against the reserve clause and the arrogant owners who have little respect for their paid employees and less for their paying customers; and against the undermining influence of television on the nation's games.

"I suppose I probably should have done more of that kind of piece earlier," he concedes. "But, then, back in the thirties and forties and fifties, *nobody* was covering sports that way." He pauses, apparently not satisfied with his own explanation. Then he brightens. "But there's another reason too: Though I've always held these views, as time has passed, I've become more and more convinced that I'm right." He grins. "It's really not so bad getting old when you get smart at the same time."

The Yankees win game three behind Mike Torrez, and Red Smith—who doesn't much care who wins the Series—is almost as miffed by the outcome as the Dodger crowd. "I had my column idea all set," he says riding the elevator down to the clubhouse level. "It was going to be built around Dusty Baker's home run (which briefly tied the game for the Dodgers). I'd noted down every pitch Torrez threw to Baker, and what Torrez did between pitches, the attitude of the crowd from moment to moment and the explosion when Baker actually hit it out. It was going to be a study of this vital moment in the ball game." He shrugs and manages a smile. "Except that it turned out to be an utterly meaningless moment in the ball game. So I'll have to start scratching around for something else."

Smith elects to begin his scratching in the interview room, where no less than 300 reporters are gathered for the standard postgame press conference with the managers and stars of the game—in this case Torrez and Lou Piniella. Red stays only five minutes. "Something like this is useful to guys on deadline who need the facts quickly," he says, moving through the corridor toward the Dodger clubhouse, "but there's precious little I can get from it."

There is not much more to be gleaned from the Dodgers. Most of them have retreated to the showers and the few who haven't sit before their lockers looking decidedly untalkative. The only noteworthy Dodger remark comes from outfielder Rick Monday after a bit of hounding from a sports writer. "Come on, Rick," urges the writer, "I can't believe *all* the squabbles are on the Yankees. There's gotta be some pricks on this club, too." "Sure there are," purrs Monday, and a half-dozen reporters start scribbling. He glances at Davey Lopes, listening in from a nearby locker, and smiles. "Hey, Lopes, you're a prick."

But that, alas, is not the stuff of a column in a family newspaper, so Smith, chuckling over Monday's remark, leaves the clubhouse, pushes his way through a sea of autograph seekers and groupies waiting in the corridor outside, and makes his way to the Yankee locker room. It is more crowded here—there are more reporters talking to more ball players in more varied stages of undress—but for a columnist who is expected to provide more than a mere account of the day's game, the pickings appear just as slim.

Smith chooses to approach Ken Holtzman, already besieged by a quartet of writers while he pulls on his socks. Though he has been a distinguished pitcher over a dozen seasons, Holtzman pitched only 72 innings in 1977 and is not expected to appear in this Series at all, and the nation's sporting press, hungry for copy, has been making much of his inactivity. But Holtzman—wisely for his own well-being, endlessly frustrating for the writers—has refused to cooperate by attacking his superiors.

"C'mon, Ken," urges one of the writers, "it's gotta be annoying."

Holtzman nods. "Sure. We have some problems, but we'll work them out."

"Mr. Holtzman," says Red softly to another reporter, "is a very discreet fellow." With that he picks up his typewriter, leaves the clubhouse, and heads for an elevator. Smith has decided to do what he has done hundreds of times before—hide away in a quiet place and pull a column out of his head and his gut.

That is a chore that, over a period of years, would suck most sports writers dry. But Red Smith never stops seeing new angles. "All you have to do to write a column," he says, moving toward the steep banks of stairs which lead to the Dodger Stadium parking lot, "is slash a vein and let the blood trickle out." He smiles. "You know, way back, when I first started covering sports, people would say to me, 'Doesn't it get dull to cover a whole season?' And I'd say, 'Only to dull minds.' Today's game is always different from yesterday's. All you need is the intelligence to discern that and the wit to express it." He pauses, "And I don't think that takes great intelligence or great wit."

He reaches the steps and slackens his pace, mounting them slowly in silence. He stops at the top. "Oh boy," he wheezes, "the legs really are the first to go."

The time has arrived for the inevitable question: How long can he go on?

Smith laughs. "I occasionally get a letter from someone asking that, but usually they put it less delicately. Like, 'You old fart, why don't you get lost?'" He pauses and gives the question a moment of real consideration. "I'll go on until I cease to enjoy it, or until someone I respect tells me, 'You've lost it, Pop.' What the hell, when either of those things happen, I'll accept it." He continues walking toward the parking lot. Then Red Smith pauses and grins. "But who knows, maybe I'll get lucky like Granny Rice and keel over at the typewriter."

AUTO RACING

THE 500 SEEMS TO LAST FOREVER

By Edwin Pope

From the Miami Herald
Copyright, ©, 1978, Miami Herald Publishing Co.

I couldn't know how this 500 looked on delayed TV. I can only say how it was here. It hurtles at you. Pure explosion. A rush of heat and sound and color, like a suddenly fragmented blast furnace, attacks your consciousness.

They say auto racing began just after the second car was built. It has been going on here literally through the blood and guts of nearly 70 percent of this century. You can watch the race on TV or listen on radio or read about it in a newspaper. But, unlike a World Series or Super Bowl, you cannot begin to perceive the vaguest fraction of its impact on your senses until you have been right beside or over an Indianapolis 500.

It is too overwhelming to put in a box in your living room. My first reaction was numbness. Fear was next.

Finally came wonder. Wonder at the madness of 32 men and one woman driving grenades on wheels, wearing helmets as potential death masks, knowing there can be only one winner, which was Al Unser, the "quiet" Unser, a wink in front of Tom Sneva and Gordon Johncock.

I hung over a rail 40 feet from machines lighter than Volkswagens and faster than some airplanes and noisier than banshees.

I saw—felt, really—Danny Ongais whoosh by after stealing the lead from pole-sitter Sneva.

Heard a gasp rise like a Gargantuan burp from one nearby batch of the 350,000 people here.

"Ongais is crazy," a man said.

"The others aren't?" I asked.

The 500 seems to last forever (by the clock, Unser finished in three hours five minutes 54.99 seconds) but never long enough to fill the hunger of its fetishists.

After a while, the onlooker sinks into a state just short of hypnotic. His head wags like a mechanical dog as one aluminum-clothed projectile after another blurs past.

I saw Spike Gehlhausen hit a wall and get by with it. A Mexican standoff. He lost his car and saved his life.

I thought about what Jimmy Clark said after winning Indy in 1965, before racing got him for good on a German afternoon in 1968, an April day that should have been beautiful for a beautiful little Scot, but was deadly instead.

"The crowd is disappointed if there is no accident," Clark had said. "They look forward to crashes and, yes, maybe even seeing people killed."

I used to believe that. Without arguing with Clark's memory, I don't believe it now.

Much of the 500 infield—so vast that a nine-hole golf course takes no more than a tiny swatch of it—is a babbling, drunken, filthy parody of humanity.

Some infielders look as though they were let out of a pigpen for the day. Out there you are overdressed in a T-shirt and cutoffs. It makes the infield of the Kentucky Derby look like Parliament in session.

Still, I can't convince myself that either these slobs or the 257,500 people on the seats want to see anybody die on a racetrack.

Hoosiers in general may be the kindest and friendliest of Americans. It is very hard to assign any innate viciousness to most of the crowd.

Truly, for certain among them the 500 is a motorized Sodom and Gomorrah. They come here to become semiconscious. They could not care less that the 500 is the only competition that starts at 80 miles an hour. Or that Ongais, after his wild early sprint, goes out after 145 laps of the 200-lap grind with a busted rotor on his turbo-charger.

Whatever that is.

I've seen people drink whisky straight at football and baseball games, and especially, at hockey games. They take it straight out of the bottle in parts of the Speedway infield with cars blazing by like groundbound UFOs.

They are so far gone by early afternoon that even the women are unaware that, with 35 laps to go, Janet Guthrie is tenth and ahead of four-time winner A. J. Foyt and two-time champion Johnny Rutherford and another Indy king named Mario Andretti.

Guthrie finishes eighth. She has come a long way, baby, and if she never climbs into another racecar, which she surely will, this lady of poise and courage has cut herself an immensely satisfying slice of history.

At last she has made her mark on the classic where more cars go faster in front of more folks who see less of what they paid for and more writers who don't know what they are doing than any place in the world.

Oh, a few writers do. Like maybe one from *Popular Mechanics*. Or the Massachusetts Institute of Technology. Bob Collins of *The Indianapolis Star* does. Collins once said Bobby Unser, Al's big brother who came in sixth Sunday, "could swagger standing still."

I tagged along with Collins to Rutherford's garage a couple of hours before Mary Hulman, old Indy owner Tony's widow, agonized through: "Lady and gentlemen, start your engines!"

Rutherford, one of the good guys, was standing there wearing his lopsided grin and polishing his helmet. Not daubing at it. He was bearing down on the helmet, searching for spots. Then he would twist a rag and grind them off like a man smashing fleas on a dog.

"Why?"

"It's an edge," Collins said. "Even a tiny speck on his helmet could mean that much more wind resistance. I know it sounds ridiculous. But they do that."

Didn't help. All that rubbing never erased the lousy luck from Rutherford's hat. He was thirteenth.

Then, in the last grit-spraying howl of the five hundredth mile, here came Al Unser, 170 pounds of smile.

Al is the youngest of three racing brothers. The oldest, Jerry, was killed here in 1959. In practice.

HORSE RACING

THE IRISH HABERDASHER'S DREAM

By Jim Murray

From the Los Angeles Times
Copyright, ©, 1978, Los Angeles Times
Reprinted by permission

It's a hard-luck race in a hard-luck town. "My Old Kentucky Home" is a rooming house. With the bath down the hall.

The grass isn't blue. Neither is the sky. They make America's whisky here. It's America's still. "The Dark and Bloody Ground" they called it in the days when the men wore coonskin caps and carried long rifles. Now, you're better off carrying your own deck—or dice.

It's a crapshooters town, the only way you could get here was by river. And most people dropped off because of a busted flush. It's the pickpocket capital of the world on the first Saturday in May. Ripoffsville, USA. They put a quarter's worth of bourbon in a five-cent glass, some weeds, and a lump of sugar and get three bucks for it. And that's the bargain of the week here. You can get a dime-store locket for 20 bucks. Of course, it's got a picture of a horse on it.

This whole grift was the brainstorm of a portly little Irish haberdasher in the days when it was a lousy little three- or four-horse little race for $2,500. Matt Winn had 10 kids to support and he showed Louisville a way to pick America's pockets. The Kentucky Derby became an American tribal rite. Matt Winn made the seventh race at Churchill Downs on one Saturday in May into the most important two minutes in sports. He convinced everybody that this rotting old pile of lumber in this humid river town was the fount of racing.

It's not only in the wrong place, it's at the wrong time. It disenfranchises half the horses born. A filly simply cannot contest with a colt in the spring of the year—even though one did. But only one. Regret in 1915. They don't even try anymore.

The race doesn't prove much. A 90–1 shot won it. A lot of horses that couldn't draw into a Caliente overnight have won it. Lots of horses who won it never won another race.

"If Native Dancer can't win that race, no one should," his trainer, Bill

Winfrey, said sadly. Native Dancer didn't win it. The horse who did never beat another horse.

Discovery couldn't win this race. Kelso couldn't even get in it. Neither could Man O'War. But Cannonade could. And Dust Commander. And field horses. And Hoop Jr. But Bold Ruler couldn't finish in the money. Round Table barely did.

Some great jockeys have never won this race. But Bill Hartack won five. Hard-knocking owners couldn't win it. Alfred Vanderbilt couldn't. Neither could Paul Mellon, Ogden Phipps. But auto dealers from La Crescenta could. Colonel E. R. Bradley, who ran gambling casinos in Florida on the side, won four.

Nobody ever got caught fixing a Kentucky Derby, but the gold-leaf sign on the clubhouse designating Forward Pass as the 1968 winner is a lie. Forward Pass was in the 1968 Derby, but he won it in 1969—when the courts threw out Dancer's Image, the real winner, for using a drug that's now legal.

Not even the war could cancel the Kentucky Derby. Louisville was more afraid of losing fresh money than of losing a war. It's impossible to estimate exactly how much a Kentucky Derby pours into Louisville. For years, every brothel within a three-state area emptied for Derby week and its attractions poured into Louisville on every Greyhound bus wearing their best boa feathers and ankle-strap shoes. Families vacated their stately homes to turn them over to corporations for $2,000 a week for Derby week. Louisville's hotels were the first to treble and quadruple or even sextuple daily rates for Derby week, although Augusta and Indianapolis, Daytona and other permanent venues now do it. A three-day rate in the finest hotels now is $265.

People at Kentucky Derbies, for some reason, eat their fool heads off. The Stevens Company's five dining rooms have long waiting lines. Some 60,000 hot dog rolls are consumed. You can buy anything from a $1 beer in a cardboard carton to a $500 mint julep in a 14-karat cup. You get to keep the cup. And the mint.

During Derby week, horse trainers are bigger celebrities than movie stars. Four-foot jockeys are social lions. Horse owners who would be shown the door by the butler the rest of the year are announced like royalty.

The fields are too big. There is a saying around a track, when you get five horses in a race, the best one will win. When you get 23, a burro might win it. All a horse has to be is get in a Kentucky Derby is a horse.

Still, it's a race which was won by Citation, too. And Whirlaway. Twenty Grand. Secretariat and Count Fleet. And the 1978 field looks vintage. Not since the year when Swaps, Nashua, and Summer Tan were in the gate, or the year when Gallant Man, Round Table, and Bold Ruler started, have there been more promising colts than Affirmed, Alydar, Believe It, and Sensitive Prince.

But a Kentucky Derby doesn't want a truly run race. That's not the stuff of legend, the bin of anecdotal lore. The Kentucky Derby wants a jockey who stands up in the stirrups at the eight pole. It wants Don Meade and Herb Fisher trading whip slashes at the finish and snatching saddlecloths. It doesn't want Gold Coast millionaires making polite speeches to some governor of Kentucky; it wants Carry Back to run away from the pride of the

Lexington breeding pens. It wants Donerail paying $184.90 straight, $41.20 place, and $13.20 show. It wants a South American dark horse that stood in quarantine in Miami for 48 hours to get lumped with the field horses and win by three.

It wants an odds-on choice to get washed out in what the theater calls "flop sweat" in the claustrophobic paddock, which is the nearest thing to a Tijuana jail you will ever see on any racetrack.

These are the things that made Matt Winn's race a genuine part of American folklore. This is what lets Holiday Inns charge $80 a night and helps cab drivers put their kids through medical school. This is what brings the beautiful people, the well-heeled, the sensation seekers pouring into this whisky town and out on Bardstown Road and drinking bourbon with grass in it and leaking money as they go.

The race lasts one minute and 59 seconds if the day is dry and the track fast. But if you paid 10 bucks to join the swarm in the infield, it wouldn't matter if it lasted an hour and 59 seconds, or a day and 59 seconds, all you'll see is somebody's navel.

If you can't make it, don't despair. Just get in a crowded elevator with a hangover, set fire to $500, and do without sleep for three days. If you don't want to do that, just send a check and tell them to split it equally among touts, pickpockets, bar girls, bellhops, cabbies, and guys selling maps to buried treasure on the corner of Fourth and Walnut. Put a Stephen Foster record on the gramophone and try not to remember he died in the hallway of a flophouse with a losing ticket where his watch used to be.

WORLD SERIES (Game III)

THE INCREDIBLE GRAIG NETTLES

By Hal Bodley

From The Wilmington (Del.) News-Journal
Copyright, ©, 1978, The News-Journal Co.

It was a night when the toast of Broadway didn't have it.

But the curtain went up at warm Yankee Stadium last night and Ron Guidry made it through the ordeal and the Yankees are back in the race, back in the seventy-fifth World Series.

Guidry pitched a courageous 5–1 victory as the Yankees reduced Los Angeles' edge to 2–1 in this autumn tournament, but had it not been for the vacuum cleaner at third base in the person of Graig Nettles, the New Yorkers might be looking at a 3–0 Dodger advantage today.

Nettles made four incredible plays to the delight of the howling Yankee Stadium mob of 56,447, snuffing Dodger rally after Dodger rally.

Not since 1970 when Baltimore's Brooks Robinson set the standard for third basemen in a World Series, has there been such outstanding play.

And no one in Yankee pinstripes appreciated it more than Guidry.

"He was inhuman out there tonight," said Guidry in the noisy, happy Yankee dressing room. "All the ones he missed during the regular season he got back tonight. He was fantastic."

"In all my years in baseball I've never seen such a performance by a third baseman in a World Series," said Dodger Manager Tommy Lasorda. "We thought we were going to be able to get some runs off Guidry tonight, but Graig Nettles had other ideas. I can't begin to tell you how many runs he saved."

Nettles's plays came when the Yankees were protecting a two-run lead and it appeared Guidry might not make it to the final curtain.

But in the third, with a runner on second, Nettles speared Dave Lopes's drive. Moments later with runners on first and third and two out, he made a sensational stop of Reggie Smith's grounder and forced the runner at second to end the threat.

In the fifth, he kept Smith's ground single from going to the outfield with runners on second and third and picked up Steve Garvey's grounder to throw out the runner at second.

The most spectacular play came in the sixth. With the bases loaded and two out, Lopes hit another shot down the line. Nettles lunged to his right, stopped the ball and, after falling to the ground, picked himself up and rifled to second to get the force.

"I've always considered myself a pretty good fielder," said Nettles. "Tonight, they were bang-bang plays. It's hard to explain. The ball is hit, you react. Your instincts and coordination take over.

"I've had good defensive plays before, but you have to do it in a World Series to get the recognition. People think that I have become a good defensive player the last three years. I was pretty good when I was in Cleveland. I led the league one year, but nobody knows it because we had a lousy team and Cleveland is a bad-media town."

Nettles refused to compare himself with Brooks Robinson.

"You'll have to ask Paul Blair," he said, with a sheepish grin. "Paul played with Brooks over in Baltimore. He'll have to tell you. He seemed to get better with age. I hope I do, too. In a sense, we are both a lot alike. We both are not afraid to get our uniforms dirty, to go after balls. I do think I can handle my position with anybody."

"I can't recall a third baseman ever doing any better," said Yankee Manager Bob Lemon. "He saved some runs tonight. I was getting a little nervous about the way Guidry was pitching."

"Nettles ought to get a save," said Guidry, who walked a season-high seven while spacing eight hits. "I was confident I would be able to stay in, but my location was not that good. I was high and I'm not the type of pitcher who can be effective when I am high."

But on a night when Ron Guidry didn't have his good stuff, Graig Nettles kept shutting off the bad guys. At every turn.

"I'm not taking anything away from Guidry, but the Series score is really Dodgers two, Nettles one," said Reggie Smith. "Fifty-six thousand people out there know who won the game for the Yankees."

Interpreted, what Smith was saying was that had Nettles not had such a spectacular night, this Broadway show might be closing late this afternoon.

BOXING

AND STILL CHAMPION

By John Schulian

From The Chicago Sun-Times
Copyright, © , 1978, The Chicago Sun-Times

There were two movie screens in the flower-laden banquet room and the film clips being shown on them were old and jumpy. Each clip was of a different fight, but the ending was always the same. Joe Louis was always the winner.

With every opponent who fell, a fresh cheer rose from the captains, kings, and queens who had paid $500 a plate to hail this heavyweight champion for all time. Up on the dais, with his wife to the right of him and Frank Sinatra to the left of him, Joe Louis was shivering in his velvet-trimmed brown tuxedo. You wanted to think it was because he was thrilled by the sight of old glories and the outpouring of rekindled love, but you knew better.

Joe Louis is sick and feeble, far older than his 64 years, and soon there was someone by the side of his wheelchair covering him with a yellow blanket. It was as sad a sight as you will ever see. Joe Louis, etched in the nation's consciousness as all-powerful, couldn't handle the blanket himself.

It has been like this, and worse, for a year now. That big heart of his gave out, and when the doctors in Las Vegas said they couldn't save him, his well-heeled friends flew him to Houston and Michael DeBakey, who could. They were preserving a living monument, if you will, a part of our heritage. But only barely.

"I wanted to go visit Joe, but the people around him said I couldn't," an old foe turned friend was saying the other day. "They don't even know if he's going to make it through the week."

And still Joe Louis came to the dinner his admirers threw for him Thursday night, came to be treated royally in Caesars Palace, where he was once a human ornament. The first glimpse of him was the one people seized on. They used it to reassure themselves that he was all right, that he was not afflicted with mortality as they are. After that, however, they should have closed their eyes and ears. Frank Sinatra wheeled Joe Louis onto the dais, held his hand in the air to acknowledge a standing ovation, and uttered two sentences that said more than he could have imagined.

"This night has been a long time coming," Sinatra said. "We should have done it a long time ago."

It was a confession that our preoccupation with the present and the future has made an afterthought of everything Joe Louis accomplished in the past.

He fought his way out of a Detroit ghetto to become, at 23, the youngest heavyweight champion ever. There was never a challenger he ducked. He fought them all—Max Schmeling, Tommy Farr, Jersey Joe Walcott, Two-Ton Tony Galento—and he beat them all.

"He musta used an ice pick," said the dazed Galento.

It was a special era for the fight game, an era for Buddy Baer and Lou Nova and Billy Conn. Joe Louis flattened them, too, without ever doubting that he could. Think of how he approached the nimbly treacherous Conn. "He can run," Joe Louis said, "but he can't hide." Unlettered and unpolished, the man was the essence of pith.

America likes its heroes that way, likes them strong and silent. The other major stipulation in the thirties and forties was that they be white. Joe Louis surmounted that one with the sheer force of what he was. He was a rock to cling to when the depression robbed the country of money and heroes. He was the good citizen who joined the army when there was a war to be fought. He was everything white people thought a man could be. And he was even more to blacks.

"He came forth," the Reverend Jesse Jackson said Thursday night, "and the cotton curtain came down."

At last, blacks could see one of their own rising above the hate and squalor that was supposed to be theirs eternally. Breaking color lines in sports, integrating schools and lunch counters, getting to the front of the bus—all that would be for the pioneers who followed. Joe Louis was blazing a trail for them, showing them that it could be done, and doing it in the only way this curiously divided nation could accept. Muhammad Ali explained it best Thursday night when he said: "Even the Mississippi redneck Ku Klux Klansmen got to love Joe Louis."

Maybe that was what made Joe Louis's fall from grace so hard to take. Suddenly the man who symbolized bravery and success was being called a tax dodger, a drug abuser, a loser. He became a professional wrestler. He thought there was a Mafia plot to exterminate him. He suffered emotional breakdowns and personal affronts. Granted the people he greeted in the lobby at Caesars Palace still called him "Champ," still wanted his autograph. But when his back was turned, he was someone to be looked down upon.

The pity and disdain must have chewed him up. You can only hope he understood how fickle America is about its heroes. You can only hope he realized what was happening Thursday night when every big name, pretty face, and old fighter available turned out to honor him.

GOLF

MAN ON A CRUSADE

By Jon Roe

From the Minneapolis Tribune
Copyright, © , 1978, Minneapolis Tribune

Gary Player was a man on a crusade Sunday. And a rousing, soul-stirring, gut-wrenching crusade the wee South African put on as he appeared almost magically out of the Georgia pines to capture the 1978 Masters.

He claims that dedication is his secret and yesterday he seemed to will the golf ball into what was needed to win his third Masters green coat.

He clenched his fist and thrust his arm. He fell to the ground and kicked his feet when a shot didn't fall that he had willed should. He covered his eyes in disbelief when an eagle putt didn't find the hole. And when, at long last, he knew he had won HIS Masters, he plunged his hand out to accept congratulations.

Player's determination had left three mere mortals in his wake. He won the Masters with a scintillating eight-under-par 64 in the final round, tying the course and tournament record. Left one stroke behind to find their own solace were Hubert Green, Tom Watson, and Rod Funseth. Player had 277 for 72 holes, 11 under par, while the three runners-up had 278s.

Player, at 42 the oldest man ever to win the Masters, ripped a six-under-par 30 out of the Augusta National Golf Club's back nine to make up the seven shots by which he had trailed when the final round began. And after he had willed his final birdie putt of the day into the eighteenth hole, he watched with a stern face as first Watson, then Funseth, and finally Green saw their last chances to tie slip away.

It was the Masters at its best. Player, who started the day at three under par, made few ripples as he toured the front nine in 34, two under par. Green carded an even-par 35, still good for a five-shot lead. And Watson, Funseth, and a myriad of other pros were still to be hurdled.

But then Player made a birdie at the tenth and nearly chipped in for another at the eleventh. It was then that he fell to the ground, twitching his legs and feet in despair. "I'm not proud of what I did," he said. "I suddenly realized I was at the Masters and you don't do that here. But I was very tense and I couldn't believe that the shot didn't go in after it seemed to disappear into the hole."

He regrouped and made a 15-foot birdie putt at the twelfth and then threw his arms over his eyes when an eagle attempt at the par-five thirteenth didn't fall. Still, he had another birdie. And another when he two-putted at the par-five fifteenth. When he used his vast knowledge of the Augusta National to sink a 15-foot birdie at the par-three sixteenth he was tied for the lead.

"Here it is 17 years later, but I remember back in 1962 that I had the exact same putt and left it two inches to the right of the cup," he said. "Arnold Palmer had just chipped in for a birdie and I felt the putt would break to the left. It didn't, but I remembered that today. It's a straight putt."

He faced another downhill 15-footer at the eighteenth. Again, he had a similar putt years before and he used that knowledge to ram it home. He had his 64, he had a share of the lead, but he still needed more if he was to add to his 1961 and 1974 green coats.

And one by one, the challengers fell. Watson, the defending champion, nearly became the second man in Masters history to win successive tournaments. But semidisaster struck at the fourteenth. He seemed ready to make a six-foot birdie putt only to three-putt instead.

"It's a putt that Gene Littler [Watson's playing partner] said he has tried only once to make," said Watson. "I thought I had made it, but it didn't go. The second putt was only three feet, but I shoved it a little and it missed the whole hole."

Still he came back with a birdie at 15 and another at 16. He was again tied for the lead. But his tee shot at 18 ("I made a bad swing") was in the pines to the left and his approach shot left him 80 feet to the left of the pin and off the green. He managed to get within 10 feet of the hole, but he couldn't save par and force a sudden-death playoff.

Neither could Funseth, who had been expected to self-destruct long before he came to the sixteenth and eighteenth holes. "I hit two good putts on those holes," Funseth said. "But I can't say I'm disappointed in not winning because I didn't throw anything away. It's just that after a while I realized the way Gary was playing that pars weren't going to be any good."

As Green discovered. He, too, was tied for the lead after getting a birdie at 15. But his second putt, about three feet from the hole at 16, was in a depression—possibly a spike mark—and it squirted to the right for a bogey.

Then he hit a shot that should have been good enough to give him a chance to be fitted for his green coat. He lofted an 8-iron to within three feet of the hole at 18 and the first sudden-death playoff in Masters history seemed imminent. If he sank the birdie attempt, he would be tied with Player.

Green had faced the same type of putt last June and sank it to win the U.S. Open at Tulsa. He poised over the putt, then backed away.

"I thought the putt should be hit in the right-center of the cup and so did my caddie," said Green. "I backed off because I heard Jim Kelly [a radio broadcaster] talking up in his booth. He did nothing wrong. He was supposed to be there and when you back away from a putt, it's your fault if you miss it."

And Green did. "I didn't want an excuse," Green said. "I didn't win and I should have. I made some mistakes out on the golf course today and I had to pay for it. I really didn't play well enough to win, that's all."

Player watched the drama unfold on television in the clubhouse. He never smiled until he knew he had won.

"It's awfully hard to smile when you're choking to death," Player said. "I can only try to sympathize with Hubert, Tom, and Rod. Second place is the lowest place to finish there is. You wish you had finished fourth or fifth.

"You have to be lucky. Look, here's another major championship and it seems like all of them are decided by a shot. Yes, you have to be lucky. And I was. You know, my record in sudden-death playoffs isn't very good. I've lost 17 straight."

The crusader marched off, leaving the mere mortals to wonder if it would have been 18 straight.

FOOTBALL

LOVE HIM OR HATE HIM

By Joe Lapointe

From the Detroit Free Press
Copyright, ©, 1978, Detroit Free Press

Of his days as an Ohio State Buckeye, Tom Skladany remembers "Michigan week" best of all. During that week, coach Woody Hayes would show his team a special film of "highlights" from past Michigan-Ohio State football games.

"The first scene would be a picture of Archie Griffin running up the middle," said Skladany, who is now with the Lions.

"You'd see a blatant foul, a Michigan guy twisting Archie's knee. Woody would say, 'Look at this, look at that.'

"He'd run it back in slow motion and he'd say, 'See? See? See what kind of a team you're going to play?'

"Next, you'd see one of our players making a clean tackle and helping a Michigan guy to his feet.

"Then, there'd be a Michigan player hitting our quarterback and jumping up and down over him, waving his finger like 'No. one, No. one.'

"This would be followed with a picture of Tim Fox, our safety, making a clean tackle and trotting back to our huddle, real calmlike.

"Then came the best scene of all. It was a film of me getting smashed by a Michigan guy in 1973. He hits me from behind and my legs buckle and crack under me. Woody would shout, 'See? See? Look what they did to our punter!'

"It was great, it was great! He'd bring up seniors like Archie to cry and pound on the desk and tell what it meant to beat Michigan. At practice, he'd pipe in a tape of 87,000 fans cheering, so loud that you had to scream to be heard.

"He'd have cops in the dorms and the windows draped. It was hell week, that's what it was! It was like a war! It was crazy! He'd get 150 percent out of every player. It was playing for a legend. Woody is the greatest coach of all times."

Some would debate Skladany's conclusion. And in this, his sixty-fifth autumn, the dean of Ohio State's football department isn't coaching as much as he used to. That fact was illustrated on the sideline of Ohio Stadium during time-outs in a recent game against Northwestern.

With the Buckeye quarterback at attention, assistant coach Alex Gibbs led the discussions of the day's plays. Not included in the group was the short, stocky, head coach with the red jacket and the black cap over his white hair. Hayes stood 10 yards away, almost alone, his only company a young aide who held a seldom-used telephone connected to the press box.

Assistant Gibbs told why.

"In a game, things happen so fast it isn't fair to Woody," Gibbs said. "He's not . . . [Gibbs snapped his fingers] on top like he used to be. We don't have time for debate on the sidelines during a game."

In a more crucial game, Hayes might get more involved, Gibbs said. But for most of the season, it has been Gibbs directing what has become a passing offense during the benign neglect of Hayes. A 34-year-old assistant in his fourth year at Ohio State, Gibbs stresses that Hayes retains a sharp football mind in teaching situations.

"His concepts are sound, they are vast concepts," Gibbs continued. "When he talks, you better listen. W. W. Hayes is very aware of everything that goes on. How many coaches have gone through male menopause at age 55 and have still maintained good records? Woody and Bear Bryant. Most of the others get out at that point.

"Maybe male menopause isn't the right term, but I'm talking about that period of age when you become paranoid and you don't trust people. Woody learned to live with it. He's still a great coach."

Gibbs stressed that his view of Hayes is balanced.

"People have this fixed image of this wild man who will tear up tables and break yard markers," Gibbs said. "But Woody is also a bright, energetic, caring person. The public doesn't know about a guy with a big heart who helps young waitresses through school and visits crippled kids."

Still, Gibbs admits, "This job is no merry-go-round. There are times you'd like to kill him. All that crap about him mellowing? That's a bunch of baloney."

Mellow or not, Hayes, 65, is nearing the final gun of a brilliant career. Saturday's Michigan-Ohio State game will be his twenty-eighth, and probably one of his last. But anyone who brings up the subject of retirement had better be prepared for consequences Marty Reid faced.

Reid is a sportscaster for Channel 4 in Columbus, Ohio, a middle-American city that is the capital of the state, the birthplace of *Hustler* magazine, and the headquarters of several insurance companies.

One of its best-known restaurants is the Jai Lai, a pink building with velvet drapes, a big aquarium, and a larger-than-life, black-and-white photograph of young coach Woody Hayes. The face in the photograph is gruff and frowning and it greets the reporters every week when Hayes holds his Monday press conferences at the Jai Lai.

Sportscaster Reid didn't need to view the picture because he dealt face-to-face with the real thing when he asked what the coach thought was an improper question.

Reid began by mentioning that in a recent survey on cable television, 56 percent of the Columbus citizens who responded thought Hayes should retire. "Well, I don't much care," Hayes began. "There's nobody around in this league or any other league that has won as many games as I have. I'm not going to let their opinion decide a thing.

"And if you're one of the 56 percent," he said to the sportscaster, "I don't give a damn about you either. Good day."

But it wasn't going to be a good day for Reid. Hayes walked across the floor with teeth clenched and eyes blazing. He approached the 25-year-old sportscaster. "If you don't like it, you can go straight to hell," he snarled.

"I'm sorry you . . ." the sportscaster began.

"I wish you were bigger and stronger," Hayes continued. "You're young enough . . ."

Reid tried again.

"Coach, I'm sorry you feel that way . . ."

"Yeah, yeah, talk, that's all you do well," Hayes cut in. "You're sorry, you're sorry. You're a pip-squeak."

It was a classic performance, calculated to generate both fear of Hayes and loathing of his enemy. Later, Reid would receive death threats on the telephone. His car would be vandalized. Other reporters would snub him. He would realize, he said later, that "any member of the Columbus media who is not a cheerleader is an outcast."

Victorious again, Hayes then headed to the Jai Lai parking lot to pick up his own four-wheel drive vehicle. Like many cars in Columbus, it is painted the Ohio State colors of scarlet and gray. Like many citizens of Columbus, the tall, skinny kid in the parking lot hustled to serve the angry coach. The kid earned a tip for his effort and he watched Hayes drive away.

"If he's with a bunch of people he gives you a dollar," the kid said. "But if he catches you alone, he only gives you a quarter."

These media confrontations are easy for Hayes, as easy as beating Northwestern by 43 points. In the past, Hayes has punched reporters, photographers, and TV cameramen—not to mention Buckeye players, doors, blackboards, yard markers, and his own face.

His most mild media dealings are every Saturday night during football season on "The Woody Hayes Show." It appears at the same time as "Saturday Night Live" and it is much funnier. No "pip-squeaks" bother Hayes on his show because Woody asks all the questions and gives most of the answers.

After the Northwestern game, he showed a video tape of the Wildcat quarterback trying to draw the Buckeyes offside. As he stood waiting for the center snap, the quarterback bobbed his head, shook his behind, and violated Hayes's sense of propriety.

"Watch his head, watch his body," Hayes sputtered. "It's illegal as the devil. It's unethical. It's unsportsmanlike. Why the rules committee allows that kind of junk, I don't know. Horrible, horrible, horrible, horrible! It's unsportsmanlike, unfair and it's just not right."

Since Ohio State won that afternoon, 63–20, Hayes quickly ended his condemnations and moved to the interview portion of the program. He lined up five of his players at a time and asked them long, rambling questions. The players answered him with "Yup . . . nope . . . uh-huh . . . right, coach . . . yes, sir . . . I dunno." After the session, Hayes laughed and said to them: "You fellas didn't get a chance to talk much, didja?" On camera, but behind his back, some of the players were giggling and snickering, but they stopped when Hayes asked for a volunteer to "deliver the valedictory." After one player shied away, a brave lineman spoke up.

"Coach," he said. "It's just great to be a Buckeye." The audience cheered and the director cut for a commercial.

It's not always that great to be a Buckeye, Billy Long remembered. For a time, Long was a favored protégé of Hayes. He was the starting quarterback in 1967. He was a frequent guest in the Hayes home for dinner and he had a warm relationship with the coach.

But then Rex Kern came along and Hayes judged Kern to be a better quarterback. So Hayes pulled the rug out from under Long. Suddenly, the coach didn't have time for Long, who became a nonperson on the scrub team.

"My senior year was the worst year of my life," said Long, now a public relations man for one of Columbus' insurance companies.

"To this day, my parents still resent Woody for what he did to me. As much as Woody hurt me, I can't lose respect for him. One side of me doesn't like him and one side of me does. He's the classic case of the split personality, football and nonfootball. He doesn't have a private life. As far as I'm concerned, Woody ruined all my chances of a professional career. But he helped me get into law school."

Years before that, Hayes had recruited Long at a Buckeye basketball game. At half time, Hayes took him upstairs to his office at St. John's Arena.

"He gave me a vocabulary test," Long said. "He'd give me a word and say, 'What does this mean? Use it in a sentence.' [Until last year, Hayes taught an English class for his players.]

"I couldn't believe it. This is how we spent the entire second half of the game," Long said. But other memories are of the bully Hayes, such as the time fullback Jim Otis fumbled three times in the first half of a game.

"Woody went nuts at half time," Long said. "He leaps over the first row, hanging over guys' shoulder pads. Bam, bam, bam, bam, beating Otis in the face with both hands. Assistant coaches were trying to pull him off."

It was all calculated, Long said, to motivate the others.

"Woody is a psychologist. He knows who he can do it to and who he can't. He wouldn't do things like that to Jack Tatum, or some of the black players. But he could intimidate some of us, including me. He knows how far he can go.

"Woody detests softness. He'd open all the windows when it was 40 degrees outside. He likes his image. When they built the new athletic facility, he said he wouldn't mind if they called it 'Stalag Hayes.' He was only half-jesting. I remember once we had an hour-long meeting on how Hitler took France on a 40-trap. The 40-trap was one of our plays."

Long also recalled one of Hayes's most memorable moments where Michigan fans are concerned. It was the day Hayes destroyed the sideline markers to protest an official's decision at Ann Arbor in 1971. "The sideline markers are the nice side of Woody," Long said. "What you see on TV is absolutely nothing. For Woody, the ends justify the means."

Hayes has survived one heart attack and Long fears that his ex-coach will "die on the sidelines." Some other former players voice similar worries. One is Brian Baschnagel, who now plays for the Chicago Bears.

"There were times I was concerned," said Baschnagel. "Like at practice, when he'd start punching himself in the face and biting his own hand. I didn't want to see him get hurt. I virtually love the guy."

So do an interesting variety of other people. Hayes's list of impressive friends includes former Presidents Gerald Ford and Richard Nixon. Hayes calls Bob Hope "the greatest living American." His other heros include generals. Assistant coach Gibbs says Hayes lectures his coaches on battle plans of the German commanders of land and sea. "You try to see through a man by the people he admires," Gibbs said.

One who admires Hayes is Bob Greene, a nationally syndicated newspaper columnist who grew up in Columbus. In a recent column, Greene wrote:

> *To those who despise him, Hayes stands for everything that is backward, outmoded, right wing, stubborn, and violent in America. He is a bad loser, a terrible loser in fact; he takes pride in this, because he feels that when his team loses it diminishes him as a man . . . . Those who see him as some kind of dumb, plodding monster would be surprised to meet him. He is a reader. He quotes historians and philosophers at a dizzying pace. He reads himself to sleep every night . . . . He is the quintessential square, and proud of it; almost nothing he does is in fashion, and yet he will never go out of style himself . . . . Why is it that I'm so drawn to him? In the end, I guess I don't know, except that whenever I'm around him I find myself grinning and shaking my head and thinking, "Here is a man."*

GENERAL

BEHIND THE SCENES AT BALTIMORE'S BIG BOWL

By Michael Nelson

From Baltimore Magazine
Copyright, ©, 1978, Baltimore Magazine, Inc.

It is 6:10 A.M. on Thursday, September 22, 1977. The Baltimore Orioles are as close to first place as they've been in a long time. At this time yesterday, the Birds were three games back, a gap that was starting to look unbridgeable at so late a stage in the season. But last night they shut out the Toronto Blue Jays 4–0 while Boston was beating the league-leading Yankees 3–2, and all of a sudden New York writers were booking reservations on the Metroliner to come see the club they'd been referring to as "That Other Team in the Race."

Calvin Woodward doesn't know about last night's games. What Woodward knows is that he is standing in front of a locked gate "getting soaked out here and those fools on the radio are still saying 20 percent chance of rain." Woodward helps sweep the stands at Memorial Stadium, and until his boss arrived to let him inside, he is going to keep on getting soaked. And then he is going to get a sore back. Hot dog wrappers get heavy and peanut shells stick to the concrete when it rains.

By the time James Laney arrives with the key at 6:30, a small crowd of sweepers has gathered by the main entrance to the stadium. He leads them to the storeroom in the stands behind home plate and hands out the brooms and assignments. "Don't give me no yellow seats, Laney," a woman calls out. "I'm about crippled from yesterday." The new yellow chairback seats in the outfield and upper-deck grandstands are a boon to the fans but a curse to the sweepers, because the spaces between them are so narrow. An older man who is told to clean the dugouts and the press box—choice assignments on a rainy day—laughs and shakes his head. "I don't know who's the biggest slobs—the reporters with their beer or the players with their sunflower seeds."

For the next hour, the sweepers are the stadium, and their sounds—the rustle of brooms, the quiet curses, the loud catcalls, and laughter—are its only sounds.

8:00. Bill O'Donnell steps outside his house to bring in the newspaper. O'Donnell's actual workday won't begin for almost 12 hours, when he and Chuck Thompson open their radio broadcast of the game, but the preparation starts now. He opens to the sports section and methodically charts in his scorebook such details as how every pitcher did last night against every hitter in every major-league game. "I won't use even 25 percent of that stuff," he says, "but if I ever get into a situation where I need a bit of information, I'll have it."

8:05. Orioles' public relations director Bob Brown is shaving. And straining. He is straining because one of his duties is to come up with an interesting baseball question to flash on the scoreboard in the seventh inning tonight, and after 152 games, Brown is just about out of interesting questions.

8:10. Over at the Cross Keys Inn, Toronto's Jerry Garvin is setting what may be a major-league record for getting up early. What's more, he is happy about it. He is happy because he pitched a one-run victory against the Orioles on Monday, he is meeting later this morning with some agents who want to represent him—and his wife of 10 months is here in Baltimore beside him.

8:15. Pat Santarone, the head of the Orioles' ground crew, is not so happy. Santarone is driving in from Baltimore County, where it did not rain last night, to the city, where somehow it did. He is getting angry, and a little worried. There had not been even a hint of rain in last night's forecast, and as a result, Santarone had decided not to lay out the massive tarpaulin that covers the infield.

8:25. Santarone's seven-man ground crew sits in their locker room under the box seats near the left-field pole, laughing and joking nervously. Ordinarily, they would be outside raking and manicuring the field to putting-green consistency, but today they can only wait for the dark, intense Santarone to arrive and give them instructions. At 8:30, he explodes through the door and hurries grim-faced into his office to call the weather bureau. It tells him there is a zero percent chance of rain tonight. "Why should I believe you now?" he barks, and slams down the phone.

9:15. In the windowless Orioles' front offices, the rain is the least of anyone's concerns. Coming into this series, the club had needed to average only 6,000 attendance per game for the rest of the season to break its previous attendance record of 1,203,000. Nothing had seemed more certain than that it would do so; after all, the Birds were in the final days of a miraculous drive for a pennant. But on Monday, 3,325 had shown up; on Tuesday, 4,301; last night, 4,237. The calls begin coming in from newspapers around the country to Beverly Weston's switchboard. "This is a misprint, right?" one editor asks. "You mean 42 thousand, not 42 hundred, right?" "It's like the bottom is falling out," says general manager Hank Peters. "Like the end of the world. It's—embarrassing."

9:52. Outside, the rain has stopped. Quickly, Santarone sends the ground crew into action. Ricky King begins painting the left-field foul line, which is made of wood; Larry Washington hoses down the bases—also wooden—and paints them; others remove the small tarpaulin from the pitcher's mound and start the slow process of packing the mound down with clay and shaping it to conform with major-league specifications.

Al Scrimger, the stadium electrician, ambles out to the scoreboard to find out which of its 8,610 lights are malfunctioning—a chronic problem.

10:50. Everybody heads back inside; the rain has resumed. Everybody but the sweepers, that is, some of them covered by plastic trash bags with holes cut out for their heads and arms. "It's rain or shine work," sighs Laney. "I can't call the game."

11:00. Rich Dauer, the Orioles' rookie second baseman, gets up out of bed in his Cockeysville apartment. He thinks of his wife back in California. For Dauer, who initially had seemed the most likely of all the team's rookies to make it, the season had started out like a nightmare. At one point, he was actually hitting his age—.024. But gradually he had put it together, won back his starting job at second, and brought his average up around a respectable .250.

Dauer is looking forward to tonight's contest. He has hits in each of the three games in the series so far, and three of his four home runs in 1977 have come off Toronto. But first there is housework to do.

11:10. "Got it, got it," chortles Bob Brown. What he's gotten is tonight's scoreboard quiz question.

11:15. The first of a small daily procession of amiable cranks wanders into the Orioles' front office and, as usual, is directed to Helen Conklin's desk in the public relations office. This one had found some old Orioles' pictures in his attic and is trying to find out who the players are. Every successful identification by Conklin gets the same response—the old man hits himself in the head, bellows "of course, of course," and tells Conklin everything he remembers about the player, with long digressions on what was happening in his own life at the time. She listens patiently and eventually he leaves, smiling.

12:30. An Orioles executive storms out of his office, waving a copy of the *Evening Sun*. "Did you see Jackman's column today?" he shouts, red-faced. "That creep. I hope Earl Weaver backs him up against the wall and kicks the crap out of him. What a moocher. All the beer I've seen him sit in that press lounge and drink, and then he turns around and knocks the club. What kind of man is that?"

The provocation was Phil Jackman's annual "Dump Earl Weaver" column, which the executive, consumed by an image of Jackman pounding it out on his typewriter while drinking beer the club has paid for, considered rank ingratitude. The press lounge is a small restaurant the team operates for reporters, free of charge. "It's an old sports tradition," says Bob Brown. "I think both the club and the press take it for granted. No self-respecting writer is going to pull his punches because he got a free dinner." Not everyone, apparently, agrees that that's the way it ought to be.

12:45. Umpire Al Clark, who will be working at first base tonight, is downtown touring the frigate *Constellation*. "Umpires are a little different from the ball players," he says. "They spend half their time on the road; we spend all our time on the road. So we take better advantage of the time we have."

1:00. Jim Tyler unlocks and enters the visitors' locker room, which is buried under the stands behind the first-base dugout. Though the Toronto players don't have to be at the stadium until 5:00—two-and-one-half hours before game time—most of them will arrive by 2:30. Life on the road is one of endless boredom for most baseball players; by getting to the ball park early, they can be bored together.

Clay Reid gets to the Orioles' locker room a little bit later, and immediately starts cleaning up the mess left by the players the night before.

He has another problem to face: uniforms. Not long ago, every team wore baggy white flannels at home, baggy gray flannels on the road. Now they wear form-fitting double knits. Reid has to decide whether it will be the new orange jerseys or the white ones for each game. "I got to be a damn color coordinator," he snorts. "When the White Sox come we never wear the orange because it clashes with their navy blue." Toronto wears light blue. Reid decides on orange.

2:10. "What's the best you got?" a customer asks Tim Geraghty at the ticket window. "First-base side," says Geraghty. "First-base side is almost always the best because the other team's dugout is there. A lot of people ask for the Orioles' side—the third-base side—so it fills up quicker."

2:30. Jerry Garvin walks around the Mormon temple in Washington with his new bride. "It was a little hard in baseball at first," he remembers. "I grew up with Mormons, and when I left to play ball for the Wisconsin Rapids, it was a whole new world for me. It was a way of life I'd never seen before. But I got used to it and now I'm finding that religion is becoming more and more accepted in baseball."

2:35. Most of the Orioles don't come in until a couple hours after the visitors. True to form, Ken Singleton is early. Singleton has been the undisputed star of the club this season. He leads the team in hits, runs, walks, and runs batted in, and his .335 batting average is second in the league.

Only a few people know that Singleton is playing in agony. A chip the size of a pencil eraser has grown in his elbow and is rubbing on the ulnar nerve, at a spot popularly known as the funny bone.

So far, at least, a cover-up is working—opposing teams haven't caught on, and Singleton has been able to play almost every game in right field. On Monday night, before the first game of the Toronto series, he had uncorked a powerful throw in fielding practice, merely to deceive the Toronto coaches. "It got to a point where I felt like every peg would be my last," he would say after the season.

Ralph Salvon, the Orioles' trainer, arrives a few minutes after Singleton. The right fielder climbs onto the training table, stretches out, and sighs blissfully as Salvon applies the ultrasound deep-heat machine.

3:05. Earl Weaver arrives at the stadium and immediately tours the field with Pat Santarone. "Looks pretty good, looks pretty good," he decides, but takes Santarone's advice and calls off batting practice.

3:10. Tim Geraghty and Bud Freeman, the ticket manager, make their crowd estimate for the game. They make it by doubling the advance sale and bracketing it a thousand either way. Their estimate for tonight is 3,000–5,000, which means fewer police, ushers, and ticket-sellers will be hired for the game. It also means the Orioles won't break their season attendance record. The bad news is sent to the front office.

3:20. Nelson Briles, a veteran pitcher, has just been picked up from the Texas Rangers to help out in the stretch drive. At a time like this, young teams like to have players who have been through it all before. "Hey, Clay," he yells to the clubhouse man, "this orange jersey doesn't fit." The Birds will wear white tonight after all.

3:55. The tarp crew starts to arrive. Most of them, like Buddy Bresnich, are high school and college students. During the game they sit out by the left-field foul pole and, says Buddy, "pray it doesn't rain." The tarpaulin they spread out over the infield when play is stopped weighs 11 tons when wet.

4:15. Weaver bustles into his windowless office near the locker room. "Running out of time," he mutters, as he sits down at his desk to make out the lineup for tonight's game.

4:30. Rich Dauer comes into the locker room, one of the last of the Orioles' players to arrive. Like his teammates, he is disappointed to hear that batting practice has been canceled. "Everybody loves batting practice," he says. "It's so much fun to swing at a ball that the pitcher wants you to to hit. And the guys who aren't starting need it to keep up a competitive edge." The substitutes, who hit first, team up in pairs and play against each other. A "hit" counts one point, a home run two. The losers fetch Cokes for the winners in the locker room.

Dauer reads his mail, gets half-dressed, and heads over to the locker room's pinball machine, where the competition is getting rough.

5:30. Players from both teams amble out onto the field to stretch, play catch, and run sprints across the outfield. Jim Palmer warms up by the Orioles dugout. Palmer had rested yesterday after getting his eighteenth win against the Blue Jays on Tuesday; today, his four-day cycle calls for a stiff workout.

Mary Mehalick, a business major at Towson State, gets her orange cap out of the ushers' locker room before heading up to section 35 in the upper deck. Until recently, ushering had been an all-male preserve at Memorial Stadium, mostly retired men and students. This was a little unusual, as well as being discriminatory; most stadiums were not only hiring women as ushers, but they were emphasizing the fact by dressing them in short skirts.

The sex barrier fell, almost accidentally, in 1974, a year I was working as an usher. The Orioles had reached the American League playoffs that year, and the club needed to hire extra help to accommodate the expected crowds. I have even heard—wrongly, as it turned out—that they had hired women ushers in the past to fill out the playoff ranks. So I didn't think anything of it when I told Deborah Kelly, a friend and fellow student, about the job.

Debbie, who is unmistakably female in person, has a husky voice that sounds even huskier on the telephone. Which accounts for the consternation that ensued when she called the stadium to apply for the job.

"All right," the man on the phone said, "but tell me how long your hair is."

"It's pretty long," said Debbie.

"Well, we have a rule that it can't reach down to your shirt collar."

Debbie paused, stunned. "But my hair reaches down my back."

"What are you, a queer?"

"No, I'm a woman."

"A woman?" said the club official. "We don't hire women to be ushers."

Debbie hit the roof, I made some phone calls, and eventually she got hired. The Orioles were semigracious losers. They eventually offered to hire Debbie for the next season (but not me); they also dressed her as a man and made her tuck her hair under her jacket.

By the time Mary Mehalick has arrived in 1977, the sex barrier is thoroughly broken. "I don't think my being a girl made any difference at all," she says. "But I do wish they'd let me wear something besides men's clothes."

5:55. The first fan of the night pulls into the parking lot. "What do we do, bump them?" yells one attendant to another. "No, space them. Small crowd tonight." When the crowd estimate is 14,000 or more, cars are parked bumper to bumper, which means that nobody leaves until everybody leaves. When a small crowd is expected, cars are allowed room to pull out.

For the next hour, the stadium functions by ritual. Players toss balls back and forth or play pepper on the field. Reporters pull them aside for interviews, then head up to the press lounge for supper. Kids with gloves and autograph books lean over the edge of the stands, pleading for attention. Umpires settle into their little room under the stands and rub up the five-dozen baseballs they will have for tonight's game. Fans trickle in slowly, are parked and seated. The concession stands open up, and vendors spread out through the stands. Eight huge light towers are switched on to take the place of the sun, which is starting to disappear behind the third-base stands. Baseball is a relaxing game, but never so much as in that hour that passes before everyone realizes that there is business to be transacted tonight, not a game, but an official game, to be played.

7:15. Robert Washington lays down the white lines that form the batter's box. "I don't know why they do this," he says, "because when that first player comes up, he's going to kick dirt all over the lines anyway."

7:20. "Ladies and gentlemen, Wild Bill Hagy!"

The crowd in the upper-deck right-field grandstand cheers and laughs as Wild Bill, tank-topped, beer-bellied, bearded, and wearing a cowboy hat over his balding head, climbs up to his seat. Wild Bill is the Orioles' unofficial cheerleader; every couple of innings he stands up and spells out the team name with his body while the fans spell it out with their voices. A Dundalk cabby, Wild Bill is surprisingly soft-spoken, even shy . . . when he's not going berserk.

7:25. Dick Young, the star sports writer for the New York *Daily News*, hurries into the press box and takes his seat. He looks around the stands below in openmouthed astonishment. "I don't understand it," he says. "Either people in Baltimore don't know they're in a pennant race or there's 50,000 of them here disguised as empty seats."

7:29. The Orioles take the field and public-address announcer Rex Barney gets everybody up for our national anthem. And then keeps them up for the Canadian national anthem.

7:33. Gary Woods steps into the batter's box for Toronto. He kicks dirt over the white lines Robert Washington had neatly laid out. It doesn't help. He looks at a third strike.

7:45. Still no score after three innings, and Rex Barney decides to liven the crowd up. He announces: "The car with New York tag REG 44 will have to move," and the fans, recognizing the name and uniform number of their archenemy, Reggie Jackson, laugh and boo.

8:28. The Orioles are on the scoreboard, but they're frustrated. Eddie Murray led off the fourth with a single, and after two infield outs and a walk to Mark Belanger, catcher Dave Skaggs brought Murray home with a bloop single to center. Then Al Bumbry ripped a single of his own. But before Belanger could cross the plate with a second Oriole run, Skaggs was picked off rounding second.

Between innings, Bob Brown lobbies Henry Heckt of the New York *Post* on behalf of Eddie Murray's candidacy for Rookie of the Year. "Here's the clincher," he says. "In five of the eight games we beat the Yankees this year, Murray had the winning hit."

8:33. Another one-two-three inning for Oriole pitcher Mike Flanagan. In five scoreless innings, he has walked none, struck out four, and given up only two singles.

Down behind home plate, a woman stands up and starts cursing. Like crazy. At the top of her lungs. Police Lieutenant Philip Farace sighs and hurries down to her seat. He speaks quietly to her, and she sits down. "This is getting to be an every night thing," he sighs. The woman is retarded.

8:44. There are two down in the bottom of the fifth, and the Orioles come alive. With Lee May on second and Murray on first, Andres Mora slices a double past right-fielder Otto Velez, bringing both runners home. Wild Bill and his friends sing: "When the moon hits the sky like-a-big-a-pizza pie, that's-a Mora." Orioles 3, Jays 0.

8:53. The Orioles have already scored one run in the sixth. A hand over each ear, Bill O'Donnell talks rapidly into the microphone. Chuck Thompson slips him a note: "Vukovich warming for Toronto."

One more fastball, and Lee May has his twenty-sixth home run of the year, scoring two runners ahead of him. Vukovich comes in from the bullpen, a tad too late. Orioles 7, Blue Jays 0.

9:06. Bob Brown's baseball quiz question flashes up on the scoreboard before the top of the seventh inning. "In the 24 years Baltimore has been in the American League, the Orioles have compiled winning records against all but two opponents. Can you name those two teams?"

9:13. Otto Velez's home run in the seventh has made it 7–1, but the fans—all 4,951 of them—are stomping and clapping to the sound of John Denver singing "Thank God, I'm a Country Boy."

The baseball quiz answer appears a few minutes later, provoking all the appropriate responses:

New York Yankees (Booooo)
Wrong (Yaaaay)
The Orioles are 235–217 against them (Yay)
Would you believe?
Boston Red Sox 229–231 (Booo)
Cleveland Indians 225–227 (Ahhhhh)

9:30. One of the problems with being Dick Young is that every other sports writer wants to come by and talk to you. "How did Toronto get that run?" he asks his neighbor, startled to see that a one had appeared on the scoreboard while he had been holding court.

9:41. Velez pops to Bumbry, ending the game. The Orioles are within a game-and-a-half of first place. It is the closest they will get this season.

2 A.M. The players, ushers, fans, reporters, and everyone else are long gone from the darkened stadium. By all rights, night watchman Bill Barry ought to be hearing nothing but his own footsteps as he makes his rounds. But he hears more than that—footsteps, voices, doors slamming, laughter. "I half expect to see the ghosts of the old ball players floating by," he says, and continues on through the rooms and corridors of Memorial Stadium.

TENNIS

MARTINA IS PROUD

By Barry Lorge

From The Washington Post
Copyright, ©, 1978, The Washington Post

When it was over, after she had come back from 2–4 in the final set by serving impenetrably and outsteadying as well as overpowering Chris Evert, Martina Navratilova thrust her arms straight up in the air. She turned to her friends, applauding wildly in the competitors' guest box above Center Court, and glowed.

Even in her private reveries, she had not been able to envision herself actually doing what she had just done: crack a big first serve down the middle and drill away a deep backhand volley on the last point of the women's singles final at Wimbledon.

The 14,000 spectators who witnessed Navratilova's thrilling 2–6, 6–4, 7–5 triumph yesterday will remember her ecstatic expression at the finish, the smile that outshone the sun popping in and out from behind the mass of billowy white clouds over the All England Lawn Tennis and Croquet Club.

They will recall the flood of tears she shed into a towel immediately afterward, her puffy eyes as she received the champion's gleaming gold plate from the Duchess of Kent. The jubilant little dance step she did as she posed victoriously for the gang of photographers jostling each other behind a restraining rope.

"I thought I could win before the match, but I didn't really believe that I could be the Wimbledon champion," said the chunky 21-year-old left hander who defected from Czechoslovakia to the United States in September 1975 and now lives in Dallas.

"It's only once a year that you get the chance, and this was the first time that I was in the finals. Most people thought that Chris would win, but I came through." The most important believer had believed.

"I always wondered what it would be like. If I could sleep the night before: How it would feel going on the court? If I could keep walking if I had to serve for the match? What I would do if I ever won. It's very different from what you think . . .

"I don't know if I should cry or scream or laugh. I feel very happy that I won, and at the same time I'm very sad that I can't share this with my family."

Navratilova has not seen her father, Miroslav, an "economic engineer" in the office of a Prague factory and her first tennis coach, her mother, or 15-year-old sister, Jana, in nearly three years.

She talks to them frequently by telephone, but she has been unable to visit them since being granted political asylum in America during the 1975 U.S. Open tennis championships.

Their applications for tourist visas to the United States and England have been rejected. Martina's attempts to secure them a permanent visa so they can settle in the United States also have failed.

Her victory might help in these efforts, and in that sense it was far more precious than the $32,000 first prize and the incalculable professional self-esteem that comes with winning the oldest and most cherished title in tennis.

She is the second expatriate Czech to win Wimbledon. Jaroslav Drobny captured the men's singles title in 1954, while traveling on an Egyptian passport.

"I like the United States very much. The people there have been very good to me. But deep down I will always be a Czech, just as Drobny was always a Czech," she said.

Navratilova had a right to be proud as well as joyous. After losing four straight games from 2–0 to 2–4 in the third set, she did not unravel.

On her own serve, she played brutally aggressive tennis. On Evert's, she was firm and patient in deep, fiercely contested baseline rallies, awaiting her opportunities to smack an approach shot and press the attack from the net.

She played with unshakable resolve when everyone expected her to get nervous. She looked Evert, the champion of 1974 and 1976, straight in the eye, and it was the legendary Ice Maiden who cracked.

Navratilova, whose emotions once overwhelmed her abundant talent, won 12 of the last 13 points. She held at love the last two times she served, missing only one first serve.

It was Evert who made three unforced errors in the end, losing her serve to 5–6 in the most crucial moment of the absorbing one-hour 43-minute match.

"I was just a notch better at the closing stages, which is the only thing that matters. I was able to raise the level of my game and Chris kind of stayed the same or even got worse," Navratilova noted, correctly.

Evert agreed. The championship had hinged on a wholly unexpected psychological role reversal.

"She's just tougher than I am right now," Evert said. "In the past, the shoe has usually been on the other foot. I've been the consistent one. But she's really matured—on the tennis court and off—and it showed up," said Evert, 23.

"She used to be very emotional and moody. Now she seems relaxed. She's been through a lot in the last couple of years—a lot of bad feelings, hurt and loneliness as far as her defection is concerned. Now she seems to have it all together.

"A couple of times I heard her talking to herself, but she didn't get flustered at all," Evert continued. "At 2–4 she could have gotten discouraged. Two years ago, I think she would have. She might have given up a little bit, made a lot of errors, gone for impossible shots. But she played consistently and forced me into errors."

The tennis was patchy, especially in the first two sets, largely because of a swirling wind that rustled the green canopy over the royal box.

Both players had some difficulty finding the range on groundstrokes in the first set. In the second game of the second set, Navratilova even suffered the embarrassment of shiffing completely on an easy overhead.

She took her eye off the ball, and a gust caught it. She swung and missed, whirled and desperately tried to get to the ball after it bounced, but couldn't. Then she stood with head in hands for a few moments, stunned.

Evert—who lost her serve at 15 in the first game of each set—buzzed a backhand cross-court passing shot on the next point to break back to 1–1. But the enormous error actually may have helped Navratilova. "It kind of woke me up. After that I paid more attention to the ball," she said.

By her own admission, Navratilova played "in a bit of a daze" in the first set. She did not move well. She held her serve only once. When she was broken from 40–0 for the set, in a game in which Evert got two lucky net court winners, depression seemed to be setting in.

She sulked and sent a couple of persecuted, hangdog glances toward the guest box where Sandra Haynie, the friend who shares a house with her in Dallas and manages her business affairs, was seated.

But after losing her serve in the game of the ignominious whiff, Navratilova settled down and played much more positively. The looks toward Haynie, who has been an important stabilizing influence in her life, were more optimistic.

Navratilova played an attacking game to break for 2–1, crunching a backhand volley that Evert couldn't handle. After blistering a short second serve at 15–40, she held her serve at love with a spinning drop volley and raised her arms triumphantly as if to say, "I finally held an advantage."

She fell behind, 15–40, in her next service game when Evert, having followed in a near-perfect drop shot, drilled a forehand volley that hit her in the ear. Navratilova took two steps and dropped to her knees, rolling her eyes and feigning death by shooting.

Evert, at first concerned, smiled, reached across the net, and patted her opponent playfully on the head. It was that kind of a sporting and good-natured match between good friends. Navratilova later insisted that a point on which Evert got a bad call be replayed, but when the laughter died down after the "killer" volley, Navratilova put in six straight first serves to dig herself out of trouble, holding for 4–2.

An athletic 5-feet-8 and 145 pounds, Navratilova has the oppressive weight of the hardest shot in women's tennis today. Her powerful serves and telling volleys were there when she needed them. She put in only 14 of 31 first serves in the first set, 27 of 42 in the second, 22 of 35 in the third, including seven of the last eight.

After trailing, 0–2 in the final set, Evert temporarily picked up the pace and accuracy of her groundstrokes. She played her best game to break for a 4–2 lead, blasting two return winners off first serves to get to 0–40, then lacing a backhand cross-court for an outright winner off a fierce, scrambling rally.

But Navratilova broke right back to 3–4, even though Evert put in five of five first serves. Navratilova remembered their only previous meeting this year, on grass two weeks ago at Eastbourne, when she recovered from 1–4 in the final set and saved a match point in beating Evert, 9–7, in the third.

Evert held for 5–4 after saving a break point at 30–40 on another magnificent all-court point. Navratilova hit a smash down the middle, Evert drilled the ball right back at her with a forehand, and Navratilova slashed a low, forehand cross-court volley that looked like a sure winner. Evert got to the ball and, on the dead run, cranked an impossible backhand cross-court passing shot that bit into the turf, a foot inside the sideline.

That, however, was Evert's last hurrah.

Navratilova, damning the torpedoes and boring full speed ahead as she served to save the match, held to love.

She played steadily in the next game as Evert made those three unforced errors to lose her serve, sailing a forehand on the last point.

GENERAL

THEY'D WIN IN ANY GAME

By Leigh Montville

From The Boston Globe
Copyright, © 1978, The Boston Globe
Courtesy of The Boston Globe

I'm building my team, you see. I'm not having any tryouts. I'm just picking people. I don't even care about the sport. I'm just building my team, you see.

Earl Weaver is my coach, my manager, whatever.

Red Auerbach is my general manager.

I'm not renegotiating any contracts, I'm not guaranteeing any contracts (except for injury), I'm not giving any incentive bonuses. Nobody is going to be allowed to open a supermarket or speak to a Rotary Club except on his off day.

I want Gerry Cheevers. I want Luis Tiant. I want Kenny Stabler. I want Paul Silas.

I don't want Pete Rose. I suppose you do, but I think Rose is a midwestern boor and a showboat. I want Joe Morgan from the Cincinnati Reds.

I want Julius Erving.

I think I want Guy Lafleur.

I don't want any vegetarians. I don't want any religious zealots. I don't want any extremes, except in professionalism and the ability to laugh at life. I don't care if a guy smokes or drinks, as long as he doesn't do it at second base.

I want Billie Jean King, not Chris Evert. I want Bjorn Borg, not Jimmy Connors. I want Lee Trevino. I want Roberto Duran.

A. J. Foyt definitely drives the team bus.

I don't care if Bill Walton suddenly is healthy and would play for nothing. I don't want him. I wouldn't walk across the street to sign Bill Walton.

I don't want anything to do with Reggie Bars, Billy Martin, or just about anyone in pinstripes. I want Mark Belanger. I want Vida Blue. I want Butch Hobson and Carlton Fisk.

I want Al Oerter. I wouldn't touch Dwight Stones or Houston McTear.

I want free swingers. I want guys who finish the game dirty. I want chewers, spitters, and colorful cursers. I don't care if anyone spikes the ball in the end zone or does a victory boog-a-loo, but I don't want any exaggerated home run trots.

I want Lynn Swann to catch the long balls. Russ Francis to catch the short ones and Fred Biletnikoff to catch the ones across the middle. I want Wonderful Harvey Martin to rush the passer.

I would take O. J. Simpson, if only he would stop endorsing every product that ever has been invented. For some reason, I don't want Walter Payton.

John Havlicek, if he'll come out of retirement, is my man for the end of the game. If he doesn't, the job goes to Carl Yastrzemski.

I don't want Kareem Abdul-Jabbar.

No designated hitters. No field-goal kickers who remove their shoes. No goons except, maybe, Dave Schultz. I'll take Dave Schultz.

I don't care if everyone else seems to have doubts about him, Ernie DiGregorio has a place. Bobby Orr does, too, even if he never laces up another skate. Ted Williams, fat as he is, also can put down his can of worms and pick up a bat at any time.

Everyone has to know how to bunt.

Every skater will wear a helmet. Except, maybe, for Dave Schultz.

Ali is a definite starter. George Foreman, never. I'll wait a year on Leon Spinks and see what happens. No to Sugar Ray Leonard.

No figure skaters. No swimmers. Definitely no platform divers.

I want a solid poker player. I want a pool shooter. Is Larry Mahan the champion rodeo guy? I want Larry Mahan.

I don't want Pele, but I want the Russian weightlifter. My distance runners will come from Kenya.

I would like the Dave Cowens of three years ago, but I'll take the one of today. I'll take the happy Jim Rice, the one his teammates see more often than the press does.

I want Willie Shoemaker instead of Steve Cauthen. No harness racers, never, but if Downing wants to stay in action I'll supply the Alpo. I want Willie McCovey, Pete Maravich, Earl Monroe, Brad Park, and Billy (White Shoes) Johnson.

I don't want cheap-shot guys, even if they'll make me a winner. I don't want garbage men. I don't want anyone who can't whistle.

My team never is going to play on synthetic surfaces. Except, maybe, artificial ice. A good proportion of the games are going to be played on afternoons, rather than nights. Every game is going to be on home television.

The uniforms are going to be something like the Oakland A's. My cheerleaders are going to be the Dallas Cowgirls, never the Embraceable Ewes or any of these other slapdash imitations. Linda Ronstadt is going to sing the national anthem, backed by the Grambling marching band. The warm-ups shall be run to rock 'n' roll. Not rock. Never disco. Just rock 'n' roll.

Frank Deford is going to write the long story about my team. Red Smith is going to write the short one. The book will be written by John D. MacDonald, if we can get him out of Florida. Don Meridith and Tony Kubek will be the television announcers and I don't care if they ever give the score. Woody Allen already owns the movie rights.

Our road trips are only going to be to either coast or Chicago. No Cleveland. No Detroit. No Columbus, Ohio, never. All charter flights. All four-star hotels. The training table certainly shall feature french fries.

I figure we'll have a good bunch of guys. I figure the other teams never can put their pants on more than one leg at a time. I see the cup coming home, wrapped in the gonfalon, cheered by the multitudes.

Spring training should begin any day now on some sandy beach. Then maybe we'll have a quick European tour. Just to get loose for the regular-season grind.

HORSE RACING

DIARY OF A TRIPLE CROWN WINNER

By Jim Bolus

From The Florida Horse Magazine
Copyright, ©, 1978, Florida Breeders' Sales Company

May 18—It's foggy this morning in Baltimore. So foggy that nobody knows Affirmed's time in a half-mile breeze at Pimlico.

"I see the stretch only," trainer Laz Barrera says back at the barn. "The fog you cannot see from here to there. No way anybody could get any time. I saw the last eighth of the workout. I hear him from the quarter pole, because I know the way he hit the track. Through my ears, I know it was him coming, but I don't see him. The beat of his legs, he's so smooth on the track. He don't hit the ground too hard. I think the way he was running in front of me, he have to go a half a mile in 52 or 51—something."

Barrera, who has won two Kentucky Derbies and one Belmont, is bidding for his first Preakness victory. Affirmed's opponents in the second jewel of the Triple Crown will include Track Reward, trained by Barrera's son, Albert.

Somebody asks Laz if Albert calls him and asks for advice. "Yeah, we talk a lot," Barrera says. "Listen, I love my children [he has three]. The only thing I did all my life was work for them."

Laz explains that Albert once attended the University of Miami. "He quit school after three years of college," Laz says. "He want to be on the racetrack. I go to see him because he no get the good marks. I got the report card from the school. I stopped by the school to check with him. And he got a lot of Racing Forms in the room. Was going to the races at Hialeah. I tell him if he want to be on the racetrack, go ahead and work on the racetrack."

Barrera adds that he wasn't "going to break my neck paying $5,000 a year" to keep Albert in college. So Albert left college and went to work for his father. He learned from the best.

The Preakness horses are stabled in Barn E, and down the way from Barrera is Alydar's trainer, John Veitch, talking to another group of reporters.

Veitch says that he has received more than 100 letters since the Derby.

"Dear John . . ."

It seems that some folks have offered suggestions, encouragement, and/or criticisms to the Calumet trainer.

"A few were critical of Jorge [Jockey Jorge Velasquez], a few were critical of me, some of them were disappointing, others were encouraging," Veitch says.

Veitch says that he doesn't know any of the persons who have written to him. "You didn't recognize my handwriting," cracks Ed Comerford, racing writer for *Newsday*.

Veitch notes that Admiral Gene Markey, whose wife owns Calumet Farm, received "a telegram from somebody who said we ought to give Velasquez back to Panama and keep the canal."

Velasquez, a native of Panama, has been unjustly criticized in certain corners because Alydar lagged far back in the early going of the Derby. Veitch says that he doesn't blame Velasquez for Alydar's defeat.

"Jorge being the rider and the horse being so far back, it was only natural that people would say, 'Boy, did he screw up. He was overconfident and let that horse [Affirmed] slip away from him.' But that wasn't the fact. He knew he was too far back, but there was nothing he could do about it. It was not his fault."

According to the Daily Racing Form chart of the Derby, Alydar trailed the leader by 17 lengths at one point. Veitch wants Alydar much closer to the pace in the Preakness. "I would hope not to be more than three or four or five or six lengths off the lead horse going down the backside in the early stages of it," Veitch says. "And I would hope to be right on top of the lead horse at the head of the stretch."

The fog now has all but disappeared and trainer W. C. (Woody) Stephens sends Believe It to the track. The colt steps three furlongs in a rapid 34 3/5 seconds. "He went just a tick fast," Stephens says, "but the way he did it was fine."

"Going into the Derby," a reporter asks Stephens, "didn't you favor Alydar over Affirmed a little?"

"Well, I did for one reason," Stephens says. "I saw Alydar run in Florida, and I hadn't been around Affirmed any since New York in the fall. But when I saw Affirmed in Louisville and I saw him work five eighths of a mile and then I saw how he behaved himself in the paddock, I changed my mind a little. Because he's a wonderful-dispositioned horse in the paddock, that's for sure."

At 9:58 A.M. the draw is held for Preakness post positions. Affirmed gets the No. 6 spot in the field of seven, Alydar No. 3. Believe It, the only other horse with a chance, draws No. 2.

The other four entered are Noon Time Spender, Track Reward, Indigo Star, and Dax S.

"The first three I wouldn't want to meet in a dark alley," says Nathan Scherr, who owns Dax S. in partnership with his brother, Robert. "But we'll try the other three any time."

"Fourth money would be a major victory," interjects Mel Gross, the trainer of Dax S.

With a grin, Gross adds, "I'm scared to death."

Dax S. is a come-from-behind horse whose style has been to run last in the early stages of his races before making his move. "He thinks his name is And Dax S.," quips Gross, meaning that when the track announcer gets around to calling the colt's name, he is running in last place.

A prediction: The Preakness horses will finish in alphabetical order— Affirmed, Alydar, Believe It, Dax S., Indigo Star, Noon Time Spender, and Track Reward.

May 19—The traditional Alibi Breakfast is held at Pimlico.

Comedian Red Skelton gets up and entertains the gathering with some jokes.

Of the Cross Keys Inn motel in Baltimore, Skelton says, "The security there is really nice. They knock on the door and say, 'You got a girl in there?' You say, 'No.' They throw one in."

Again on the Cross Keys: "They've got a real bellhop up there. This guy's got one leg."

Skelton says he doesn't drink. "Why I don't drink: Somebody will say to me, 'Have a drink.' I say, 'No, thanks.' They say, 'Oh, come on, have one to be sociable.' So I take one. A few minutes later, they say, 'Can I freshen that up?' The next thing I hear is somebody saying, 'Did he have a hat?' "

After the breakfast, Laz Barrera returns to his barn and talks about Preakness strategy. He suggests that running closer to the pace in the Preakness might backfire on Alydar.

"He might lay third or fourth," Barrera says. "If he goes easy to that position, that's OK. But if you have to rush him, you change your style on him after you teach him so long to rate him and bring him from behind. If you have to keep punching to keep him close, that can be a very dangerous thing because probably he don't gonna have no kick in the end."

Barrera figures that Believe It will set the early pace.

"Woody Stephens try his horse from behind in the Derby," Barrera says. "He got to my horse and my horse run away from him. He have to do some changing. And the change I'm expecting him to do is to send to the lead. And he work him yesterday with that idea."

Pimlico throws its annual party at the Suburban Country Club this evening. Women, many in long dresses, and men, mostly in sports coats, enjoy themselves eating and drinking and talking about horses.

Howard Cosell is there. Among other things, he is talking about sports writers. And what he says is not particularly complimentary. Not that what he says is particularly important.

A Louisville writer is introduced to Cosell. Big deal. In a short time Humble Howard is looking directly in the writer's eyes and saying, "You've just been introduced to me and already you know that I have a brilliant mind . . ."

Blah, blah, blah.

The writer looks down at the ground, turns his head, begins to twist his mouth somewhat, and wonders if Cosell, brilliant mind and all, realizes that he's on the verge of bursting out into laughter. The writer, however, is able to restrain his laughter. He deserves an Academy Award.

May 20—A record Preakness crowd of 81,261 turns out on a hot day.

Laz Barrera, wearing the same gray suit that he wore on Derby Day, is at his barn answering questions fired at him by a 12-year-old boy from Laurel, Md. Gino Alongi, whose father works in the mutuel department and trains one horse as well, is impressing Barrera with his knowledge of racing.

"Would you say Affirmed's the best horse you ever had?" Gino asks Barrera.

"Very hard to answer that question because I have a lot of—Bold Forbes was a good horse, J.O. Tobin is a good horse, Barrera going three quarters of a mile is a helluva good horse."

Gino asks other questions and makes enough sharp observations about racing that Barrera predicts the youth is "a cinch" to be a turf writer some day.

At 4:31, W. C. (Woody) Stephens arrives at the barn and mentions to Barrera that somebody has told him a bettor put down $40,000 on Affirmed.

Later, Pimlico stable manager Harry Jeffra, a former boxing champion, drops by the barn, shakes hands with Barrera, and says, "I want you to win today, and I'll tell you why—I won the featherweight title 38 years ago today."

Alydar leaves Barn E at 5:14. A minute later Affirmed follows him. For once, Affirmed is behind Alydar.

Jeffra shakes hands with Barrera as the trainer leaves the barn with his horse. Shortly before Affirmed reaches the track after the walk from the stable area, a boy yells from the grandstand, "Alydar's going to win this race! You better mark down Alydar if you want to win any money!"

Affirmed is now heading down the stretch, on his way to the saddling area on the grass course in front of the infield tote board. The Harbor View Farm colt looks like a million dollars, which is only appropriate. For, if he wins the Preakness, he will top the million-dollar mark in earnings. No other horse has ever achieved that mark at such an early stage of his career.

Grandstand fans, many with cameras, are leaning against the rail, looking at the Preakness horses walking down the track.

"Is that Affirmed? All right! Go Affirmed!"

"Who's that? Oh, he's beautiful!"

Affirmed is led onto the grass course and saddled for the Preakness.

Barrera then gives instructions to Steve Cauthen, which puzzles at least one Kentucky hardboot who is looking on. "Why wouldn't Laz just give Cauthen a leg up and wish him good luck?" the hardboot wonders. "Surely, he's already gone over strategy for the race and has given Cauthen his instructions."

Surprisingly, Barrera hasn't had that opportunity until just now.

"Riders up!" And the crowd cheers as the horses leave the infield and head for the track. The Baltimore Colts' band plays "Maryland My Maryland."

Mike Barry, the Louisville *Times* columnist who was the only writer covering the Derby to correctly pick the first four finishers, is on hand to watch his first Preakness in person. He is hoping to see a race in the Preakness—a head-and-head stretch battle between Affirmed and Alydar—

that many had expected in the Derby. That kind of race didn't materialize in Louisville. Maybe it will today.

It's 5:41. Post time.

They're off and running in the Preakness, and Track Reward and Affirmed are going for the early lead. Alydar, as expected, is much closer to the pace as Affirmed proceeds to move past Track Reward, setting some slow fractions.

This time the critics won't be able to say that Velasquez is too far back with Alydar. The Calumet colt is perfectly placed and he closes in on Affirmed rounding the far turn.

At the top of the stretch, Alydar is rolling, moving up to challenge Affirmed. Velasquez believes that he will win the race. Yet, he knows that Affirmed likes to wait for horses when he's in front. Velasquez is fully aware that he still has a battle on his hands coming down the Pimlico stretch.

It has now developed into strictly a two-horse race. Affirmed leading and Alydar coming on. The crowd is going wild.

Both jockeys are working on their horses, getting every ounce of energy out of them. After looking around just before the quarter pole, Cauthen hits Affirmed six times, hand-rides a few strides, hits him four more times, and then hand-rides him the last few yards. Velasquez hits Alydar twice left-handed at the top of the stretch, then 10 times right-handed the rest of the way.

Two weeks ago in Louisville, the Derby was decided at the eighth pole. Affirmed had already put the race away, and inside the final furlong, Mike Barry yelled from the press box, "Way to ride him, Stevie, way to ride him!"

But with an eighth of a mile to go in the Preakness, Affirmed hasn't won. Not with Alydar alongside him, he hasn't. And Barry is yelling, "Hold him, Stevie! Hold him!"

They're nearing the finish now, a classic duel between two horses running as fast as their legs and bloodlines will carry them, two horses running their hearts out, two horses staging a memorable battle.

Affirmed still is leading, but Alydar has dead aim on him. All Alydar has to do is pass his rival and go on and win the race.

But he can't.

At the finish, it's the same old story: Affirmed first, Alydar second. The margin of victory is a neck. A long neck. And it's a long way back—7½ lengths—to Believe It in third.

The race has been a great one, and up in the press box many writers are all shook up. The excited Barry is babbling, incoherent. A veteran turf writer on one side of him says, "I'm wound up so tight I can't breathe!" A man on the other side of Barry says, "I was afraid my heart was gonna stop!"

Affirmed is a horse who will run as fast as he's forced to run and today, with Alydar putting pressure on him, he has had to run plenty fast. The time of 1:54 2/5 ties Triple Crown champions Seattle Slew and Secretariat for the second fastest in Preakness history.

When Cauthen brings Affirmed back to the cheers of the Pimlico crowd, the young rider spots Larry Barrera on the track, and the two 18-year-olds do what comes naturally to them. Cauthen reaches down from Affirmed and slaps hands with his friend, who is the son of Laz Barrera.

Velasquez dismounts from Alydar and talks with Veitch. Then heading back to the jockeys' quarters, Velasquez is asked by a reporter, "Did you get the lead on him?"

"No, I never. The closest that I got to him was in the last sixteenth coming to the wire."

Velasquez walks into the jockeys' room, and soon is surrounded by reporters. He has no alibi.

"I just got beat," Velasquez says. "My horse really run a very good race. I couldn't find no excuse. When I asked him to run, he responded. He come on, but the other horse kept going."

Velasquez explains that the idea was for Alydar not to drop back like he did in the Derby "and then people criticize me because they thought I took him back. And that's bull. I didn't take him back. He took himself back. He wasn't trying that day. But today he was trying. And I have no excuse, I got beat."

From the presentation stand, Cauthen is taken to the press box.

"I was waiting for Alydar the whole race," Cauthen says. "He came to me at the top of the stretch. He [Velasquez] set his horse down and I set my horse down. I opened up a length on him but he came back to me. They fought it out after that. And I beat him. Today, he had no excuse."

Meanwhile, over at the detention barn, Veitch is with Alydar.

"When you come that close, I ain't afraid of him," Veitch says of Affirmed. "We'll catch him someday. We're going to try him in three weeks again."

Referring to the Belmont, a reporter asks, "Do you think the added distance of——"

"I don't have any idea," Veitch says before the question is completed. "Affirmed is a very, very tough racehorse, and there's no telling how far he'd go. So, we just don't make it today and maybe next time we will. Affirmed's a very fine horse."

Just then a young man who apparently has enjoyed himself thoroughly in the infield walks over and, at first, takes part in the interview. Later, he takes it over. (For lack of a more appropriate name, the youth will be referred to as Intoxie.)

"Hey, what's your name?" Intoxie asks Veitch.

"John Veitch."

"John Veitch, is it? Yeah . . . . You train who?"

"Alydar."

"Ayeedar. Yeah, I'm glad to meet you . . . . What happen? Where'd he run?"

"Second, second."

"Yeah. By how much?"

"Half a length . . . a neck."

"Well, we'll get him in that damn Belmont, right?"

"Well, all we can do is try. We'll lay on him in the Belmont."

Veitch is incredible. Here he has just lost the Preakness after a hotly contested stretch battle and he is handling this situation beautifully. Many other trainers would walk away from Intoxie or tell him where to go. Not

John Veitch. He is patient and understanding. Most of all, he is demonstrating what he is—a true sport.

Veitch tells a reporter, "Jorge rode a perfect race and the horse ran a perfect race, I thought. You know just——"

Intoxie interrupts and says, "Jorge—he handled the horse good."

"Perfectly," Veitch replies.

"Yeah . . . excellent job."

"He's a good rider," Veitch says. "He——"

Again Intoxie interrupts, this time saying, "What do you think of Cauthen?"

"He's an excellent rider, too," Veitch says.

"Yeah," Intoxie says, "what do you think of Affirmed?" Intoxie not only is monopolizing the interview by asking most of the questions, but now he is even providing the answers because before Veitch has a chance to say what he thinks of Affirmed, Intoxie comes back with, "We'll get him NEXT TIME, right?"

Intoxie is overbearing, but his actions can be excused. He is, after all, literally caught up in the spirit of the day, as evidenced by his next question to Veitch: "Would you like a cold beer?"

"No, sir," Veitch replies. "Thank you, no."

Veitch then inquires of Intoxie, "Was it hot in the infield?"

"Oh, sir. It was somethin' . . . . Man, this one guy got a bottle thrown, and it hit him right in his face—blood."

Later, Intoxie asks Veitch a question that he has asked earlier. "How far did you get beat?"

"Neck."

"Oh, man, that's a shame. That is a damn shame."

"It was a good horse race," Veitch says.

To which a reporter says, "This has got to be the——"

Once more, Intoxie interrupts. "It's got to be the best race ever . . ."

"Are you going to go in the Belmont?" a reporter asks Veitch.

"Yes, sir. When you only get beat like that, there's no telling every time you meet who'll come out on top. And what it's going to come down to at the end of the year is probably whichever horse is really the strongest over an extended period of time."

"So this is going to go on and on and on," Intoxie says.

"Yep," said Veitch.

"Until ALVADAR ends up champ," Intoxie says.

"As far as you're concerned," a reporter says to Veitch, "the war's not over."

"That's right," Intoxie says.

"It's only a battle," Veitch says, managing to squeeze in an answer.

"I can even answer you there," Intoxie tells the reporter, "because I love Alvadar. I love Alvadar. That's my horse."

So much for that interview.

It's 6:35, less than an hour after the Preakness, and Laz Barrera is heading back to the barn, his arm around his wife. He is miffed.

It seems that a not-so-funny thing happened to Barrera on the way to the press box for a postrace interview. He didn't make it. The press box elevator was so crowded that Barrera wasn't able to get on it. Cauthen, however, was on it. Moreover, Barrera had waited for the elevator to stop again on his level, but it didn't. A proud man, Barrera's pride has been hurt by this incident, and he walks disgustedly back to the barn.

But not without saying what's on his mind.

"They only worry to take Steve Cauthen [to the press box]," Barrera says. "It looks like Steve Cauthen was the only star in this show."

Barrera goes back to the barn and, at 6:39, Charlie Rose, the exercise rider for Alydar, returns with the Calumet colt from the detention area. On his way past Barrera, Rose walks over and shakes hands with the trainer. "Congratulations," Rose says.

"Thank you, my friend," Barrera says. "Thank you. It's too bad that we have to get these two horses the same year."

Moments later, Barrera shows his displeasure with Cauthen. Or rather with Cauthen's agent, Lenny Goodman.

"I know he's a big star," Barrera says of the celebrated rider, " . . .but he should have been in this barn this morning to listen to the instructions because I have to give instructions running around in the paddock. I don't blame Steve. I blame his agent because he should have known that. Should have brought him here this morning."

May 21— The morning after.

John Veitch reiterates that he is not throwing in the towel against Affirmed. "I'm not going to concede anything at this point," he tells reporters. "We've got a long year yet to go. This is only May. A lot of racing and a lot of racetracks to run over.

"I will concede that he's a damned fine racehorse, Affirmed. Maybe a tad better than I thought he was."

At the end of the interview, reporters thank Veitch for his patience and wish him luck down the road. Mike Barry, the Louisville *Times* columnist, says something to Veitch that pleases the Calumet trainer. "John, it's ridiculous to come around and offer sympathy to a man that's got a horse as good as yours."

Barry returns to Louisville and writes that he's never seen a better race than the Preakness. And he's seen thousands of races through the years.

"I'm almost back to normal now, at least what's normal for me," Barry writes. "And, now that I've had a day and a half or so to think about it, there's no doubt at all. The one-hundred-third Preakness has got to be the best race I've ever seen, because I can't think of a better one. Or a race as good, for that matter.

" . . .This was a race to remember. I don't think I'll forget it, ever."

June 5—Jorge Velasquez is one of the coolest, calmest jockeys in America. But even he can lose his cool.

Following his second-place finishes aboard Alydar in the Derby and Preakness, Velasquez was the victim of some booing and nagging comments from New York racing fans. The fans kept reminding Velasquez that 18-year-old Steve Cauthen had finished ahead of him with Affirmed in the Derby and Preakness.

"Every time I was coming out on the track, they were booing me," Velasquez says in an interview. "And people were telling me, 'You can't beat the kid.' And, 'Watch out. Steve is in the race.' And, 'Here comes Steve.' It was bugging me. It was some people, they were just getting to my nerves sometimes, and they just annoyed me. You know how New York fans are. But they're not booing me anymore."

Maybe Velasquez's recent hot streak—he rode the winners of four straight stakes races at Belmont Park—has reminded these fans what kind of jockey he is. Not that he needs to establish his credentials as a top rider. He has been one of the country's very best riders for some time.

Velasquez says that his irritation following the Derby and Preakness losses stemmed from the fans' booing and barbs and not from his attitude toward Cauthen. Velasquez stresses that he doesn't have anything against the young rider from Kentucky. "We get along good," Velasquez says. "We get along very nice."

Despite his fine overall record as a jockey, Velasquez thus far has missed out on one goal. He has never won a Triple Crown race. His combined record in the three races is 0 for 15. He is hoping to end his Triple Crown jinx this Saturday in the Belmont Stakes, once again riding Alydar against his nemesis, Affirmed.

"I'm anxious to win this race," Velasquez says. "Of course, the Affirmed people are anxious to win it, too, because they already won two, so naturally they'd like to win the third one, too. But I feel the same way. I feel like I want to win the race, too, and I'm gonna be trying my best."

June 6—Given your choice, which horse would you select—Affirmed or Darby Creek Road?

Stupid question, huh?

Well, now it is. Now that Affirmed has done as much as he has, winning the two-year-old title in 1977 and the first two legs of the Triple Crown.

But last summer everybody wouldn't have chosen Affirmed over Darby Creek Road.

Tony Matos, for one, didn't.

Matos, agent for Angel Cordero, had to decide during the 1977 Saratoga meeting whether his jockey would ride Darby Creek Road or Affirmed. Matos has been right many times, but on this occasion he made a mistake. He chose Darby Creek Road.

"I thought Darby Creek Road had a better pedigree and I thought he would mature into a better horse, but he didn't," Matos now says. "Affirmed turned out to be the best horse."

Darby Creek Road tries his best, but that's not good enough against Affirmed. Or against Alydar, either. Darby Creek Road has raced against those colts four times each. In each race, the son of Roberto has finished behind them.

Darby Creek Road is owned by James W. Phillips, son-in-law of John Galbreath, the master of Darby Dan Farm. "We ride a lot of horses for Darby Dan," Matos says. "As long as I've had Cordero, I think they have been my best customers. The whole family has been very good, and the trainer, Lou Rondinello, I have a lot of respect for him."

Matos has the highest respect for Laz Barrera.

"I think that Lazaro has really done a helluva job with Affirmed," Matos says. "He had a rough time in California with the mud, and he had all the bad weather out there, and he couldn't get a race into his horse until real late. And he still held his cool. He didn't panic with this horse.

"I think he had him up for the Triple Crown just as good as anybody could have any horse. I think that Laz Barrera is probably as good a trainer as we've ever seen. I think the whole key to this whole Triple Crown is Laz Barrera. I think he's a super horseman."

June 7— A reporter from Kentucky arrives in the Big Apple and asks a New York cab driver, "Do you go to the races?"

"No, I don't."

"Who do you like in the Belmont?"

"I only know the headlines—Affirmed and the other one. What's his name?"

"Alydar."

"Alydar. That's right. I don't think he's going to do it. He's had two chances. For the Derby, I read up on it and I thought Alydar would win it. Which one do you like—Affirmed or Alydar?"

"Affirmed."

June 8—At the Calumet barn this morning, exercise rider Charlie Rose gets some laughs by telling newsmen, "I thought we were a mortal lock in the Derby. The Preakness, I thought, we were a cinch. And I view the Belmont with guarded optimism."

Calumet trainer John Veitch isn't using such words as "mortal lock" or "cinch" to describe his feelings about Alydar's chances in the Belmont, but he's still supremely confident.

"I'm going to take the blinkers off Alydar, but I'm not going to change tactics," Veitch says. "It's a stamina thing and it's a strength race." Veitch believes Alydar is a stronger horse than Affirmed—"going a mile and a half, I do."

Besides, Veitch says that Affirmed "is not going to be able to use the speed he's got. It's not going to be as big a factor as it was in the other races, because he's just not going to be able to use it. If he uses it and tries to get away and uses too much of himself up early, he's going to have Alydar breathing down his neck the last eighth of a mile pretty heavily. He can't run the same way Bold Forbes ran, because if he runs that last quarter of a mile the way Bold Forbes did, then he's not going to beat Alydar."

Bold Forbes who was trained by Barrera, ran the 1976 Belmont's last quarter of a mile in 27 1/5 seconds, but he still managed to win over some mediocre opponents.

Veitch doesn't think there's any question about which horse will set the early pace in the Belmont—Affirmed. "I don't think there's any other horse in the race that will even come close to it."

Five horses are entered in the Belmont this morning. In the draw for post positions held at a Belmont press breakfast, Affirmed lands the No. 3 spot, Alydar No. 2.

The other three—Darby Creek Road, Noon Time Spender, and Judge Advocate—don't have a prayer.

This one-hundred-tenth Belmont is being billed as Close Encounters of the Affirmed-Alydar kind.

Affirmed is bidding to become the first Florida-bred horse to win the Triple Crown, racing's most coveted prize. Altogether, 10 horses have won the Triple.

"The Triple Crown is everything to me because it's what I've been working for," Barrera says after the breakfast. "For anybody who's in this business, when he's got a chance to win a Triple Crown, it's the greatest thing that can happen to you."

Affirmed has never raced with blinkers and, of course, he won't in the Belmont either. "I don't have to worry about changing equipment or putting blinkers on or making him relax," Barrera says. "My horse relax naturally. He never need blinkers, and he don't have to do any adjustments."

At the Preakness, Barrera was upset with Cauthen because the rider didn't drop by the barn the morning of the race to get instructions. But Barrera says there's no friction between the two of them.

"Steve Cauthen is like my son," Barrera says. "All I can say is if I have to call his attention to something I think he do wrong, I want to because it's like I'm talking to my young kid. But not because of any friction. There's no way in the world you can get friction with a rider who wins so many races for me."

June 9—Watching the races this afternoon from a Belmont clubhouse box is Ivan Parke, who trained Affirmed's sire, Exclusive Native, for Harbor View Farm.

Asked if Affirmed is similar-looking to Exclusive Native, Parke replies, "They are a little similar. I believe that Exclusive Native's head is a little larger than what Affirmed's head is."

Parke says that Affirmed likes to play the waiting game just as his sire did. "Exclusive Native used to go to the front and he would open up maybe four or five lengths. Then he would pull himself up. Affirmed, he'll take the lead and he'll wait for horses the same as his daddy would."

A Belmont prediction from Parke: "I feel like Affirmed will win it, I feel like he's the best horse."

June 10—"Kindly bring your horses to the paddock for the eighth race, please. Kindly bring your horses to the paddock for the eighth race."

At 4:59, the announcement is heard in Barn 47. Six minutes later, Affirmed is led from stall No. 3 by Juan Alaniz, his groom.

Affirmed is on his way to the paddock, on his way to his date with destiny.

Two Pinkerton guards who had been stationed close to his stall accompany the colt on the walk to the paddock. One is walking behind Affirmed, the other in front and off to the left of the colt.

The walk is a quiet, uneventful one. Near the end of the long trip, Affirmed and his handlers pass Charlie Rose, Alydar's exercise rider, who is standing off to the side of a walkway. Rose reaches out and shakes hands with Jose Ithier, Affirmed's exercise boy.

Affirmed now is walking down a tunnel that leads to the paddock. Two Pinkerton guards are standing above the tunnel, looking down at the colt.

"Alydar?" one guard says. "Who is that? Alydar?"

"The other one," says a reporter who is following Affirmed.

"Affirmed," the guard says.

"Right."

Sharp guys, those Pinkertons.

Affirmed enters the paddock at 5:21. A minute later, Alydar arrives. Fans cheer both horses.

The horses are saddled, and before long, a familiar cry lets everybody know that it's time for the jockeys to mount their horses.

"Riders up!"

With the horses heading for the track, fans yell at the riders of the Big Two.

"Good luck, Jorge!"

"Bring him home, Stevie!"

A banner is held up in the crowd near the winner's circle. Printed on the banner are these words:

STEVE

AND

AFFIRMED

#1

The banner is pink with black letters. The same colors of Lou Wolfson's Harbor View Farm.

Excitement can be felt in the air. Everybody seems to sense that something big is about to happen. The dramatic confrontation between Alydar and Affirmed is much like a heavyweight championship match. The archrivals are preparing to do battle, and the tension has gripped many.

The crowd of 65,417 is beginning to get all worked up as the horses are led into the starting gate. Assistant starters are needed to force Alydar into the No. 2 stall.

Affirmed, ever relaxed, walks into the gate like an old cow.

As Alydar and Affirmed are loaded into the gate, the crowd noise is getting louder and louder. People are actually beginning to cheer this race, and it hasn't even started yet. Unbelievable.

They're all in the gate now, and soon they'll be off and running. Oops. Judge Advocate, a horse who doesn't even belong in the race, slams through the gate. He has to be brought back around and reloaded.

Now they're all in, once again. It's 5:43, and starter George Cassidy sends them on their way.

Affirmed takes the early lead with Judge Advocate running second and Alydar third. Cauthen moves Affirmed through the first quarter in 25 seconds, exceedingly slow time. Affirmed takes another 25 seconds to cover the next quarter. The pace is slow, and the longer Cauthen is able to keep Affirmed taking it easy on the lead, the better it is for him. But Velasquez has had enough of these slowdown tactics and he does what he has to do—he goes after Affirmed with Alydar. Racing down the backstretch, Alydar draws up alongside Affirmed. No introductions are needed. These two colts have met before, and now the race is on.

Things start speeding up. They cover the third quarter in 24 seconds, the fourth in 23 2/5.

Affirmed and Alydar round the sweeping far turn, drawing away from their hopelessly beaten opponents, and reach the top of the stretch locked together in a two-horse duel that is so reminiscent of their past races.

But will they stay locked together? Going into the race, some observers figured that it wouldn't be possible for Affirmed and Alydar to run the length of the long Belmont stretch battling head and head. Surely, one of them would crack under the demands of this race.

Cauthen is going to the whip. He hits Affirmed some nine times right-handed from the top of the stretch to about the three-sixteenths pole. Velasquez whips Alydar only twice during this time.

In a smart riding tactic, Velasquez moves Alydar so close to Affirmed that Cauthen can no longer use the whip on the right side. Cauthen has never whipped Affirmed on the left side, but now he has no choice. Alydar has taken a slight lead on Affirmed near the three-sixteenths pole, and Cauthen must do something to get his colt moving. So he switches his whip to his left hand and he goes to work.

The fans are on their feet, yelling and screaming as the two horses thunder toward the finish line, running side by side, each reaching out and straining, each determined to beat the other. It's a rousing finish, a stirring windup to a brilliant Triple Crown series. Clearly, a man with a heart condition has no business watching a race as breathtaking as this one.

Cauthen keeps whipping Affirmed on the left side, and the colt is responding. He is coming back. In two or three strides he is back even with Alydar, and in a few more strides, Affirmed regains the lead. But Cauthen can't feel certain of victory. Velasquez is working on Alydar, whipping him almost every stride. Alydar isn't finished.

Two of America's finest jockeys are riding America's two finest three-year-olds for all that they're worth, and the crowd is going absolutely crazy. Many are pulling for Cauthen and Affirmed to win—"Come on Stevie!"—while others are hoping that Alydar can pull this one out—"Get him Alydar! GET HIM!"

These two colts have battled before, but never as fiercely as this over such a long distance. They're saving the best for last. Contrary to the belief of some, neither colt is going to crack. They have too much courage, too much heart for that and now, with just a sixteenth of a mile to go, Affirmed and Alydar are going to battle each other every last inch of the way.

Affirmed is tired, but he's come too far now to call it quits. Tired as he is, he digs in even more and fights. Alydar is in a fighting mood, too, and here they come, Affirmed on the inside and Alydar on the outside, just yards away from the finish, drawing closer and closer to the wire.

Finally, the race is over . . . and the finish is close. Close enough for the "photo finish" sign to be lit up. But not so close that those with the right vantage point don't know who has won.

Charlie Rose, the Calumet exercise rider, knows. He's been in the sport for 31 years and, for the first time, tears come to his eyes after a race.

Jorge Velasquez knows, too.

So does Steve Cauthen, who thrusts his left hand up high in a victory salute immediately after the finish. It's only appropriate that he raises his left hand because it was Affirmed's response to left-handed whipping that has gained the nod.

Laz Barrera's son, Larry, hurries to the track and excitedly shakes hands and accepts congratulations.

Rose steps onto the track, too.

"I'm sorry, Charlie," a reporter tells Rose. "This was a great race."

"I can't even talk," Rose says softly.

The numbers go up on the board: 3-2-1-4.

It's 5:48, and now everybody knows. Affirmed has won the Triple Crown. His time is an excellent 2:26 4/5, third fastest in Belmont history.

The scene is wild and frantic in the winner's circle.

It's much more quiet in the jockeys' room, where Velasquez is greeted with such comments from riders and valets as:

"Hey, Jorge, great race."

"You rode a horse race, Jorge."

"Jorge, that was one of the best I've ever seen."

Velasquez forces a smile as he goes about the business of changing silks for the last race on the card.

"These horses, I don't know, they got to be the greatest around," Velasquez says. "When I got close to him, they started rolling. They started ROLLING when I got close to him, and they FINISHED running. They're for real."

Though the Daily Racing Form chart-caller is in the process of writing that Alydar "reached almost even terms" with Affirmed near the three-sixteenths pole, Velasquez says that he thought his horse pushed ahead by a "big nose" for "maybe a couple of jumps" at that point.

Standing nearby is Angel Cordero, who finished a distant third on Darby Creek Road. The jockey who gave up the mount on Affirmed last summer praises the new Triple Crown champion—and Alydar, too.

"I think at this stage he [Affirmed] compares with Seattle Slew and Secretariat," Cordero says. "Why not? And Alydar, too. I think they BOTH could run with them two horses."

Back at his barn, John Veitch somehow manages a smile.

"What are you going to do? You do the very best you can," he says. "My horse ran his guts out."

His opinion of Affirmed? "He's just a damned fine racehorse."

Affirmed now has beaten Alydar in seven of nine meetings. Does Veitch believe Affirmed is better than Alydar?

"He has been these three races," Veitch says, referring to the Derby, Preakness, and Belmont. "We'll wait until the fall and see if he can keep it up."

Veitch says that he talked by telephone to Mrs. Gene Markey, the

Calumet owner, and her husband after the race. They watched the Belmont on television in Lexington, Ky.

"They were disappointed, of course," Veitch says, "but they thought their horse had acquitted himself very noble, very bravely. He did the very best he could and he never gave an inch all the way.

"It was a damned fine horse race. I'll run against him again and we'll have the same type of race, and hopefully if we have a little bit of luck we'll come out in front. I'm certainly not going to stick my tail between my legs and go find an easier place."

Up in the press box, Barrera and Cauthen are talking to the writers.

Barrera calls the Belmont the best race he's ever seen in his life.

Cauthen describes his whip action in the stretch. "At the head of the lane I was hitting him on the shoulder. At the three-sixteenths pole, Alydar got in front of me and he was real close to me and I switched my stick and hit Affirmed left-handed. And he really seemed to respond good from it. He was digging in like he always does, but he seemed to dig in a little more with the left hand. I've never hit the horse left-handed in my life."

Barrera then takes the microphone from Cauthen and says: "Steve, let me ask a question to you. How do you feel to win the Triple Crown?"

Reporters break up with laughter.

"Very good," Cauthen says with a smile.

How sweet it is!

FOOTBALL

MOON, STARS, AND ROSES

By Phil Taylor

From the Seattle Post-Intelligencer
Copyright, © , 1978, Seattle Post-Intelligencer

Washington, building up some early reserve by drawing to a couple of inside straights, saved the last big Rose Bowl pot yesterday when Michigan, an unaccustomed gambler, failed to fill one like it.

One unbelievable defensive play by Mike Jackson, always the most reliable man in such a situation, finally put it away for the Huskies, 27–20, and stuck yet another dagger into Bo Schembechler's Wolverines, who now have knuckled down to the Pacific Eight Conference four times in as many tries.

It all concluded in a termination almost as eerie as the gathering twilight of the Arroyo Seco, and it kept all 105,312 souls in attendance restless in the pews.

It was sweaty-palm time—for both sides.

Washington, choice of almost no one, had ruptured the supposedly invincible enemy fortress early, put together a 17–0 half-time lead, built it to 24–0, then 27–7 behind some cunning and guile, before Bo finally turned loose his troops in a desperation game of catch-up.

This is not Michigan's strong suit, but the Wolverines very nearly pulled it off.

Quarterback Rick Leach, advertised as a guy with a pretty solid wing, began to demonstrate it, and the foe stormed back in the final period.

The Wolverines closed it to 27–14, then 27–20, and were on the move again as the lights cast a weird glow in the field and the seconds ticked off the clock.

Some 2:46 remained as Michigan took over on its own 42 and advanced to the UW eight with a first and goal. Folks began to envision a Michigan go-for-two to win it all.

Jackson never let it happen.

Leach drifted around in the secondary, then dinked a little pass in the direction of tailback Stanley Edwards. It hit the Wolverine back on the shoulder pad and bounced in the air a couple of times.

At about that time Jackson arrived on the scene and wrapped his arms around Edwards as the two headed for the turf. The ball rolled over Edwards's back and Jackson, in one instinctive move, cradled it in his arms for the interception.

There was 1:21 left.

Washington failed to make a first down and had to punt it back to the enemy, but Nesby Glasgow, flying deep alongside Edwards on a long Leach toss, snatched the ball to put an official end to the proceedings.

So those maligned kids from the Northwest, the mismatched cannon fodder for the mighty men of Michigan, closed out their incredible season, one somehow destined for success from the advent of the year's fifth game.

And, as always, it was Warren Moon, voted outstanding player of the game, who had another big hand in the richly deserved windup. He scored two touchdowns and passed for a third in delivering some staggering blows to Michigan. Officially he was 13 for 24, good for 234 yards, and his generalship hardly could be faulted.

But this game belonged, really, to all 90 members of the team, though some were along only to hone the regulars razor-sharp for the combat.

The offensive line, especially in the first half, took it right to Michigan and had the upper hand. The function of this unit was to give the ground troops some opportunity to run and thereby open up the passing lanes.

Washington's trenchmen accomplished just that.

Joe Steele, playing with a hip pointer, pulled groin, and God knows what else, stiff-legged and stiff upper-lipped his way to 77 yards in 13 carries. His replacement, Ron Rowland, added 32 and Ron Gipson contributed another 48.

The defense, while giving ground reluctantly in the late going, was only marvelous in the first half. Then, backed to the wall on its own 11 after a Michigan interception early in the third period, it held fast one yard short of a first down.

With that kind of established field position, the revved-up offense promptly drove 97 yards for a touchdown that, in all likelihood, proved Washington really was going to win.

To single out names would require too much space and would inadvertently leave out deserving citizens, in all probability.

It was, in the best tradition of the cliché, a team effort.

Statistically, there wasn't much to choose between the two ball clubs. The figures: first downs—Michigan 22, Washington 17; net yards passing—Michigan 239, Washington 234; and total net yards—Washington 398, Michigan 388.

Washington, so superbly prepared—parking lot practice and all—by Don James, showed early it was on hand to prove something.

It didn't take long.

Michigan, halted in its first series at the UW 38, went into punt formation, but John Anderson's knee hit the ground as he reached for the low snap, turning the ball over to the Huskies at the Michigan 49.

Mixing it up, passes and runs, Moon sent his forces toward the goal, the key being a 19-yarder to Spider Gaines at the Michigan three. The boys from the Midwest were to see this combination again.

On second and goal from the two Moon swung left on a pass-run option, suckered the opposition with a couple of little pump fakes, then wedged himself into the end zone between two tacklers. Steve Robbins, letter perfect in a day that included field goals of 30 and 28 yards, added the seventh point.

They struck quickly early in the second period, the eventual field goal set up by a 62-yard Moon-to-Gaines completion as the Spider Man took the ball on the run behind Dwight Hicks and Jim Pickens. Pickens ran him down on the Michigan 17 and the Huskies settled for Robbins's first three-pointer.

Before the half had ended Moon snuck over the middle for the final yard of a 60-yard drive. Gipson and Rowland were the most active ballcarriers on this foray, which also included the inevitable Gaines reception for a key 13 yards.

The key 97-yard drive was a long, gutty effort of 12 plays and it rubbed considerable salt into the wound. You are not supposed to do this to Michigan.

Steele, back in the contest after special padding had been supplied to protect his ailing hip at half time, carved out 46 of those yards and Gipson and a couple of Moon passes provided the rest as the team advanced to the Michigan 28.

Then, on first and 10, Moon found Gaines in the corner of the end zone behind wolfman Derek Howard for another six-pointer. He caught the ball on the move and crashed into the restraining wall. Gaines was momentarily stunned, but soon regained his feet.

That made it 24–0 before the Wolverines, so dormant most of the day, awoke from their slumber.

Leach, catching the UW secondary in a rare lapse, spotted flanker Curt Stephenson behind the last defense. The Michigan receiver caught the ball on the run on his own 45 and had no one to beat to the goal line. The play covered 76 yards, a Rose Bowl record. The extra point by Greg Willner was good.

But after the second Robbins field goal moments later from 28 yards out made it 27–7, Michigan went 78 yards in 11 plays, with fullback Russell Davis leaping over center for the final two yards at the outset of the final period.

Another drive—70 yards in eight plays—narrowed the gap to 27–20 as a bad snap from center prevented the extra-point conversion.

The payoff covered 32 yards as Leach, after scrambling around in the backfield, lofted a pass to Edwards, behind the spread-out UW defenders on the 20, and the fleet Michigan halfback took it in for the score.

That left time for a lot of dry throats and the final Michigan thrust that just missed.

So Washington has finally and completely blotted out all the stigma and stain that covered the Huskies at their darkest hour. They never lost faith. They never gave up.

That sometimes can take you a long way.

Almost never has a team come farther.

FOOTBALL

GRANT TEAFF AND HIS AMAZING WORM ACT

By Blackie Sherrod

From the Dallas Times Herald
Copyright, © 1978, Dallas Times Herald

It was with considerable curiosity and not a little squeamishness that us traditional codgers read about Grant Teaff and His Amazing Worm Act. You know, about how the Baylor football coach inspired his charges into upsetting the Texas Longhorns by dropping a real live earthworm in his mouth during his pregame sermon. Correction: real dead earthworm. Big ole rascal, Teaff said with a certain pride.

The coach's act was a demonstration, don't you see, of some Aggie joke about how a successful fisherman kept his bait warm in the winter. If you haven't heard it, stop me for goodness sakes. None of us wishes to go through that again.

Teaff, if you didn't know, has gained a reputation around the country for his inspirational messages, both to religious bodies as a stimulant to their faith fervor, and to business groups as a motivating force toward success. Some of his motivation talks are recorded as albums and sold. So you're not dealing just with a carnival geek, eating live pullets for a pint of wine, but a professional motivator.

Besides, it was just an act.

"I didn't swallow it," said Teaff. "Honest, I didn't."

There are those naturalists who will probably hold that a nice clean earthworm is a lot better for the system than a wad of chewing tobacco in your trough or a pinch between cheek and gum or, for that matter, a ladle of four-alarm chili. I can remember the immortal words of the late Benny Bickers, a midnite philosopher hereabouts, who once said, "Dammit, it's my mouth. I can haul coal in it if I want to!"

There are those who claim Teaff's Amazing Worm Act was designed not only to whip his Bears into a glorious froth, but to attract heavy newspaper ink that would aid his recruiting program, just now swinging into earnest action. After all, the coach of a 2–8 team normally doesn't make the headlines all that much unless he wrestles an alligator at half time or rents a hotel room and smokes in bed.

("If that's what it takes to coach," said A&M's Tom Wilson, "then I'm in the wrong business.")

Frankly, some of us fail to recognize how the Amazing Worm Act can help Baylor recruiting. Oh, Grant might attract an early bird or two, but he could also find the modern jock will opt for Barry Switzer doing the Hustle on the parlor carpet or Lou Holtz springing a nice clean card trick at the dining room table. The Amazing Worm Act demands a specialized audience, preferably one that hasn't just eaten. You must hand it to Teaff for taking a calculated risk. He could have hiccuped.

Still, the Amazing Worm Act is a noteworthy milestone, I suppose, because it marks a definite stage of progress in motivation talks. There was a time when a little frog-voiced coach could pull out his handkerchief and ask the boys to win one for the Gipper, and let it go at that.

Gosh, once Abe Lemons's Oklahoma City basketball team got 20 points behind at half time and Abe, of all people, was stricken mute for a motivating talk in the locker room.

"I had a speech for 10 points behind, or 11 or 15," said Abe, "but I never figured on 20." So Abe silently motioned his cowering lads back to the court and held a scrimmage until the other team showed up to start the second half.

Tom Landry, once trying to goad his laggard Cowboys into furious shame, made a show of removing his championship ring at half time. It made the squad mad alrighty, but not at the other side. At him.

Darrell Royal was never one for half-time oratory, but at one Cotton Bowl intermission, he suggested to the Texas squad: "There's a helluva fight going on out there on the field. Why don't you fellows join it?"

Once the Fighting Irish were stirred to fanatical delivery when after a long wait, Knute Rockne stuck his bald head in the door and removed his hat. "Pardon me, ladies, I thought this was the Notre Dame dressing room," he said and left.

But now motivation is big league. It was only a few years ago that Al Conover, trying to spur his Rice Owls to wilder efforts against Arkansas, grabbed a chair and threw it through a locker room window. Then you may have read last year about the high school coach somewhere who brought a live chicken to the practice field and ordered his players to kick it to death to demonstrate their determination.

And just last season, a Florida high school coach bit the head off a live frog to illustrate what could be done if a person set his mind to it.

Doubtless all these audiences were stimulated to superior performance. Certainly it seemed to work at Baylor. According to witnesses, when Teaff finished his act, the Bears almost tore the walls down in their rush to get on the field and whomp the Longhorns. Personally I don't much blame them. If a man is standing there biting on a live frog or dropping worms in his mouth, I wouldn't be too eager to stay in the same room with him, either.

GOLF

THE ENIGMA OF JOHNNY MILLER

By Nick Seitz

From Golf Digest
Copyright, ©, 1978, Golf Digest, Inc.

Johnny Miller is golf's rejoinder to that little girl in the nursery rhyme who had a little curl. When she was good, she was very, very good, but when she was bad, she was horrid—and presumably could not break 80. At his best, Johnny Miller may be the finest player ever. He can be, in the carefully chosen words of sporting historian Herbert Warren Wind, "almost confoundingly brilliant." But at his worst Miller can disappear from contention and public view.

Miller has shot more near-perfect rounds than anyone else active today. When he's hot, he can "run the table" in the vernacular of pool players, pool being one of Miller's several avidly pursued diversions from golf. He came from well back in the pack to romp away with the 1973 U.S. Open at Oakmont, shooting a shocking final-round 63 that is the lowest score of all time in our national championship.

Monumental though that round is, it practically pales in comparison with what Miller did to start the 1974 tour season. He won the opening three tournaments—the Bing Crosby National Pro-Am, the Phoenix Open, and the Tucson Open—and shot par or better in his first 23 rounds! He ultimately finished the year with eight victories and a tour money record, still standing, of more than $353,000!

As comfortable in the desert as a cactus, Miller started the following season nearly as fast, winning at Phoenix by 14 strokes with a 24-under-par total of 260 and at Tucson by nine with a 25-under 263. All eight rounds were in the 60s, and he shot a 61 each week.

But, at the other extreme, Miller can miss putts by gaping margins, play far below his peak in one major championship after another, and just generally disappoint himself and his followers for months on end. In 1977, unbelievably, he was a distant forty-eighth on the money list, with earnings of only about $61,000, and he failed to win a tournament.

Can this be the same Johnny Miller who so often makes a mockery of par? Who, when he's on, perhaps has no peer? How will he start 1978, with a bang or a whimper?

If Miller's sporadic brilliance is confounding, his not-infrequent slumps are even more so. His inconsistency baffles astrologers, graphologists, bio-rhythmists. He is an enigma wrapped in an enigma.

Why is Miller so streaky?

"I think it's in the level of his desire to play," says Rod Funseth, a fellow tour player who lives near Miller in Napa, Calif., alongside the Silverado Country Club course. "I can pretty much tell how he's going to play by how enthused he is. If he feels like playing, he's liable to have one of those lights-out days. I played with him in Arizona when he was on one of his tears, and I don't think anybody's ever played that well. It was early in the year and he was rested and fired up, and he just about knocked down every flagstick. The amazing thing when he's playing like that is how accurate he is with his distance on iron shots. He's never 20 feet long or short. Even though you know the exact yardages, you still have to visualize the shot and feel the swing before you make it, and he does that better than anybody. I've also played with him when I got the impression he would just as soon have been somewhere else, not playing golf. You have to understand that Johnny genuinely enjoys himself at home. He likes his family and he likes hunting and fishing and he likes driving fast cars and motorcycles and working around the ranch near his home.

"Some people thrive on being in the limelight, but Johnny Miller doesn't. I think Johnny's on the shy side. When his game isn't good, he gets a little embarrassed and down.

"I've never seen him work very hard at his game. The year he won eight tournaments, he'd take a lot of time off and get completely away from golf, then go back out on tour and pick up where he left off. Now he's 30 years old and finding he can't do that anymore.

"There could be another factor. Johnny is bigger and stronger than people think—he's no skinny kid. To build up his endurance he's worked on his ranch and lifted weights, and I think some of his muscles got too tight for golf.

"But there's still plenty of greatness left in Johnny. One good round can set him off. His confidence soars and he's unbeatable. He knows what he has to do. At first he didn't care. Now he cares, but he can't get his swing going."

Miller's fluctuating motivation long has been suspect among other tour players. One tournament winner says, "He lacks the tenacity and dedication of a Ben Hogan. If he had Hogan's determination, he might never lose." Allowing for a touch of overstatement there, it certainly is true that Miller's attitude has been the reverse of Ben Hogan's work ethic. If Hogan finished fourth in a tournament but felt he was not striking the ball purely enough, he would cancel out of the next two tournaments, go home, and do little but beat practice balls for two weeks.

Hogan had an understanding and enduring wife and no children. Miller, by contrast, is torn between his allegiance to home—because, in his view, there's no place like it for being with your wife and kids—and to the tour—which makes him wealthy and gives him a chance to fulfill his foremost talent, in the sport he loves. So far he has been unable to strike the proper balance, in his own mind, between the two pulls, and that has to confuse and perturb him although he is careful not to let any inner turmoil show.

"My attitude toward life isn't affected too much by what happens on tour," Miller says matter-of-factly, as he carries his own bag across another in a long gray line of locker rooms. "If I'm playing well, it's nice. If I'm not, the world isn't going to stop turning."

After a decade of intrigued Miller-watching, I reflect on remarks like those with mixed sentiments. I often wonder if "he doth protest too much" when he downplays the significance of the tour—or of the major championships, which he hasn't won as often as some other people who speak of them as the be-all and end-all. But I am convinced that Miller is a sincere family man who can live, at peace with himself, without the trappings of fame. His religion—he is a Mormon—is no small influence on his philosophy. "I am a man in the world but not of the world," he says.

I cannot conceive, though, of Miller forsaking the tour at the age of 30 to go off and lead a life of anonymous domesticity on the ranch. The game means more to him than he lets on, and he is committed to starting the 1978 schedule with a blast of rockets.

"I worked on my game more in 1977 than I had since I turned pro," he says. "I got heavy—over 190 pounds—and I ran and lost weight. I got stronger as well as bigger, and that quickened the tempo of my swing. I was lunging on the downswing. I studied pictures of my swing, before and after. I hit a lot of balls. I'm paying the price."

Miller's controlled monotone seldom varies, and his detached expression rarely changes, but when he's excited the words tumble out in an inadvertent rush that gives away fast-running undercurrents of emotion.

"It was a crazy year," he says of 1977, "but there comes a time when you have to realize that no job is easy. I'm not going to rebuild my game completely—I'm patient and my play goes in cycles—but you have to work at it. I wasn't willing to do that a while back, but my attitude has changed. It all goes back to motivation. Nicklaus said he went through the same adjustment when he was about my age. The last two years I lost motivation. I had a bad shoulder and wrist for a while, but they didn't hamper me as much as my attitude did.

"This slump didn't start in 1977—it started in 1976. I won the British Open and made pretty good money in the U.S. in 1976, but I thought I had a poor year. I think after those good years in 1974 and 1975 I just got burned out. You have to realize I've been playing golf intensively for over 20 years—that's a lot of shots. I even thought about quitting. But a couple of weeks off the tour and I'm chomping to get back. Sometimes we have to be shaken to realize how good we have it."

A few experts who have watched Miller's game develop allege that he sometimes is too self-reliant when it comes to repairing his swing. He's knowledgeable about the golf swing, they concede, but his is a big, bravura action that leaves a good deal of room for error, and lately it seems to have lost a measure of the exquisite balance on which it is heavily dependent.

When Miller wants help with his game, he still goes to John Geertsen, the longtime teaching professional at the San Francisco Golf Club who has been tutoring him for 23 years, since Miller was seven. Miller considers him a second father. Geertsen recalls, "I met him not long after tragedy struck his family and more or less brought us together. Johnny's older brother fell off the rocks fishing in the ocean, and drowned. I knew the parents, and not long afterward I saw them at church and inquired about Johnny. It turned out his father had been teaching him golf on a mat in the garage since Johnny was five. I invited Johnny over to the club and began working with him three or four times a week. He was one of the littlest fellas for his age I've ever seen, but he took a long swing to get distance, and by the time he was 10 he had an excellent action that basically has stayed with him.

"I think," continues Geertsen, "John decided he wanted to be the greatest golfer in the world shortly after the first time we worked together. His dad, who is a security officer for RCA in San Francisco, talked to him from the onset about being the best, and made sure he worked at what I told him to do. His father sometimes forced him to practice more than he wanted to—he had Johnny at it all the time—but that brought Johnny along, and Johnny never resented it.

"It helped John growing up that he was able to play a lot at good courses like San Francisco Golf Club and Olympic, which gave him a junior membership. Those are U.S. Open-type courses where you have to drive straight, hit your irons high, and putt fast greens well. I'll never forget following Johnny when he played in the 1966 Open at Olympic. He was only 19 and a sophomore at Brigham Young University, and he'd planned to caddie in the tournament until he qualified for it. I remember him saying he wanted to make some date money so he didn't have to bum it off his dad. The last day, an incident occurred that shows what a great attitude he has for this game. On the fifteenth hole, a medium length par three, he overshot the green and was in that thick, long rough the USGA grows for the Open. His ball was two feet in front of a gallery rope, and the marshals laid down the rope so he could play the shot. But on his backswing, somebody accidentally pulled the rope, and it came up and caught Johnny's club. He hit the ball only six inches. He just walked away from the ball calmly, looked at the shot again— and plopped the ball out of the rough and into the hole for a par! That clinched low amateur for him, and he decided to try to birdie every hole the rest of the way, which was a mistake. He took a couple of bogeys and finished eighth. But that's one reason Johnny makes low scores—he's not afraid to shoot a really low number like a lot of players are. If he makes three birdies, he doesn't get conservative. He tries to make three more.

"Knowing him as I do," concludes Geertsen, "I think he's worked harder to get where he is than anybody else ever has. You can get to a point, you know, where you have a fine golf swing and can practice too much. Johnny's a great believer in mental practice. He'll sit at home analyzing his game in his head for an hour and do more good than he could by hitting a thousand range balls."

Miller has said much the same thing, which has done absolutely nothing to endear him to the other pros. When he was on top, he gave the impression the game was as easy for him as letting his blond hair grow, and players who were struggling cultivated a keen dislike for him. His candor and outward aloofness makes him probably the least popular superstar among the players.

"I guess some of the things I've said sounded cocky to some people," he says. "You know, the brash kid who hadn't paid his dues. I was 26 when I won the Open. If I'm playing super I'll say I can win. But I've never said anything intended to be disrespectful. I respect these guys. I just say what I believe is right.

"I'm not as popular as most guys, but I might be a better father. A lot of the guys who came on tour with me are getting divorces. I'm still happily married, and that's more important to me than sitting around the clubhouse shooting the breeze with other golfers after a round. A lot of people think I'm aloof, but I don't mean to be. I don't socialize much because I would rather be with my wife and kids. My oldest boy has started school and my family can't travel with me as much, and that bothers me.

"It upsets some people that I don't play in many tournaments and don't practice as much as other players. They can't accept that I could be successful, and they've had to hope I was a fluke."

Miller smiled, and a sense of humor surfaced. He giggled boyishly and said, "After the year I had in 1977, they ought to like me better."

Miller's principled world view leaves him open to snide remarks about "Johnny Miller, All-American boy." And there is nothing in his makeup to belie the image. He is the tour's Mr. Clean—he doesn't smoke, drink, curse, or wink at strange girls. He plays pool—but only in his recreation room. He is an active Mormon who attends church twice on Sunday when he's home, for 90 minutes in the morning and 90 minutes in the evening, and frequently turns up at a week-night service in a tour city to give a short inspirational talk and field questions. "The best thing he does for the church," says a Mormon spokesman, "is set an example by his very life-style. He exemplifies the clean living that the church recommends." Tithing from his formidable earnings surely doesn't hurt, of course.

All of this came as a severe blow to the young single women of America who watched a 23-year-old Miller stalk dashingly across their television screens and into the national consciousness in the 1971 Masters which he nearly won, wearing brightly hued clothes, his surfer's hair voguishly styled in a Prince Valiant cut. They quickly learned Miller was a swinger on the golf course but not off it.

Of his colorful outfits, Miller says, "I like them because they cheer me up and they're good for color television. I enjoy experimenting with clothes." Especially, he might have added, clothes made by Sears, Roebuck & Company, which pays him something like $170,000 a year to wear its latest shirts and slacks and pose for advertisements, Miller's slender, 6-2 frame being almost mannequin-perfect for modeling. No company has used a golfer as extensively as Sears uses Miller, and one can envision even now the collector's item Sears catalogs of the next century featuring the young Johnny Miller (will he ever age?) posing in leisure wear designed for breaking 65.

Making so much money off the course can be a two-edged sword, however. "It takes away from your golf time," Miller admits, "and it distracts you. It's my biggest problem. If I weren't making as much money as I am, a bad slump might be driving me crazy, but as it is it's hard to get that worried about it. I have plenty of money no matter what happens on the golf course. I'm set for life."

Actually, says Miller's business manager Ed Barner, Miller does not have enough money to be set for life—not, at least, if he continues living in the luxurious style to which he has become accustomed and not at modern inflation rates—but he is in wonderfully sound financial condition. "His big contracts, with Sears, Ford, Gillette, and Princess Hotels, are solid and long-term," says Barner. "A slump can cut into his exhibitions and personal appearances after a while."

In the final analysis, Miller's business involvements could rekindle his motivation to keep winning in golf, because the former ultimately depend on the latter, and Miller—for all his homespun virtues—is uncommonly fond of expensive cars, boats, and houses.

It is his manager Barner, a Mormon like Miller and as close to him as anyone, who gives the clearest insight into the seeming enigma that is his client. "The thing is, he is a simple person, in the best sense of the word, and people try to make him out to be overly complicated. He doesn't care if there's a courtesy car to meet him at the airport when he arrives for a tournament. His game goes up and down, and he doesn't know why and doesn't run to the practice tee. In a sport where everybody wants to be your friend, he's secure in his own company—he's most happy when he's alone. That's the real Johnny, and he isn't about to start pretending to be somebody he isn't. When he's through with the tour, I think he'll work actively in youth programs. He's really comfortable coaching youngsters who have some talent and want to become good golfers. He has the desire to teach, unlike most top players, and he has the patience."

If Johnny Miller can strike a meaningful balance between his professional life and his personal life, it is that temperament that could enable him to play with confounding brilliance for years and years to come. Some of the time anyway.

MARATHON RACING

THE REAL BOSTON MARATHON

By Joe Soucheray

From the Minneapolis Tribune
Copyright, ©, 1978, Minneapolis Tribune

The part of the Boston Marathon you may have seen on television Monday night was beautiful. Bill Rodgers came flying across the line to defeat Jeff Wells of Dallas by two seconds, the closest finish ever in the 82-year history of the world's most popular footrace.

Up the line on Lake St. and at Coolidge Corner and farther back toward the start at the village green in Hopkinton, bands played and old men perched atop stepladders with water hoses aimed at the runners. Even the helmeted riot police tried to smile. You saw the spectacle of 4,764 runners running for the fun of it. It made a nice picture, great film footage.

But you didn't see the real Boston Marathon. The Boston Marathon of record is contained in the precise times clocked by stopwatches. The real Boston Marathon, the one the television cameras never saw, began early in the morning when nearly 1,000 runners packed into the high school gymnasium in Hopkinton. Many were naked. They rubbed protective creams on their bodies. They taped the nipples of their breasts to prevent bleeding. Other runners were outside on the grounds and in the parking lot, and as the noon starting time drew near, they threw their baggage into the trucks that would transport it back to Boston.

The real Boston Marathon was not the early race between Rodgers, Frank Shorter, and Esa Tikkanen of Finland. That group broke clean and free of the pack and ran with the wind at its backs. Those runners would be fresh at the end, two hours later. For the real Boston Marathon runner, the guy from the suburbs someplace, the afternoon was torturous and sometimes frightening. A crowd of as many as a million people narrowed the course. Bicyclists, on the course illegally, often bumped runners into the crowd. Wheelchair contestants sped down hills and nearly were run over by police cars and the two buses that were allowed on the course to carry officials.

The best picture of the real Boston Marathon should have been taken in the underground parking garage near the finish line on Commonwealth Av. That garage resembled the burning-of-Atlanta scene in *Gone With the Wind*.

Runners collapsed on makeshift cots. Some had the skin worn off their feet. Others were frozen into grotesque poses—one runner posed for nearly 30 minutes in the manner of a man about to break out of the blocks for a 100-yard dash. They tried to help each other up. They tried to help each other spoon the traditional Boston Marathon beef stew into each other's mouths.

"Was it worth it?" a man asked one of the contestants huddled on the floor in a fetal position. The runner began to weep.

Some men and women were not designed to run 26 miles and 385 yards and this year's Boston Marathon proved it. You would think after its long reign as the world's most treasured amateur race that the Boston Marathon would have exhausted its capacity to surprise and to provide drama. But this year's race was street theater, for good runners and bad.

Rodgers had stopped short of predicting his victory, which he achieved in 2:10:13, 18 seconds off his 1975 record. This year Rodgers had competition from Shorter, who was attempting to become the first Olympic gold medalist to win at Boston. Rodgers, Shorter, and last year's defending champion, Jerome Drayton of Toronto, those runners were from a different world.

At the first checkpoint in Framingham, Rodgers was running abreast of Shorter and Drayton. Rodgers wore white gardening gloves against the 46-degree cold and overcast skies. At the second checkpoint in Natick, Rodgers and Shorter were joined in a pack that included Kevin Ryan of New Zealand, Tikkanen, but no Drayton. Drayton had dropped out of the race, still suffering from a hamstring muscle he had pulled in Toronto 10 days ago.

At Wellesley, where schoolgirls lined the street, Rodgers, Ryan, and Tikkanen were alone in front. Shorter had faded badly. Rodgers made his move at Braeburn Hill, the first of three increasingly steeper hills that lead to the crest of Heartbreak Hill near Boston College. It was on those hills that a cyclist bumped Tikkanen into the crowd and John Thomas of Boston, the eventual fifth-place finisher, had to leap over a wheelchair contestant who had swerved to avoid Tikkanen.

Rodgers was alone and in familiar territory. The 30-year-old lives in Melrose, Mass., and yesterday's course took him by his own running-equipment store on Chestnut Hill Av. in Brookline. On Heartbreak Hill, Wells, a 23-year-old student at Dallas Theological Seminary, passed Ryan, Tikkanen, and Jack Fultz of Franklin, Pa., the 1976 winner.

Over the final three or four miles, Rodgers was not even aware that Wells was his closest pursuer and closing. Rodgers had opened up a 500-yard lead on the hills, but because of some maneuvering by the official buses, Rodgers was never able to see who was running behind him. Wells, meanwhile, was cursing himself for feeling so strong. He had plenty left but couldn't tell where Rodgers was.

It wasn't until Rodgers turned onto Commonwealth Av. for the stretch to the finish that he saw Wells. Neither of them had seen a real Boston Marathon runner since way back in Hopkinton. Tikkanen was third in

2:11:15 and Fultz finished two seconds behind him. Shorter was the twenty-third runner across in 2:18:15.

"What happened?" Rodgers asked. "I thought I had a big lead. The last guy I ever saw in second place was Tikkanen and then I saw Wells and I got afraid. I didn't want to lose, but this was the hardest marathon I ever ran. From 20 miles on, I was in pain and gutting it out."

"What about Shorter?" somebody yelled.

"I saw Frank breathing hard at the halfway point near Newton Lower Falls," Rodgers said. "I knew he was in trouble."

"And Tikkanen?"

"That Finn knows how to bide his time," Rodgers said. "I saw him get a drink at the 16-mile mark and he was smiling, like he was just waiting for his break. But when we came into the hills, I was fortunate to be strong. I train in those hills. But I never even knew about Wells. A cop on a motorcycle told me there was a guy behind me and closing fast. I was falling apart thinking about losing. I just gutted it out."

Wells had entered the garage and headed for the medical facilities looking for a place to rest. He was not injured, but the people around him were moaning, clutching their legs, and talking about their failed dreams.

"I had too much left at the end," said Wells, who finished twelfth here last year. "I should have been burning that energy up earlier on the course. I should have pushed harder. I'm grateful and I'm exhilarated, but I should have pushed harder."

Shorter was trying to drum up some companions for a beer. He is a good loser. "I just tightened up," Shorter said. "I haven't run a marathon since the fall of 1976, and, hey, you've got to train for these suckers. I was in over my head."

So were most of the real Boston Marathon contestants. Runners were still crossing the line a full five hours after the start. It had started raining hard by then and the wind increased and a spooky fog rolled over the Charles River, but they were out there and they would crawl in if they had to.

BOXING

ALI'S LAST HURRAH

By Bud Collins

From The Boston Globe
Copyright, ©, 1978, The Boston Globe
Courtesy of The Boston Globe

Luis Sarria, a wizened black Cuban—the Artur Rubinstein of rubdown men—is playing Brahms' Lullaby on Muhammad Ali's back, a private concert repeated innumerable times over the years in innumerable small rooms attached to innumerable fight gyms. Ali groans as Sarria hits a sour note just below the left shoulder blade.

Sarria, an ageless artist who has been rubbing the fighters Angelo Dundee trains for nearly 20 years, speaks English never and Spanish seldom. He nods, pours a little more fluid from a small bottle (Benjamin's Healing Oil, says the label) onto the 36-year-old body, and resumes with chords.

"I'm tired," says Ali. He is bored and aware that there's more of him for Sarria to tend than when their association began 15 or so years ago—a larger keyboard in front. "Gonna fast tomorrow," says Ali. "I can lose five pounds a day doin' that. But," he sighs, "soon's I eat, most of it comes back.

"But I'll be ready for Spinks." His voice is lifeless. "Don't worry 'bout that."

Approaching fast is the day of Ali's (announced) Atonement against one of the country's better known delinquents, Leon Spinks—also holder of Ali's Allah-given heavyweight championship.

"September 15—the biggest event in the history of the earth—and I'll show everybody I'll be king again," Ali mumbles.

Right now, however, a triple-ripple belly tells Ali and the few observers that he is "maybe 15 pounds too heavy. 'Bout 229. Long as I get down into the teens I'm OK. I can dance." Until the first of September, Ali will remain here at Deer Lake, in the gentle hills of Pennsylvania Dutch Country, ensconced like Abe Lincoln in a log cabin (an air-conditioned one, however). This is his camp—"where I have peace and the best fresh air to breathe. That's important.

"Am I gonna miss boxing? Whooooee, no. But boxing's gonna miss me. I'm tired of it. Other things to do. Ambassador of peace. That's what Brezhnev called me when I visited the Kremlin."

He is brightening. Sarria has finished the lullaby, and Ali sits up on the table. "Man, that Brezhnev follows my career. He knew my accomplishments." Ali is talking about his recent trip to Russia and the audience with the boss. "I told him Americans and Russians can get along." He seems to have had greater success with Lovable Leonid than Grinny Carter—of course, Ali's record is considerably more impressive than Carter's.

Now that he's up, Ali is in better position for sidelong glances at his favorite companion: a mirror. Mileage is beginning to show on him. Humidity has zitzed up his complexion and he is—relatively—flabby. Still, he remains the ultimate objet d'art on display in our sporting galleries.

"When I'm gone . . . nobody can replace me. The world's gonna miss me."

Certainly the immediate world, the retainers of his court who look to him for moral support in treasury green. After the Spinks rematch, will their log cabin Camelot—with Ali ringing the giant and hugely welcome dinner bell himself—be reactivated again? Is it all over for them? Has the gravy train rusted out for this corps of fetchers and finders, fondlers and flatterers? They move about the camp in their lumberjack-chic costumes—heavy on boots and Ali T-shirts—as though these are the last days in the Berlin bunker.

Several have been with Ali for years. "He ain't gonna be ready this time—don't quote me," says one of the less dependent, a man who has seen the aging on the wall mirror, too, and has opened a shop in Harlem. The real world looms. Bundini Brown, the Medicine Man who coined "Float Like a Butterfly, Sting Like a Bee!" has lost a few flaps in his own wings. No longer the jovial one. Less fun now. "We going just one fight at a time," says Bundini, so worn out he sounds as dull as a football coach.

The show has gotten old. At present, Ali tries to start something, ever the genius of press-agentry. "Look at this, man," his voice rises, he points to a good-looking dude who has entered the room. "Got to beat him after I whup Spinks. Look out, Ken Green. I got to get you off my conscience. Anybody beats me I got to whup them eventually. Like Spinks. Like you, Ken Green."

Green smiles. He had a win over Ali back in the middle ages, when they were amateurs. "Twenty-seventh of February 1958 in Chicago," says Green. "Stopped him. I'm 1–0 against you, Ali. I'll give you another shot."

Considerate. Green stopped fighting 11 years ago, but "Ali has promised I'm next." Why not? But first . . . Leon Spinks.

"If Spinks gets outa jail, I'll whup his tail!" Ali shrieks. The laureate has dressed and is walking outside the gym toward a group of tourists who have watched his workout. He is turned on and up again. Fatigue vanishes when he has an audience of more than one. Sarria's lullaby fades.

The lecture begins. Outrageous and shopworn (yes, he does not forget "I'm still The Greaaatest!"). Yet, to those hearing it for the first time—and in person—the harangue is spellbinding, awesome.

Sarria sits on a nearby woodpile, smoking his pipe. His Benjamin's Healing Fluid has been put away until today's recital. Sarria knows Ali is tired, but probably Lawrence Welk is tired, too, and he keeps cranking it up.

Luis Sarria smiles at the noise Ali is making, shakes his head approvingly, and puffs. He doesn't understand what Ali is saying—maybe it is better that way. Sarria may have fingered unresponsive fighting muscles, but he hears his piano thundering and knows at least the vocal muscles will never be out of tune.

SOCCER

THE WORLD'S FINEST SOCCER PLAYER FINDS PEACE IN AMERICA

By David Hirshey

From Sport Magazine
Copyright, ©, 1978, David Hirshey

Bursting from a side door of a Toronto hockey hall, the Warner Communications security force makes a flying wedge with a dozen Canadian Mounties, cutting through the crowd toward the New York Cosmos' team bus. At the wedge's center is Franz Beckenbauer, a trim, sweet-faced man who has just watched a closed-circuit telecast of a soccer game in which his former West German teammates struggled to a 0–0 tie with Poland in a lackluster opening game of the World Cup. Gazing straight ahead, Beckenbauer seems oblivious to the maelstrom around him.

"VERRATER!" A man's voice screams above the din. *Traitor.*

Within an arm's reach of the procession, an old German man with a face like a crumpled brown bag is holding a photograph of Beckenbauer. The old man tears it, flings the pieces to the ground, and spits on them.

"VERRATER!" he screams again. "DU SOLLTEST IN ARGENTINIEN SEIN!"

You should be in Argentina. That is what everyone is telling Franz Beckenbauer. They had screamed it in the theater. They're yelling it in the streets in Toronto and Munich. And if that isn't enough, a pack of German journalists has dogged Beckenbauer to Toronto where he is playing with the North American Soccer League's Cosmos to constantly remind him: *"You are the finest soccer player in the world. At 32, you are at the peak of your career. You are German. So what are you doing here playing for American dollars, sitting in a Toronto hockey hall and watching your national team go scoreless in the sport's most important tournament."*

VERRATER. The cry hangs in the air like a vulture.

Climbing over the equipment of two camera crews in the aisle, Beckenbauer eases himself into a seat on the bus. Patiently he answers the reporters' questions. Yes, it is strange to be playing on a raggedy field against—what's the name?—the Toronto Metros-Croatia. Strange, when his friends, the men he captained to the last World Cup in 1974, are competing in Argentina. Yes, there were negotiations between West Germany and the Cosmos to "borrow" him for one last time, but no, it could not be arranged. This is—what is the right word?—unfortunate. He is maybe a little sad. But he cannot worry over what might have been.

"I am not a dreamer," he says, "I am a realist."

The floodlights click off and Beckenbauer sinks back into the shadows. Though his face is calm and impassive, dark perspiration stains have spread down both sides of his light-beige shirt.

"These people," he says, referring to the angry German fans, "these people talk bad against me because suddenly the little boy maybe doesn't act the way his public expect him to act. This happens when you become too successful. You must work very hard to obtain success, but harder to keep it."

Beckenbauer's success comprises many things. His national team won a World Cup Championship. His Bayern Munich team was an international power. He was twice named European Footballer of the Year (1972 and 1976). He was called "Der Kaiser" in Germany. He is perhaps the finest soccer player in the world. And, at a salary of $2.8 million over three and a half years, he is the third highest-paid athlete in America, behind basketball's David Thompson and football's O. J. Simpson. Beckenbauer, last year's Most Valuable Player in the NASL, is the set piece of the glittering Cosmos franchise, the 1977 NASL champions who are favored to repeat this year. Success has earned Franz Beckenbauer all this and more.

On several occasions, success has also made him miserable.

Plucked from the highest levels of international competition at the prime of his career in 1977, Beckenbauer played his first American season in the shadow of Pele. Though captain of Bayern for ten years, Beckenbauer is not consulted by either his Cosmos coach or his teammates. His body (5-11, 165 pounds) has been punished by substandard American fields and the vicious fouls of substandard players. Sold to the American public as the most perfect soccer machine on God's green Astroturf, he has been booed lustily for one slightly errant pass. Still, Franz Beckenbauer says this has been "the most wonderfullest year in my life."

"Come to my hotel room," he whispers on the bus while writing his room number on a piece of paper. "I will try to explain. Talk to me before the Germans can find me. Once they do, I cannot breathe."

He is sitting in his Toronto hotel room, about to plunge his left foot into a bucket of ice. The foot is small, size 7½, very smooth and perfectly shaped, nothing like the gnarled deformities that most veterans of soccer wars limp around on.

"Everybody write about how shy I am," he says quietly. "This is wrong. I need people. I believe in them. But I'm not gullible. I'm not blind. You learn to be careful if you have been hurt. But I like people very much."

But tonight, while his teammates are scattered in outdoor cafés, Beckenbauer is alone with his thoughts. He wriggles his foot deeper into the ice and begins to unravel the roots of his discontent.

Beckenbauer first ran into what he calls "the underside of glory" in 1974 when he captained the West German team to the World Cup. Soccer fever had turned into an ugly nationalist disease. "I don't like to remember it," he says. "Our training camp was like a prison with barbed wire, dogs, police, roadblocks. There were threats on my life. We were forbidden to see our wives for four weeks. Soccer in Germany is a religion. I was beginning to think it is a little . . . not correct."

Back on his Bayern Munich team, the glory had begun to fade as well. By 1975, though he was still at the peak of his form, the proud dynasty had become just another team as the players aged and no new stars replaced them. So when the then Cosmos president, Clive Toye, began offering sackfuls of dollars to play in New York with Pele, Beckenbauer cocked an ear.

Things got ugly when word leaked out about the Cosmos negotiations. Beckenbauer was branded a Judas and pilloried in a press campaign. In April 1977, a newspaper article headlined "The Kaiser's Private Life Is Tense" portrayed Beckenbauer as a hideous man who had left no sin untried. The article accused him of adultery, tax evasion, causing the bankruptcy of Bayern and, worst of all, betrayal of the national team. Beckenbauer had his manager call Clive Toye and tell him Der Kaiser would play for the Cosmos.

"I am always a man of the middle," Beckenbauer explains. "I like to work, to practice, to play soccer. I like to be a normal man. For the last 15 years I try to follow the idea of live and let live. This is impossible in Germany. Envy is a very pronounced thing there."

His departure was planned with swift efficiency. Then bit by bit, the old life was dismantled. His villa outside Munich was sold to pay a $240,000 tax levy; his savings were shifted to Swiss bank accounts; and his wife, Brigitte, and three sons were moved to Switzerland where they remain. The Cosmos paid Bayern a transfer fee of just under $1 million and a plane flight out of West Germany was arranged under heavy security.

"Naturally," says Beckenbauer, "I had envisioned my departure differently. Every player dreams of having a testimonial game. Is like a girl who dreams of the white wedding gown."

It took Beckenbauer a very short time to learn that the glory of American sport has its underside as well. His new team was in astounding turmoil when he joined them in late May.

"In the first three weeks after I come to America I see a president [Clive Toye] fired," says Beckenbauer. "I see fights in the locker room, fights on the field. I see a coach [Gordon Bradley] fired. And from all this I see Pele cry. Never do I see anything like this."

He stumbled through his first game. The language barrier confused him, and the disorientation was complete when new coach Eddie Firmani, without consulting Beckenbauer, ordered him taken out of the sweeper position he had made into an art form and moved to midfield.

The sweeper is the last link between the defense and the goalkeeper. He roams behind his team's three fullbacks and picks up anything that gets through them. Beckenbauer had added an offensive dimension to the sweeper position—in much the same way Bobby Orr did in hockey—by often moving upfield with the ball and launching offensive sorties with passes or solo runs.

But to orchestrate the attack from his new midfield position, Beckenbauer must first take possession of the ball with lots of chasing and hard tackling over a larger area of the field. It is a position he feels taxes his lungs more than his skills.

"At sweeper I could see the whole field in front of me and I would touch the ball 85 to 90 times a match," Beckenbauer says. "At midfield, my vision is limited and I make contact with the ball only about 30 times. I don't know. Midfield may turn out to be a good school for me, but the transition is hard. I have to change my style and this is very frustrating. I run left. I run right. I run up the middle and still I don't get the ball and I say, 'Shit!' " He stops himself, worried perhaps that he has said something wrong. Distracted, he pulls his foot from the ice and examines his toenails, tinged violet with cold. "This running, running," he mutters. "It is sometimes very hard."

"Sure, he'd like it better at sweeper," Firmani said, explaining the switch. "It requires less running, less work. But his talents were wasted playing in the back. His superb passing and vision benefit us best at midfield. He's working harder now than he has for years."

"At Bayern Munich," says Beckenbauer, "the coach come to me and we talk about the team. We talk about the opponent and what's best style to play. Last year, we have four world-class players—Pele, Giorgio Chinaglia, Carlos Alberto, and myself—and Firmani never comes to any of us except Giorgio for advice. I think this is very strange."

Friction between Beckenbauer and Firmani erupted last fall during a postseason exhibition tour in Brazil. The matter was trivial but the wider issue was authority. Firmani had imposed annoying curfews for what the team felt was a meaningless game. Beckenbauer ignored the orders and went to a party at the Rio home of Carlos Alberto. This year the relationship has been civil if not cordial. Beckenbauer has a streak of quiet pride that sometimes leads him to set his own course.

"He plays his own tune on the field," says Terry Garbett, Beckenbauer's hardworking English partner in midfield. "Sometimes you'd like him to play a different tune. I know I'd like him to be more aware of picking somebody up tighter on defense. But then he makes a pass that is from another world and you're willing to run your ass off for him."

The brilliance and professionalism of Beckenbauer's play have earned him his teammates' respect. He has willingly assumed a leadership role on the field. But there is another role he is not eager to fill—the tiring, hype-ridden role of legend-in-residence. Understanding that Pele was the catalyst that ignited the soccer explosion in this country, the Cosmos and the NASL have designated Beckenbauer as Pele's logical successor, a visible hero in whose image children build their dreams. But Beckenbauer has proved a reluctant heir.

"Last year, when Pele was here, everyone looked for him," he says. "People only expected a good game of me then. But now they expect more. I am very critical of myself. Pele is Pele and I am Franz Beckenbauer. I think it is wrong to try to make a copy. I have never been a killer on the field like Pele. He would decide a game alone with maybe four, five great scoring chances. I always try to build a goal, to give good passes. I am a play-maker. And I can never be Pele."

Some of his teammates would thank him for that. Comparing Pele and

Beckenbauer, one player said, "Franz may not say much, but his emotions are honest. With Pele, it was impossible to tell where his act ended and his personality took over."

When I relay this remark to Beckenbauer, he is visibly upset. "How can anyone say this?" he asks. "Pele is the most perfect man I know. I could never hope to be his equal."

Clearly there is only one way to deal with such frustrating modesty, and this is to give the man a formal coronation in spite of himself. And so it was decreed. With the aid of the New Jersey State Senate, the Cosmos had May 19 declared "Franz Beckenbauer Day" now and forever in the Garden State.

Franz Beckenbauer Day dawns warm and cloudless, a perfect afternoon for a testimonial game. More than 71,000 fans have turned up at Giants Stadium to see the Cosmos play the Seattle Sounders. The crowd listens to a pregame concert by the world famous Fischer Choir—flown in from Germany for this occasion—and, at the appointed moment, Beckenbauer materializes on the Astroturf, arms outstretched, smiling beatifically. He stoically endures the ceremony, his arms folded across his chest, his eyes staring into a phalanx of 200 cameras. Over the PA system he tells the crowd that he is very embarrassed by this honor, but that for him it is a wonderful day. He accepts embraces from Pele and from league commissioner Phil Woosnam. He receives the keys to a new car, which he donates to the Special Olympics. Finally he trots off. Back in the dark shelter of the tunnel, Beckenbauer wipes a sheen of sweat from his forehead.

"I am glad this is over," he says. "I worry for days that I say the wrong thing. I am not a speaker. I am a soccer player."

Seattle's All League defender, Mike England, overhears this and smiles. "On the field, Beckenbauer is a man of vision," he says. "He can be looking you straight in the eye and know exactly where his teammates are *behind* him. Give him any time at all and he'll tear you apart. What he's shown Americans is that if you play intelligently and quickly, the ball does the work for you. Americans want to see him beat four or five guys one-on-one like in basketball. But what he does is much harder. Simplicity is what makes him so great."

"Everything he does looks so easy, people think he's not trying hard," says Cosmos goalkeeper Jack Brank. "But it's just that he's playing on a level so much higher than the rest of us."

Whether Beckenbauer is advancing boldly into attack or distributing the ball from in front of his own goal, he plays with the leisurely flair of a man who knows he is the best in the world at his craft. Style is what sets him apart. It is apparent when he gets the ball during the game that afternoon.

He gathers in the ball with as little movement as possible, as if to make sure no muscle moves without a sense of purpose. The Seattle defender backs away as Beckenbauer begins his move. With a sudden burst, he fakes shoving the ball to his right with the left foot but actually steps over the ball. Then, carried forward by momentum, he gently taps it in the opposite direction with his right heel. Deceived, the defender lurches back toward the ball. Too late. Beckenbauer is past him now, surging through a small space between the arms and legs of two Sounders. In a split second he is free, open, poised to shoot, when he spots Chinaglia running goalward. With a casual flick of the ankle, Beckenbauer lays the ball down the middle two steps ahead of Chinaglia, who collects the ball without breaking stride and hammers it in for his third goal of the day. During the game, Beckenbauer handles the ball 38 times—and misplays it only twice. The Cosmos go on to win 5–1. Afterward, Chinaglia acknowledges Beckenbauer's assist. "He is still the best," he says.

"It was a perfect pass," England says later. "One millimeter to either side and our defenders would have had it."

But Beckenbauer says: "I could have given Giorgio a better ball."

"Franz looks for perfection in everything he does," says Werner Roth, Beckenbauer's good friend and roommate on the road. "If he doesn't talk much, it's because he's afraid his English is less than perfect. And when he makes mistakes on the field, you can see him get angry at himself. He just doesn't want to do anything wrong."

At last, the Franz Beckenbauer Day festivities end, and the comfortable routine resumes. Beckenbauer has agreed to a final interview after a midweek practice in Giants Stadium. He has learned to trust the American press because, he explains, it has been considerate of his private life. Most of the reporters are aware of his blond girl friend, Diane Sandmann, who is Beckenbauer's nearly constant companion during the season. But here the affair isn't headlined the way it is in West Germany.

When I meet Beckenbauer after his practice, he is apologetic as he leads the way to his metallic-blue Mercedes parked outside the players' entrance. It is raining, and if he had been able to find my phone number, he would have called, told me to meet him in the city and avoid the trip. "So sorry," he says. "You should have no inconvenience."

Despite rainy-day traffic, the ride into Manhattan is smooth. Beckenbauer says that in Germany he could get away with driving 90 mph on such a road, but here he never exceeds 50. It is the law. Beneath the dashboard is a stereo cassette player, and the glove compartment is filled with classical music tapes.

"You would like to hear some music?" he asks with a mysterious smile. He pushes a button, and a nasal voice says: "Good morning. How is the weather this morning? Good? Or bad?"

"Very bad," Beckenbauer answers, and then he laughs. It is a language tape, part of the homework for the English courses he takes every available afternoon with Carlos Alberto and goalkeeper Erol Yasin. Beckenbauer has the best attendance record.

As the Mercedes slides out of the Lincoln Tunnel, Beckenbauer cranes his head out the window to view the Empire State Building. He smiles like a delighted child.

"In Germany, I hear a lot about New Yorkers as the ugly Americans," he says. "I expect a very dangerous city. Killing. Like Wild West. Boom. Boom." He makes guns with his fingers. "Really, I am very surprised at how friendly people are here. I love it. New York has given me the chance to lead my own new life. "

Beckenbauer says that New York has given him two things that were denied him in Germany: freedom and privacy. He revels in the cloak of anonymity he wears in New York, delights that a switchboard operator asks him to spell his name. "In Germany," he says, "people follow me into the bathroom. In the middle of the night, they come to my hotel. Here, I go to a restaurant. I see Woody Allen and Diane Keaton at the next table. Nobody bother them. Surely nobody bother me."

No longer bound by his role as Der Kaiser, he is free to be just Franz. His life is looser, more relaxed. He has bought blue jeans and T-shirts. His teammates have coaxed him into junking his blow drier and letting his curly brown hair dry *au naturel*. He visited a Greenwich Village club to listen to Carly Simon, and three times he has been persuaded to visit Studio 54, the chic Manhattan disco.

At Studio 54, Beckenbauer installed himself in the balcony, content to watch other athletes—such as tennis star Vitas Gerulaitis and heavyweight boxing champion Leon Spinks—boogie below.

"This is not my life," he says of his fling at the disco whirl. "My trips into these worlds of money, nobility, and society have been described often in the press. You know, the soccer player from the blue-collar neighborhood in Munich becoming the beautiful person. The truth is, I feel more at home in that workers' neighborhood than I did at the wedding of Egyptian president Anwar Sadat's daughter."

"This is a man who stood in a block-long line for extra tickets to Pele's farewell game rather than use his influence," says Werner Roth. "When we room together on the road, he returns every phone message he gets at the hotel, whether he knows the person or not. Once, he disappeared from dinner for half an hour to take a phone call. When I asked who it was, he shrugged and said it was just a local fan who wanted to talk soccer."

Beckenbauer's character has remained rooted in the sober Protestant ethic of the German working class. He tries to avoid ostentation. Though he is freer and happier than he has been in years, Beckenbauer maintains his standards; it is imprudent, maybe even dangerous, to let them down.

"He's a typical German guy," says Bobby Smith, the Cosmos' free-spirited fullback. "He's very straight, hard to know. He seems very concerned with doing the right thing. Still, I detect a little bit of satire. Sometimes I'll catch his eye and I know he's laughing inside. Like when Eddie [Firmani] gets on him to do something on the field, Franz will look at me and grin. If it wasn't for that smirk, I couldn't like the man."

There is, then, a tiny fissure in that impeccable propriety. Humor bubbles up through it; occasionally, anger does.

"Yeah, I've seen Franz angry once," says Terry Garbett, citing an incident in Toronto when Garbett made a nasty retaliatory foul. "He was pissed. He gets this look on his face like he's going to eat you. He thought that what I did was unprofessional. He said there was no need to fight when we were ahead 3–1. But what he doesn't understand is that not all of us can keep our emotions under such tight rein. There are some excitable boys on this team."

One of those excitable boys is Giorgio Chinaglia, who leads the Cosmos in scoring and controversy. I remind Beckenbauer that last year Chinaglia complained that the Cosmos should have bought young American players instead of another superstar like Beckenbauer. But those who predicted a clash between Giorgio and Franz were wrong. This season Beckenbauer has fed Chinaglia a steady stream of perfect passes. Since Beckenbauer moved to midfield, Chinaglia's point total has soared just as Chinaglia's good friend Eddie Firmani promised.

"Good friends?" questions Beckenbauer. "I don't know if they are still such good friends. After Eddie pulled Giorgio from a bad game in Memphis [in early June], Giorgio said, 'When Firmani come in the dressing room, I punch him.' These are good friends?" Beckenbauer is laughing. "I don't know the Italian style, but I can't criticize a person one day and the next day be his friend."

The talk is still of Chinaglia as we enter Alfredo's, an elegant Italian restaurant on Central Park South just two blocks from Beckenbauer's apartment. Chinaglia is well known here, one of the select few instantly recognized and whisked to a front table.

"Becking-bower?" Frowning, the maître d' locates the name in his book and waves us imperiously toward a table in the back. Amusement flickers across Beckenbauer's face.

Over lunch Beckenbauer judiciously sips a first, then a second glass of white wine. A busboy has recognized him, and soon the word is out. Three times, just as he brings the same piece of prosciutto and melon to his lips, he is interrupted and asked for an autograph. A busboy. A waiter. And, finally an apologetic maître d'. Someone asks if the Cosmos can repeat as champions.

"You know," he says when they have gone, "I can compare the Cosmos to Bayern Munich before I left. When we are on top, everyone wants to beat us. Other teams play over their heads. You can't be afraid to fight back."

This, he says, is why other teams may beat the Cosmos, who have spent most of the season so far making a mockery of the rest of the league with a 16–3 record in late June. "A coach can tell his team to go out and run 90 minutes, fight 90 minutes," he says. "Do lots of tight marking and then you can win against the Cosmos. We play for the eyes very well. But sometimes we don't have enough here." He thumps his heart.

He seems to catch himself again, as if he has said something wrong. There is some banquet he has to attend tonight and he must excuse himself to go home and rest. "Fancy people," he says of the evening's affair. "Big names. Pele. Ali. And this man who played baseball. I think a pitcher. Henry somebody. He is bigger than Babe Ruth, no?"

With a satirical wink, he is off, strolling through the lunch-hour crowd. Not a head turns.

WEIGHTLIFTING

LADIES IN WEIGHTING

By Amanda Bennett

From The Wall Street Journal
Copyright, ©, 1978, Dow Jones & Company, Inc.

Move over, Vasily Alexeev. You've got some new competition.

Me. And the 67 other women who competed Sunday in the International Women's Powerlifting Championship here.

Well, maybe we wouldn't be much competition yet for the likes of Russian champion Alexeev. But even the tiniest women here were swinging some fairly substantial weights and having fun doing it.

Although woman athletes have often trained with weights to improve their skill in such sports as skiing and gymnastics, only in the past three years or so have they begun entering contests in weightlifting.

If my experience is any guide, the sport will catch on with women. Despite being a jogger and having participated in some intramural sports in college, I don't consider myself athletic. I've been practicing lifting weights for two months in preparation for this article. But now I like lifting so much (and I did have a degree of success against the top competition here) that my assignment may turn into a hobby.

Women's weightlifting may not be sweeping the country, but gyms and health clubs say the seeds of a popular sport have been sown. "We had about three women in our gym up until this year," says Ken Sprague, owner of Gold's Gym in Santa Monica, Calif., where famous male body builders train. "Now, about 150 of our 1,200 members are women."

The contest here drew all kinds of women competitors, from an 18-year-old high school student to a 51-year-old magazine writer. A feminist women's health center in California raised money to send a group of lifters. Purdue University fielded a group, as did the YMCA in Canton, Ohio. An Australian health club held raffles to send two women, and a Florida-based cook drove for two days with her husband and two little sons to compete.

The meet, held in a large community hall here, was the first women's meet approved by the Amateur Athletic Union, a governing body for amateur sports. Each competitor performed three lifts: the squat, in which the women lifted the bar from a high rack onto the back of their shoulders, did a deep-knee bend, and then stood erect; the bench press, in which they lay on their backs and lifted the bar from a rack onto their chests and then fully extended the arms; and the deadlift, which involves lifting the bar from the floor to knee level.

Although some of the competitors had trained for three years or more, many, like me, had been lifting or training for only a short while. Most of the women, even the super-heavyweights (over 181¾ pounds), would never be taken for weightlifters because of any special bulkiness.

Jan Todd, a Nova Scotia schoolteacher, who set the world women's deadlift record at the meet, is larger than the average woman at 5 feet 7 and 195 pounds. ("I have some trouble buying clothes," she says.) But her shape, like the shape of most competitors here, is unmistakably feminine.

She lifted 453¼ pounds—about the weight of two linebackers—to set the deadlift record. The 25-year-old Mrs. Todd, whose husband, Terry, is a former champion weightlifter, can perform such other feats of strength as bending large spikes in half and bending bottlecaps with the fingers of one hand.

Some other women lifters, however, were so tiny that they looked as though they would break under the large weights. Pam Meister of Canton, Ohio, is 22 years old, 105 pounds, and less than 5 feet tall. But she lifted a combined total of 680 pounds in her three lifts. Terry Dillard, a 24-year-old Iowa speech therapist, set a 270-pound record in the squat among competitors weighing less than 114½ pounds.

Unlike most of the competitors, I was unaccustomed to competition. When I lined up with the other women to be weighed at 8 A.M. my reportorial detachment vanished, and I was terrified. Women were there with their coaches kneading their muscles, which intimidated me.

I had had dreams the night before of falling and being crushed under the weights. I was relieved to see the burly men assigned to be spotters, to come to the rescue when competitors buckle under the weight. As the women began choosing their weights for the first attempt at each lift, I was afraid the women would laugh at the minuscule weights I chose for my first attempts. The scrambled eggs I had had for breakfast sat heavily in my stomach.

For the first two lifts, I was so nervous I almost couldn't climb up to the stage. I missed one attempt on the bench press and one on the squat because I was so nervous I completed the lift before the official signal to begin. But by the deadlift, the final lift of the three, my nervousness dissipated. For my last deadlift of the day, I chose 250 pounds, 10 more than I had ever tried in practice. In mid-lift, it sounded like every voice in the audience was urging the weight up, and it helped. I did it.

The audience of about 200, which stayed nearly 12 hours to watch the meet, was wildly enthusiastic for all the competitors.

"I felt like I screamed the bar up the last three inches for every competitor," one woman in the audience said. This enthusiasm contrasts with the hostility some lifters recall from a couple of years ago. "At first, people would yell, 'Hey, where do you wrestle?' when I stepped into the gym," recalls Cindy Reinhoudt, a psychologist in New York State who was named best lifter at this meet. "Even other sportswomen used to think women who lift are a little strange," says Mrs. Reinhoudt, a former javelin thrower.

Other initial difficulties stemmed from the lack of specific rules for women. Men's rules require contestants to be weighed nude, and at a recent meet in Iowa, Miss Dillard and three other women were weighed nude before three male officials. "They said we couldn't lift unless we went by the rules," Miss Dillard says. "I wanted to lift, so I did it." Other women have been required to wear athletic supporters, simply because the rules stated that contestants must wear them.

But competitors here were weighed by women officials. And recently adopted women's rules help to settle problems of dress. Only the basic format of lifting outfit was prescribed, though, so there was a wide variety of colors and shapes of lifting garb at the meet here. I was fairly drab in a black leotard and gymnastic slippers, although I put on some white eyeshadow for the occasion.

Other women wore brightly colored lifting suits, which look like old-fashioned bathing suits, with legs. One woman had hearts and flowers painted on her belt (competitors wear wide leather belts to support their backs and abdomens). Many wore makeup and earrings. One wore a T-shirt with "Wonder Woman" emblazoned across the back.

While "98 percent of the men lifters are now for women lifting," says Joe Zarella, national powerlifting chairman for the Amateur Athletic Union, some men object to the attention given women who lift what the men consider insignificant amounts.

At a recent meet in California, women lifters were followed by television cameras and journalists, while nearby Bruce Wilhelm, a U.S. super-heavy-weight lifting champion, competed unnoticed.

"All a woman has to do is get out there and shake and rattle a bit and the cameras crawl all over her," Mr. Wilhelm complains. "I could use the publicity more myself; I'm serious about the sport," the 330-pound lifter says.

No one really knows yet what levels trained women lifters can achieve. "I didn't even know I was strong until I tried lifting in a contest," recalls Rebecca Joubert, 22, from Tennessee. At her first meet, she dead-weight-lifted over 300 pounds. At Sunday's competition, she just missed setting a 330-pound world record in her 148-pound weight class.

Women so far generally haven't come close to lifting the weights attained by men. Lack of male hormones keeps women's muscles from growing bulky with exercise as men's do. A controversy has arisen in women's track and swimming in recent years over whether some women athletes, especially East Germans, take male hormones. They deny it, and the women weightlifters here who were asked all denied using male hormones.

Male hormones tend to change the physique, and the feminine figures of most of the competitors here attest to their disclaimers.

In fact, many of the women began the exercise to cut down on their body weight. "I have to work to stay over 110 pounds when lifting," Miss Dillard says.

In most cases, women's lifts are about 60 percent of the totals of similar-sized men. But Mrs. Todd's record total of 1,041.8 pounds for three lifts at one meet would have earned her next-to-last place in her weight class at the recent men's international powerlifting championships.

Some experts debunk the widely held theory that women will never come close to lifting the weights that men do. They note that some women, without much training, are approaching men's levels. Jan's husband, Terry Todd, the author of several books on strength, says that women's lower-body muscle structure may in fact be stronger, pound for pound, than men's. "When they get going, they just might surprise us," says Murray Levin, Olympic weightlifting chairman of the Amateur Athletic Union.

I have to agree. In my first meet, I did a 150-pound squat, a 100-pound bench press, and a 250-pound deadlift, for a 500-pound total. This earned me a two-foot-high trophy as the fourth best lifter among the 10 or so foreigners here (I'm a Canadian resident), and I was eighth among the 15 competitors in the under-123½-pound body weight class. By next year's meet—who knows?

BASEBALL

MIGHTY LIKE A ROSE

By Peter Bonventre

From Newsweek
Copyright, © 1978, Newsweek, Inc.
All rights reserved
Reprinted by permission

Outside, vendors were hawking long-stemmed roses and banners reading, "Do It, Pete." Inside the ball park, Pete Rose of the Cincinnati Reds was opening good-luck telegrams from Governor James Rhodes of Ohio and a woman who bills herself as Morganna, the Kissing Bandit. "She's a stripper," Rose said with a wink. The night before, Rose had tied the modern National League record by hitting safely in 37 straight games. It was set in 1945 by Tommy Holmes of the Boston Braves, and most players would be jubilant about having matched a record that stood for 33 years. But not Pete Rose. "I don't think you accomplish anything by tying someone," he said. "I gotta go out there and break it."

And that's exactly what Rose did last week. On a breezy night in New York's Shea Stadium, in his second time at bat against New York Mets pitcher Craig Swan, Rose lined a single to left field and had the record all to himself. Standing on first base, he waved his cap to the thunderously cheering crowd. Tommy Holmes himself was present and he sprinted onto the field and shook Rose's hand. Rose offered Holmes the record-breaking ball. "No," replied Holmes. "It's yours. You keep it."

"I hit the damned thing, so I will keep it," Rose said with a laugh.

The following night, after extending his streak to 39 games, Rose had everybody wondering if he could surpass Joe DiMaggio's mark of 56 straight games, set in 1941. That is the one record that oddsmakers have long predicted will never be broken, and even Rose's staunchest admirers weren't giving him much of a chance. "DiMaggio's streak, in my opinion, is untouchable," says Reds manager Sparky Anderson. "Pete can't convince me any different until he gets up to 50."

"I'm just starting now," Rose says. "I heard that DiMaggio said if anybody breaks his record, he hoped it would be me."

So do a lot of people. Other ball players obviously admire Rose, and nobody appreciates him more than the everyday fan who carries his lunch pail to the job and works overtime to make a few extra bucks. Running to first base on a walk, sliding on his belly, tumbling into box seats after a foul pop—these are Rose's trademarks. And when Rose crouches low at the plate with his bat almost resting on his shoulders, he gives the impression that he wants to hit more than other players want air to breathe. He gets upset if he doesn't bang out at least 200 hits a year, and earlier this season, his sixteenth in the big leagues, he joined a distinguished circle of players by accumulating the three-thousandth hit of his career. "What makes this streak special," says Rose, "is the fact that I'm 37. I'm supposed to be too old to play the way I am."

At any age, Rose's streak is a remarkable achievement.

"I just don't know how he's doing it," marvels Minnesota's Rod Carew, who is widely regarded as the best hitter in baseball. The pressure of trying to get a hit every day and coping with all the press attention is enough to rattle even the toughest psyche. But what other players call pressure, Rose defines as fun. "I enjoy having my back to the wall," says the chunky third baseman, "and I enjoy having a goal to shoot for. A lot of the fans are on my side, and their cheering stimulates me. That's a big advantage."

Rose has also counted on other advantages during his streak. As Cincinnati's lead-off batter, he usually gets an extra turn at the plate. And because he is a switch-hitter, neither lefties nor right handers tend to bother him unduly. "People talk about needing a lot of luck," says Rose. "But I haven't had one lucky hit, nothing that scooted off a player's glove or leg. They've all been in there."

Six times, Rose kept his streak alive with hits in his final turn at bat. Once, he fouled a pitch by Houston's Joe Niekro off his right ankle, and it promptly swelled like a balloon. "I got my butt right back into the box before Sparky could put in a pinch hitter," he recalls. "The next pitch, I got my hit and Sparky brought in a runner for me." Later, against Philadelphia, Rose was still hitless in the eighth inning when he drew a walk. But his teammates got a rally going, and he came up in the ninth inning with two outs—and placed a perfect bunt down the third-base line.

Rose capitalized on Phillies pitching again last weekend, extending his streak to 42 games and surpassing Ty Cobb and George Sisler. He then aimed his bat at Wee Willie Keeler's mark of 44—but Rose still had a long way to go before proving the oddsmakers wrong.

GENERAL

THE IMPORTANCE OF BEING HOWARD

By Murray Olderman

From Newspaper Enterprise Association
Copyright, ©, 1978, Newspaper Enterprise Association, Inc.

Howard Cosell may be the unhappiest man I know. Howard, who has thrived on being the man everybody loves to hate, really hates not to be loved.

He has what ostensibly every successful man yearns for. He makes half a million dollars annually as a broadcast journalist (Howard will love that job description!) and, at his age, pushing 60, wouldn't have to work another day in his life. He has a supportive wife, a stable home life, and he is famous far beyond his early dreams.

The first time I met Howard was at the Polo Grounds, which no longer exists, watching a New York Giants baseball game. Garry Schumacher, their old public relations man, had graciously set me up with two tickets right behind home plate. This was long ago when getting a pair of freebies was not deemed a heinous violation of human nature.

My wife, who basically couldn't care less about sports, or even about Howard Cosell, didn't and still doesn't know much about baseball. So I was patiently explaining the nuances of Willie Mays gloving a fly ball like he was using a peach basket, or Eddie Stanky crowding the plate to make the pitcher nervous.

But every time I volunteered a pearl of information, this guy in the box seat on the other side of her would contradict my information or, at the very least, embellish it.

It turned out he was a lawyer. He was, he noted, the lawyer of Monte Irving, the fine black left fielder of the Giants (now an aide in Commissioner Bowie Kuhn's office).

You guessed it—he was also a lawyer on the way to becoming TV's Howard Cosell.

I don't have to detail how from that point Howard got to be one of America's genuine and notorious media celebrities. How he changed his name from Cohen to Cosell, put on a toupee, and proceeded "to tell it like it is."

He took personality gimmicks—stridency, pomposity, and bombast—and parlayed them into a communications figure, who may be the most imitated by such noted mimics as Rich Little and Frank Gorshin in bistros from Las Vegas to Atlantic City.

It should not be forgotten, however, that Howard is also a very bright, glib, retentive, generally unflappable man. These qualities, too, have helped him to become the most recognizable sports communicator in America.

But Howard's problem is that basically he is not what he wants to be. Howard has this ego. He not only wants to be famous and make huge amounts of money; he wants to be important.

That accounts for his flirtation with the idea of running for the United States Senate, an idea that turned out to be abortive.

That accounts for his disastrous sidestep into an imitation of Ed Sullivan and his flop as a Saturday night variety show host.

That accounts for his relished appearances before Congress whenever a controversial sports issue arises.

That accounts for his taking on a guest lecture course at Yale University.

All these would serve to give him credentials that transcend the world of fun and games on which Howard is so dependent for his *raison d'être* and which he pontifically calls "a microcosm of society."

But in the final analysis, Howard can't avoid sports as his basic milieu. (I once caught Howard misusing "milieu" when he was trying to flaunt his erudition before Frank Gifford in a New York football locker room one day when Frank was still a Giants player and trying to break into broadcasting.)

Anyhow, Howard's quest to be accepted among the great conflicts with the performance of his job. You see, when he has to describe how someone named Tom Veryzer went into the hole to rob someone named Chuck Hartenstein of a "bingle," that makes Howard less important than either Veryzer or Hartenstein, who aren't exactly household names.

And when Howard, who can get into Studio 54 with a flick of the wrist, has to interview an 18-year-old amateur boxer, probing for the latter's innermost thoughts, that very act constitutes deference to the obscure fighter.

All of which is why Howard is basically unhappy. He is extremely sensitive to criticism, especially from the print media, which because of natural envy and because of Howard's egregious putdown of sports writers, has been generally stinging in its appraisal of his role on the American sports scene.

The intimation that a sports event doesn't really count unless Howard is an appendage of the game has never set well with the men in the press box.

Also, Howard has been guilty of some execrable taste in his assaults on athletic figures while posing as an interviewer. Particularly remembered is his sniping barrage at Stan Wright, the hapless assistant track coach of the American Olympic team at Munich in 1972 after Stan's mistake caused two U.S. sprinters to miss their quarter-final heats in the 100-meter dash.

I never found anything amusing about his verbal jousts over a period of years with Muhammad Ali, which gave the latter a forum for his personal, racist propaganda. And Howard has had a penchant for arrogant, patronizing approaches to his interview subjects, sometimes under the guise of humor.

Why do they take it? Because they respect Howard's power as an image-maker and are afraid of him. Also, because he overwhelms them intellectually. They're not used to or don't know how to cope with his polysyllabic jabs.

The fact is, despite all that verbiage flaunted as erudition, Howard frequently mangles the English language. His syntax is gross.

Let's give him his due, though. He brought a spirit of iconoclasm to electronic broadcasting of sports. He did his homework, and he was not afraid to ask questions, impertinent or otherwise. That was something new to sportscasting, too.

The private Howard Cosell can also be likable and amusing and a good friend. There've been insinuations that his co-workers have not exactly liked him, have resented him, have even hated him. But Chet Forte, who has been a director for ABC for years and worked 80 percent of his telecasts, asked Howard to be the best man at his wedding. And his cohorts behind the microphone, while kidding about their relationship, have never publicly blasted him—he's been like the eccentric uncle whose excesses at the family reunion are tolerated and later remembered fondly.

The miracle of Howard Cosell is that he has had a remarkably long tenure as an influential, important sports broadcaster whose style has never wavered. His timing has been perfect. He came along when sports pro-liferated as a programming commodity on television, and you could say that Howard, if only because he was there, was partly responsible for that growth.

The analogy isn't perfect, but almost a generation ago, a broadcaster named Mel Allen had the same kind of pervasiveness, at least in the New York market, where Mel handled the broadcasts of the New York Yankees and where Howard also has his power base.

Allen was less abrasive, but no less gabby, and one day he woke up and found himself without a job. It shattered his psyche.

This is not to intimate Howard is going to be lopped off suddenly, though you hear intimations he might be cut back.

Nevertheless, behind the hard, brusque shell of Howard Cosell there is a sensitive man who, above all, wants approval.

FISHING

SALMON OF THE TUNDRA

By Jack Samson

From Field & Stream
Copyright, ©, 1978, Field & Stream

No balmy New Brunswick, Canada, where the summer temperatures soar into the high 90s, the land of the tundra salmon is harsh, beautiful, and as unforgiving as any arctic area of the globe.

At the southern end of Ungava Bay, about seven degrees south of the Arctic Circle, two huge salmon rivers empty into the chilly salt water. They are the George and Whale rivers of northern Quebec, and they pour into the bay after running northward for several hundred miles through some of the most rugged and stark terrain on the face of the North American continent. This land of rolling foothills and steep valleys is covered with slippery, spongy caribou moss, stunted bushes, and gnarled trees—all buried for most of the year beneath the thick layer of arctic snows. But for a few short months each year—part of June, July, and August—the earth tilts its northern axis just enough toward the sun for the warm rays to melt the snow and cause the land to burst into life.

Caribou and ptarmigan feed on bright berries that splotch the gray-and-green landscape like millions of tiny rubies and garnets. The white gyrfalcons build their nests on the ground and perch on lichen-spattered rocks to look for rodents and ptarmigan, which they will kill and feed to their young. The snowy owls are also nesting then and their huge shapes float over the land at dusk as they search for food.

And it is then that the great schools of salmon make the swing around the northern tip of Newfoundland and enter the Hudson Strait between the northernmost tip of Quebec and Baffin Island. These are late-spawning fish, heading up the great, wide rivers as late as September, while their southern cousins have surges up rivers with names like the Restigouch, Miramichi, Matapedia, Grand Cascapedia, and the Tabusintac to spawn as early as May and June. No gill nets, trap nets, or drift nets threaten the salmon at the mouth of the mighty George River, although there are a few on the Whale. This is Eskimo land, and they only set up temporary tent camps along the two big rivers in July and August to work for the few outfitters who cater to the salmon fishermen and caribou hunters who come to this land each summer from far to the south.

The Eskimos have their headquarters at Fort Chimo, about 25 miles west of the Whale and almost 100 miles west of the George. There they take all the salmon they need with nets from their home river, the Koksoak, as they have for centuries. They have no problem securing enough caribou during the annual migration to provide them with meat and skins for the winter. The sportsman who is fortunate enough to arrive in the area when both the salmon are running and the caribou migrating will think he has died and gone to heaven. Caribou, following ancient migration routes dating back to the retreat of the glaciers, pour across the tundra like the herds of bison once did in the American West. The migration, depending upon weather and temperature, usually takes place in the latter part of August or early September. A hunter who simply wants to kill a caribou for meat has only to wait until a good bull comes by. Those hunters who want a trophy rack along with their meat would be wise to take along some photographs of what a trophy head really is. There are so many good heads passing by in the vast herds that it is difficult to judge a trophy unless one is thoroughly familiar with the body markings of old bulls, the number and spread of tines and forward-jutting shovels.

But for the salmon fisherman who comes to the great rivers there are a few problems—unless one considers drowning or freezing something less than a problem. The George River is as much as a quarter of a mile wide in many areas and the pools may run 15 to 20 feet deep in spots. Even the Eskimos don't know all the runs and where the salmon lie. Few outfitters claim to know much about the huge rivers outside of their own leased areas. It has only been in the last dozen years or so that any concerted effort has been made to set up Eskimo-run tent camps along the river. Before that, the few camps there were leased from the provincial government by wealthy American and Canadian individuals or companies. In the early 1960s, the government organized the North Quebec Co-Operative, whereby some of the revenue produced by the influx of American and Canadian hunters and fishermen would go to the Eskimos themselves. In addition, Eskimos built cooperative stores, such as the one at Ft. Chimo, where they derive income from the sale of Eskimo-made soapstone carvings and other items of native art.

The sportsman is now offered a choice of a seven-day trip to the big rivers where he or she may choose to fish for salmon and trout or fish for both and also hunt caribou. Compared to the stratospheric prices being asked today to fish salmon rivers in southern Quebec, New Brunswick, Iceland, Scotland, Ireland, and Norway, the price here is a bargain—probably less than a third of what is being asked internationally, where the high rates are for one rod on salmon water for five days, not seven.

The Eskimos are excellent fishermen, canoeists, and guides. Unlike some of the northern Indian tribes, they are happy, friendly, hardworking, and almost childlike in their sense of humor. Short and stocky, they are immensely strong. Even an elderly Eskimo guide is capable of carrying a quarter of a caribou for hours over terrain that would intimidate a pack mule. They are good shots, although they exhibit a total disregard for the care and maintenance of guns. A gun fancier would shudder at the sight of several of their rifles lying in the boulders of the edge of the river, their stocks bleached from the sun and rain and covered with scars. The outside of the barrels are solid rust and the bolt must be forced open to insert a shell in the chamber. But when an Eskimo needs to kill a wolf or a caribou, the battered guns always seem to fire and hit where they are aimed.

Most show a complete indifference toward fly rods and, probably, consider the fly rod fisherman either a fool or a dilettante. When they want salmon, char, or trout for a meal, they either put out nets or reach for a spinning rod. These rods are almost universally battered, and the reels usually have missing parts. Most spinning reel spools contain 12- to 15-pound test leader, and the red-and-white wobbling spoon is almost the standard lure on the big rivers. There is a law against sportsmen using spinning tackle for salmon, but the Eskimos pay no attention to it. After all, they were fishing these rivers and setting their nets when the Norsemen sailed around the tip of Newfoundland and first saw the great bay about A.D. 1,000. (The impression of what the Norsemen sailed in has been a bit warped by Hollywood movies. The Viking galleys, rowed by huge oars, were only used as raiding warships. For exploration, they used a stubby single-masted sailing ship called a knoor, which was extremely seaworthy and 40 to 60 feet long. With these the Norsemen sailed westward from Norway and colonized Iceland, discovered Greenland, and even landed on the northeast coast of Newfoundland. It is doubtful that the Eskimos regarded these bearded and skin-clad foreigners much differently than they do the fly fisherman or big-game hunter who visits their country today.)

Over the hundreds of thousands of years since the remote ancestors of the modern Eskimo crossed via the Aleutian Island land bridge to North America from Asia, the people here have adapted marvelously to their cold, snow-clad environment. The eyesight of an Eskimo is a constant source of wonder to the "civilized" sportsmen who hunt and fish with him. He is able to spot caribou where we see only tundra and, even at that distance, can distinguish bulls from cows. An Eskimo will stand on a rock beside the river and point to a spot in the fast current.

"Salmon," he will say. "Two."

And we will stand beside him for minutes, wearing polarized glasses and staring vainly at the spot. Finally, after the guide has reached out an arm with instructions to follow where he is pointing, and has said "head" and "tail—there," the salmon will suddenly become visible against the shifting light, the mottled bottom, and the changing shadows of rushing water. But the two fish are as visible to the Eskimo as goldfish in a bowl are to us.

Like all true fishermen, Eskimos never tire of watching other anglers catch fish. They thoroughly enjoy watching a fly-rod fisherman battle a leaping, fighting salmon. They get the same enjoyment watching one fight a large char, brook trout, or lake trout that has struck a trolled streamer fly from behind the canoe. They are agile while wading, even in rubber boots, and most are experts with the big aluminum nets needed to scoop up a tiring salmon in shallow water.

When fishing the George one never knows what one will take on the next cast. Unlike most salmon rivers, where only an occasional small trout is likely to make a pass at a salmon fly at the bottom of a float, the George is full of surprises. The river is full of battling brook trout which may run to considerable size. On one trip in the late 1960s, I caught a 17-pound lake trout from a pool above Helen Falls Camp. Last year, I caught one that weighed 14 pounds, and Jim Bashline lost fly, leader, line, and 250 yards of backing to a fish which took everything downriver after one thrash on the surface. We both wanted to believe it was a 50-pound salmon, but since it never jumped, we surmised it was probably a huge laker. But who knows?

Most of the salmon we caught—and we caught and released more than 40 in four days of fishing—were in the 12- to 15-pound class. But a number of 30- to 40-pound salmon are caught regularly. The Quebec government allows one to bring out about 75 pounds of salmon. Jim and I brought home four each that weighed about 20 pounds apiece. Our head Eskimo guide, Conolusi, who spoke very good English, told us one evening that several years ago his uncle caught a 50-pound salmon on a red-and-white spoon just below an island in the center of the river about half a mile upstream from our camp. When asked how he knew it weighed 50 pounds, he told us it was thrown on the freight scales used to weigh baggage and freight going aboard the bush planes. The rusted scale—which we looked at—was probably at least 5 pounds off, one way or the other. Conolusi is known as an honest man and the rest of the Eskimo staff backed up his story. The scales may have been off, but suppose they were off on the downward side. The fish could have weighed 55 pounds. Eskimos have no interest in weight of salmon. To them it is simply a main source of food. They are about as interested in the weight of an individual fish as we would be in how much a head of beef weighed before it was converted into steaks.

Of all the salmon streams I have fished—and I have fished them in Quebec, New Brunswick, Iceland, and Scotland—I would rather fish the George than any other. It is so awesome a river that it frightens me at the same time it intrigues me. The water temperature is always somewhere in the mid-50s in August and if one should suddenly fall in, the chill would not take too long to paralyze. The current is so strong and the water so deep that a fisherman wearing hip or chest waders would be swept down huge chutes and dashed against sharp boulders. Unless an Eskimo guide could get to a fisherman in a few minutes, it would be too late. And many an Eskimo guide has been known to nap comfortably in the shelter of some rocks while the angler fishes.

My last day on the George last year was the finest I have had on a salmon stream in a lifetime of fishing for the magnificent Atlantic salmon. We had hunted for caribou for three days, and one of our party had taken a trophy bull. Jim and I had not seen a bull worth taking and had really come up for the salmon fishing anyway. We fished three days under clear sunny skies with a chill wind blowing down the canyon of the George—gusting at times to 20 knots or more. Casting was difficult in the wind, and the wind-chill factor brought the mid-50 degree temperature down considerably lower. I had been fishing with felt-lined footed hip waders, long underwear, a heavy wool shirt, and a down jacket. We had taken fish up and down the river, but it had been fairly slow fishing for that part of the world.

The last morning, September 5, we awoke to rain pounding on the tent. Outside, the temperature had risen a few degrees, but heavy clouds hung low over the foothills bordering both sides of the river. The river was black and sullen-looking in the early morning light. I felt better. No one else did. Most decided to hunt caribou. But this, to me, has always been ideal salmon fishing weather. Many salmon fishermen love the warmth of the summer sun on clear water. Perhaps it is my Scot ancestry, but I feel more at home standing in dark water and casting to fish under rainy skies. I caught more fish under those conditions when I fished the River Spey in Scotland, just inland from the cold waters of the North Sea. I caught more and better fish in the rain on the Grimsa, Nordura, and the Haffjardara in Iceland, too.

Digging out a hooded rain poncho and a pair of thin calfskin gloves, I headed upriver with my guide after breakfast. I took a sandwich and a Thermos of coffee—sufficiently spiced to keep damp wind and frigid water from penetrating the bone marrow while I waded. The guide and I pulled the big canoe ashore on a long, slender island near the far shore about a mile above camp. We could just make out the white triangles of the tent camp on the bluff above the river far downstream. The guide pulled his down parka hood over his head and huddled in the lee of a large boulder as I waded into the dark water and began false casting with the nine-foot graphite rod. I was using a Black Rat, my favorite fly for the George in this type of weather.

"Black flies for black water and black skies," a Scotch gillie had told me once on the river Test. The advice worked on the George better than on any other river I had fished. The water below the island fanned out over a long pebbled bottom dotted with occasional clusters of submerged boulders. The water ranged from a few feet deep close to the island to black depths a dozen yards out into the stream. I was able repeatedly to fish a shore area perhaps 40 yards long. After methodically working down as far as I could safely wade without danger of losing footing and being swept away, I would wade ashore and repeat the performance.

Ah, what a marvelous day that was! I hooked and released eight salmon—all silver colored and fresh from the sea—that morning and killed only one. That one weighed 27 pounds. In addition, I hooked and released two big lake trout, half-a-dozen char, and a couple of small brook trout. The salmon all fought spectacularly—taking the black fly on the swing in several feet of water and then moving off into deep water when they felt the bite of the hook and the pressure of the line. After realizing they were in trouble, they would start upriver until they felt the pressure of the graphite rod and the big reel. Then they would begin the fight by hurling themselves into the air—cartwheeling until they crashed to the surface, and then tearing off line on one magnificent run after another. By noon, when it was time for the guide to eat lunch, my arm was tired from fighting salmon. I reeled the line in and lumbered over to where the guide was seated, water running from his parka hood. He was a young man, about 18 years old, with a handsome face and quick smile.

"Charlie," I said, squatting down beside him. "You take the canoe and go back to camp for lunch. OK?"

"You no eat?" He looked puzzled. I pointed to the small pack with the sandwich and the Thermos.

"I had cook make me lunch," I said. "You go back and eat. Take your time. I want to fish until 5 o'clock." It was then noon. The past three hours had gone so rapidly they had seemed like an hour at the most. "You understand 5 o'clock?" I asked holding up five fingers. He nodded.

"I no come back after eat?" he asked.

I shook my head. "No. You stay in camp and keep warm and dry. I don't want to keep any salmon. Just hook and let go. I won't need you to net. Just leave net here. OK?"

He nodded and began sliding the big canoe into the river. "OK," he said. "I come back 5 o'clock."

I watched him start the 40 hp outboard motor, swing the dark-green canoe in the current, then head into the rain and mist for the camp. Then I sat down on the rock and began to open the sandwich. It is not often a man gets five hours alone on a huge river filled with salmon. Guides are a great help in netting and tailing fish, but there is much more pleasure in fishing alone. The sandwich tasted good and the Irish coffee flooded me with a warmth I had not felt since finishing breakfast.

As I waded back into the shallow water and began casting, a sense of contentment came over me. I had five hours of freedom ahead. Five hours where no conversation was necessary and no voice other than my own would be heard across the small island and the surface of the huge river. The wind had picked up a bit and the rain fell steadily. Overhead two big herring gulls flew slowly up the river from the bay far downstream. They craned their necks as they passed over me—one species of fisherman inspecting another—and perhaps wondering what sort of a fool creature would be out in such weather.

The pickup of the fly at the end of the float, the false cast, and the next forward cast—all became a smooth rhythmic motion. After each cast there was one step sideways downstream and the beginning of a new series of casts—lengthening the distance about a foot each time to cover as much of the water as humanly possible.

The rain fell steadily, the wind ruffled the dark surface of the river, and the clouds scudded overhead. Periodically there was the heartstopping tug of a strike, the sudden and incredibly powerful first rush, and the breathtaking thrill of a leaping fish. The whoops of pure joy were unheard by any mortal man but me. Each fish was released as it finally, reluctantly, came into the shallows and turned on its side, gills flaring. After breaking the leader at the fly, I would watch each fish swim slowly back into the main current.

Two salmon broke off, one a monster that could have gone 35 to 40 pounds and snapped the 15-pound leader 150 yards out in the middle of the river on the fifth towering jump. It took shaking hands a good several minutes to tie on another fly and tippet—this time a 20-pound one. The "purist" may fish for Atlantic salmon with tiny bamboo rods and 8-pound-test leaders. I have done it, but no longer—not on rivers like the George— nor will I, for that matter, on the Restigouche or the Kedgewick or a number of others where salmon may run 40 pounds or more. The big reel carried No. 11 weight-forward intermediate floating line with a sinking tip. Behind that was 350 yards of 15-pound-test Dacron backing. Anyone who thinks that tackle is too heavy has never been fast to a 40-pound Atlantic salmon on a river the size of the George!

The hours passed like minutes. Fish struck, fought, tore off line, leaped, thrashed in the shallows, and finally quit, but only after fighting until near exhaustion.

No track was kept of how many fish were hooked, fought, and released. It was no longer important to count. As the day wound down and the darkness began to set in after 4 P.M., the world had been reduced to a 40-yard stretch of a tiny island in the black current of a mighty Arctic river. There was nowhere else that mattered, though that world was coming to a close, far too soon, in the cold rain and gusting wind.

Without turning around, it was not difficult to imagine the figures, some sitting on the big boulders, others leaning at ease against a slab of rock or squatting in the gravel, smoking their pipes and watching—all shrouded in the mist of gathering darkness.

There would be the occasional nod of approval at a well-handled cart- wheeling jump of a good fish—but probably more frequently a tolerant smile and a shake of the head at a foolish and clumsy mistake. It was not necessary to see them to know they were there—salmon fishermen from other times and other far-distant places, who would rather be here on this river than anywhere else.

FOOTBALL

"SWIVEL THOSE HIPS!"

By Jeff Meyers

From the St. Louis Post-Dispatch
Copyright, © 1978, St. Louis Post-Dispatch

While news reporters can sink their teeth into a daily diet of crime, corruption, and sex, sports writers must make their contribution to society by explaining the 3–4 defense and translating athletes' quotes into English. It's not often that we get to write about a great moral issue—or even a small one. Once in a while, however, something comes along that makes editorial writers twitch and compels investigative reporters to visit the sports department on the pretense of acquiring passes to the racetrack.

A recent example is the dilemma facing professional sports: Should women reporters be allowed in locker rooms? It is a subject that transcends sports and arouses the patriotism in people who believe the fate of the nation is at stake.

Last week in New York, a judge ruled that women sports writers no longer can be barred from the clubhouse of the New York Yankees. The ruling surprised me because I never knew they were kept out. I had always assumed that women stayed out of steamy, clammy locker rooms in order to keep their mascara from running.

A locker room is not as glamorous as the public thinks. First of all, the place apparently was designed to retain and preserve odors for future generations to appreciate. In addition, the athletes don't adorn their lockers with *Playboy* centerfolds, nor do they do anything more notable than towel themselves after showering. Is it worth hanging out in locker rooms to get an occasional interesting quote? Hardly, especially if you mildew easily.

But women sports writers insist on access to the locker rooms despite angry protests from outraged players, their wives, and club owners. One side argues that women should have the same rights as men, the other side says that athletes have the right to privacy. The women are afraid of not getting the same priceless clichés as their male counterparts, and the athletes are afraid that women are going to peek or perhaps tell them to scrub behind their ears and straighten up their lockers.

It's understandable why the players object to strange women seeing them without clothing—hey, I still blush in front of my mother. But how can owners become indignant? These are the same fine citizens who are bringing us half-naked cheerleaders who wriggle suggestively during a game in the name of good, clean, wholesome voyeurism.

The owners, however, will have the last word. There already has been a confrontation between management and women's lib, and management won. After a football game in Miami between the Cardinals and Dolphins, a woman reporter for a Florida newspaper tried to get into the Big Red locker room. Larry Wilson guarded the players' honor by keeping her out.

There is always the chance, of course, that some curious woman reporter is going to want access to the locker room for more than just a simple interview. For example, take an incident that occurred at a recent Pro Bowl. It involves a woman television reporter and a locker room full of football players.

Here's what happened: An interview session with the entire media was forced inside because of rain. The players, in uniform, were interviewed at their lockers. In about 30 minutes, most of the reporters had gone. Within 45 minutes, the only reporter left was the TV woman, who was fiddling with her equipment. The players fidgeted for another 20 minutes, then began peeling off their clothes.

"We watched her and she was checking us out as we walked to the shower," one of the All-Pros said, incredulously.

It is obvious that somebody is going to have to resolve the locker-room dilemma before an uppity woman reporter gets punched out by a security guard. The owners have suggested that all reporters be barred from the locker rooms. In other words, equal rights for men and women sports writers. No more cheap thrills for anyone, the owners say. Fine with me. I never liked interviewing naked men in the first place.

The best solution would be to set up a postgame interview room and bring in selected athletes in an orderly fashion. Only open the locker room 30 minutes after the game when, presumably, the athletes would be showered, dressed, and sitting demurely in front of their lockers. By then, they would have a better, less-emotional perspective on the game and would have had time to think up something clever to say.

Why hasn't someone thought of this before? Why is sports the only legitimate business in which reporters are permitted to watch the principals take off their clothes? Do members of Congress invite the press into their bathrooms for a story? Has President Jimmy Carter ever held a press conference in the raw? Does Farrah give interviews in the shower?

The alternative solution, of course, would be to open locker rooms to reporters of both sexes. Bashful athletes could put on black masks like those you see in X-rated movies or wear their uniforms home. Uptight owners could erect waist-high barricades in front of the players' lockers. In today's laid-back society, however, nobody should be embarrassed, except those male sports writers who kept getting scooped by the women.

If the alternative solution were accepted, it would be only fair that professional women athletes permit men sports writers in their locker rooms. But this possibility is certain to be greeted with yawns by the men sports writers. Let's face it: While men athletes fit the general stereotype of the ideal male body, women pros are known more for their skills than their figures.

Which brings up another story, this one hopefully apocryphal: It seems a man sports writer somehow got into the locker room during a women's pro tournament, and joined a seminary the next day.

TENNIS

BIG-TIME COLLEGE TENNIS: THE INSIDE STORY

By Tim Noonan

From Tennis Magazine
Copyright, ©, 1978, Tennis Magazine

The first major college tennis match I ever saw took place on the shiny black asphalt courts on the back tier of the Los Angeles Tennis Club in March of 1967. I was a high school freshman then, but I had fled the harsh snows of New England on the strength of an invitation to work out during my spring break under famed University of Southern California coach George Toley. And I watched in awe that day as the mighty Trojans, led by All-Americas Stan Smith and Bob Lutz, soundly trounced the University of Tennessee 8–1.

Nor were Smith and Lutz the first big tennis stars to play for USC. Alex Olmedo won the men's singles at Wimbledon while still a student there. Dennis Ralston and Rafael Osuna won the men's doubles at Wimbledon before they even enrolled at USC. And the Trojans were then defending NCAA team champions, a title they had won four of the five preceding years. But, besides myself, only about 20 mildly interested fans walked down the breezeway from the clubhouse to catch a bit of the match.

By the time I entered Stanford three years later, though, college tennis had changed a great deal and it's changed even more since. USC now has a new on-campus tennis stadium that it frequently fills to capacity. Stanford annually draws 20,000 or more to a series of weekend tennis matches against USC and the other big Southern California tennis power, the University of California at Los Angeles. Tennis has gone big time and college coaches all across the country are pursuing the choicest high school talent with big promises—hoping that if they do catch a star they can keep him on campus for at least a couple of years before he goes after the really big money in the pros.

"No, tennis doesn't quite pull its own weight yet," says Stanford assistant athletic director Don Tobin, "but it's third behind football and basketball, and way ahead of all the other sports." The need to succeed has, in fact, become so great that for many players college tennis represents the most intense and longest continuous pressure situation they will ever face.

And that's true not only of the men but the women, too. The passage of Title IX, guaranteeing equal rights for women athletes, has seen to that. "When I was here," says USC women's coach Dave Borelli, himself a former USC tennis star, "you were hardly aware that there was a women's team. Now the women share the spotlight with the men—scholarships, practice facilities, uniforms, travel, publicity—everything."

The pressure can actually begin long before a player walks on campus. Five or 10 years ago, for example, when there were virtually no restrictions on recruiting, Stanford coach Dick Gould wooed many of us in high school with almost weekly letters. Some of the decidedly blue-chip prospects, like Roscoe Tanner and Sandy Mayer, might hear from Gould even earlier—in junior high. One of my 1974 teammates, Paul Sidone, received his first letter from Gould when he was in only the seventh grade, before Gould had even become the Stanford coach.

By the time you got to be a senior, you could be getting these letters almost daily—not only from Gould, but from other top coaches like Toley of USC, Glenn Bassett of UCLA, and Clarence Mabry (since succeeded by Bob McKinley) of Trinity. And one of the things you soon discovered was that some of them just wouldn't take no for an answer.

When I was a senior in prep school, there was one coach at an eastern college—a place I had expressly said I was not interested in attending—who went so far as to fill out an admission application in my name, complete in every detail except for my signature. He did it, he explained, "just in case I changed my mind." And later on he offered to fly me in and arrange for me to work out for a week with one of the top 10 players in the United States.

My own modest recruitment was nothing, though, compared to that experienced by such top prospects as Jimmy Connors, Dick Stockton, and Harold Solomon—who probably had 50 or 100 schools competing for their services. I have no idea what inducements they might have been offered. Whether they included flagrant recruiting violations involving cars, money, or women, such as you find in other "major" sports, I honestly can't say. But I do know that they included a lot of what might be termed quasi-legal temptations.

One such case involved Mayer, who was later a teammate of mine at Stanford. He was invited to spend a recruiting weekend at Rice University in Houston and, while attending a basketball game there, was asked to pick out the prettiest cheerleader. He did, and the girl then became his date for the weekend. Sandy really fell for her and after that they started writing back and forth. But when the time came, he finally chose head over heart and signed with Stanford, where he had intended going in the first place. End of romance.

Sometimes, recruiting doesn't stop even after a player enters college. At one point in my career at Stanford, when I wasn't playing much, a coach from an East Coast college made some unsubtle overtures to me about transferring to his school, where he said I would have a top slot on the team.

Needless to say, such tampering is frowned upon. Indeed, during the past several years, the rules on recruiting have been tightened all down the line.

"Lately," says Gould, "we can't talk to a kid unless he's at least a junior in high school, and we're allowed only two personal visits. After that, contact must be kept to a mere salutation. In addition, we've cut back to five scholarships now, which isn't even a whole team. That means I have to zero in on the top five or six graduating high school seniors, of which only two or three may be academically eligible for Stanford. That tends to focus recruiting on a couple of individuals. It's no longer a broadly based canvassing."

Recruiting violations still do occur, of course, but these are kept to a minimum, Gould claims, by the shortage of funds at the college level and the small fraternity of the sport.

"I don't think there are any violations that I know of—at least, out here," says Gould. "I have a high respect for both Glenn [Bassett] and George [Toley]. I tell any kid that if someplace is offering him something, first get it in writing. And if you aren't getting the same thing from us or USC or UCLA or Cal, then you should be careful."

OK, you've been careful, you've compiled a brilliant record in the juniors; you've been heavily recruited, and you've finally made your choice. So by the time you arrive on campus, you should have it made, right? Well, maybe. But not if your experience is anything like mine.

When I enrolled at Stanford in 1970, I suddenly found myself in the midst of a glut of tennis players consisting of at least 12 feasible All-Americas, all vying for just six varsity playing spots. These included Tanner, Mayer, and Jim Delaney, who were guaranteed starting berths on talent alone; the rest of us had to fight it out week after week in challenge matches to see who would get to play.

Except for the Stanford team this year, clearly one of the best in tennis history, no college team may ever have been as deep. But there are so many good players these days at so many colleges around the country, the intensity of competition must be just as severe now as it was then. And it was plenty severe, then, believe me.

The first challenge matches started in the fall—played out on angry, fiery afternoons—and grew in ferocity as the year went on, reaching fever pitch with the approach of the biggest team matches of the year. Hurled rackets and vocal outbursts grew more and more common. And on one particular afternoon, two players who had been doubles partners and best friends for years finally started fighting about a disputed line call. No one was hurt, fortunately, but that was only because a couple of guys grabbed them and said, "Hey, let's mellow out here."

On another occasion, two players from the same Pacific Eight team met in a California state tournament and ended up in a shouting match that eventually embroiled both their coach and the father of one of the players who happened to be there. The result of that was a rift that wasn't settled until both players were out of school.

But if teammates occasionally get mad at each other, it's nothing compared to the common anger they frequently feel toward their coach. One reason for that is the fact that in college, as opposed to tournament competition, a player's standing is often determined—or seems to be determined—subjectively by his coach. The coach, thus, becomes a convenient and logical scapegoat for the disgruntled player who feels that he should have had another chance to challenge the player directly above him, or that he's not playing well because he has not been allowed to play in enough matches, or that he ought to be playing in the first spot, against topflight competition, instead of fourth against some hacker.

The coach's toughest job, it seems, is to keep all his players happy while fielding his best team—a near-impossible task when dealing with so many ambitious people. In 1974 at Stanford, in fact, it did prove impossible. That was a year in which we eventually won the national title, but feelings ran so hot that our top player quit in midseason, hardly anyone was talking to anyone else by the end of the campaign, and college officials ultimately decided to cancel our end-of-the-year banquet.

All of that is not to say college tennis is a nightmare of tension. It's not. In fact, it can be just the opposite at times—especially when you're playing for a tennis power and you get into the regular schedule of dual team matches, many of which are against lesser foes.

At Stanford, USC, UCLA, Trinity, or Miami—even North Carolina or Arizona—you know that at least 80 percent of your team matches will be nothing more than casual warm-ups for tougher opponents. You can play in a fairly relaxed and confident frame of mind. So great is the disparity that the Big Three in California rarely trot out their big guns except for each other and a few other powerhouses, preferring instead to give their outstanding but lower ranked team members a chance to compete.

One year that I was at Stanford, ostensibly the eighth-ranking member of the squad, I played in more varsity matches than any of the top three players (again Tanner, Mayer, and Delaney), splitting my time between all six positions. Where I played depended on how tough our opponent was and who the coach wanted to use in that match. We never lost against secondary competition, and regarded such matches as almost a part of practice. If we wrapped up the win during singles play, as we often did, we'd generally go off for a real workout against each other and leave it to the jayvees to finish off the doubles.

One task we all had to face, though—whatever our ranking—was simply that of getting through school. After all, we were supposed to be getting an education. Perhaps surprisingly, most of us did. But there were others. . . .

Academically, college tennis players can probably best be broken down into two groups—the relatively small percentage who turn pro early on, and the vast majority who play all the way through school until they get their degrees. Seven years ago, Connors was about the only college player good enough to cast his lot with the pros. But as more and more money became available to more and more players, the list of collegians-turned-pro grew tremendously, and last year Tim Wilkison became the first U.S. youngster to play-for-pay directly out of high school. It's almost a foregone conclusion now that the best players will jump before the end of their college careers, as John McEnroe of Stanford already has.

Most of the players do get an education, though, and do get their degrees. In the 10 years he's been at Stanford, says Gould, "68 of my 70 players have graduated, and in a questionnaire given out earlier this year, five of my top eight said they were planning on going to grad school sometime in the future." And while those facts may reflect more on Stanford than on tennis players, it's true that during my years there most players were concerned as much with achieving academic success as athletic success.

Gene Mayer, for instance—one of Stanford's recent standouts—was one of the hardest working students on campus, although he tried to conceal it at times for fear of being called an egghead. His brother Sandy, an NCAA champion in both singles and doubles, has long pointed toward a career in law. Several of my teammates were in honors programs, and others—like Gerry Groslimond, now manager and director of tennis at Atlanta's mammoth Peachtree World of Tennis complex, and Craig Johnson, a stockbroker in San Francisco—have put their undergraduate degrees in business to good use in the outside world.

Still, people wonder how an athlete can keep up with his schoolwork when he or she is gone for several weeks, or even an entire quarter, to play tournaments in some remote corner of the world. The answer to that is that 10 or 15 years ago, before academic curricula became as flexible as they are today, it was difficult. But now, if absences can be anticipated, a player's schedule can be arranged to give him a lighter workload or more independent study to allow for travel. This year at Stanford, for example, McEnroe, Matt Mitchell, and Bill Maze managed to squeeze in a couple of midyear tournaments each at places as far away as Nassau and Great Britain, while still carrying full loads including courses such as "Radical Thought in Literature" and "Macroeconomics."

Again, this diligence is not entirely the rule. Tennis players, the same as everyone else, are not above "dogging it" now and then with "mick" courses. And once in a while a player will attempt to loaf along all the way through school. But the idlers are offset by the occasional tennis-playing intellectual—like concert pianist Jeff Borowiak, a former NCAA singles champion, and the brilliant Ferdi Taygan, a four-time All America, both of whom played at UCLA.

It's been my experience that really when you get right down to it, the dumb jock who needs tutoring and academic string-pulling to remain eligible just doesn't exist in tennis. Tennis players can often be narrow-minded and overly tennis-oriented, but most of them seem as bent on achieving good academic records as any other students in school.

The other side of the eligibility coin, though, is professionalism, and that's an area where college tennis players have had to resort to some creativity to maintain their "amateur" status. Major violations, because of tennis' glass walls, are relatively nonexistent. "If there have been any violations," says Gould, in reply to a question about large under-the-table payments, "I've never known about them. And I don't want to." There is, however, a growing problem with minor violations.

When I entered college, the rules were rather vague, stating something to the effect that a player, when competing off-campus, could accept only expense money, which theoretically had to be arranged with a tournament director before the tournament in question began. What usually happened was that a player would win, say, $350 in such a tournament, and then he and the tournament director would sit down and work out a list of expenses— $200 for air fare, two nights at a hotel at $50 a night, and $50 for meals. That would come out to $350; that's what he would get, and no one would be the wiser.

Since then, though, the NCAA has established a strict set of per diem amounts that are supposed to limit expense payments—but rarely do. No one has ever gotten rich from these small money situations; a college tennis player's overall costs usually far exceed whatever he makes. But a strict interpretation of the rules, if he ever got caught, could put him in a lot of trouble.

Another rule that creates a worse problem is the one that prohibits a player from accepting gifts of any kind from a manufacturer or distributor of tennis equipment. Such a gift is considered promotional in nature and, therefore, makes the player a pro. But it's a rule that's unfair.

A football player, for example, doesn't need a full set of equipment to go out and throw a football around all summer; all he needs is a football. But a tennis player often needs hundreds of dollars' worth of rackets, clothes, shoes, and balls before he can step onto a court to play. Fortunately, just about every talented junior player in the nation has been getting this kind of help. There is hardly anyone who doesn't, or hasn't, accepted equipment. The NCAA rule just makes it more difficult for players to get the kind of help they need, and needlessly turns just about everyone into an offender.

What the NCAA fails to understand, or take into account, is the competitive nature of tennis which permeates the sport at every level. For both men and women, college tennis is just one more long competition among many—a way station on the trail that begins with the juniors and leads through the various levels of the game, eventually, it's hoped, to the top of the pro ranks.

If the NCAA fails to recognize that, though, the coaches do. And as a result, the sense of the individual is rarely lost in college, even in team practice.

Gould ran our practices at Stanford, and runs them today, pretty much the same as other coaches. Practice begins officially around 3 P.M., although some get out to hit a few or play a set earlier. In the fall, he works the team on drills he sets up, uses videotapes or ball machines where he thinks it will help, works in some doubles, and ends up each session with some tough physical conditioning. But as the year goes along, the players are left more and more to their own devices, to practice almost any way that they feel is best for them or will help them the most.

To the outsider, a practice session like that can appear unstructured to the point of chaos. But Gould recognizes that it has to be that way. "I don't police much," he says. "Everyone's pretty good about hitting serves and returns every day, and after that I leave it up to them a great deal."

Toley of USC, rated by many the best coach in college tennis, stresses the individual even more so. "I'll lose a year of matches with a kid," he says, "to get him to improve a facet of the game in which he's lacking. If the kid only feels secure at net, then I'll make him play back all year, even if he loses for a while, because that's the only way he'll ever become a complete player."

With all the competition, with all the players working so hard on their own, with the increased exposure college tennis is getting these days, you'd think that the quality of collegiate play would be on the rise. But Toley, for one, says that's not the case at all.

"Even though there are more good players," he says, "the top players are not as good as they used to be. Just at UCLA about 15 years ago, they had four kids at one time ranked in the top 20 in the country—[Arthur] Ashe, [Charlie] Pasarell, [Dave] Sanderlin, and [Whitney] Reed. Another seven or eight, like [Clark] Graebner, [Marty] Riessen, [Frank] Froehling, and [Chuck] McKinley, were scattered around the country. Perhaps 12 or 14 of the top 20 in the nation were in college." That compares with only two collegians in the U.S. top 50 this year—McEnroe at No. 10 and Eliot Teltscher at No. 23.

Part of the reason is that the better players turn pro sooner. But there's more to it than that, says Toley: "The competition today wrings kids dry. Before, when all those players could go out and win tournaments and then return to school confident and sitting pretty, so to speak, they could thrive on success. Today, there's too much competition all around the world at all times from too many players for that sort of thing to happen. The collegians get beaten down, and it takes them longer to mature."

Toley's views further illustrate one intractable axiom about college tennis—that its fate is inseparably tied to that of the pro game. But that, in the long run, may not be bad. Agent-promoter Donald Dell insists, in fact, it could be a big plus for college tennis in years to come.

"Five years from now, when purses have doubled and there's a big tournament every week," he said recently, "there is little chance that collegians will rule the game as they once did. But, still, the college game will be healthier than ever before. The campus has been returned to the true amateur, and a wise policy of recruiting restrictions and scholarship cutbacks is beginning to spread the talent out. The California schools will be tough, but they should find some company at the top soon. And in another parallel to the pros, women's tennis will add an exciting new dimension to intercollegiate athletics and provide academic opportunities for a whole new group of people."

For now, though, big-time college tennis remains a four-year pressure cooker that attempts to harden young athletes as heat tempers steel. Some will take it and thrive; others will fall by the wayside. But I guess when you're shooting for that pot of gold at the end of the rainbow maybe that's the way it has to be.

TROTTING

WHY HORSES DON'T BET ON PEOPLE

By D. L. Stewart

From The Dayton Journal Herald
Copyright, ©, 1978, The Journal Herald, Dayton, Ohio

In my behalf, it should be pointed out that the area of Cleveland in which I grew up was not your basic bluegrass country.

The only horses that ever made it to our neighborhood came in dog food cans. You could live on my block for two or three lifetimes without ever seeing a saddle, bridle, or a pile of fertilizer. In my crowd, we figured the only reason to ride a horse was if you were too dumb to hotwire an ignition.

None of which prepared me for the experience of driving a harness horse at Lebanon Raceway.

The concept of taking a harness horse for a few quick laps first comes up at a cocktail party this past summer. It doesn't even sound like a good idea at the time.

"There's nothing to it," insists Jerry Nardiello, the Lebanon publicity man. "There's absolutely no danger. I guarantee it."

The longer the cocktail party lasts, the less hazardous seems the idea of driving a harness horse. Cocktail parties have a way of doing that to me. Sometimes in the final stages of cocktail parties I am convinced I can thrash the stuffings out of Muhammad Ali and/or Mean Joe Green.

I have a vague recollection, therefore, of telling Jerry Nardiello that, if he can find an owner dumb enough to risk a horse, I will be glad to drive it. And/or thrash the stuffings out of it.

Two days later, my tongue has returned to its normal size and I have forgotten all about my promise. Jerry Nardiello, unfortunately, has not.

"It's all set," he says when he calls me early in October. "I've got you a horse, a sulky, and even a set of silks for you to wear."

"Yeah, but, Jerry you don't understand. You see, my columns are written pretty far ahead. By the time I could get around to writing about driving a horse, I'm sure the weather will be too cold."

"Not at all," he says. "Our season goes on until December 2. Maybe longer if we can get an extension."

"Gosh, that's, uh, great. And you say you have silks for me to wear? What color are they?"

"Mostly yellow."

"Good choice."

Several days later I am in Lebanon, sitting with Jerry Nardiello and Mahlon Nixon, the track's director of racing. We are having lunch and discussing my impending ride, which is scheduled to happen as soon as we are done with our meal.

"You're absolutely sure this is safe?" I ask Jerry Nardiello again as the waitress serves our soup.

"Well, nothing is entirely without danger. There's always the slim possibility of mishap."

"When was the last time the slim possibility of a mishap took place here?" I demand.

Jerry Nardiello stares into his soup. "Let me think a second."

"Tell me the truth," I demand, jabbing my salad fork in Mahlon Nixon's direction, "how much danger is involved in driving a harness horse?"

"Well, if a horse is 'on the bit,' he might pull your arms out of their sockets," he says. "If that happens, remember you're not allowed to leave your arms on the track.

"More likely, though," he continues, "you could get thrown from your cart. If that happens, sometimes the shafts splinter and horses run over you. Up in Chicago one time, I saw a driver flip in the air and come down on another horse's back. Damnedest thing you ever saw.

"Also, you want to stay away from the rail. You get thrown into the rail and you can get a pretty good concussion. Mostly, though, you'd probably just break something. Old Elmer Conrad, from over in Indiana, he's had three or four broken legs."

"But not all at the same time," Jerry Nardiello puts in, hastily.

Despite my suggestion that a third dessert would be nice, lunch comes to an end and it is time for us to drive to the track. To take my mind off splintered shafts, flipping drivers, and old Elmer Conrad's hobby of breaking his legs, I review the research I have done in preparation for this afternoon.

Harness horses, I learned, come in two varieties: pacers and trotters. Pacers, the faster of the two, move the front and back legs on the same side of their bodies forward at the same time. Trotters don't.

Horses that carry little men on their backs are known as thoroughbreds and trace their lineage back to three Arabian stallions: Darley Arabian, Q Godolphin Barb, and Byerly Turk.

Harness horses, on the other hoof, are called standardbreds. Ninety-nine percent of today's standardbreds trace their lines back to Hambletonian, who was born in 1849.

All of this is very important to horse owners, although there is no reason to believe that the horses themselves care much one way or another.

We arrive at the track, where we are directed to the barn in which the horses belonging to the Jim Ferguson Stables are located. The Jim Ferguson Stables, I am told, have agreed to provide the horse I will drive.

"I wonder why they'd be willing to do that?" I ask.

"Jim's out of town," someone says.

We walk into a large, incredibly clean barn, where the sulky and the silks are waiting for me.

"The name of your horse is Choo Choo Time," a groom tells me. "She's a six-year-old mare with bowed tendons who just had a foal."

"She sounds like a mess. Maybe you ought to put her in the sulky and let me pull."

"I don't think you'll want to do that. She's about 16 hands high."

"Is that big for a horse?"

"Fairly big. Take a look for yourself. She's over in that stall there."

By "fairly big," the groom means "just slightly smaller than the state of Idaho." Choo Choo Time, I suspect, is the one who pulls the Budweiser wagon on the Clydesdales' day off.

"Do you want to open the door and bring her out of her stall?" the groom asks.

"Why should I open it? If she wants out, she can just step over it."

Eventually, Choo Choo Time is led out of her stall and attached to the cart. It is a jog cart, which is different than the sulkies used in actual races.

"How is it different?" I ask Mahlon Nixon.

"A jog cart has bigger tires," he says, "and it's larger. That gives you a more comfortable ride. Plus, you sit a little further back from your horse, which is nice when she lifts her tail."

"What do you mean 'when she lifts her tail'? What happens then?"

"Oh, nothing much," Mahlon Nixon shrugs, "it's no big deal."

I am still pondering that as the groom shows me how to get onto the cart, sitting on it backward first and then swinging my legs around to the front. When I am securely in place, the groom unties Choo Choo Time's halter line and leads us out of the barn. At least, I assume there is a groom leading us. When you are sitting in a little cart behind a 1,500-pound horse with middle-aged spread, your horizons are somewhat limited.

Suddenly we are on the track. We roll past Jerry Nardiello. We roll past Mahlon Nixon. We roll past the groom. Wait a minute. That can't be right. If the groom is behind us, that means . . .

Then we are on our own, just me and Choo Choo Time and the knot of fear in the pit of my stomach.

It is, I am surprised to discover, not all that unpleasant an experience. The gentle motion of the cart. The bracing wind in my face. The rhythmic clop-clop-clop of the horse's hooves. It is all so enjoyable that, midway through the first lap, I make a decision. I will open my eyes.

As we come out of the turn and approach the finish line, I spot Jerry Nardiello. He is waving his arms.

"Take her around for a few more laps," he shouts.

"She needs the exercise."

On the second lap, I notice more than the bracing wind in my face. Choo Choo Time's hooves are kicking up gravel that flies back in the breeze. And her mouth is producing little specks of foam. By the time we are in the backstretch again, the little specks are becoming a horizontal shower. I haven't seen that much spit since the World Series. There is a pair of goggles on top of my helmet, but the thought of taking one hand off the reins and reaching up to pull them down is not worth serious consideration. Besides, it could be worse.

On the third lap, it is worse. Choo Choo Time lifts her tail. Mahlon Nixon was wrong. It is too a big thing. And getting bigger every second.

I'm not sure who it was that first came up with that line about not putting the cart before the horse. But I'm pretty sure he never drove a sulky.

HOCKEY

THE PUCK STOPS HERE

By Jack Mann

From The Washington Post Sunday Magazine
Copyright, ©, 1978, The Washington Post

"Success is failure turned inside out," one of the photocopied inspirations on Tom McVie's desk exhorted iambically. "You never can tell how close you are. It may be near when it seems so far."

Light-years, it seemed to McVie, 42-year-old coach of the Washington Capitals of the National Hockey League, the least successful aggregation of professional game-players in the history of the jockstrap. The night before the Caps had failed to win for McVie for the one-hundred-thirtieth time in twenty-five months, snatching a tie from the jaws of victory with two seconds left on the clock—at home.

"It is," McVie said softly, "like trying to win the bleeping Kentucky Derby with a bleeping mule." He ignored the loud bang on the door of his office and told how, during his team's recent twenty-game winless streak, "There were times—people will think this is bull—I wished I'd die. I just became an old man." Another bang on the door.

But the flaky kid who dived into the white water of the Columbia River for the hell of it had lived to be a coach in the big league of jet lag and room service. McVie was reminded of one of pro sports' hoarier clichés, that being in the big league is like sex: when it's good it's very good, and when it's bad it's not bad. Weren't columnists in places like Seattle still writing their amazement that the Joy Boy of the Western League had been anointed a leader of high-priced men? Two more bangs on the door.

"A lot of people," McVie said, "didn't think I would ever make it to be an ordinary citizen." Bang. Bang.

The little coach opened the door to the dressing room and beheld the pinkish mass of Robert Picard, wearing nothing but a sheepish smile and holding a hockey stick ready to slap another puck against his boss's door. The Quebecois, Washington's prize in the 1977 amateur draft, is 20 years old. By the time he is 25, Abe Pollin and his associates will have paid him about a half-million dollars to do what he can in their defense.

"Rookie," McVie said as he closed the door. Then he smiled. "I have to remember that he's a little boy—a big little boy. I have to remind myself.

"I like all these kids," said the coach, whose income in 17 years as a hockey player peaked at $14,000, "and made me feel like I'd pulled a Brink's job.

"I'm glad they have their big contracts and their cars," he went on. "But sometimes, when they tell me what they think is a sad story . . . that their girl friend is coming in at Dulles, so if they go to practice there'll be nobody to pick her up . . . well, I feel like saying come in my office and I'll tell you some stories that'll make you cry."

Perhaps the young man could not relate to the dangers McVie has passed, e.g., a near-miss at ending up a skeleton in the Canadian Rockies or, perhaps worse, a hockey bum. If not, Tom could bring in his wife, Arlene. She could tell them about riding five days in a car, sitting on a pillow, from Toledo to Seattle, because the firstborn son in her arms was barely two weeks old. "We'd have to stop at gas stations where they had a coal or wood stove, to heat a bottle," she recalls. Mrs. McVie had to leave the hospital the third day (a short stay for maternity in 1957) because International League player contracts did not provide Blue Cross, or much else. The hospital warned the young father it would not release the patient—he still wonders which one— without full payment. Tommy tapped all their money from the bank and borrowed another hundred.

McVie was raised to hard times. One day when he was nine years old McVie had an experience that had an impact on his young mind as searing as the guided tour of the Inferno that Virgil gave Dante. He grew up in the company (Consolidated Mining and Smelting) town of Trail, British Columbia. McVie's father worked in the melting room, at 150 degrees or so, pouring molten zinc into 140-pound ingots. The elder McVie was neither absent nor tardy—Coach McVie's driven, disciplined flock of Capitals will roll their eyes at this—for 40 years, and the day he finally felt he couldn't hack it he went to the office and retired. During World War II, C.M. & S. was the largest smelter of its kind in the world and production demands were high. One day McVie's father sent a message down the hill that he'd be working 16 hours and would need an extra lunch.

"I carried it up there," Tommy recalls, "about 11 o'clock at night. The security guard let me in and I saw my dad in his asbestos clothing, with the furnaces blazing behind him. Kids in the town would quit school in the tenth grade and go into the mine; it was the only thing to do. But I knew right then, whatever I did with my life, that wasn't going to be it."

The alternatives were limited. The only opportunity to go abroad from Trail was the annual excursion on the company train to Nelson, 40 miles away, where there was a lake. Young Tom learned to dive in the company pool and at 15 the company sent him 90 miles to Kelowna to win the British Columbia (it's the size of Texas) junior springboard diving championship.

McVie in recent years has watched his three sons swim from Sandy Island, a sort of beach made by a gentle eddy of the surly river, "and had my heart in my throat." He has not forgotten his family's flight to higher ground when he was 13 and the Columbia poured five feet of white water into their homestead on its bank. Tommy was 12 the first time he swam the mile-wide river. "The normal current was about 15 miles an hour, so it could take you five miles downstream." The swim was, naturally, a rite of passage for the company town's lads and from time to time a pubescent body would wash up on Dead Man's Eddy, three miles down.

But however hairbreadth some of the margins have been, Tommy McVie is a survivor and how are you going to keep them down in the mine after they've seen Kelowna? So it was in 1951, at the end of tenth grade, just before his sixteenth birthday, that Tom, and a buddy who had a little English car, set out on one of the two uphill roads that led out of Trail to somewhere else. Anywhere else.

"It was time to go," McVie explained. "My father knew that; he left home in Scotland at 14. Scotch people don't hug and kiss like the French and Italians, but I think it was one of the happiest moments of my father's pretty lousy life when he saw me getting away from the mine.

"And my mother never cared much for me anyway." Tom's mother in two marriages had five daughters, all older than her one son, and never really came to understand why a boy would jump off the roof of the company ice rink, bashing his face with his knees when he landed, just because somebody said he wouldn't do it.

"The town was getting too small for me," Tom decided at the time and the town was beginning to agree. With one movie theater burned down and the other flushed out by that 1948 flood, the only entertainments were the live shows the company brought into the rink. McVie and his chums gained free admission to some of those by measures that could be construed, by a harsh critic, as breaking and entering. Then they took some stuff from a grocery and got in some other troubles and in a small town everybody talks. It seemed to Tom that his parents were always mad at him.

So by midsummer of 1951 he was employing his 5-foot-nothing, 135-pound body to push and shovel wheelbarrows of wet cement at a construction site somewhere north of Edmonton, Alberta, for something like $1.35 an hour. McVie thinks of that adventure these days, driving through the road construction on Central Avenue, on the way to the Capitals' morning practice at Fort Dupont.

And his players hear about those road workers: "I see those poor bastards out there, up to their ass in mud. I saw them when I came out here and they'll still be there when I go back. And in between all I'm asking you guys to do is concentrate for an hour and a half on playing hockey. If you can't do that, don't waste my time." Give up playing games, McVie clearly implies, and go to work. It is an abhorrent concept to a career jock, especially one who can offer no more employable skills than Tom McVie had in 1951.

He did not think of himself at 16 as a hockey player, though he had been "one of the best three or four" in the peewee, bantam, and midget competitions around his hometown. One truth McVie had come to accept was that he was too small. But construction work that summer had put 15 pounds on him and, with overtime, more than $400 in his pocket. So he hopped a bus to Medicine Hat, Alberta, to try out for the Tigers of the Western Canada Junior League.

Tom did not survive the final cut. ("And they didn't make any mistake," he says, with characteristic, sometimes jarring candor. "There were better players there.") While the training camp lasted, however, Tommy went first cabin. That four hundred bucks burned at both ends and they still talk in Medicine Hat of the lovely light it gave. "I don't know how a guy can be a hero when he's cut from the team after one game," hockey reporter Bob Fachet of *The Washington Post* said after a tour of the Canadian prairies, "but McVie is a legend in Medicine Hat."

"I blew it all," McVie recalls, not remorsefully, "eating and drinking. They still tell stories about me out West." They do, and a number of them read like final chapters, particularly one all-she-wrote ultimatum from his wife. "I think now," Tommy said recently, "that I wasn't really having such a good time all those years." It would take him 17 years of minor-league hockey to reach that conclusion.

"If I had my life to live over," McVie's introspection continued, "I'd always be a hockey player. But if I changed one thing, I'd be a straight arrow. In L.A., Portland, Medicine Hat, everybody has a Tom McVie story. It's taken six years to shake the reputation."

McVie was never really a crooked arrow. He was always free of the satyriasis that opportunity inflicts upon so many professional athletes and his drink was beer. But he was a funcoholic, a clown, who frequented bars because they were laughing places, men's places, where you could sing and tell jokes "and just screw around." Hockey needed those six years to be able to take Tommy seriously.

"When you're winning," McVie said recently, talking about the curfews, rules of dress, and other behavior limitations he imposes on his Capitals, "you can do a headstand on the bar and sing, and nobody will say anything." McVie has done headstands on bars, singing.

It was the man-to-man fun that was narcotic to Tommy. While hockey players may be the most obscene of athletes (using the present participle of that four-letter, not-really-Anglo-Saxon verb as an inscrutable part of speech: "I'm bleeping going home"), they are otherwise little different from baseball players in their dressing-room persiflage. They caress each other with personal insults that would start fights in genteel society and it is great fun.

But then it ends. "When a practice or a game was over," McVie recalls, "and the guys would finally be dressed and start going home, it would break my heart." That brittle camaraderie was Arlene McVie's rival for all the 14 years in the Western League until the season in Phoenix, which for her was the last ho-ho. The money, in keeping with Tommy's 400-goal status, was good, but nothing else was. "It was a new franchise and it wasn't competitive," McVie says now. "Not as bad as here, but bad. A bunch of Good-Time Charlies, too much happiness. My bride said, 'That's it. You play here another season and I won't be here.' I think she meant the end of everything."

La commedia e finita. There were some scenes in her hockey-wife career that Arlene wouldn't care to rerun and the Phoenix experience is No. 1. "The team was a lot of guys out to have a ball. I liked them personally, but they were there strictly to have a party. The situation wasn't that great for Tommy."

It was another close call. McVie got himself traded to Seattle, stopped drinking beer (he still doesn't), and started thinking. "If I hadn't been such a comedian," he thought, "if I'd been a little more dedicated, maybe I'd have been on one of those six teams. You never know."

If McVie had trained on prune juice and thought beautiful thoughts all his years as a left wing, he still would have been a long shot to make the teams in Montreal, Boston, New York, Toronto, Detroit, and Chicago, which were all the cities the National Hockey League comprised in those years. Now there are 18 franchises, but by the time the league was expanding, Tommy's powers were contracting.

At age 36, he voluntarily went down a rung to play against 20-year-olds in the International League, for about a quarter of the money he'd been making as the most rewarded member of the Western League. "I was campaigning," McVie said, "for the new Tom McVie." New Tom was elected. John Ferguson, now general manager of the New York Rangers, nominated McVie to manage the Boston Bruins' International League team at Dayton. "Is he drinking?" was the only question Bruins' general manager Harry Sinden asked.

"Every day I go to work I'm grateful to those two guys," McVie says. "After 20 years, it seemed like I couldn't get a job in hockey. And I don't know what else I could have done."

Those were the same circumstances McVie, "a 16-year-old man," had faced 20 years earlier, after playing big spender in Medicine Hat. Stony-broke, Tom didn't know how to get out of town, or where to go. Nick Yanchuk, also cut from the team and also broke, was given a bus ticket because the Tigers had invited him to try out; McVie was a walk-on. But Nick proposed they hitchhike to Yanchuk's home in Vancouver. That was about 700 miles, over the Rockies, and it was October, the beginning of Canadian winter.

"We got a ride from some guy who must have been a forest ranger," McVie said. "He turned off and left us nowhere, about 10,000 feet up in the Rockies, snowing. We were beginning to think seriously about freezing to death when a guy came along in a Ford Meteor. He said he was going to Vancouver and we said 'So are we.' Then you could see him thinking, 'Oh-oh,' about picking up two young animals like us. It took about 200 miles before he was convinced we weren't going to rob him."

The Yanchuks, a generous family, took Tommy in and he didn't think seriously about hockey for that winter or the next. He got a job as a redcap, then in the freight department, of the Canadian Pacific Railroad, paid $50 a month board and played hockey for fun in the city league. "Life was OK," McVie recalls. He could see no future in hockey; he had tried out on the prairies and been found wanting. "Anyway, I was a midget."

But he wasn't suddenly. At 19, with a year's eligibility in junior hockey remaining, Tom McVie was nearly 5-10, nearly 180 pounds, "nearly the ideal size for a winger." Clearly, it was time for another narrow escape— from the OK life.

Kenny Ullyott, coach of the junior team at Prince Albert, Saskatchewan, gave McVie a tryout. "And surprise! I was a good player. I didn't know it until I heard the guy on the radio say, 'The hottest prospect in camp is this kid from Vancouver.'"

McVie made the team and the all-star team. His "amateur" contract was for $175 a month. After the first month he asked for $225 and got it. (Ullyott, having observed the hot prospect's fluidity in the beer parlor, put $75 a month in the bank for him.) Then Tommy's hockey career ended again. He was caught in a pub, under age, and Ullyott bounced him off the team. One mistake, McVie pleaded. "You didn't show me you wanted to play," Ullyott said.

The Capitals moaned two years ago when "Simon" McVie ordained that all their practices, including the 45-minute passing-shooting drill on game day, would be conducted not in sweat suits but in full, 14-pound combat upholstery. "A batter don't swing a little piece of pulp in the on-deck circle and then pick up the real bat to hit," McVie analogized. The players were not only inconvenienced but, like Marines ordered to carry full field pack on parade, insulted. The Caps were easily inconvenienced in those days. "They'd come to practice at Tysons Corner rink a half-hour late," McVie remembers sourly, "and explain there were barrels on the road [Beltway construction barricades]. 'Then get up earlier,' I said." On his sixth day as coach, at game 17 of a 25-game winless streak, McVie called for unheard-of twice-daily practices. "It was," team captain Bill Clement said, "downright painful. You could see it in our faces." And hear it in their voices. The out-of-shape Caps lost a collective 160 pounds in McVie's first month, with the coach weighing them personally. And they grumbled and moaned.

It would be an exaggeration to say the midwinter climate of Prince Albert, on the banks of the Saskatchewan River, is as severe as Murmansk's. Actually the prairie town is at 53 degrees north latitude, like Petropavlovsk on the Siberian steppes. A steppe is a prairie is a steppe. It was 60 degrees below zero when Tommy McVie went out to skate, wearing all the socks and underwear he had. "I know I was the only person in town who was outdoors," McVie recalled. "They say after it gets lower than 20 degrees below it don't make any difference. Well, they don't know. When you breathe in at 60 degrees below, you don't feel cold; you feel like a hot poker is being shoved down your throat.

"And there I am out there, doing sprints and stops. Ullyott came out in his car to watch me. He was there just a few minutes and I could hear the crack when his tires broke away from the ice." McVie believes he scourged himself to his mortal limit: 30 minutes a day of swallowing the hot poker, for three days. "And the third day I had my mind made up: If he don't take me back, that's it. I ain't going to do any more."

His first game back as a Prince Albert Minto ("I don't know what a Minto is; I never asked"), Tommy scored four goals including the winner as the Mintos beat Humboldt in overtime, 7–6. So the McVie career was launched one more time. As New York Ranger property, he would get a call from general manager Muzz Patrick. Tom summered in Vancouver, working in construction to build himself up, skating every day at a rink (where he met

Arlene, an eight-hour-a-day skater about to join the Ice Follies chorus), and waging box lacrosse, a sideline that would keep the McVie ménage solvent for a decade. There was no call, but a letter from Patrick: sorry, but the Rangers had too many guys in their camp. And McVie, it said between the lines, had only one of three years' junior hockey experience that was, and is, considered requisite. Tom was 20 and it was too late.

The next season Andy Mulligan gave McVie a chance with his International League team in Toledo. Two chances, really. "At the [roster] cutoff date, it was between me and another guy. I know the other guy was better," McVie declared. "But Andy kept me, because of my hustle—and because Tommy was going to be born in February. I didn't set any records in Toledo but I busted my ass for him." It was Mulligan who put up the extra hundred bucks to ransom Tom McVie IV from the hospital.

"Hustle," says one of the photocopied inspirations McVie has handed out to his team, "is maximum effort joyfully expressed."

Like George Allen, whom he admires, McVie believes winning is a matter of motivation. "And after what I went through, I think I can motivate people. I'm tough with these players; I stand up to them. But somebody stood up to me at Prince Albert, didn't he? and made me prove I wanted to play hockey?

"And hockey may have saved me from . . . I think it was that close."

Something in Tom McVie's shtick worked. In his first full season as coach of the Capitals, a team that won 19 games in its first two years of existence, he led them to a 24–42–14 record. A Coach of the Year poll had him second to Scotty Bowman of Montreal, which wins as many games as it wants. McVie was doing something right, despite a beginning Les Canadiens might call gauche.

"All I can say," McVie said as a preamble to recounting the embarrassing experience, "is that my enthusiasm was pure." Watching from a Capital Center Sky Suite with General Manager Max McNab as Montreal blitzed the Caps, 6–0, McVie could see exactly what needed to be done. After two successful campaigns coaching the Dayton Gems, he said, "I believed in myself. I really thought that in about a month and a half I'd have the whole thing straightened out and we'd be winning on a regular basis."

The team McVie took over on December 30, 1975, was 3–28–5. He would coach 12 games in the big league before he won one. "But I bounced out of the Sheraton-Lanham every morning for the first three or four days," McVie recalls, the trace of a blush around his boneless nose. " 'Gentlemen,' I would say, 'I have these things planned for today. We'll do some two-on-ones, some three-on-ones . . .' And I saw the looks on them, like 'this guy is bleeping crazy.' I went on with it and they just leaned on their sticks and listened. Finally I asked if anybody had anything to say."

"Why are we doing all this," inquired defenseman Bob Paradis, who had become a Capital just in time to be in on the winless streak, "when we know we're going to bleeping lose anyway?"

"Well, then," said McVie, "why don't we all go to Mr. Pollin's office and tell him we are disbanding the team?" Then, cooling down, he said: "You may as well get used to it. I'm not going to get any different."

He didn't. McVie took 60 people to camp at Hershey, Penn., last fall, worked them from 6 A.M. to midnight and came back to Washington feeling he had picked the right 20. "We've done our work," he said to McNab after the Caps had held Montreal to a 4–3 score "and shoulda won it."

And then they didn't win for 42 days: 20 games without a victory.

"God," McVie said to McNab as the winless streak rolled on, from October into December, "we've won two games. We could have done that without having a training camp. We coulda gone out and got drunk and won three or four, couldn't we?"

McVie fudges the question whether his team has ever made him cry. "I've walked off with tears in my eyes," he said. "It's a hurtin' you can't believe. Nobody will ever know: not Max, not my wife." Certainly not the players.

"I can't explain it," said McVie, his eyes seeming darker and deeper, "and I guess I shouldn't say this, but that [20-game slump] done more hurt to me than anything in my life and we had a baby boy die, just a couple days old."

The coach says things he shouldn't say, the most famous being, "I'd rather find out my wife is cheating than go on losing like this."

"Good line," Arlene said. "I was in Portland when somebody told me about it and I said, 'Oh, God, that sounds like something he'd say.' He's a very funny man and it [losing] has not taken away his sense of humor. We never argue. We make smart remarks at each other all the time, but that's not arguing.

"In fact Tommy is a nicer person since he's been coaching. He's a very poor loser, but he was that as a player and I'm used to it. I'm sure people think he must be a maniac at home, but he's learned that all the players aren't made like him; they can't try as hard as he does.

"When he comes home after losing," McVie's wife said, "he sits and stares into space for a while and then he becomes tolerable. I pretty much ignore him because I don't have the answers to his problems.

"I'm just pretty careful to do and say the right things," Arlene McVie concluded.

Arlene's mother tries, too. One night in the latter throes of the 20-game streak Tommy came home and his mother-in-law greeted him with the thought that "it's just a game."

"It was a tough line to top," McVie said, "but she did it." He came home with deep, dark eyes the night of the most unkindest cut: The Caps had their expansion peers, the Colorado Rockies, beaten at 19:58 of the final period and had to settle for a tie.

"Another day," his mother-in-law said as Tommy stared into space, "another dollar."

"I wish I'd said that," Thomas Ballantyne McVie said, and went to bed.

GOLF

RAGGEDY ANDY'S CLOSING CHARGE

By Joe Gergen

From Newsday
Copyright, ©, 1978, Newsday, Inc.

The rules of the United States Golf Association do not specify that the U.S. Open should be a classic. And it's fortunate for all concerned that they don't. Otherwise, the 153 shot-makers who started the seventy-eighth Open would be forced to return to the Cherry Pits Country Club today and keep playing until they get it right.

And hardly anyone was eager to play another 18 at Cherry Pits, not even if it meant a championship. When Andy North dropped a 40-inch putt on the seventy-second hole after what seemed an interminable wait, J. C. Snead and Dave Stockton appeared to be as relieved as the winner. Had North missed, there would have been an 18-hole playoff. "I told Dave just before the shot," Snead recalled, " 'I don't know if I want a playoff or not.' "

Snead's reluctance was understandable considering the conduct of yesterday's final round. Had the course been a few holes longer, they would have needed stretchers for the survivors. As it was, the top three barely finished on their feet. The closing charge by Raggedy Andy went like this: Bogey, double-bogey, par, par, bogey. And he almost was blown off his Foot-Joys by the wind as he stood over the winning putt.

It was the sort of Open which will not be chiseled into America's consciousness. It was an Open in which no player matched par, in which one player was assessed a two-stroke penalty for delay of game, in which two players disqualified themselves for incorrect scorecards and left others wishing they had thought of that, in which two players completely whiffed on balls in the rough, in which the most memorable swing was a tee shot which slammed into a lake and then miraculously reappeared on the fairway. It was a gas.

Consider that the last Open at Cherry Pits was so scintillating that a memorial to the event was constructed by the old first tee, honoring Arnold Palmer for his victory and his achievement of driving the first green. This time around it has been suggested a similar plaque be placed on the Port-a-John alongside the thirteenth tee where Nicklaus apparently left his hopes for a fourth Open title during Saturday's third round. He entered the water closet even par and said later he lost concentration, triple-bogeying the hole. He finished four shots back.

Was he sorry he went to the bathroom? "No," he said. "I had to go."

There was one other possibility for a permanent marker. "I think they should put a monument in the lake on 18 where J.C.'s ball hit," Stockton said. Snead, in his best aw-shucks manner, allowed as how it wasn't anything special. "I saw Dave choke and hit one over in the rough," Snead said, "so I just played a little low shot and skipped it over the water." And then both men laughed at the implausible finish.

Snead was thankful to finish second. He played almost the entire final round without putting his spikes to a fairway. He spent so much time in sand that if you held his wedge to your ear, you could hear the ocean. He discovered 18 different species of flora and fauna the membership did not even know existed. "We'd have finished a half hour earlier," Stockton cracked, "if J.C. hadn't been all over the course." And that's the man who finished in a second-place tie with a one-over 72 yesterday.

Stockton also had a final 72, which was admirable under the circumstances. Among the finest shot-makers in the world, Nicklaus had a 73, Johnny Miller a 74, Gary Player a 77, Severiano Ballesteros a 77, Tom Kite a 77, and Mark Hayes a 79. The only charges made at Cherry Pits yesterday were for impersonating a contender. Almost everyone was found guilty.

Although North took the bows, the real winners were the 18 scenic holes hacked out of a cherry orchard under the supervision of noted architect Bill Flynn (who was largely responsible for the design of Shinnecock Hills in Southampton) and recently remodeled by Arnold Palmer and partner Ed Seay. Unfortunately, it was impossible for the USGA to call each hazard up to the clubhouse for a pat on the back. But I would like to take this opportunity to note the part they played in this tournament.

Let's have a hand for the deceptively simple bank around the fourth hole, where Nicklaus double-bogeyed yesterday by sculling a pitch shot. And, of course, the trap on 15 which cost North such grief. And, well, what can you say about the lake at 18 that hasn't been said? Certainly the rough and its keeper deserve special praise.

Certainly, Arnie finished a winner, even if he failed to make the cut. His finishing round of 65 in 1960 was never threatened. Nor was his final score of 280. Not only did no one drive the first hole, many were thankful to get there in two. Lee Trevino required five strokes to reach that green on Saturday. So Palmer, the golf-course designer, succeeded admirably.

Trevino had predicted earlier in the week that a lot of his fellow pros would be "leaking oil" marching up the eighteenth fairway Sunday. And he was right. A few could have used lube jobs, as well. And then there was Player, who reasoned that a man who needed a par four on 18 to win the tournament would find his "tonsils talking." North's tonsils were singing all the way home, and all he needed was a bogey.

And that's the way it was at Cherry Pits in 1978, the year the Open was won by a man who only the previous day had been misidentified as Andy Bean by a newsman. RaggedyAndy held on to win the Open which everyone seemed determined to lose. "Thank heavens," the winner said, "it's over."

TENNIS

COURTING THE STARS

By Pete Axthelm

From Newsweek
Copyright, ©, 1978, Newsweek, Inc.
All rights reserved
Reprinted by permission

The U.S. Open had barely begun last week when the enormous pressure of the occasion descended upon Lornie Kuhle. Jimmy Connors, Lornie's friend and hero, was not in a good mood. First, Connors vented his anger by whipping a hapless first-round opponent. Then he decided that he wanted to slip away from fans, reporters, and other annoyances. That was when he turned to Lornie, Jimmy's personal version of a familiar phenomenon in modern tennis—the Walk Around Guy.

As the name suggests, the Walk Around Guy can usually be found striding just behind the modern tennis prima donna. He or she may be called a coach or cornerman, Svengali or sycophant. But whatever the title, the requirements of the job are fairly standard: Bags must be toted, backs slapped, players reassured about how great they are. And when a tough match is over, the Walk Around Guy must be able to say—and truly believe it—"We won it."

Kuhle, a 34-year-old veteran who once walked around with male chauvinist profiteer Bobby Riggs, rose quickly to Connors's challenge last week. He had already surveyed the grounds of the brand-new National Tennis Center in Flushing Meadow, N.Y., so he knew the best escape routes for his pouting friend. He ushered Jimbo into a waiting limo and locked the car door with a note of finality. When an eager young girl thrust a phone number toward Connors, Lornie opened the window and grabbed it without a wasted motion. When Jimmy recalled that he had left a case of steaks behind in the locker room, Lornie hustled away to retrieve the meat. And when Jimmy finally smiled with satisfaction, Lornie smiled with him.

I watched this performance with more than casual interest because I was about to fulfill a minor fantasy and become a Walk Around Guy at the Open. In other years, when the tournament was held amid the stately if cluttered elegance of Forest Hills, I never experienced a desire to venture very far from the pleasant clubhouse bars. But slick and modern Flushing Meadow, with its sharp-edged functional architecture and fast artificial court surfaces, inspired me to plunge more deeply into the life-style of contemporary tennis. Since the entourages of most stars had long since been stocked, I cast about briefly for a position. Then I settled on fourteenth-seeded JoAnne Russell, a 23-year-old Floridian noted for hard hitting, lengthy if nonalcoholic hanging out in East Side bars, and a love for Steve Martin humor that made her just wild and crazy enough to take on an unschooled rookie racket carrier.

"You'll have a chance to break in slowly," Russell reassured me. "While the famous bagmen are in the stadium, you'll be practically alone with me. They usually put me on a court you have to travel to on a shuttle bus."

"Maybe you'll get more respect now that you're not carrying your own stuff," I said hopefully.

"I could use it," she sighed. "I'm getting tired of calling, 'Ball, please,' and having the ball boy yell back, 'Get it yourself.' "

My new role required some changes in my Open customs. First, there was the question of wardrobe. Because most Walk Around Boys hope to be mistaken for players while they tote rackets around, they wear sweat suits. But when Russell and I almost bought a flashy green and yellow number for me, she demurred because she didn't want to be mistaken for the owner of a 220-pound parrot. We opted for a standard safari shirt because it had many pockets in which to carry her wallet, sweat bands, and other necessities.

As a reporter, I could have watched matches from the stadium press box, a towering structure puzzlingly designed to overlook precisely one and one-half of the 27 courts in the center. But as Russell's Walk Around Guy, I got to sit around the players' lounge and rub tennis elbows with the masters of the art. After a few minutes in that heady atmosphere, one is overcome with the realization that while hangers-on are present in every sport, they are the very foundation of tennis.

Most awe-inspiring of the cast is Ion Tiriac, who peers through brooding eyes from behind his bushy beard, then makes subtle slashing hand motions that convey secret inspirations to sensitive, poetic Guillermo Vilas. Most serious may be Lennart Bergelin, longtime coach of Bjorn Borg. While Bjorn has risen to new heights in tennis, his coach has achieved some medical wonders of his own; by a unique symbiotic process, when Borg injures a part of his body, Bergelin winces at precisely the same spot. In the category of most adoring, it is hard to separate Kuhle from Billie Jean King's two-platoon system of Marilyn Barnett and Ron McCabe—although McCabe gets a special citation for wearing a little sign proclaiming himself Billie's "road manager." Finally, the most beautiful entourage belongs to Vitas Gerulaitis, who eschews individual bagtoters in favor of a starlet-strewn traveling squad from Studio 54.

Walking into such company, I quickly made a few rookie blunders, the worst coming when I purchased wristbands in a color that clashed with Russell's tennis dress. "Are you color-blind?" JoAnne snapped during her first-round match. "Lornie would be fired for this."

That was true. But it also made me think about the Walking Around relationship. Before she accepted her small new entourage, Russell had been a funny, noisy, independent young woman. Now, she was suddenly critical and bossy, in the habit of throwing towels in my direction to get attention. It was all part of our joking act, of course. But it made us both wonder. "If somebody really spoiled me like this," JoAnne mused, "maybe it really could make me into a bitch." We had assumed that tennis prima donnas demanded sycophants around them, but perhaps the sport's Walk Around Guys are actually to blame for creating its more petulant heroes.

Having absorbed that little lesson, I am retiring from walking around. It is often boring and degrading and it takes place too far from the bar. Still, it gave me moments to treasure. Wielding my lucky horseshoe, I felt possessed with truly Tiriacal spells. Lighting my victory cigar duing the final points of JoAnne's first-round victory, I felt awash in coaching cleverness. And at last, when JoAnne served an ace to win that match, I sniffed the very essence of my new profession, turned to some friends, and announced with great sincerity, "We won it."

BASEBALL

CUBAN BASEBALL: AIR HORNS AND RASPBERRY-CLAD UMPIRES

By Thomas Boswell

From The Washington Post
Copyright, ©, 1978, The Washington Post

The sugarcane fields are ablaze here in Pinar Del Rio, Cuba, their scorching sweet smoke rolling down the barrancas, a sign that the rich, hard weeks of harvest have come.

This island has two obsessions, two sources of sustenance, two causes for annual celebration: sugar and baseball.

Both have reached their season of fruition. Both are on fire now—cane by day, baseball by night.

"That's one sugar on Juan Castro," crackled the voice of Sala Manca, the baseball radio announcer for all Cuba. "The fish has bitten the hook."

From easternmost Point Maisi to the Isle of Pines in the west, perhaps half of Cuba's 9.6 million people are listening to Sala Manca's voice as he tells them in his rolling, idiomatic Spanish that the count on Juan Castro is one strike.

In the batter's box in Pinar Del Rio Stadium, Castro steps out. The bases are loaded and so is the air—with a crescendo of sound.

Women beat on 20-gallon tin cans. Enormous air horns, outlawed as hearing hazards in the United States, pierce the lush night. It takes three men to lift the largest horn. The leader of the trio is still in his cane-cutting field clothes with gaucho straw hat. He smokes a foot-long Cuban Hupman cigar and smiles blissfully.

Banners flap above the Pinar dugout: "Juan Castro, with your home runs, you put rhythm back in the dance."

"Castro fouls the second pitch into the crowd. Two sugars on Castro," Sala Manca tells Cuba. "Now the fish is in the pan."

The crowd of 30,000 *beisbol fanaticos* filling every bench seat in the beautiful, spanking modern stadium, pleads with Castro.

The precious foulball that Castro had hit into the stands is thrown back into play. A soft ripple of cheers acknowledges the gesture, for baseballs, like many commodities here, are hard to come by. A man in white gloves so that only clean hands will touch the ball collects the *pelota* for future use.

The moral mandate to return fouls is just one Cuban incongruity to northern eyes. All fans get in the stadium free—first come, first seated. Cows graze only a few feet away from the open stadium gates, and occasionally must be dissuaded from wandering into the park.

Once inside, the single-deck stadium offers no advertising, no ushers, no concessionaires, no hawkers, no panty-hose night, no exploding score-boards, no inessential public-address announcements.

The game is the only focus and it is played quickly, usually in two hours or less. Strong, sweet hot tea is passed through the stands in small cups during the middle innings. A few drink Cabeza de Lobo—Wolf's Head—beer, but they do it surreptitiously. Baseball is thought to be sufficient inebriation for any Cuban.

The Havana manager, hoping to squeeze the two-strike tension around Castro's throat, calls a long mound conference with his pitcher, Juan Pedro Oliva, brother of former big-leaguer Tony Oliva.

The party caucus at the hill is enormous—six players and a manager. But Pinar del Rio shows Havana what a real conference is like: all three base runners, two coaches, the on-deck hitter, and the manager surround Castro at home plate, patting him on the back, giving advice.

If Havana can have seven on the mound, Pinar can have eight at the plate.

Finally, all four umpires—dressed in outrageous raspberry suits so they look like four fat popsicles—congregate on the mound to break up a meeting that now seems to have enough members for a coup d'etat.

Sala Manca tells the masses every detail. In the morning at 5 A.M., the laborers will be back in the cane fields stripping the burned leaves off the cane stalks with their machetes. Until sundown, they will work, often scrambling in mountainside fields. The baseball games at night are their release, their joy.

Sala Manca knows. The Cuban government knows. "Baseball helps the harvest," says that other Castro, Fidel. "It is tied to the heart of our economy."

When the "Game of the Night" has ended, Rebel Radio will flash around the island, picking up other games in progress until the last out in Cuba has been recorded.

"Will the fish be fried?" asked Sala Manca as the huge conference disperses. "Will it be three sugars on Castro?"

Castro lunges at a curve, catching it flush on the fat of his aluminum bat.

CLANK! Although his swing was off balance, the lively metal bat and the even livelier Batos ball produce a soaring fly to the left garden. The white baseball hangs high in the constellation-filled Caribbean sky, flying toward the only two signs (one says, "Harder work produces better-quality tobacco" and is signed with one word, 'Fidel.' " The other is a 40-foot-high mural of a local revolutionary).

Cuban crowds never make a mistake on fly balls. It is shameful to stand and scream for a fly ball that dies at the warning track. Only Sala Manca is extended the privilege of doubt.

"Se va, Se va (It's going, It's going)," he screams as an estimated 5 million Cubans listen. "No se va (It's not leaving). Si, se va (Yes, it is)," he plays the cat-and-mouse game.

The crowd roars. The ball disappeared over Fidel's name on the sign. Sala Manca cannot keep his secret any longer.

"Good-bye, my dear Lolita," he says, laughing to show that he knew it was a grand-slam home run all the time.

So no one cares that a marriage of an aluminum bat, a rabbit ball, and a short fence (345 feet to left center) have combined to create this moment of madness.

Cubans demand excitement, scoring, base stealing, strategy—therefore, all the conditions of the Cuban game promote offense. A 1–0 pitcher's duel is worse than cutting cane. Fans leave early en masse in disgust.

A grand slam like Juan Castro's produces a minute of near-national euphoria. All along the winding 200 kilometers of road from Pinar del Rio to Havana, people are in the streets, at gas stations, in front of diners, listening and cheering.

This ball will not be returned by the children outside the stadium.

The noise in the Pinar del Rio stands is shattering. This has always been called the "Cinderella Province" because it has produced great athletes despite its rural spareness, its ancient housing, its legacy of brutal labor in the cane and tobacco fields.

It has been a generation since the Vegueros (Greens) had a champion. Good players, sí, Island-wide supremacy, no.

Now they have a champion. When the youthful Pinar fuzz-beards (average age 23) startled the nation by winning the 18-team Series Nacional in March, there was a holiday in the province.

Cane-cutters, with their machetes raised, formed a phalanx of honor to escort the team into town.

People rode horseback, the players stacked themselves on jeeps. Beer and rum and pork and dancing filled the streets all night.

On this night, the greeting for Juan Castro as he runs out his grand slam is a continuation of the same celebration. Pinar del Rio has moved up into the same rarefied air of the Series Selectiva—the six-team national World Series when the stars of all 18 provincial teams are consolidated.

Beyond all expectation, Pinar now leads the Series Selectiva, as well, holding a cane-stalk-thin two-game lead over the menacing maroon-clads of Havana.

Before Juan Castro reaches second base, the entire Pinar team has exploded from its dugout and waits for him—not at home plate, but strung out the entire length of the third-base line. As soon as Castro's foot hits third, his hand is grabbed in the first of 25 soul shakes.

At the plate, the three men who were on base wait with their arms linked around each other's shoulders. They are bouncing as they wait to give Castro his final embrace.

It is only the first inning.

It would dismay Cuba to think that any country could match its love for baseball. Relative to its population, this nation is convinced that neither the United States, Japan, nor any Latin neighbor is its equal in per capita frenzy—either in playing the game, watching it, or dissecting it.

Baseball in Cuba is a unique three-part blend, as pungent as the land's omnipresent espresso coffee.

That mixture is one part century-old tradition, one part artistic Latin temperament, and one part first-generation communism. No other country offers the old game in such a challenging and often perplexing form.

More than 100 years ago an American Merchant Marine ship sailed into Matanzas Bay. On a hilltop overlooking one of the most breathtaking natural harbors in the Caribbean, the U.S. sailors planted a huge seed exactly the size of a baseball.

On that hill above Matanzas, a town called "the Athens of Cuba" for its beauty of its setting, the islanders built their first baseball stadium, Palmar de Junco, and inaugurated it in 1874.

Today, Palmar de Junco is a preserved relic, a museum, an academy for young players of the Matanzas province.

During its first 100 years, the park played host to scores of legendary Cuban players from Adolfo Luque (194 major-league victories) and Martin Dihijo (Hall of Fame), through Camilo Pascual and Minnie Minoso, down to the last pre-revolutionary contingent that included Tony Perez, Mike Cuellar, and Luis Tiant.

One need look no further than ancient Matanzas to discover the importance of baseball in Cuba under Fidel Castro.

The town itself is as physically repulsive as its setting is magnificent. Public housing is Cuba's major embarrassment, and no better example than Matanzas need be looked for. The one-story row housing makes Appalachia look like a resort.

The people in those houses, however, are fiercely dignified. The gutters are spotless and the children who pop out of the dismal doorways are like so many neat pins.

In the midst of this cramped world of narrow streets, tiny and overcrowded houses and antique U.S. automobiles of the forties and fifties, rises the Estadio Victoria de Giron—a 30,000-seat memorial to Cuban baseball and to the American defeat at the Bay of Pigs.

The park looks a bit like Chavez Ravine with a hint of the enclosed coziness of Fenway Park. That is to say, it is more pleasing to the eye than half the stadiums in the U.S. majors. And it also looks like it cost more to build than all the pinched houses in Matanzas.

Baseball may be the only facet of Cuban life that comes close to transcending politics. Other sports bear the stamp and rhetoric of a severely disciplined party line. There is an approved state way to do every push-up, and if a child anywhere in Cuba chins himself, there seem to be two adult trainers on hand to graph his progress.

Baseball, however, has a degree of autonomy. True, Cuban sports writers have been instructed to stop using personal nicknames since the team, not the individual, is of primary importance.

"We must help the people to learn to think collectively," says Cuban sports writer Jose Luis Salmeron.

Also, Cuban pitchers who are yanked by their managers or players who are called out wrongly by umpires show incredible restraint in sublimating their anger to respect for authority.

Cuba's top hitter, Wilfredo Sanchez, was once called out by a "blind" umpire in Matanzas when he was safe by a yard, leaped high in the air, spun around, and made the psychic transformation from complete disbelief and fury to resigned composure before he returned to earth. He walked off the field without any show of displeasure except that four-foot vertical catapult when he first saw the umpire's thumb.

The contrast between crowd behavior in Cuba and in its spitting-distance neighbor, the rowdy Dominican Republic, is almost total. The Dominican Republic surpasses even Puerto Rico for incipient fan violence, fields ringed by police, and a suppressed sense of danger.

Cuban ball parks may be the only ones in the hemisphere that combine rabid partisanship, ferocious noise, and umpire baiting with a sense of total personal security.

The crowd has its right to yell, "We are being robbed" and, "We are playing nine against 13." But when the ump has heard enough, he calmly raises a hand like a school principal and the sound turns off like a faucet. It is an impressive and somewhat unnerving sight.

Even after a controversial game, the umpires walk slowly, face up, into the crowd, without a policeman in sight. The children throw harmless wads of paper . . . at their feet.

Whatever subtle political and psychological realities may lie below the surface of baseball under Fidel, the exterior of the game is idyllic.

All the Cuban players must work at other jobs. Many also continue their schooling through their 20s. Members of the national team, which has won six of the last nine world amateur titles, supposedly work as dentists, accountants, dock workers, and the inevitable legion of physical education instructors.

No Cuban baseball player has publicly said he has any interest in U.S. major-league money in 17 years. On the contrary, Cuban stars spit out the word "professionalism" like a curse. If their stream of pro patria words is said with anything other than considerable conviction, they are even better actors than athletes.

The unpaid Cubans say they play for pride, patriotism, incalculable public adoration, and government fringe benefits that would seem paltry to a Big Ten football player.

Nevertheless, even more unusual than the Cuban players are the fans of every hue of pigmentation coexisting in the stands, without a hint of an argument, other than in jest. And without a gendarme, an usher, or any official personage in view.

Like the fans of Puerto Rico, the people of the Cuban provinces split their parks down the middle into cheering sections. But unlike Puerto Rico, they throw only words across the dividing line.

"I have no interest to play anywhere else," says Cuba's top hitter, Wilfredo Sanchez, 28, whose .332 career average for 10 seasons is the highest in Cuban history. "We give to the people and they give us back things that cannot be measured."

"We all await the day when we can play against the North American Great Leaguers. We know that they are better than us. We have much to learn from them. And perhaps they have things to learn from us. We have many stories to tell each other."

FOOTBALL

NOAH JACKSON WAS NOT INHIBITED

By Jill Lieber

From the Milwaukee Sentinel
Copyright, ©, 1978, Milwaukee Sentinel

Noah Jackson was not inhibited. The Chicago Bears' burly guard raced into the outer entryway of his team's locker room last Sunday afternoon with nothing on but a raincoat.

"A lady wants to talk to me?" he asked with a smile as wide as his oversized waist. "No lady ever came in here after a game before. Let me shake your hand."

Jackson was right. The Bears' public relations people had informed me in the Soldier Field press box before the game that I was the first woman sports writer who had ever covered their team and needed to get into the locker room after the game. And Ted Haracz, the Bears' director of public relations, was a bit edgy about the whole thing.

Haracz had read about women sports writers being physically thrown out of NFL locker rooms. To a PR man, articles like that are horror stories. Haracz was also familiar with the suit that was filed against major-league baseball last year by Melissa Ludtke of *Sports Illustrated.* That was the last thing he wanted.

I admitted to Haracz that I, too, was a rookie at NFL postgame interviews. I told him that I would not demand to be allowed inside the locker room, but that I also did not want to wait outside the door with a wind chill of nine below zero and 300 fans screaming and clawing at the players as they came out.

So the Bears went to great lengths to make my job easier and less frustrating. They had the coach's quotes tape recorded, and they personally brought out all six players that I requested.

I had no locker room problems Sunday. In fact, I probably had more fun than a lot of men writers. I was a novelty.

"A lady in our locker room?" punter Bob Parsons shrieked. "We've waited too darn long for this, haven't we, Noah? Well, Miss, you're welcome back anytime."

"Hey, Noah," Bear running back Roland Harper kidded. "What you got on under that raincoat?"

"Noah," defensive back and special teams player, Steve Schubert yelled. "That's the first woman I have ever seen who wanted to talk to you."

Jackson was a funny sight. He huddled inside the lightweight coat, dancing back and forth from one foot to the other trying to keep warm.

"Wo-o-o-o, it's cold in here," Jackson said. "I don't think I'll thaw out until I get some beer in me. But you? You must be freezing. Here, let Noah take you where you can warm up."

Faster than I could decline, I found myself being dragged toward the shower area of the locker room. And all 6-feet-2, 275 pounds of Noah Jackson was shaking so hard with his loud, raucous laughter, that I was sure his raincoat would fall off. But I knew Jackson was just teasing, and I stopped him before he could get to the end of the last dividing curtain.

When I got back to the entryway, I had to wait awhile before Schubert, Brad Shearer, Mike Hartenstine, and Mike Phipps were dressed and could come out to be interviewed. And while I was waiting, I noticed a smaller man looking at me. His head was cocked, and he watched me out of the corner of his eye. Obviously, curious. Even while the other players talked to him as they walked out the door, he kept right on staring.

"How you doing?" he said softly, making me realize just who he was. "I haven't ever seen a woman in here before." He paused and smiled. He seemed a bit shy. "What's your name? Who do you write for?"

Just as I began to answer, he put his hand on my shoulder and moved closer to my ear. "This is a hard business for a woman, isn't it?"

That question made me smile. Maybe he really understood. "Not today," I said. "Today this is lots of fun."

"It won't always be like this," he said. "A lot of the time it isn't even fun for us players. But you can't ever let any business get you down. In the end, all the heartaches, all the losses, are worth it."

And with that, Walter Payton patted me on the back and walked out into the cold, dark stadium.

GENERAL

"HOW ARE YOU GOING TO DO IN THE BIG GAME?"

By Loel Schrader

From the Long Beach (Calif.) Independent Press-Telegram
Copyright, ©, 1978, Independent, Press-Telegram, Long Beach, Calif.

My ophthalmologist quickly scanned the file.

"Oh, yeah, you're the sports columnist. You must meet some interesting people."

I thought back to something I had read over the weekend.

It was a piece on why Prescott Sullivan had retired from the *San Francisco Examiner* sports department after 53 years.

"I was 71 years old and I had to walk up to some sweaty kid who could have been my grandson and ask, 'How are you going to do in the Big Game?' " said Sullivan.

"That was it. I decided it was time to take it easy, just as if I hadn't been taking it easy all these years. Somehow, 53 years at the ball park seemed like enough self-indulgence."

Interesting people, eh?

Sure. Take Reggie Jackson. As he entered the Yankee clubhouse at Anaheim Stadium last week, I walked up to him with notebook in hand and said: "Do you have a few minutes to chat?"

Jackson, hero of the 1977 World Series, reacted as though I had asked for his life. Or at least his wife.

A half-sneer froze on his face.

"Who are you?" he demanded.

"Loel Schrader of the *Long Beach Independent, Press-Telegram.*"

He tried to stare me down.

Finally, Reggie said: "I'm not even acclimated yet. The least you could do is let me get acclimated."

"Fine, take all the time you need to get acclimated."

A couple of other writers were standing about 15 feet away, out of earshot but clearly within range to gauge Reggie's sneer. I walked over to them.

"Maybe you would be better off trying to get him at the batting cage," one suggested.

"No, I'm going to let him get acclimated."

Jackson kept staring our way, with that half-sneer. God knows why, but he did.

He went about his business, taking care of ticket requests and opening letters.

When he was about half-dressed, I returned to his cubicle.

"Are you acclimated?"

"Sure," he said, flashing a friendly smile. "Sit down and let's talk."

Figure that out, if you can.

About that time, the ophthalmologist stuck something into my eye and I flinched.

"Geez, what the hell was that?"

"A needle. I'm just draining a duct."

He continued with his probing.

"You must do a lot of traveling."

Between sobs, I laughed.

"Sure do."

I had figured it out recently, and it came to more than half a million air miles and five years in motels and hotels.

I recalled a flight from St. Louis to St. Paul-Minneapolis when the plane lost power in both engines at 14,000 feet during a thunder and lightning storm.

And the time a pilot tried to land a plane in Milwaukee with ceiling zero and discovered—not a second too soon, I might add—that we were missing the runway. He pulled it up, and the craft shuddered as it fought the laws of gravity.

Or the motel in South Bend, where I returned to my room late at night and discovered I couldn't shut off the air conditioning. It was about 50 degrees in the room, but the clerk said nothing could be done until morning.

As he drained my left eye, the ophthalmologist inquired: "Are most athletes pretty nice guys?"

I thought of Reggie and several others, including some Southern Californians, and chuckled. Maybe it was more of a "God help me" giggle.

Then I remembered a morning in Cincinnati with Pete Rose.

We met at an appointed time in the Reds' clubhouse, and Rose sensed immediately that I wasn't at the top of my game.

"Could I get you a cup of coffee?" he asked.

My head was pounding and my eyes were slits.

"I don't think that will do it, Pete."

He jumped up. "Well, to hell with you then."

Rose left the players' room where we were meeting, then returned moments later with three bottles, seals unbroken.

One was Aqua Velva, another was a container of Scotch, and the third was shaped like a baseball glove.

"I drink Aqua Velva," Rose snickered, getting in a plug for the product for which he does a TV commercial.

My head hurt too much to laugh. "What's in the glove?"

"Try it, you'll like it."

I poured half a paper cup of the stuff and slugged it down.

"Holy cripes," said Rose. "That's awesome."

So was the medicine in the glove. It lifted me off the chair as though it had rocket power.

I was a new man, and we proceeded to engage in a delightful interview, during which Rose revealed more of his character than all the "Charley Hustle" stuff you read.

As the ophthalmologist put a pack on my eye, I reconsidered.

"I hope I didn't create the wrong impression," I said. "There really are a lot of nice athletes and coaches around."

Enough so I can still accept Reggie Jackson's insolence.

Enough so I can still stand to ask some sweaty kid, "How are you going to do in the Big Game?"

GENERAL

ON A COLD DAY 15 YEARS AGO

By Dave Kindred

From The Washington Post
Copyright, ©, 1978, The Washington Post

It was a Sunday, 15 years ago, the Sunday before Thanksgiving. Down by a twisting creek, off in a flat and treeless corner of a farmer's pasture, a handful of men had come together, as they did every Sunday before Thanksgiving, for a turkey shoot.

The men carried old guns, the kind they call muzzle-loaders. They shot at bull's-eye targets set up by the creek, and on this day, chill and still in the country, the report of a shot rang across the hills. In an ambulance, coming over the hills toward the creek, the man heard the shots, and he smiled.

The man brought these shooters together over the years. There weren't many, no more than 20. But every Sunday, they came to shoot their muzzle-loaders. If it snowed, they wore gloves and cursed the weather, but they came anyway. They shooed away the cows down by the creek, and they shot until the daylight, or the coffee, ran out.

The man who started them shooting was always the first there and the last to leave. He brought the targets and took them home. He kept them in his garage, and he kept them in his house, and, finally, he built a room inside his house for the guns and targets and lead (he made bullets on his wife's stove).

The man had always been a sports fan. In grade school he was a high jumper. Once, he was proud to say, he made it over the bar and was able to walk back under it without stooping. He played baseball, too, and basketball, but not much. His father died at 41, and he went to work when he finished the eighth grade. He drove trucks for a while, and he was in the army for a while, and then he was a carpenter.

The man was caught up by guns when he moved his wife, son, and daughter into a big, old house and, cleaning it, found a rusting handgun. Sometime later, he began buying the muzzle-loaders, one here for $10, one there for $25, and tired of driving a hundred miles every Sunday to shoot, he made up his own muzzle-loading club.

The man was, by then, an aficionado; he ran advertisements in shooting journals, setting down the dates for his club's shoots; he took to wearing a buckskin jacket when he shot, and he always wore a black mountaineer's hat with a pheasant feather stuck in the band; he made, with his own hands, muzzle-loading guns of such precision and beauty that men offered him hundreds of dollars for them, all the while knowing the man would as soon sell his right arm as his guns.

Every spring, the man made the pilgrimage to Friendship, Ind., 300 miles from home, for the national championship muzzle-loading matches. He drove a pickup truck, and his wife sat in front with him, and his son and daughter rode in the back in a cabin he built for them. He entered the benchrest matches, those in which the shooters put their guns on a table to shoot them. He never won, but he never cared, and in the winter, looking at his magazines, he would announce to his family the dates for the spring nationals.

And then, 15 years ago, when the doctors told him he had cancer, and he had two weeks to live, no more, the man thought of his turkey shoot down by the creek. He would go, he said, to the turkey shoot if he had to go in an ambulance. And on that Sunday before Thanksgiving, he went.

Coming over a hill in the pasture, the ambulance rolling silently over a path worn dusty by the shooters' cars over the years, the man heard the guns of his friends, and he smiled. He wore his black mountaineer's hat (his wife once caught him unawares and took his picture when he wore white long johns and the black hat). And when they lifted him out of the ambulance on a stretcher, he told his son he wanted to sit up, dammit, so he could see.

He hadn't spoken in the ambulance during a half-hour's drive to the shooting range. Once there, he laughed and talked and had his picture taken with his friends and family making a semicircle on either side of his stretcher.

He didn't talk going back to the hospital that Sunday before Thanksgiving, and he died on Tuesday, and I thought of all this again on another Sunday before Thanksgiving when, late at night, my son, 16, said, "I love you, Daddy." That's what I said, on that ambulance ride 15 years ago, to my father.

BASEBALL

TOUGHNESS

By Randy Smith

From the Journal Inquirer, Manchester, Conn.
Copyright, ©, 1978, Journal Publishing Co. Inc., Manchester, Conn.

Toughness.

New Yorkers, including the defending World Champion Yankees, thrive on it. Californians, including the Los Angeles Dodgers, are repulsed by it.

Toughness.

New Yorkers relish it as a necessary part of life. How else can you survive on the street? Californians shy away from it and who cares anyhow, let's go to the beach.

Toughness.

The Yankees have it. The Dodgers don't.

The World Series weekend in New York proved beyond the slightest doubt that you can take the Dodgers out of Los Angeles, but you can't take Los Angeles out of the Dodgers. Nice guys won't always finish last, but in New York, the best they can hope for is a distant second.

Toughness.

The Yankees took that quality and in three straight games, shoved it down the throat of the Dodgers. Behind 2–0 in games, the Yankees needed Ron Guidry Friday night, but got Bud Daley instead. Guidry, with no fastball and a slider he couldn't control, walked seven and was in constant trouble. Graig Nettles, at third base, made more stops than an Amtrak commuter, and Guidry somehow pitched a 5–1, complete game victory.

"He beat the best team in the National League with nothing," catcher Thurman Munson said.

Nothing, but toughness.

In game four Saturday, the Dodgers built a 3–0 lead against Ed Figueroa, who can put away his hair drier for another year. Yankee reliever Dick Tidrow bailed out Figgy with three innings of scoreless work and the Yankees clawed their way back in it. Roy White, overlooked and unnoticed until it's time to pull a putter out of the bag, delivered a single and a sacrifice bunt. Reggie Jackson provided a run-scoring single and a hip check which flattened a sleepy umpiring crew. And Munson—if Jackson's "October's Child," then Munson's a close neighbor down the street—produced a two-strike double which knotted the game. Lou Piniella, another Yankee who doesn't bet to place or show, climaxed the comeback with a tenth-inning single for a 4–3 victory.

Toughness.

In game five Sunday, the Dodgers cracked, wide open like delicatessen eggs, the ones used to make omelets. Bill Russell, Reggie Smith, and Steve Garvey made errors, and starting pitcher Burt Hooton was fried in less than three innings. Munson, who probably could have stayed the full 15 rounds with Apollo Creed, too, knocked in five runs and White drove home three more in a 12–2 win sweetened from the Yankees' viewpoint by Ivy Leaguer Jim Beattie's first complete-game victory.

Toughness.

In New York, it comes with the territory.

The Series shifts to Los Angeles Tuesday for game six. The Yankees have selected Jim Hunter to shoot the nine-ball, while the Dodgers most likely will tab Don Sutton to shoot the eight. If Hunter misses and Sutton clicks, it will be Guidry against Tommy John in game seven Wednesday.

"We beat Boston in Boston and we can beat Los Angeles in Los Angeles," Yankee shortstop Bucky Dent said Sunday.

Toughness.

The Dodgers are returning to their beloved, the 3.3 million faithful who patronized Walter O'Malley's Shangri-La this year. It's a Never-Never Land, Dodger Stadium is, where the comfortable go to gain further comfort. The Dodgers won't be booed or hissed at and their infield might even turn a double play or two. But the California coast, let it be said loud and clear, is a long, long way from the Bronx, and not in miles alone.

Second-baseman Davey Lopes, for one, has seen enough of New York.

"They should drop a bomb on this place," he said after Sunday's game.

The Dodgers, in a sense, did, exposing themselves as the fabricated team they are. No team, in any sport, is so contrived as the Dodgers. O'Malley and son Peter virtually handpick prospects who are good citizens first, good players second. They spoon-feed the youngsters, nurturing them in Dodger history, Dodger strategy, Dodger decorum, and Dodger blood.

"What do you want to be, Davey Lopes?" Manager Tom Lasorda screams.

"I l-o-o-o-o-v-e to be a Dodger," Lopes screams back.

But not in New York.

Toughness.

The Dodgers, better than any of their opponents, realize they lack the killer instinct, the stick-it-in-his-face vulgarity which characterizes the great competitor, like a Munson. They tried Dick Allen and they tried Frank Robinson, but neither studied the Dodger missal, so off they went. They threw the dice again on Reggie Smith and so far, it's been a good roll. But one slipup—a bad year, a bad comment, a bad act—and he'll be gone, too.

Analyze the seventy-fifth World Series as you wish, but when you finish sifting through the hit-and-runs and passed balls and missed opportunities, you'll find at the core a tale of two cities, two cultures at the opposite ends of the spectrum, two completely different ball clubs.

Los Angeles is a vacation.

New York is survival.

Los Angeles is bean sprouts and health food.

New York is a bowl of chili and can't you make it any hotter?

Los Angeles is Russell, Garvey, and let's do the best we can, fellas.

New York is Munson, Jackson, and what have you done for me lately?

Los Angeles is Disneyland and Malibu Beach.

New York is Harlem and the Bowery.

Los Angeles is crème de menthe on the rocks.

New York is a shot of Four Roses and a beer chaser.

Los Angeles is a picnic basket and a bottle of suntan lotion.

New York is a hot, roasted pretzel and a bottle of Pink Pussycat.

Los Angeles is Doris Day.

New York is Neil Simon.

Los Angeles is a mineral bath.

New York is a shower at the YMCA.

Los Angeles Dodger crowds are white, warm, and adoring.

New York Yankee crowds are all colors, hostile, and critical.

Los Angeles is a backyard swimming pool because the Pacific Ocean's too cold.

New York is a fractured fire hydrant in the dead heat of August.

Los Angeles is Charlie's Angels and Universal Studios.

New York is Andy Warhol and a Forty-second Street peep show.

Los Angeles is jogging and birds chirping at early morn.

New York is spitting on the sidewalk and a police siren.

Los Angeles is a starlet who will turn into a hooker.

New York is a hooker who used to be a starlet.

Los Angeles is a palm tree and a beachball.

New York is a tenement and a crap game in the alley.

Toughness.

Toughness.

Toughness.

New Yorkers, including the Yankees, thrive on it. Californians, including the Dodgers, are repulsed by it.

And you wonder how in the world the Yankees could have taken three straight.

GENERAL

THE LEAST PLAUSIBLE DATELINE

By Si Burick

From The Dayton Daily News
Copyright, ©, 1978, Si Burick

HIROSHIMA, Japan—
Of the millions of words that have emerged from my portable typewriters, this dateline seems the least plausible.

What am I doing, anyway, covering baseball in Hiroshima, scene of the World War II tragedy, where the United States broke Japan's back and will by dropping the first atomic bomb?

Please forgive a note of personal reference. This, for me, is an incredible anniversary, a milestone with an ego syndrome.

On November 16, 1928, my first sports column appeared in *The Dayton Daily News*. Except for illness, emergencies, and vacations, these effusions have appeared here regularly ever since. This covers 50 years, mind you; *half a century*.

A few days earlier, the late Dan Mahoney, Sr., the general manager, advised that the publisher, Governor James M. Cox, wanted to see me. Mr. Cox was referred to as "The Governor" by all of us. He had spent three terms in the governor's mansion in Columbus. Then he ran for president on the Democratic ticket in 1920. A disciple of President Woodrow Wilson, he firmly believed in the League of Nations.

Governor Cox was defeated by Senator Warren G. Harding, also an Ohio publisher from Marion. The country, wearied of the internationalism that inspired World War I, turned isolationist. But, "The Governor" believed to his dying day that U.S. participation in "The League" could, or would, have prevented World War II.

Anyway, eight years later, he was offering a shy 19-year-old with scarcely 18 months experience on the paper, the sports editorship, replacing M. Carle Finke, who was leaving to go into business.

I had been working "temporarily" to raise enough money to continue a premed course at UD, which I had left after a year. There were plans for medical school somewhere in my future.

Now I firmly believe that this strange twist, the switch from early ambition to become a doctor to a sports-writing career, was a boon to humanity. Pity those might-have-been patients. I took the job and, of course, never left it. After five decades, I confess there have been no regrets on my part.

I defy anyone in any field who has had more fun than I have on my job in what Red Smith has called the "Toy Department" of a newspaper. Following the Reds on this trip enhances the feeling, although the "fun side" is tempered at the moment by the horror of Hiroshima's history.

When I broke in, sports writing was a mass (or mess) of clichés. Literacy did not become a virtue in this field until much later. One bit of idiocy required that you did not repeat the same word even if it properly told the story. Use a synonym.

My column was called Si-ings and this was to remain so for many years. Writing was horribly stilted. Consider this lead paragraph in the first Si-ings column November 16, 1928:

"Like the rest of the country, Dayton 'grid' fans will watch for the result of the Iowa-Wisconsin 'clash' with unabated interest."

I didn't say "football" or "game." There were further references to the affair, tilt and, finally, game. Grudgingly used, I suppose.

Later, that first-ever Si-ings noted that Carnegie Tech would be playing Knute Rockne's Irish at Notre Dame, which hadn't lost a home game in 23 years. Guess what? Tech won, 27–7. (Carnegie, now called Carnegie-Mellon, plays Dayton in the Division III playoffs Saturday.)

Our Sunday paper reported that the UD Flyers "sang a victory song" over Ohio Northern, 41–0, for its fifth "win" of the year.

That's how sports writing went. Even for the worst of us, it has improved vastly. Not that all clichés have disappeared, but certainly it is aeons ahead in literacy.

After the kid enjoyed a brief apprenticeship, "The Governor" ordered him to "broaden your viewpoint; don't confine yourself to local interests, but don't ignore them; cover a big event out-of-town now and then." What an invitation!

So there were trips to and with Ohio State; to Notre Dame; to various places with UD. Because both Governor Cox and Dan Mahoney were boxing buffs, I began covering heavyweight title fights early; and these assignments have endured from Max Schmeling's time to Muhammad Ali's.

I got to my first World Series in 1930. There have been 46 since. In 1929, I covered my first Kentucky Derby. There have been 48 by now. I was assigned to go to spring training with the Reds and later to travel with them during the season. There were pro football championships in my future. Virtually all of the college football bowl games; all 12 Super Bowls.

A special big moment: my first Olympic Games assignment in Rome in 1960; in 1972, the tragedy of Munich. In basketball, the NIT and NCAA came along; some big tournaments in golf.

And here, on my fiftieth anniversary of sports columnist of *The Daily News*, I'm with the Reds in Japan, still in love with my job and, believe me, feeling few of the pangs of age. Not yet, anyway.

BASKETBALL

THE END OF A 10-YEAR QUEST

By Paul Attner

From The Washington Post
Copyright, ©, 1978, The Washington Post

Wes Unseld ended a 10-year quest for the National Basketball Association title last night when he sank two free throws with 12 seconds remaining to give the Washington Bullets a heart-pounding 105–99 victory over the Seattle SuperSonics.

Unseld's dramatic foul shots, which came 14 seconds after he had missed two attempts, wrapped up the best-of-seven series, 4–3, and ensured Washington's first professional major sports championship since 1942, when the Redskins won the National Football League title.

Unseld, who finished with 15 points and nine rebounds, was named the series' Most Valuable Player by *Sport Magazine* in a vote of sports writers. Ironically, the Bullets tried to get him out of the game just before he was fouled, but the team failed to call time-out and Seattle immediately smacked him.

The victory ended a long and amazing comeback by the Bullets from a disappointing regular season ruined by injuries. They finished only third in the Eastern Conference, but upset San Antonio, Philadelphia, and now Seattle to overcome the odds and win their first NBA crown.

The Bullets made the 36-year wait by area sports fans for this ultimate pro triumph worthwhile with their gutty performance against a Seattle team which had won 22 straight on the Center Coliseum floor. In the fourth period, the Sonics had erased all but two points of what had been a 13-point lead before Unseld ended their rush.

When it was over, Coach Dick Motta and his assistant, Bernie Bickerstaff, embraced at midcourt before Motta pranced to a nearby room to receive the NBA championship trophy.

Team owner Abe Pollin, overcome by emotion, could only mutter, "unbelievable" about the club's victory, which rewarded his 14-year struggle to win a league title.

Twice before, the Bullets had made it to the finals, only to be shut out, 4–0, both times—in 1971 by Milwaukee and 1975 by Golden State.

Unseld quietly suffered the heartbreak of those losses. But last night the veteran center, who might have played his last pro game, let himself become emotional for one of the few times in his career.

"It's a great feeling," he said, "it's hard to describe. It's something I've always wanted."

The Bullets had hoped their experience, especially along the front line, would hold up under the intense pressure of this final game better than Seattle's youth.

Their hopes bore fruit. Bob Dandridge, a nine-year veteran, and reserve Charles Johnson, who has been in the league six years, had 19 points each, including nine by Johnson in the last period. Ten-year veteran Elvin Hayes, bothered by foul trouble throughout, contributed 12 points and eight rebounds before picking up his sixth personal with 8:05 left in the game.

With Hayes shackled, other Bullets picked up the slack. Mitch Kupchak overcame turnover problems to score 11 second-half points. Tom Henderson turned in another fine defensive job and also directed the team down the stretch while adding 15 points. And Johnson provided the outside shooting Washington needed in the absence of Kevin Grevey, who did not play in the second half because of his sore left wrist. He had six points in the opening 20 minutes.

Of the Bullets' final 20 points, 18 came from Kupchak, Johnson, Unseld, and Henderson. Of these only Johnson had scored consistently during the playoffs.

Of Seattle's young players, only Marvin Webster (27 points and 19 rebounds) and Jack Sikma (21 points, 11 rebounds) played well.

Dennis Johnson, who had been the Sonics' star through the first four games of the series, exemplified Seattle's frustration by missing all 14 of his field goal attempts. He finished with only four points after averaging almost 19 a game the first six contests of the series.

Seattle's back court, which had been carrying the club, made only 13 of 44 shots. It was that poor marksmanship—the Sonics hit only 39 percent for the game—that ultimately finished Coach Len Wilken's team against the strength of Washington's powerful inside attack.

But before the Bullets could become the NBA's eighth different champion in the last nine years and before they could begin counting the winners' pool of $150,000, they had to survive an incredibly tense final four minutes.

Washington, which had blown a 19-point lead in the opening game, entered the final 12 minutes with a 13-point bulge. But that lead had shrunk to two points with four minutes left.

Then Seattle, behind Webster and cagey Fred Brown, who had 21 points, began creeping back, urged on by the wildly cheering sellout crowd of 14,008.

The Sonics ran off a 12–4 burst, with Webster and Sikma getting all but one of the points, to close to 98–94 with 1:45 to go.

Then came the play that might have saved the title for the Bullets.

Charles Johnson, whose long-range shooting had kept the Sonics at bay earlier in the period, fired up a jumper that didn't reach the rim.

The shot hit off the hands of Webster and Sikma and bounded to the floor. Tom Henderson dove, knocked the ball between the legs of Webster, and into the hands of Kupchak.

Kupchak grabbed it and put in a lay-up as he was fouled by Webster. With 90 seconds to go, he sank a free throw for a 101–94 Bullet lead.

Again, Seattle rallied. Brown could convert only one of three free-throw attempts but after a Charles Johnson miss, he sank an eight-footer.

The Sonics had to foul to have any chance of winning. They decided to hack Unseld, a 54 percent free-thrower. Sikma did the chore and Unseld, who had hit four of eight from the line in the series, didn't clear the front rim on either attempt with 26 seconds left.

Brown was taking over the Sonics offense now. He fired up a long jumper, which missed, but Paul Silas, who had only four points, grabbed the rebound and put it in. Now the lead was down to 101–99 with 18 seconds on the clock.

Motta screamed for a time-out so he could remove Unseld. But the Bullets didn't hear him. They tossed the ball in bounds, and within six seconds, Silas grabbed Unseld in the back court far away from the ball.

The crowd, sensing a potential Seattle victory, screamed at Unseld as he stood on the line. His first attempt rimmed the basket and fell out. The fans waved banners and yelled even louder. Unseld looked at the bench, took a deep breath, and swished his next try.

The Bullet bench erupted in celebration and Motta called time-out. When the teams returned to the floor, Unseld again was true from the line and Washington was up by four.

Seattle tried one more shot, but Brown missed, Unseld pulled down the rebound and fed Dandridge breaking downcourt. Dandridge took the pass and dunked the ball with three seconds left. One more shot by the Sonics came after time had expired.

Webster, who had been shackled throughout the series by Unseld's physical defense, had his finest game. He poured in eight fourth-period points and had 15 in the last half. Brown added 11 and Sikma had 10.

But the Sonics waited long. For three quarters, they played tentatively, showing the effect of the final-game pressure.

They never were able to get their running game started or break off any long scoring bursts, something they had done in their three victories in the series.

Instead, they shot horribly at the most critical times. When the Bullets were building a 41–33 lead, Seattle missed its first nine second-quarter shots and was one for 12 at one point in the period. Washington wound up leading, 53–45, at the half thanks to 12 points by Dandridge, 11 by Unseld, and 25 percent shooting in the second quarter by the Sonics.

Dandridge and Hayes combined for the Bullets' first nine points of the third period to move the advantage to 11. And when Seattle moved to within five, Kupchak responded with three quick baskets. Ironically, Motta was going to replace Kupchak with Greg Ballard because he had turned over the ball twice in a row, but he put in a rebound and Motta changed his mind.

Seattle, which made only three of its first 10 shots after intermission, fell behind by 13 as the quarter ended when Charles Johnson sank a beyond-half-court, one-handed prayer shot. Before Hayes fouled out in the final period, he made back-to-back shots and it seemed Washington was ready to coast home. Then Seattle began its rally.

But when Unseld converted those pressure free throws, Motta's famed fat lady could begin singing. Before the trophy presentation, Motta asked Unseld to lift him up onto a high platform where league Commissioner Lawrence O'Brien was waiting.

"I haven't got enough energy," Unseld replied, laughing.

"I told Wes he missed those two early free throws on purpose," kidded Motta. "He just wanted us to sweat. And we did.

"But this is sweet, I've waited a long time for it. I'm just glad it's over."

And then Motta, Pollin, and Unseld all embraced.

BOXING

GENE TUNNEY: A MAN IN SEARCH OF OBLIVION

By Shirley Povich

From The Washington Post
Copyright, ©, 1978, The Washington Post

Gene Tunney should have been the living portrait of the certified American hero. He was the young, handsome, stalwart fighting Marine of World War I, square-jawed and fearless. He reached for the heavyweight championship of the world and won it, from Jack Dempsey.

He also beat the big odds that said this New York Irish kid, this high school dropout of 15 would never master Shakespeare and be asked to lecture at Yale. He made a million dollars in one fight, and poor no more, married the heiress of his dreams, Andrew Carnegie's niece.

He was all of these things, but complete admiration escaped Tunney. The flaws were two. He was the man who beat a popular idol when he twice destroyed Dempsey. And there was a personality defect. Unlike hi-ya-guy Dempsey, he lacked the common touch, choosing to hang out with scholars.

In his pursuit of culture, Tunney took a walking tour of Europe, cultivated Yale professor William Lyon Phelps, and went swimming with George Bernard Shaw. To the genus fight fan this added up to uppity.

These are some of the recollections prompted by Tunney's death this week at age 80. I was at ringside that September 19, 51 years ago in Soldier Field, Chicago, when the battle of the long count saved Tunney's title and gave America one of its most enduring debates. There also is a vivid memory of Dempsey fans screaming, "Come on, Jack," after he floored Tunney in round seven, more cheers for Dempsey in that one round than for Tunney in the eight he won in the 10-round fight.

At Chicago there was a carry-over resentment of Tunney among many Americans. When he out-pointed Dempsey the year before in Philadelphia, it was the first time that the heavyweight title had been won by a decision.

There was a wide, if mistaken belief, that this wasn't right. The heavyweight title should be won by a knockout. What happened to macho? As an on-points heavyweight champ, Tunney was diminished in the minds of many.

This, it must be remembered, was the mid-twenties, the so-called golden age of sports, and Dempsey-Tunney was part of it. This was the era of Babe Ruth and Bobby Jones and Bill Tilden and Red Grange and Helen Wills. Only a week before the long count in Chicago, Babe Ruth hit his sixtieth home run in Yankee Stadium against the Senators' Tom Zachary.

Sport's idols were fewer but they were giants. The irreverent Westbrook Pegler called it the Era of Wonderful Nonsense.

In the same methodical manner that he hung out in libraries to soak up knowledge, Tunney set his sights on Dempsey's title after turning pro following the war. He was ring-wise when he met Dempsey, having fought 77 bouts and losing only to Harry Greb, whom he twice licked in return bouts.

For all the luster of his won-lost record, Tunney was a "made " fighter. He lacked the natural moves of a Dempsey and others. He was his own creation, a stand-up counterpuncher who made a science of his style, took no fear into the ring with him, and in his training camps practiced at great length the backward moves that ultimately helped him keep his title in round seven at Chicago.

There was a discomforting irony for Tunney with both his fights with Dempsey. Here he was the World War Marine who had seen combat action and was decorated. Dempsey, in contrast, was under slacker charges in 1918 when he was caught posing as a shipyard worker, but in patent-leather shoes. Yet, less than a decade later, it was Dempsey the people's choice and Tunney the hooted one.

The now-popular art of psyching an opponent may first have been practiced by Tunney. For his first Dempsey fight, he brazenly flew by small plane from his Stroudsburg, Pa., training camp to Philadelphia in a driving rain, a bravura stunt in 1926. If Dempsey wasn't wholly impressed with Tunney's gutsiness, promoter Tex Rickard was. With a $2 million stake in the promotion riding in Tunney's plane, Rickard was reported airsick despite never leaving the ground.

It was a proper beating Tunney gave Dempsey at Philadelphia in 10 rounds, fending off Dempsey's rushes and handling him in the clinches. He targeted Dempsey's face with straight rights and left it a bloody mess. The unanimous decision was unquestioned.

Because Dempsey was fighting after a long layoff, the cry for a rematch was instant. Rickard put it in Soldier Field and pegged the price at an unheard of $40 top for ringside. Dempsey trained at a racetrack. Tunney hied himself to a Chicago suburb and indicated he didn't want fight writers around by giving out false workout times, working in as much privacy as he could get.

In Soldier Field, 104,943 saw the fight, some from such distances in the stadium they claimed they were in Evansville. They paid a then-record gate of $4,658,600. Tunney was to get an almost tax-free check for $999,000.

It was the first fight ever broadcast by a commercial broadcaster.

Eight of the 10 rounds were won by Tunney, yet ultimately he won on luck. In the seventh round when Dempsey suddenly came to life and relived it up with a flurry of the same murderous punches that floored Jess Willard and Luis Firpo, Tunney was caught off guard and clobbered. The first two

Dempsey punches on either side of the head caused Tunney to sag. The descending Tunney then was clubbed on top of the head by a dozen Dempsey blows and was on his pants, hurt and groggy with one arm groping for the lower strand of the ropes.

Dempsey, who should have known better, hovered over him. The instructions to retire to the farthest corner in case of a knockdown had been spelled out for both fighters by referee Dave Barry in the prefight instructions. Ironically, Dempsey himself had inspired the rule by his actions in the Firpo fight when he stood over the fallen Argentinian in readiness to swat him again as his foe tried to rise in their Jersey City fight. Yet, Dempsey didn't remember the rule until Barry almost physically directed him to the farthest corner.

By that time, the count against Tunney had reached five, and now reverted to one with Tunney getting the benefit of it. I was positive then, as now, that Tunney would not have been up at a proper count of 10, but those precious seconds were heaven-sent for him, and at nine he made a gutsy rise to his feet.

The retreats he had practiced in training now paid off for Tunney, who backpedaled out of danger for the rest of the round. At the round's end, it was Dempsey who was spent from his exertions, and he was reduced to beckoning in vain for the canny Tunney to "come in and fight."

Tunney ran away to fight another round and another and another and at the end of 10 was the clear winner over an exhausted Dempsey.

In later years, Tunney could live with the disputed count graciously, but sometimes he would say, "Everybody forgets that I floored Dempsey with my first punch in round eight."

Tunney made one more fight before he retired, picking apart plodding Tom Heeney in New York and knocking him out in round 11. This was another Tex Rickard promotion, with Rickard learning that Tunney, without Dempsey, was not box office. Rickard lost $132,000 on the fight.

Following that fight, Tunney married Polly Lauder in Rome and retired to a new world of dinner jackets and, later, corporate board meetings. He had refused a $100,000 endorsement from a cigarette company and wrote a "don't smoke" article for *Reader's Digest*.

On one trip to Europe, he told assembled news photographers, "If my picture is taken again, it will be without my consent. In England, if a person announces he is retiring to private life, they respect him."

In 1945, Tunney wrote the segment on boxing for the Encyclopedia Britannica but otherwise retired to his Connecticut country home in what appeared to be a search for oblivion.

Former heavyweight champion Gene Tunney remains an enigma to the boxing world in death just as he had in life.

Boxing's "royalty" stands ready to pay its final tribute to the former Marine who beat Jack Dempsey in two of boxing's most famous bouts. But Tunney's family, speaking through the Knapp Funeral Home, refuses to reveal any details of Tunney's burial service.

"Under no circumstances will we give out the time, place, or day," a spokesman for the Knapp home said. "That is all we have to say."

MARATHON RACING

THE CRAZINESS OF THE LONG-DISTANCE RUNNER

By Vic Ziegel

From New York Magazine
Copyright, ©, 1978, New York Magazine Co., Inc.

Staten Island: Mayor Koch is minutes away from firing the cannon that will start the New York City Marathon. The mayor is wearing a dark-green corduroy jacket and a jolly yellow-and-brown knit tie. He has his back to 9,875 people in T-shirts and shorts.

RADIO INTERVIEWER: Do you think you'll ever run in the marathon, Mayor?

KOCH: I jog for exercise, but I couldn't possibly run in this. So I think I'll just shoot off the cannon for the next 12 years.

A man and woman are at the mayor's side. "We're from Washington," the man says, "and we remember you down there with great affection."

The mayor reaches for his hand. Smiles. "Wasn't I a good congressman?"

RADIO INTERVIEWER: A beautiful day, isn't it, Mayor?

KOCH: I declared by proclamation that it would be a sunny day and, of course, it is sunny.

Someone suggests that the runners aren't too happy about the warm weather. "Well, I wish they would have told me," the mayor says. "I would have made it cooler." The mayor smiles again. He moves toward the cannon. He has a full schedule: a groundbreaking in Brooklyn and then the trophy presentation to the marathon winner. The mayor has a ride. The radio interviewer will watch the race from the press bus. There are two flatbed trucks for photographers. Motorcycles for the police, helicopters for the sponsors, ambulances for the runners.

BOOOOOOMMMMMM!!!!!!

"What's taking them so long?" That's what Bill Wiklund wants to know. He is on the third floor of marathon headquarters, the New York Cultural Center, the Friday before the race, waiting for 1,134 women runners and 4,005 first-time men starters to pour from the elevators. They have to pick up their numbers, the T-shirt from Perrier, the cap from New York Telephone, the tray from Manufacturers Hanover with a brief history of the race on the back.

Wiklund is 71, the Crusty Old Marathoner Lending a Hand. "What? Run. No, I can't run. I've got an artificial hip. Ten-inch stainless-steel shaft. They operated on me in February. May 24 I ran 10,000 meters. Had a bet with my doctor I'd be able to finish. Cost him $10. I was training for the marathon last month. Stepped on a stone."

A woman steps off the elevator.

"Check the wall for your number," Wiklund hollers. "Go to the proper table." She tells one of the people behind a table that she's a volunteer too.

"They get off the elevator and stand there like sheep," Wiklund says. "You got to tell them what to do. They're wonderful kids. But it's like a picnic to them. When I ran they were all runners. Ran the Boston Marathon when it used to be the qualifier for the Olympic team. I was the third American to finish in Boston in 1944 and what do you think happened? The only time I made it, they cancel the Olympics."

No. 301 F is Janet Bailey, a 22-year-old secretary at the United Nations, blond, perky, June Allyson's stand-in for the race. "It took me two years to run five miles without dying. January I broke through. Now I run about 40 miles a week, which really isn't enough for a marathon. I'm starting to get · tense about it. I know I can do it, but after I ran my only marathon last spring I was destroyed for about six weeks. Sleeping a lot, eating a lot, no energy, depressed. I really want to do well this time. I can't imagine living in New York and missing it." She glances at her number, her cap, her shirt, her tray.

"It'll definitely hurt."

Charles H. McCabe, Jr., is proud of the tray. The vice-president and director of marketing for Manufacturers Hanover says, "We get some business from the race but nothing that's going to affect the bottom line or put Tim Conway out of work." McCabe budgets $75,000 of his bank's money on the marathon and admits, "We'll probably go over that figure. But I couldn't spend a hundred thousand in paid-for media and get that kind of coverage. My selfish desire is to have the bank's name on the winner's shirt. It's on all the numbers, the mile markers, the kilometer markers, the start, the finish . . . I just couldn't buy that kind of publicity."

The *New York Times* page one for October 24, 1977, is framed on his office wall. The photograph at the top of the page is of Bill Rodgers crossing the finish line, winning the marathon. "He had the bank's name on his number. If the camera had come in just a little closer . . ."

McCabe accompanies his visitor to the elevator and they meet Fred Lebow, president of the New York Road Runners Club, the marathon organizers. Lebow is wearing a green expensive-looking warm-up suit. McCabe isn't a runner. That doesn't mean he wouldn't want a green, expensive-looking warm-up suit.

"Adidas is giving one to every top official of the club," Lebow says.

McCabe is fingering Lebow's sleeve. "I'd like one of these. Couldn't you make me an honorary official?"

"I'll see what I can do."

The banker nods. "They'd make great pajamas."

Lebow is on the move. There's a meeting with the Police Department to discuss the marathon route in the Bronx. To help the flow of traffic the police suggested an alternate street for the runners. Since it seemed to be a parallel route, Lebow agreed. And then discovered it would add 159 yards to the marathon. He measured it 11 times. Hated it every time. "I would rather not run a marathon than run one that was 159 yards off," he insists. "What can I do? I don't know. We'll fight over it."

He makes a stop at marathon headquarters. The hospitality suite. Apples, bananas, cheese, Perrier, peanuts, old runners, young runners, runners with beards, runners staring at other runners. Sitting on a couch is Lasse Viren from Finland, a double gold-medal winner in the last two Olympic games. He's not too many cushions away from Eugene Schapiro, a 60-year-old accountant from Roosevelt Island who began running after open-heart surgery.

Michael Weinstein is an advertising man who thought he would break three hours in his first marathon. He ran 20 miles every Sunday during the summer. "The first time I tried it, all I could think of was going to Baskin Robbins for a root-beer float. The second time was easier. After that it was a piece of cake. Three Sundays ago I was running and I got bad stomach pains. The next thing I remember . . ."

He was in the emergency room at New York Hospital saying good-bye to his appendix. And the marathon. "All I could think of was the days I ran in 95 degrees, the nights when it rained. A friend in the race visited one morning and then he called me at night. He said, 'Guess what? I'm in the emergency room.' He tore ligaments in his ankle and couldn't run either. That made me feel a little better."

Lebow recognizes one of last year's runners. "Didn't you finish the race on crutches?" Michael Levine raises a withered arm, gnarled fingers. "Not me," he says. "I can't control crutches."

Levine was born with cerebral palsy on the right side of his body. "Right hemiplegic, they call it. I'm an epileptic too." He smiles. "I don't want to be maudlin about it to an uncalled-for extent. Well, maybe to a called-for extent. I run the way I walk, and it's not pretty. That's one of the reasons I train at four in the morning. Nobody watches me. I've been laughed at all my life and it bothers me. Sure it does. Kids laugh at me because they don't know any better. I guess you heard about last year's race."

He was running through Brooklyn when a couple of Boy Scouts came out of the crowd carrying a stretcher. They were going to save Levine's life. "They thought I was flailing. And I was flailing. But that's how I look when I run. That's my style."

Bill Rodgers, winner the last two years, makes one final prerace appearance. Bloomingdale's. To sell. The Bill Rodgers shirt is $10; the Bill Rodgers warm-up suit, $60. He has two equipment stores in Boston, another on Martha's Vineyard. Rodgers, 30, blond, runner-skinny, is talking about the weather.

"If it's over 70," he says, "that's really nasty. For me, that's drastic. If you're hot, you're pouring water over yourself and you're sweating a lot more and you get more water in your shoes. That's depressing, isn't it?"

The crowd murmurs agreement. This is, after all, Bill Rodgers talking. The doyen of distance. If he's depressed, none dare smile.

"That's part of my strategy," Rodgers says. "I depress people."

The runners meet again in the courtyard at Lincoln Center, where city buses shuttle them to the starting line. "Sunny and warm," the radio has said. "High in the 70s. Unseasonably mild." That's later. At seven in the morning, with the only light coming from dawn's rosy finger, the runners are cold, nervous. The conversation is tenuous.

"Does that work?" He's pointing to a clip on the tongue of Philip Held's shoe. It holds his house key.

"Ask me two hours into the race," Held answers.

"I was told to tie my key to my laces but I'm afraid it would flap."

"I run with my key in my hand."

. "Did you read *Papillon?*" says Held. "This morning, when I slipped my key in there, I felt like Papillon with his charger."

"What's a charger?"

"That's the little container the prisoners put their valuables in. They keep the charger in their anus."

Held finds a seat at the rear of the bus. His neighbor is Mike West, a junior high school English teacher. "I hope they give us coffee," Held says. "I just read an article in *Runners' World.* The new thinking is that coffee is good for you two hours before a marathon."

"There's always something new," West says. "I read how I got to watch out in this race because the pavement is hard. Hey, I live here. I know the pavement's hard. Then they tell you to watch out for potholes. Hey, I know I got to watch out for potholes."

Held has decided. "I'm going to try the coffee. The only thing that bothers me is that coffee makes me pee."

The runners fill an open field at Fort Wadsworth. T-shirt humor is everywhere: "I spit to the right." "Escargot" (front), "Escargone" (back). "I love you, Cincinnati." "Love animals—don't eat them." "I'm from Boston but I love the Yankees." "Girl friend wanted." "Duryea for governor." "Tylenol." "I'd rather be in Tucson." "Olympics Da Moscow Nyet."

The "Running Rabbit" T-shirt walks past a "Superman" shirt and cape. "I plan to fly around the course a few times," Superman is telling a reporter. "Then I'll come back here and start the race with the mere mortals."

Three runners glance in his direction. "What a jerk," says one.

"Makes us all look stupid."

"Yeah, but look at his number. Pretty low. I guess he can run a little."

The Road Runners processed applications from more than 11,000; almost 2,000 didn't show. Who will wear their shirts, their caps, drink their complimentary Perriers? The runners I talked to all started, and all of them finished.

"I was debating whether to start," said Gene Schapiro, the open-heart patient. "There was pain in my feet all week. Shins, knees, ankles. But I did it. Not as fast as I would have liked, but it was tremendous. Only one thing surprised me. Going through Harlem, people were calling me 'Pops' and 'Grandpa.' I always prided myself on looking younger than my age. 'Pops.' It sort of bothered me."

No Boy Scouts came after Michael Levine. "I was in Harlem and I saw a kid who stopped his brothers from laughing at me last year. When I went past him this time he said, 'I remember you, I remember you.' I remembered him too. I smiled at him. The only thing that was bad was that there were too many runners in too little space, not enough room to pass. On First Avenue a few people stopped for water and I crashed into them. It was my fault. I don't have that much control of my muscles and balance. But I'm the healthiest person you know with one foot in the grave."

Perky Janet Bailey is wondering "if I'll ever do it again. I've got a headache, I hurt inside, the works. At the end my body was crying with pain."

Mike West, who knew about potholes, reached the finish line when the digital clock read 3:30.37. (Rodgers's winning time was 2:12.12, the slowest of his three marathon victories. Not so depressing.)

"There wasn't too much joking going on at the finish," West said. "The runners just hit the grass like they were in a battle. I was a little disappointed in my time, but it doesn't matter. It was terrific, wondrous. It put you one up on the guys in the old neighborhood. I'm not O.J. or Kareem, but I ran 26 miles. I'm an athlete. I'm a runner."

The last time he saw Phil Held, who read *Papillon*, who was determined to drink coffee, was at the start. They thought they might pace each other, stay close. It didn't work out that way. As the runners waited for the cannon, jumping with excitement, stretching one time, peering up at the helicopters, aching to begin, Phil Held realized he had to pee.

BOOOOOOMMMMMM!!!!!!

BASKETBALL

JACK'S THE RIPPER

By Billy Reed

From The Louisville Courier-Journal
Copyright, © 1978, The Louisville Courier-Journal
Reprinted with permission

The pesky Duke University Blue Devils kept the party from starting until the very end of the long, crazy, wonderful University of Kentucky basketball season.

But once the game was over, once the Wildcats had proved to everyone that they are the best college team in all the land, coach Joe B. Hall and his players proved they also could smile and hug and party as well as anyone.

The celebration began before the final seconds had ticked off the clock in UK's 94–88 victory over Duke in the final game of the 1978 NCAA tournament before an SRO crowd of 18,721.

With only moments left, UK's James Lee, the bullish 6-foot-5 senior from Lexington, got behind Duke's frantic press, took a pass, and roared in from the left side of the hoop for a smashing dunk that put the exclamation at the end of a game, and a season, that Wildcat fans will remember for a long time.

The dunk brought Hall off the bench, his arms raised toward the ceiling in joyous celebration. Moments later, the final horn sounded and then the party began in earnest.

The first order of business, of course, was to cut down the nets. At the sight of senior forward Jack "Goose" Givens rising to the shoulders of his teammates, the UK partisans broke into a frenzy of pompon waving and filled the arena with the chant of "Goose! Goose! Goose!"

In his last game in a Wildcat uniform, the soft-speaking, soft-shooting native of Lexington was absolutely, positively magnificent. Besides scoring a career-high 41 points—mostly on his soft little jumpers from the foul lane—Givens played with uncommon ferocity. Anytime UK needed points, Givens begged for the ball. He hit 18 of 27 from the floor.

"I was ready, really ready," Givens said.

The victory gave UK its fifth national championship, but first under Hall, the bespectacled native of Cythiana, Ky., who accepted the impossible task of following the legendary Adolph Rupp in 1972. Rupp, who coached

UK's first four national champions in 1948–49–51–58, died last December 10, the night this UK team defeated Kansas, his alma mater.

Just to show that UK fans hadn't forgotten, Wildcat mascot Gary Tanner and a UK cheerleader carried a sign on the floor late in the game that said, "Win one for Rupp."

Seldom, if ever, has a UK team—or coach—gone through such a strange season. Ranked No. 1 from the very first, the UK coaches and players wrestled all season with uncommon pressure. Their victories were shrugged off because they were expected. Their two losses—to Alabama and Louisiana State—were received as if some great tragedy had befallen the Commonwealth.

Even in victory, Hall was the subject of considerable second-guessing and criticism. When UK won, either the margin wasn't enough or the game wasn't pretty enough to suit some of the fans. As a result, Hall often seemed tense and angry, and he seemed to transfer that tension to his players.

The drive toward the national championship probably began with the LSU loss in February. After the game, Hall accused his team of being "complacent" and "selfish" and he began to tongue-lash them and push them harder than ever. It was a gamble on Hall's part—the team could have quit on him.

Instead, the players responded to the pressure with a series of gritty tournament wins against outstanding competition—Florida State, Miami of Ohio, Michigan State, Arkansas and, finally, Duke.

If UK is the brawniest team ever to win the national title—shall we call it the "Physical Five"?—it also may be the most unpopular. UK's no-nonsense, all-business, deadly serious approach to the game turned off many who naïvely believed that big-time college basketball is a game more than a business.

Asked Sunday at a press conference if basketball at UK were fun this season, senior forward Rick Robey smiled and said, "Ask me tomorrow night."

Last seen, Robey was walking around the court in the Checkerdome, the remnants of a basketball net around his neck and a championship trophy in his hand. He looked as if he were having fun.

Until the end, when Duke's frantic rally cut into their lead, the Wildcats controlled the tempo of the game from the opening tip.

The first half mostly was a case of Duke's foul shooting—UK's 15 fouls allowed the Blue Devils to hit 21 free throws—against the marvelous work of Givens. Time and again, the Wildcats would work the ball against Duke's zone defense until Givens worked loose in the lane for one of his quick little jumpers. And time and again, Givens would face Mike Gminski, Duke's brawny 6-foot-11 sophomore center, and score over him.

Going into the second half, the main question for UK was whether it would be done in by foul trouble.

It wasn't.

And for Duke, the question was whether it could stop Givens.

It couldn't.

Adding 18 second-half points to his 23 in the first, Givens played as a man possessed. The only other Wildcat in double figures was Robey with 20. The Blue Devils were led by Freshman Eugene Banks with 22, Jim Spanarkel with 21, and Gminski with 20.

Banks was marvelous, especially considering a death threat had been made on his life before the game. The Duke bench was ringed with extra security.

Using their 1-3-1 zone defense to protect their foul-plagued players, and to force Duke to shoot from outside, the Wildcats clawed to a 16-point lead, 66–50, when Givens put in a Robey miss with 12:46 to go.

That would have been a good time for the young Blue Devils to fold and go home to wait for next year. Instead, they threw a furious press at UK and managed to stay close enough to delay UK's party until the very end.

"Givens did a super job," said Hall after it was all over. "He did one of the finest jobs I've every seen against a great Duke team."

With less than a minute to go, Hall pulled his starters so the Wildcat rooters could give them well-deserved standing ovations. However, he quickly put them back to ensure against disaster. The Blue Devils cut it to four, 92–88, with 10 seconds to go, but then Lee got the dunk that ended the season, cinched the title, and started the party.

"We've got a lot of stored up celebrating to do," Hall said.

HORSE RACING

THE STAKES RACE

By Randy Harvey

From The Chicago Sun-Times
Copyright, © , 1978, The Chicago Sun-Times

Horse Trading once was done much less extravagantly than at Keeneland's
Selected Yearling Sale, where proper women arrive in long evening gowns
and dignified men in tuxedoes with tails. It is an affair more appropriately
reported in society columns than *The Daily Racing Form.* Joan Louise Siegel's
name appeared in neither during the annual auction last month in Lexington, Ky., but she believes she soon will be an esteemed member of the horse
set. If the sport of kings needs a queen, she is available.

Almost everyone stared at Joan Louise when she entered the room next
to the sales pavilion on the first afternoon of the world's most exclusive horse
auction. It was immediately evident this woman was different. She was
wearing tan corduroy jeans under a blue cotton two-piece dress. The skirt
kept sliding off her waist to reveal a pink slip that matched the sweater she
wore around her shoulders. She wore a turquoise sweater on top of the pink
sweater. On her head was a yellow bonnet to protect her long, raven hair. On
her feet were orthopedic shoes. Sunglasses hid her eyes. She wore ruby red
lipstick.

She has only one visible tooth, a lower right bicuspid. Occasionally, she
lapsed into coughing seizures, which she later revealed were caused by
chestal congestion. She said the congestion also had caused her to lose weight
and make her look more frail than she actually is. She also later revealed she
is 62 years old and intends to become a rich woman before her next birthday.

Standing in line while waiting to use the telephone, the man somehow
didn't notice Joan Louise until she tapped him on the shoulder and asked
where she could acquire a catalog like the one he had in his hand. The
catalog included detailed information on the 350 horses that would be sold
during the next two days and had a color picture on the cover of one of the
auction's distinguished alumni, The Minstrel, crossing the finish line first in
the 1977 Epsom Derby. Her catalog was identical except for the cover, which
was white with orange trim. No color picture. She wanted one with the color
picture on the cover.

The man was preoccupied with his own business and was in no mood for conversation. But he told her where she could go to find the catalog she wanted. He hoped she would go soon.

It was unsettling for the man to feel so threatened by such a harmless woman. But he was afraid the others in the room would see him talking to her and consider him guilty by association. He didn't know them, either. He recognized it as a flaw in his character and made a mental note to analyze the human condition later. Meantime, he glanced self-consciously around the room as he listened to her dreams of a financial empire.

"I was living in a two-by-four room in California in 1968 while I was on medical dispensation when I was engulfed in God's power," she said, sounding like a character from a Carlos Castaneda book. "I opened the Bible to Deuteronomy and read, 'If ye double your riches in silver and gold in life, do not forget God or all is for naught.' I knew then that I would become rich. It was all very real."

It was somewhat more real than the riches she since has acquired, she admitted. But she said she plans to close within 60 days on the $30 million purchase of a Nevada gold and silver mine that is worth $300 million. She said she also is negotiating to buy a $10 billion Alaskan sulfur mine for $500,000 and a $10 billion Washington dolomite mine for $1.5 million. "My attorney told me by this time next year I'll be solid," she said.

By this time next year, she also plans to be one of the nation's foremost thoroughbred owners. She came to Keeneland last year to buy a Secretariat colt and was told she first should buy a farm on which to raise him. That is why she returned this summer, to find a farm that might be for sale. If Joan Louise went to Rome to buy a house, she would want the Vatican. If she went to California to buy land, she would want San Francisco. When she came to Lexington to buy a farm, she wanted Calumet.

Calumet Farm, the pride of Fayette County. Rolling hills, blue grass, white fences, and stately mansion. The home of eight Kentucky Derby winners. God's 100 acres that have been entrusted to the Admiral and Mrs. Gene Markey.

"It was meant for me to have," she said. "I'm going to buy 100 acres for 10."

"Ten what?" the man asked.

"Ten million," she said. "You don't know figures yet, do you?"

Figures. They are the universal language at the Keeneland Selected Yearling Sale, where millionaire horsemen come to bid at the Cadillac of horse auctions. Jess Collins came from England as a representative for the British Bloodstock Agency of London. Young and blond with his chin resting on his hand, he sat near the back of the sales pavilion on the final night of the sale and tried to attract a bid spotter's attention without attracting the attention of everyone else in the room. He raised his right hand to his coat lapel and waved his index finger. He winked. He brushed his hair with his left hand. Finally, auctioneer Tom Caldwell noticed the exasperated Briton from his vantage point on the podium and directed the spotter toward him. "Lift up your eyes to the heavens, Dale," Caldwell said. "There he is in the back." The spotter, Dale Rouk, found Collins and acknowledged his bid: $650,000.

Three men in another part of the pavilion huddled before bidding $700,000. Collins couldn't see them and didn't know who they were, but he suspected they were from the British Bloodstock Agency of Ireland. A natural rival. He bid $750,000.

The object of their affections was a bay colt for Northern Dancer, the third-leading sire in the United States, and out of Special, whose sire, Forli, also was Forego's sire.

The Irish bid $900,000. Collins countered with $905,000.

"We may be here until 3:05 at that rate," Caldwell said glancing at his watch. It was 10:20 P.M. "But I don't care."

The Irish bid $950,000.

"Give me a million," Caldwell said. "It doesn't hurt a bit if you say it fast."

Collins bid $1 million. If it hurt, he didn't let anyone else know. His eyes betrayed nothing.

The audience applauded as if they'd just heard *The War of 1812 Overture*. Music to their ears. "How about that?" Caldwell said before the bidding continued.

It is potentially risky even to watch such proceedings. Spotters are trained to distinguish between twitches and bids but sometimes are fooled. "You go on instinct," veteran spotter Charley Richardson said. "You just look for a motion, maybe a nod of the head or just a wink. But you've got to be sure." During the first session of the sale that afternoon, a woman waved across the room to a friend and two spotters recorded it as a $65,000 bid. She leaped to her feet to explain her mistake. "That woman held her arm straight up in the best imitation of a bid I've ever seen," Caldwell said. "If we catch you doing that, you're liable to end up owning a horse."

No one stirred as the English and Irish tried to intimidate each other with their bold bids. The English finally won with a bid of $1.3 million. It was the second-highest price ever paid for a yearling.

"How much higher would you have gone?" reporters asked Collins later.

"Precious little," he said.

"Was it an inflated price?"

"That's a difficult question," he said. "Maybe I'll be able to tell you in two years."

It has been two years since John Sikura and Ted Burnett of Toronto paid a record $1.5 million for one of Secretariat's first foals, a colt they later named Canadian Bound. They beat out a syndicate of Texans headed by William S. Farish and automobile racer A. J. Foyt. In retrospect, the Texans probably won by losing. Canadian Bound has not distinguished himself on European tracks. (There are just as often happy endings of such stories. Cannonero II, who later won the Kentucky Derby and Preakness, was sold at Keeneland for $1,200. Mickey and Karen Taylor bought eventual Triple Crown winner Seattle Slew for $17,500 at the Fasig-Tipton sale in Lexington after Keeneland officials declared the horse didn't even have good enough bloodlines to be sold at their auction.)

As a rule, Secretariat foals sold at Keeneland before this year at an average price of $278,808 have had disappointing racing careers, although his two-year-old filly Terlinqua has been an exception by winning all three stakes races she has entered. Kentucky breeder Tom Gentry, who sold the Secretariat filly last year for $275,000, was showing her half brother this summer. He was disappointed when the chestnut colt sold on the final night of the auction for *only* $525,000. "Some of Secretariat's charisma has worn off," said one buyer, Texan W. R. Hawn.

Most of the big spenders were saving their best bids for foals of Northern Dancer, who has sired 55 stakes winners, or Vaguely Noble, the leading sire in the United States and the only horse to sire two $1 million winners, Dahlia and Exceller. Seventeen Vaguely Noble colts were sold on the final night of the sale for $5,185,000, an average of $305,000.

Vaguely Noble's sexual proficiency pushed Keeneland toward a record sale as 350 yearlings were sold during the two-day auction for $42,479,000, an average of $121,654. Aided by the declining value of the dollar on the world market, foreign interests contributed $16,504,000. The major benefactor was Bluegrass Farm's Nelson Bunker Hunt, the Dallas oilman who already is one of the world's richest men. The owner of Vaguely Noble, he sold 21 yearlings this summer for $5,281,000. An unimpressive man physically, Hunt walked among the chic, tanned sophisticates at Keeneland wearing a soiled, wrinkled white shirt without a tie and baggy trousers that accentuated his ample midsection. Once spotted in the coach section of an airplane, he said, "My horses go first class. I go coach."

But the brunch he hosted on the lawn of Bluegrass Farm Number One the day before the sale began was nothing if not first class. It was the first and most elaborate of several parties hosted by racing's blue blood that day. A white tent was draped in Hunt's racing colors, two shades of green, and the brunch tables were centered with green baskets filled with daisies tinted green and coral geraniums. He served chicken crepes, a casserole of chicken livers, orange rind and wild-rice, Kentucky country ham, English peas, lima beans, water chestnuts, cheese grits, fresh muffins, and fruit. His guest list looked like a page from *The Social Register*.

Joan Louise said the next afternoon she didn't attend Hunt's brunch because the bus company had misplaced one of her suitcases, the one that carried her formal attire. She had taken the bus from Las Vegas to Lexington, with temporary stops in Flagstaff, St. Louis, Indianapolis, and Cincinnati. She was still complaining because she lost money in a newspaper vending machine in Flagstaff and in a snack machine in Indianapolis while trying to buy potato chips. The man offered to take her to dinner the next evening at Keeneland's Clubhouse Dining Room. On the way she found an umbrella on a bench that the previous owner had discarded because it had a large hole in the top.

"You're not going to keep that, are you?" the man asked.

"Of course," she said. "It was meant for me to have." She tucked the umbrella under her arm and continued walking. She talked about her past, a fascinating story that continued through dinner. She is an intelligent woman.

She said her father, Harry, was the first president of New York Life and her mother was a daughter to the Millers of I. Miller shoes. They lived in New York City at Seventy-second and Madison in a building she someday hopes to own.

Her family lost most of its money during the depression, but she still was able to finish college at the University of Miami and was satisfied with her sedate middle-class life until 1962 when she moved to Las Vegas and was involved in two serious automobile accidents within a two-year period. That is how she landed on welfare in the small cubicle in California, where she had the vision of herself as a millionairess.

"I was talking to a woman in the coffee shop of the Sahara Hotel in Las Vegas later that year when her husband walked in and started talking about sulfur mines he wanted to buy in Alaska," she said. "That's the way you meet people in Vegas. I didn't see any future in it at the time, but I said I would help. The man whose home I was living in at the time had a business associate who was in real estate. He referred me to a sulfur mine. The man tried to buy the mine, but his deal fell through. It was then offered to me, but I didn't get the deal cleared in time. But that started me in the right direction."

She said she doesn't actually plan to purchase the mines for which she is now negotiating because she doesn't have the capital, but she serves as the middleman between mine owners and potential investors. She figures to make a small fortune.

"Dynamic," she said. "Use that word referring to me. I was reading a social science's book in the Reno library. I opened the book to that word. The dictionary said the word meant you have motivation, incentive, and perseverance. The only problem I have is that some lawyers don't take me seriously."

"Do a lot of people take you less than seriously?" the man asked.

"You mean P-H-O-N-Y?" she said, spelling the word she didn't feel like repeating. "I don't want to hear that word again."

Keeneland officials treat her politely. They don't admit publicly they think she is P-H-O-N-Y, but it is apparent they are terrified by the thought she may not be. After dinner, she confronted a local realtor, who does a great deal of business with horsemen, in the hallway outside the sales pavilion and told him of her plans to buy Calumet. The realtor's eyes grew as large as Frisbees.

"I know the Markeys pretty well and I don't think Calumet is on the market," he said.

"The desk clerk at the Hilton told me," Joan Louise argued.

"I don't think so," the realtor said.

"You're negative," Joan Louise said. "Think positive."

That obviously is the advice she has given her attorney, Madison Graves of Las Vegas. He said last week Joan Louise's claims that she is negotiating for silver, gold, sulfur, and dolomite mines throughout the West are legitimate.

"All I can tell you is that she is counting on the deals being consummated," he said.

"What are the chances they will be consummated?" he was asked.

"Anything is possible, I suppose," he said. "I have my fingers crossed."

The last time the man saw Joan Louise she was standing outside the sales pavilion while waiting for a taxi cab to take her to the bus station. She had to catch an 11:56 P.M. bus to Albany, N.Y., where she was planning to visit her brother. She waved. "By the way," she said, "do you know where I can send a card of condolences to the Rockefellers?"

BOXING

"THRILLER ON THE RIVER"

By Paul (Tex) Chandler

From The Angolite
Copyright, ©, 1978, The Angolite Magazine, Louisiana State Penitentiary,
  Angola, La.

Men have always fought each other. There's something instinctive and natural about it. That's even more true with prisoners—fighting is a natural part of the competitive struggle for survival in prison. And every Thursday night prisoners get into a makeshift ring in the prison's A-Building to box, brawl, run, and sometimes just downright fight.

Probably the most memorable fight scene in Angola's boxing history occurred several weeks ago in the heavyweight title bout between the defending champion, Roland "Boogie" Gibson, and challenger Conrad "Big Junior" Norman. The fight pitted youth against age, upstart courage against mature determination. Pulses quickened, thoughts intensified, and adrenaline pumped through the crowd as the two fighters entered the ring, squared off, and let each other know that they were ready for whatever had to come in the fight.

Like the seemingly immortal Cochise, Boogie has established himself as somewhat of a legend in Angola's boxing world. In the ring he is a patient, confident man who moves with the grace of a stalking leopard. He is a boxer, not a brawler, yet he has knockout strength in either hand. Conrad, on the other hand, is a big, bruising youngster who keeps comin' in a style a bit similar to that of Smokin' Joe Frazier. The dress style of the two men perhaps best pronounced the difference in their styles: Boogie was dressed in the traditional red AABA trunks and wore the conservative high-laced black boxing shoes. But Conrad came out in his classy purple n' white trunks with matching white-purple stripe shoes. He had the flash of Las Vegas.

As the fighters stood facing each other at center ring, not even listening to the monotonous hum of the referee's instructions, other dimensions of the fight could be felt. The fighters themselves represented the traditional factions of the Big Yard and Trusty Yard. Boogie represented the Big Yard. He stood in his corner, strong, defiant, and ready to get down. Among men he is the kind of man who claims whatever spot he stands on, and no other man intrudes on or tries to take that spot. If they do, then they have a helluva fight on their hands. Conrad wants Boogie's spot and he challenged Boogie by calling him an "old man with arthritis." But as Conrad stood in his corner looking out across the ring at the leopard ready to pounce on him, he knew that Boogie was not an arthritic old man and that he had a hard fight ahead of him if he wanted to take the title.

With the sound of the opening bell, the fighters came out and greeted each other with a vicious exchange of solid punches. There would be no finessing, no early feeling-out, or attempts to set a style. Both men came to fight: to prove something—that each was the best. From jump-street Conrad did the only thing he could do: He took the action straight to Boogie. He kept coming, kept pressing: He crowded Boogie like the Big Yard prisoners crowded that mess hall door to see *Emmanuele* [ED. NOTE: *Emmanuele* is an X-rated movie]—and the more he crowded, the more punishment Boogie poured on his head with damaging short left hooks and occasional hard rights to the body. But Conrad kept coming, sometimes landing solid blows that caused Boogie's eyes to narrow in surprise and anger.

At the end of the first round, the fighters went back to their corners and refused to sit. The round had been hard, grueling, and contained plenty of action. The crowd was immediately on its feet following the round, clapping and cheering. Cheers from both fighters' fans tried to reach above the other's pitch. The fighters stood in their corners, glaring across the ring at each other. They were oblivious to the spectators. The fight had become very personal—it was no longer a contest for the crowd. The men were fighting for pride, for masculine dominance, and just for the simple, perhaps inexplicable man-to-man fight of it.

The second, third, and fourth rounds were almost identical to the first, only more intense and harder fought. Each round became more physical, more brutal as the two fighters continuously challenged and rechallenged each other with blows and counterblows. Boogie kept easing up a light point-lead because Conrad kept coming, taking all the blows dealt on him. In the middle of the third round Boogie landed several solid punches which nearly took the challenger out. Conrad's knees buckled and almost gave way as he hurriedly clinched, violently shook his head, and reached down in his gut to find enough stamina to survive the round. Yet, although hurt, Conrad kept coming—and the constant pressure bothered Boogie. He got more determined and more angry. He put all his strength and weight into his blows. A look of concern, blended with frustration, could be seen on his face at the end of the third round. He had hit Conrad with every blow he had, and while he nearly brought him to his knees, the challenger not only survived the attack but was actually fighting back at the close of the round.

At the start of the fifth round announcer Mark Sullivan told the crowd that Boogie had predicted he would take Conrad out in the fifth. The crowd reacted. The prisoner audience came to its feet as the fighters came out to meet each other. It proved to be Conrad's best round and the turning point in the fight. The announcement seemed to give him more determination and placed more pride at stake. He poured in on Boogie—hooking, throwing some vicious body blows, and countering with some mean head-shots. For the first time in the fight Conrad had Boogie off-key and startled—he backed, covered, and even clinched. His blows were easily deflected and warded off as Conrad kept throwing and crowding him. Finally, toward the end of the round, both fighters stood, toe-to-toe in the middle of the ring, exchanging blow for blow: There was no protecting, ducking, or dodging. There was just a brutal exchange of blow pounding after blow. The crowd loved it. Standing, they hollered and cheered encouragement to their fighters as the men kept up the vicious exchange, not even hearing the bell sound for the end of the round causing the referee to step in and separate them.

Boogie walked slowly back to his corner—a look of 10 million years of pain, hell, death, and blood etched across his face. He didn't see the crowd below him and wasn't listening to his trainer working on him. Blood poured from his mouth, dripping onto his chest. He proudly spat out his bloody mouthpiece. It was a yoke he wouldn't accept as a warrior. On the other side of the ring, Conrad stood gasping for second air as his trainer Jake Robertson frantically wiped a mixture of sweat 'n' blood from his body. He seemed confident and could sense victory: He had taken everything Boogie had to offer and he had the champ hurt, bleeding and angry.

The bell for the sixth round sounded loud as the two bulls charged out to meet each other head on. Immediately there was a vicious exchange of blows. The crowd once again came to its feet cheering. The concession stand even stopped cooking. There was no movement around the A-Building except for the two men doing battle. With each blow dealt out, the crowd could feel and sense that a death-duel was being staged before them. They collectively sensed that they were watching something rare, something unique—one of those special life-happenings which unexpectedly comes along now 'n' then. It's the kind of thing you try to slow down, to make it happen in slow motion—like a good movie, you don't want to see it end.

Suddenly, blood started to pour from the top center of Conrad's head; it was not a trickle but a flow. Both men were soon covered with blood. Conrad's purple trunks became a blotched stain within minutes as the two men fought hard, tight, and in-close. The blood bothered Conrad. He had to not only fight and defend but also wipe away blood. Boogie was on his way to his best round. He was all over Conrad, steadily dealing on him with those lightning hands of punishment. Still, the challenger hung in there with admirable courage—he took all of Boogie's blows and, somehow, managed to fight back.

At the end of the sixth round, the crowd gave the fighters a standing ovation.The trainers worked frantically on their fighters: Charles "King" Daniels on Boogie and Robertson on Conrad. Robert and Mike Paul, sponsors of the Gladiator boxing club, went to each corner to check on the fighters and raced to Colonel Pence to give him a report. The Colonel looked at both men and then said what the fighters and fans wanted to hear, "Let 'em fight." And fight they did. Having stopped some of the blood flow, the fighters came out as mean as ever in the seventh. Both abandoned all caution. It was no longer a fight to score points. The fight was to win, to take the opponent out—and although weary, hurt, and tired, the men kept the action in center ring, trading blow for blow.

Between the seventh and eighth round, both corners worked desperately on their fighters. Conrad's corner worked to clean the blood off him. Boogie's corner worked on the muscles, trying to add strength to them. But Boogie was tired, a look of weary frustration covered his blood-streaked face. While everyone had him slightly ahead on points, the young challenger just kept coming. The eighth and final round proved no differently. Conrad broke out of his corner while Boogie seemed to cautiously stalk out. He had his final strategy down pat: to stalk for the one blow that would send the challenger home. But Conrad had different plans: He knew the fight was close on points and he also knew it was a rare event in the boxing world for a champion to lose his title on points. That axiom is even more true when the champion is popular like Boogie. Conrad came for the knockout; it was his only hope to win. He quickly broke up Boogie's stalking strategy. He simply poured in on Boogie, relentlessly throwing blows. Boogie reacted as only his instincts would let him: he stood his ground, giving a blow for every blow he took. And that's the way it came to an end: toe-to-toe sluggin' until a Conrad right caught Boogie with the force of a cannon-shot. The blow was heard at ringside—and as if in slow motion, Boogie's face went blank and his entire body relaxed as he crumpled to the canvas. Conrad immediately turned his back on the fallen champion, both hands exultantly stretched to the sky in a victorious exclamation. Without having looked back at his fallen opponent, Conrad knew it was over—he had put the champ away.

It took several long seconds for it to register on the crowd that it was actually over—that Boogie was down and knocked out. As soon as the referee gave the final count, King charged into the ring in aid of his fallen fighter. Suddenly there was complete pandemonium in the ring: Conrad's supporters surged up from their seats into the ring and lifted their new champion high in the air. Some of Boogie's supporters charged into the ring to protectively huddle around their fallen champ. Colonel Pence personally reacted, leading the way up into the ring to disperse the jubilant fans and within minutes things were quickly back in order. Both fighters were taken out of the A-Building and sent to the prison hospital for examination.

In a postfight interview, Boogie told *The Angolite* that "it was a beautiful fight. That's the way I like to fight." Boogie said that he hadn't been training regularly when King told him that he would have to defend his title. He had only three weeks to prepare.

Several days after the fight Conrad was transferred to DCI (Department of Corrections Institute), leaving Angola without a heavyweight champion. On a return trip with some other DCI fighters Conrad told *The Angolite* that he had trained only four days before the fight and felt he had won the whole fight. The departed champ told *The Angolite*: "I want to give him a rematch but this time I would like to see the fight held on the Big Yard . . . that way everyone will have a chance to see it."

A rematch seems inevitable. Besides Boogie and Conrad both wanting it, there is a popular demand for it. And Angola is without a champ. But regardless of how the next one goes, Angola boxing fans will long remember the last one probably as being the best title match ever staged on the River.

FOR THE RECORD

CHAMPIONS OF 1978

ARCHERY

World Champions

FREESTYLE

Men—Darrell Pace, Cincinnati.
Women—Anna Marie Lehman, W. Germany.

BAREBOW

Men—Anders Rosenberg, Sweden.
Women—Suizuko, Japan.

National Archery Assn. Champions

TARGET

Open Men—Darrell Pace, Cincinnati.
Open Women—Luann Ryon, Riverside, Calif.

FREESTYLE

Men—Darrell Pace, Cincinnati.
Women—Winnie Eicher, Duncansville, Pa.

National Field Archery Assn.

FREESTYLE

Open—Paul Nazelrod, Cumberland, Md.
Women's Open—Beverly Stout, Clinton, Ind.

AUTO RACING

World—Mario Andretti, Nazareth, Pa.
U.S. Grand Prix—Carlos Reutemann, Argentina.
USAC—Tom Sneva, Spokane, Wash.
USAC Stock—A.J. Foyt, Houston.

Indy 500—Al Unser, Albuquerque, N.M.
Daytona 500—Bobby Allison, Hueytown, Ala.
NASCAR—Cale Yarborough, Timmonsville, S.C.
24 Hours of Le Mans—Jean-Pierre Jaussaud-Didier Pironi, France; Renault-Can-Am—Alan Jones, Australia.
ISMA Camel—Peter Gregg, Jacksonville, Fla.

BADMINTON

World Champions

Singles—Liem Swie King, Indonesia.
Women's Singles—S. Ng, Malaysia.
Doubles—Tjun Tjun-J. Wahjudi, Indonesia.
Women's Doubles—Regina Masli-T. Widiastuti, Indonesia.

United States Champions

Singles—Mike Walker, Manhattan Beach, Calif.
Women's Singles—Cheryl Carton, San Diego.

BASEBALL

World Series—New York Yankees.
American League—East: New York; West: Kansas City; playoff: New York.
National League—East: Philadelphia; West: Los Angeles; playoff: Los Angeles.

All-Star Game—National League, 7–3.

Most Valuable Player, AL—Jim Rice, Boston.

Most Valuable, NL—Dave Parker, Pittsburgh.

Leading Batter, AL—Rod Carew, Minnesota.

Leading Batter, NL—Parker.

Cy Young Pitching, AL—Ron Guidry, New York.

Cy Young Pitching Award, NL—Gaylord Perry, San Diego.

AL Rookie—Lou Whitaker, Detroit.

NL Rookie—Bob Horner, Atlanta.

BASKETBALL

NBA—Washington Bullets.

NCAA Div. I—Kentucky; Div. II—Cheyney (Pa.) State; Div. III—North Park (Ill.).

NAIA—Grand Canyon.

Women's College (AIAW)—UCLA.

NIT—Texas.

Junior College—Independence, Kan.

Women's J.C—Panola (Tex.) CC.

AAU Men—Joliet Youth Christian Center.

AAU Women—Anna's Bananas, L.A.

BIATHLON

World 10 km.—Frank Ullrich, East Germany.

World 20 km.—Odd Lirhus, Norway.

U.S. 20 km.—Peter Hoag, Minneapolis.

BILLIARDS

World Champions

3-Cushion—Raymond Ceulemans, Belgium.

Pocket—Ray Martin, Fair Lawn, N.J.

Women's Pocket—Jean Balukas, Brooklyn.

BOBSLEDDING

World Champions

2-Man—E. Scharer-J. Benz, Switzerland.

4-Man—East Germany.

AAU Champions

2-Man—Bob Hickey-Joe LeClair, Keene, N.Y.

4-Man—Wade Whitney, Keene, N.Y.

BOWLING
PBA Tour

Leading Money Winner—Mark Roth, North Arlington, N.J.

ABC Champions

Singles—Rich Mersek, Cleveland.

Doubles—Bob Kulaszewicz-Don Gassana, Milwaukee.

All-Events—Chris Cobus, Milwaukee.

Women's IBC

Singles—Mae Bolt, Berwyn, Ill.

Doubles—Barbara Shelton, Jamaica, Queens-Annese Kelly, Brooklyn.

All-Events—Annese Kelly.

Queens—Loa Boxberger, Russell, Kan.

National Duckpin Congress

Singles—Jim Simmons, Baltimore.

Women's Singles—Doris Gravelin, Jewett City, Conn.

Doubles—Don Lopardo-Nick Tronsky, Torrington, Conn.

Women's Doubles—Chickey Balesano-Cathy Dyak, Manchester, Conn.

BOXING
Professional Champions

Heavyweight—Muhammad Ali, Chicago, recognized by World Boxing Association; Larry Holmes, Easton, Pa., recognized by World Boxing Council.

Light Heavyweight—Mike Rossman, Turnersville, N.J., WBA; Marvin Johnson, Indianapolis, WBC.

Middleweight—Hugo Corro, Argentina.

Junior Middleweight—Masashi Kudo, Japan, WBA; Rocky Mattioli, Australia, WBC.

Welterweight—Jose (Pepino) Cuevas, Mexico, WBA; Carlos Palomino, Huntington Beach, Calif., WBC.

Junior Welterweight—Antonio Cervantes, Spain, WBA; Saensak Muangsurin, Thailand, WBC.

Lightweight—Roberto Duran, Panama.

Junior Lightweight—Sammy Serrano, Puerto Rico, WBA; Alexis Arguello, Nicaragua, WBC.

Featherweight—Eusebio Pedrosa, Panama, WBA; Danny Lopez, Los Angeles, WBC.

Junior Featherweight—Ricardo Cardona, Colombia, WBA; Wilfredo Gomez, Puerto Rico, WBC.

Bantamweight—Jorge Lujan, Panama, WBA; Carlos Zarate, Mexico, WBC.

Flyweight—Betulio Gonzalez, Venezuela, WBA; Miguel Canto, Mexico, WBC.

Junior Flyweight—Yoko Gushiken, Japan, WBA; Kim Sung Jun, Korea, WBC.

CANOEING

Flatwater

KAYAK

500 Meters—Steve Kelly, New York.

Women's 500—Leslie Klein, Hadley, Mass.

1,000—Steve Kelly.

Women's 5,000—Ann Turner, St. Charles, Ill.

10,000—Brent Turner, St. Charles, Ill.

CANOE

500 Meters—Roland Muhlen, St. Charles, Ill.

1,000—Jay Kearney, Lexington, Ky.

10,000—Kurt Doberstein, St. Charles, Ill.

CASTING

World Overall—Steve Rajeff, San Francisco.

U.S. Overall—Steve Rajeff.

U.S. Women's All-Accuracy—Barbara Rohrer, Santa Cruz, Calif.

CROSS-COUNTRY

World Champions

Men—John Treacy, Ireland.

Women—Grete Waitz, Norway.

United States Champions

AAU—Greg Meyer, Boston; team, Mason-Dixon AC, Washington.

AAU Women—Julie Brown, Northridge, Calif.; team, Liberty AC, Cambridge, Mass.

NCAA Div. I—Alberto Salazar. Oregon; team, Texas-El Paso.

NCAA Div. II—James Schankel, Cal Poly, San Luis Obispo; team, San Luis Obispo.

NCAA Div. III—Dan Henderson, Wheaton; team, North Central (Ill.).

NAIA—Kelly Jensen, Southern Oregon; team, Pembroke State.

AIAW—Mary Decker, Colorado; team, Iowa State.

Junior College—Odis Sanders, Hagerstown, Md.; team, Southwest Michigan.

Junior College Women—Wren Schafer, Golden Valley Lutheran; team, Dodge City.

CURLING

World—United States

United States—Superior, Wis.

U.S. Women—Wausau, Wis.

Canada—Alberta.

CYCLING

World Champions

TRACK RACING

Sprint—Anton Tkac, Czechoslovakia.

Women's Sprint—Galina Zareva, U.S.S.R.

Pursuit—Detlef Macha, East Germany.

Point Race—Noel deJonckheerre, Belgium.

Time Trial—Lothar Thoms, East Germany.

Pro Sprint—Koichi Nakano, Japan.

ROAD RACING

Men—Gilbert Glaus, Switzerland.

Women—Beate Habetz, W. Germany.

Pro—Gerrie Knetemann, the Netherlands.

Tour de France—Bernard Hinault, France.

United States Champions

ROAD RACING

Senior—Dale Stetina, Indianapolis.

Women—Barbara   Hintzen,   Grosse
Pointe Farms, Mich.

TRACK RACING

Sprint—Leigh Barczewski, W. Allis, Wis.
Women's   Sprint—Sue   Novarra,   Flint,
Mich.
Pursuit—Dave   Grylls,   Grosse   Pointe,
Mich.
Women's   Pursuit—Mary   Jane   Reoch,
Phila.

TIME TRIALS

Men—Andy Weaver, Coral Springs, Fla.
Women—Esther Salmi, Chester, Conn.

DOG SHOWS

Best-in-Show Winners

Westminster (New York)—Ch. Cede Hig-
gins, Yorkshire terrier, Barbara and
Charles Switzer, Seattle.
International (Chicago)—Ch. Kishbuga's
Desert Song, borzoi, Dr. Richard Meen,
Campbellville, Ontario.

FENCING

World Champions

Foil—Didier Flament, France.
Epée—Alexander Pusch, West Germany.
Saber—Viktor Krovopuskov, USSR.
Women's   Foil—Valentina   Siderova,
USSR.

United States Champions

Foil—Marty Lang, New York AC; team,
Pannonia AC, Philadelphia.
Epée—Brooke Makler, Pannonia AC, Phila-
delphia; team, New York AC.
Saber—Stanley Lekatch, New York AC;
team, Fencers Club, New York.
Women's Foil—Gay Dasaro, San Jose,
Calif.; team, Salle Csiszar, Philadel-
phia.

National Collegiate Champions

Foil—Ernest Simon, Wayne State.
Epée—Bjorne Vaggo, Notre Dame.
Saber—Michael Sullivan, Notre Dame.
Team—Notre Dame.
Women's Foil—Stacey Johnson, San Jose.
Team—San Jose State.

FOOTBALL

College

Eastern (Lambert Trophy)—Penn State.
Eastern (Lambert Cup)—Massachusetts.
Eastern (Lambert Bowl)—Ithaca.
NCAA Division II—Eastern Illinois.
NCAA Division III—Baldwin-Wallace.
Atlantic Coast Conference—Clemson.
Big Eight—Nebraska, Oklahoma.
Big Ten—Michigan State, Michigan.
Ivy League—Dartmouth.
Mid-American—Ball State.
Missouri Valley—New Mexico State.
Ohio Valley—Western Kentucky.
Pacific 10—Southern California.
Pacific Coast AA—Utah State, San Jose
State.
Southeastern—Alabama.
Southern—Tennessee-Chattanooga,Furman.
Southland—Louisiana Tech, Arkansas State.
Southwest—Houston.
Southwestern—Grambling.
Western Athletic—Brigham Young.
Yankee—Massachusetts.

Professional

NATIONAL LEAGUE

American Conference—Pittsburgh Steelers.
National Conference—Dallas Cowboys.
Super Bowl—Pittsburgh Steelers.

CANADIAN FOOTBALL LEAGUE

Grey Cup—Edmonton Eskimos.

GOLF

Men

U.S. Open—Andy North.
U.S. Amateur—John Cook.
Masters—Gary Player, South Africa.
PGA—John Mahaffey.
British Open—Jack Nicklaus.
World Series—Gil Morgan.
Tournament of Champions—Gary Player.
Vardon Trophy—Tom Watson.
Leading Money Winner—Tom Watson.
PGA Player of Year—Tom Watson.
Canadian Open—Bruce Lietzke.
U.S. Publinx—Dean Prince, Santa Rosa,
Calif.

USGA Senior—Keith Compton, Marble Falls, Tex.

USGA Junior—Donald Hurter, Honolulu.

NCAA Div. I—David Edwards, Oklahoma State; Div. II—Tom Brannon, Columbus Col.; Div. III—Jim Quinn, Oswego.

NAIA—Greg Brown, Point Loma.

Junior College—Jim Stuart, Alexander City, N.C.

Women

U.S. Open—Hollis Stacy.

U.S. Amateur—Cathy Sherk.

Ladies PGA—Nancy Lopez.

Leading Money Winner—Nancy Lopez.

LPGA Player of Year—Nancy Lopez.

USGA Senior—Alice Dye.

USGA Junior—Lori Castillo, Honolulu.

USGA Public Links—Kelly Fulks, Phoenix.

AIAW—Deborah Petrizzi, Texas.

Junior College—Pam Elders, Miami-Dade N.

Curtis Cup—United States.

GYMNASTICS

World Championship

MEN

All-Round—Nikolai Andrianov, USSR.

Floor—Kurt Thomas, Terre Haute, Ind.

Rings—Nikolai Andrianov.

Vault—Junichi Shimizu, Japan.

Horse—Zolton Magyar, Hungary.

High Bar—Shigeru Kasamatsu, Japan.

Parallel Bars—Eizo Kenmotsu, Japan.

WOMEN

All-Round—Elena Mukhina, USSR.

Floor Exercise—Elena Mukhina.

Balance Beam—Nadia Comaneci, Rumania.

Bars—Marcia Frederick, Springfield, Mass.

Vault—Nelli Kim, USSR.

Team—Soviet Union.

All-Round

AAU Elite—Phil Cahoy, Nebraska G.C.

AAU Women's Elite—Karen Lemond, Reno.

NCAA Div. I—Bart Conner, Oklahoma.

AIAW—Ann Carr, Penn State.

NCAA Div. II—Casey Edwards, Wis-Oshkosh.

NAIA—Casey Edwards.

USGF—Men, Kurt Thomas, Indiana State; women, Kathy Johnson, Belcher, La.

HANDBALL

U.S. Handball Assn.

FOUR-WALL

Singles—Fred Lewis, Miami.

Doubles—Stuffy Singer-Marty Decatur, New York.

Masters Singles—Rene Zamorano, Tucson.

Masters Doubles—Pete Tyson-Dick Robertson, Austin, Tex.

HARNESS RACING

U.S.T.A. Awards

Horse of the Year—Abercrombie.

Pacer of the Year—Abercrombie.

Trotter of the Year—Speedy Somolli.

Aged Trotter—Green Speed.

Aged Trotting Mare—Petite Evander.

Aged Pacer—Whata Baron.

Aged Pacing Mare—Mistletoe Shalee.

3-Year-Old Trotting Colt—Speedy Somolli.

3-Year-Old Pacing Colt—Abercrombie.

3-Year-Old Trotting Filly—Rosemary.

3-Year-Old Pacing Filly—Happy Lady.

2-Year-Old Trotting Colt—Legend Hanover.

2-Year-Old Pacing Colt—Sonsam.

2-Year-Old Trotting Filly—Ahhh.

2-Year-Old Pacing Filly—Hazel Hanover.

Leading Race Winners

TROTTING

Hambletonian—Speedy Somolli.

Yonkers Trot—Speedy Somolli.

Kentucky Futurity—Doublemint.

Roosevelt International—Cold Comfort.

PACING

Little Brown Jug—Happy Escort.

Cane—Armbro Tiger.
Messenger—Abercrombie.
Driscoll—Whata Baron.

HOCKEY

National League

Stanley Cup—Montreal Canadiens.
Regular Season—Patrick Division, New York Islanders; Smythe Division, Philadelphia Flyers; Norris Division, Montreal; Adams Division, Boston Bruins.
Leading Scorer—Guy Lafleur, Montreal.
Most Valuable Player—Guy Lafleur. Leading Goalie—Ken Dryden, Montreal.

World Association

Avco Cup—Winnipeg Jets.
Regular Season—Winnipeg.
Most Valuable Player—Marc Tardif, Quebec.
Leading Scorer—Marc Tardif.
Leading Goalie—Al Smith, New England.

Amateur

World—Soviet Union; Class B, Poland.
NCAA—Boston U.
NCAA Div. II—Merrimack.
ECAC—Div. I, Boston College; Div. II, Bowdoin; Div. III, Westfield State.
Western Collegiate—Denver.
Central Collegiate—Bowling Green.
NAIA—Augsburg (Minn.).
Junior College—New York A & T, Canton.

HORSE RACING

Eclipse Award Champions

Horse of Year—Affirmed.
Older Horse—Seattle Slew.
Older Filly or Mare—Late Bloomer.
3-Year-Old Colt—Affirmed.
3-Year-Old Filly—Tempest Queen.
2-Year-Old Colt—Spectacular Bid.
2-Year-Old Filly—Candy Eclair, It's In the Air.
Sprinter—Dr. Patches, J.O. Tobin (tie).
Grass Horse—Mac Diarmida.

Steeplechaser—Cafe Prince.
Owner—Harbor View Farm.
Breeder—Harbor View Farm.
Trainer—Laz Barrera.
Jockey—Darrel McHargue.
Apprentice Jockey—Ron Franklin.

Leading Race Winners

Triple Crown (Kentucky Derby, Preakness, Belmont Stakes)—Affirmed.
Brooklyn—Bold and Nasty.
Champagne—Spectacular Bid.
Coaching Club American Oaks—Lakeville Miss.
Flamingo—Alydar.
Florida Derby—Alydar.
Jockey Club Gold Cup—Exceller.
Marlboro Cup—Seattle Slew.
Metropolitan—Cox's Ridge.
Suburban—Upper Nile.
Travers—Alydar.
Turf Classic—Waya.
Wood Memorial—Believe It.
Woodward—Seattle Slew.
Epsom Derby—Lucius.

HORSE SHOWS

World Champions

Three-Day—Bruce Davidson, Unionville, Pa.; team, Canada.
Dressage—J. Michael Plumb, Chesapeake, Md.; team, United States.
Jumping—Gerd Wilfang, West Germany; team, Britain.

American Horse Shows Assn.

Hunter Seat—Hugh Mutch, Weston, Conn.
Stock Seat—Lisa Graybehl, Moraga, Calif.

ICE SKATING

Figure

WORLD CHAMPIONS

Men—Charles Tichner, Littleton, Colo.
Women—Anett Poetzsch, East Germany.
Pairs—Irina Rodnina-A. Zaitsev, Soviet.
Dance—Natalia Linichuk-Gennady Karponosov, Soviet Union.

Men—Charles Tichner, Littleton, Colo.
Women—Linda Fratianne, Northridge, Calif.
Pairs—Tai Babalonia, Mission Hills, Calif.-Randy Gardner, Los Angeles.
Dance—Stacey Smith-John Summers, Wilmington, Del.

Speed

WORLD CHAMPIONS

Men—Eric Heiden, Madison, Wis.
Women—Tatiana Averina, Soviet Union.
Sprint—Eric Heiden.
Women's Sprint—Liubov Sadchikova, Soviet.

U.S. CHAMPIONS

Outdoor—Bill Heinkel, Racine, Wis.
Women's Outdoor—Paula Class, St. Paul-Betsy Davis, Montclair, N.J.
Indoor—Stan Wisniewski, Sierra Madre, Calif.
Women's Indoor—Debbie Carlstrom, Des Plaines, Ill.

JUDO

National AAU Champions

132 lbs.—Keith Nakasone, San Jose, Calif.
143 lbs.—James Martin, Sacramento, Calif.
156 lbs.—Stevens Seck, Los Angeles.
172 lbs.—Tefmoc Jonston-Ono, New York.
189 lbs.—Clyde Worthen, New Milford, N.J.
209 lbs.—Irwin Cohen, Wheeling, Ill.
Over 209 lbs.—John Saylor, Columbus, Ohio.
Open—Michinori Ishibashi, Fort Worth.

KARATE

Kata—Domingo Llanos, Haverstraw, N.Y.
Women's—Ellen Beol, Barrington, N.H.
Kumite—Tokey Hill, Chillicothe, Ohio.
Women's—Rosine Hatem, Methuen, Mass.

LACROSSE

NCAA Division I—Johns Hopkins.
NCAA Division II—Roanoke.
Women—Penn State.

LUGE

World Champions

Men—Paul Hildgartner, Italy.
Women—Vera Sosulya, Soviet Union.

AAU National Champions

Men—Jim Moriarty, St. Paul.
Women—Debra Sanders, Monroe, N.H.
Doubles—John Skelton-Jim Moriarty.

North American Champions

Men—Larry Arbuthnot, Canada.
Women—Debbie Genovese, Rockford, Ill.

MODERN PENTATHLON

United States Champions

Men—Greg Losey, Napa, Calif.
Women—Gina Swift, Marble Falls, Tex.

MOTORBOATING

Unlimited Hydroplane

Season Series—Atlas Van Lines, driven by Bill Muncey, La Mesa, Calif.
Gold Cup—Atlas Van Lines.

Offshore Racing

U.S.—Betty Cook, Newport Beach, Calif.
South American—Billy Martin, Clark, N.J.

PADDLE TENNIS

U.S. Singles—Brian Lee, Santa Monica, Calif.
Doubles—Sol Hauptman-Jeff Fleitman, Brooklyn.
U.S. Women's Doubles—Annabel Rogan-Lena Perez, Los Angeles.

PARACHUTING

World Overall Champions

Men—Nicolai Usmayev, Soviet Union.
Women—Cheryl Stearns, Fort Bragg, N.C.

United States Champions

MEN

Overall—Bob Van Duren, Fort Bragg, N.C.
Accuracy—Phil Munden, Fort Bragg, N.C.
Style—Dennis Wise, Fort Bragg, N.C.

WOMEN

Overall—Cheryl Stearns, Fort Bragg, N.C.
Accuracy and Style—Cheryl Stearns.

PLATFORM TENNIS

United States Champions

Men—Herb FitzGibbon, New York-Hank Irvine, Millburn, N.J.
Women—Louise Gengler, Locust Valley, L.I.-Hilary Hilton, New York.

POLO

United States Champions

Open—Abercrombie & Kent, Oak Brook, Ill.
Gold Cup (18-22 Goals)—Abercrombie & Kent.
College (indoor)—California-Davis.

QUARTER-HORSE RACING

All-American Futurity—Lark.
All-American Derby—Medley Glass.

RACQUETBALL

United States Champions

Open—Jeff Bowman, San Diego.
Women's Open—Alicia Moore, Soquel, Calif.

Pro—Marty Hogan, St. Louis.
Women's Pro—Shannon Wright, San Diego.

RACQUETS

United States Champions

Open—William Surtees, New York.
Amateur—William Surtees.

ROLLER SKATING

World Champions

Men—Thomas Neider, West Germany.
Women—Natalie Dunn, Bakersfield, Calif.
Dance—Fleurette Arnesault, Cambridge, Mass.-Dan Little, Farmingdale, L.I.
Pairs—Robbie Coleman-Pat Jones, Memphis.

United States Champions

Singles—Paul Jones, Flint, Mich.
Women's Singles—Robbie Coleman, Memphis.
International Singles—Lex Kane, Toledo.
Women's International Singles—Natalie Dunn, Bakersfield, Calif.
Pairs—Paul Price-Tina Kneisley, Michigan.
Dance—John LaBriola-Debra Coyne, Calif.

ROWING

World Champions

MEN

Single Sculls—Peter Kolbe, West Germany.
Doubles Sculls—Alf, Frank Hansen, Norway.
Pairs—Bernd, Jorg Landvoight, E. Germany.
Pairs With Coxswain—East Germany.
Fours—Soviet Union.
Fours With Coxswain—East Germany.
Eights—East Germany.

WOMEN

Single Sculls—Christine Hahn, East Germany.
Double Sculls—Bulgaria.
Quadruple Sculls—Bulgaria.
Pairs—East Germany.
Fours—East Germany.
Eights—Soviet Union.

United States Champions

Men—Jim Dietz, New York AC.
Women—Lisa Hansen, Long Beach, Calif.
IRA—Syracuse.

SHOOTING

National Skeet Shooting Assn. Champions

Men—Walter Badorek, Klamath Falls, Ore.
Women—Ila Hill, Birmingham, Mich.

Grand American Trapshooting Champions

Men—Reg Jachimowski, Antioch, Ill.
Women—Freida Summer, Washington, Ind.

SKIING

World Cup Champions

Men—Ingemar Stenmark, Sweden.
Women—Hanni Wenzel, Liechtenstein.

World Alpine Champions

MEN

Downhill—Josef Walcher, Austria.
Slalom—Ingemar Stenmark, Sweden.
Giant Slalom—Ingemar Stenmark.
Combined – Andreas Wenzel, Liechtenstein.

WOMEN

Downhill—Annemarie Proell Moser, Austria.
Slalom—Lea Soelkner, Austria.
Giant Slalom—Maria Epple, West Germany.
Combined—Annamarie Proell Moser.

World Nordic Champions

MEN

Jumping

70 Meter—Matthias Buse, East Germany.

90 Meter—Tapio Raisanen, Finland.

Men's Cross-Country

15 km.—Josef Lusczek, Poland.
30 km.—Sergei Saveliev, Soviet Union.
50 km.—Ake Lundback, Sweden.
Combined—Rauno Miettinen, Finland.

Women's Cross-Country

5 km.—Helena Takalo, Finland.
10 km.—Zinaida Amosova, Soviet Union.

Collegiate

NCAA—Colorado.
AIAW—Utah.

SOCCER

World Cup

Argentina.

United States Champions

North American League—Cosmos.
Challenge Cup—Maccabi, Los Angeles.
Amateur—Denver Kickers.
Junior—Imo's Pizza, St. Louis.

Collegiate Champions

NCAA Division I—San Francisco.
NCAA Division II—Seattle Pacific.
NCAA Division III—Lock Haven (Pa.) State.
NAIA—Quincy.

SOFTBALL

World Champions

Women—United States.

United States Champions

MEN

Fast Pitch—Billard Barbell, Reading, Pa.
Slow Pitch—Campbell's Carpets, Calif.

WOMEN

Fast Pitch—Raybestos Brakettes, Stratford.
Slow Pitch—Bob Hoffman's Dots, Miami.
Collegiate—UCLA.

SQUASH RACQUETS

U.S. Squash Racquets Assn.

Singles—Mike Desaulniers, Montreal.
Singles 35's—Roger Alcaly, New York.
Singles 40's—George Morfitt, Vancouver.
Singles 50's—Henri Salaun, Boston.
Collegiate—Mike Desaulniers, Harvard.

U.S. Women's Squash Racquets Assn.

Singles—Gretchen Spruance, Wilmington, Del.
Senior Singles—Goldie Edwards, Pittsburgh.
Collegiate—Gail Ramsay, Penn State.

SQUASH TENNIS

U.S. Open—Pedro Bacallao, New York.

SWIMMING

World Champions

MEN

100-M. Free—David McCagg, Ft. Myers Beach.
200 Free—Bill Forrester, Auburn, Ala.
400 Free—Vladimir Salnikov, Soviet Union.
1,500 Free—Vladimir Salnikov.
100 Back—Robert Jackson, San Jose, Calif.
200 Back—Jesse Vassallo, Mission Viejo, Calif.
100 Breast—Walter Kusch, W. Germany.
200 Breast—Nick Nevid, Elm Grove, Wis.
100 Butterfly—Joe Bottom, San Ramon, Calif.
200 Butterfly—Mike Bruner, Stockton, Calif.
200 Ind. Medley—Graham Smith, Vanc., B.C.
400 Ind. Medley—Jesse Vassallo.
400 Freestyle Relay—United States.
400 Medley Relay—United States.
800 Freestyle Relay—United States.

WOMEN

100-M. Free—Barbara Krause, E. Germany.

200 Free—Cynthia Woodhead, Riverside, Calif.
400 Free—Tracey Wickham, Australia.
800 Free—Tracey Wickham.
100 Back—Linda Jezek, Los Altos, Calif.
200 Back—Linda Jezek.
100 Breast—Julia Bogdanova, Soviet Union.
200 Breast—Lina Kachshite, Soviet Union.
100 Butterfly—Joan Pennington, Nashville.
200 Butterfly—Tracy Caulkins, Nashville.
200 Individual Medley—Tracy Caulkins.
400 Individual Medley—Tracy Caulkins.
400 Free Relay—United States.
400 Medley Relay—United States.

MEN'S DIVING

Springboard—Phil Boggs, Ann Arbor, Mich.
Platform—Greg Louganis, El Cajon, Calif.

WOMEN'S DIVING

Springboard—Irina Kalinina, Soviet Union.
Platform—Irina Kalinina.

U.S. Men's Long Course

100-M. Free—David McCagg, Ft. Myers Beach.
200 Free—Bill Forrester, Auburn, Ala.
400 Free—Jeff Float, Sacramento, Calif.
1,500—Ed Ryder, Mission Viejo, Calif.
100 Back—Robert Jackson, San Jose, Calif.
200 Back—Jesse Vassallo, Mission Viejo, Calif.
100 Breast—Steve Lundquist, Jonesboro, Ga.
200 Breast—Jeff Freeman, Los Gatos, Calif.
100 Butterfly—Joe Bottom, San Remos, Calif.
200 Butterfly—Steve Gregg, Hunt. Beach.
200 Ind. Medley—Jesse Vassallo.
400 Ind. Medley—Jesse Vassallo.
400 Freestyle Relay—Florida Aquatics.
400 Medley Relay—Cummins Engine SC, Bloomington, Ind.
800 Freestyle Relay—Florida Aquatics.

U.S. Women's Long Course

100-M. Freestyle—Cynthia Woodhead.
200 Free—Cynthia Woodhead.
400 Free—Kim Linehan, Sarasota, Fla.
800 Free—Kim Linehan.
100 Back—Linda Jezek, Los Altos, Calif.
200 Back—Linda Jezek.
100 Breast—Tracy Caulkins.
200 Breast—Tracy Caulkins.
100 Butterfly—Joan Pennington, Madison, Tenn.
200 Butterfly—Tracy Caulkins.
200 Individual Medley—Tracy Caulkins.
400 Individual Medley—Tracy Caulkins.
400 Medley Relay—Nashville AC.
800 Freestyle Relay—Mission Viejo.

SYNCHRONIZED SWIMMING

World Champions

Solo—Helen Vandenburg, Calgary, Alberta.
Duet—Vandenburg-Michele Calkins, Canada.
Team—United States.

TABLE TENNIS

United States Champions

Singles—Norio Takashima, Japan.
Women's Singles—Hong Ja Park, S. Korea.

TEAM HANDBALL

United States Champions

Open—Air Force Academy.
Women's Open—Slippery Rock (Pa.).
Collegiate—Air Force Academy.

TENNIS

International Team Champions

Davis Cup (Men)—United States.
Federation Cup (Women)—United States.
Wightman Cup (Women)—Britain.

United States Open Champions

Singles—Jimmy Connors, Belleville, Ill.
Women—Chris Evert, Fort Lauderdale, Fla.
Doubles—Bob Lutz, San Clemente, Calif.-Stan Smith, Sea Pines, S.C.
Women's Doubles—Billie Jean King, New York-Martina Navratilova, Dallas.
Mixed Doubles—Betty Stove, Netherlands-Frew McMillan, South Africa.

Other United States Champions

Clay Court—Jimmy Connors.
Women's Clay Court—Dana Gilbert, Piedmont, Calif.
Junior—David Dowlen, Houston.
Jr. Women—Tracy Austin, Rolling Hills, Cal.
NCAA—Div. I, John McEnroe, Stanford; Div. II, Juan Farrow, So. Ill.-Edwardsville; Div. III, Chris Bussert, Kalamazoo.
NAIA—Francois Synaeghel, Belhaven.
AIAW—Jeanne DuVall, UCLA.
Junior College—Eddie Gayon, Sumter.
J.C. Women—Sandy Collins, Odessa.

Foreign Opens

Wimbledon Men—Bjorn Borg, Sweden.
Wimbledon Women—Martina Navratilova.
Australian Men—Vitas Gerulaitis, New York.
Australian Women—Evonne Goolagong, Aus.
French Men—Bjorn Borg.
French Women—Virginia Ruzici, Rumania.

Professional Champions

Leading Money Winner—Bjorn Borg.
Women—Martina Navratilova.
Team—Los Angeles Strings.

TRACK AND FIELD

U.S. Men's Outdoor Champions

100 M.—Clancy Edwards, Los Angeles.
200—Clancy Edwards.
400—Maxie Parks, Athletes in Action.
800—James Robinson, Inner City AC.

1,500—Steve Scott, Irvine, Calif.
3,000 Chase—Henry Marsh, Athletics West.
5,000—Marty Liquori, Florida AA.
10,000—Craig Virgin, Athletics West.
5-km. Walk—Joseph Berendt, U.S. Army.
20-km. Walk—Todd Scully, Long Branch, N.J.
110 Hurdles—Renaldo Nehemiah, N.J. Flyers.
400 Hurdles—James Walker, Ath. in Action.
High Jump—Dwight Stones, Huntington Beach, Calif.
Pole Vault—Dan Ripley, Pacific Coast Club.
Long Jump—Arnie Robinson, San Diego.
Triple Jump—James Butts, Ath. in Action.
Shot-Put—Al Feuerbach, Athletics West.
Discus—Mac Wilkins, Athletics West.
Javelin—Bill Schmidt, Knoxville, Tenn.
Hammer—Boris Djerassi, New York AC.

U.S. Women's Outdoor Champions

100 M.—Leleith Hodges, Texas Woman's U.
200—Evelyn Ashford, Los Angeles.
400—Lorna Forde, Brooklyn.
800—Ruth Caldwell, Citrus College.
1,500—Jan Merrill, Waterford, Conn.
3,000—Jan Merrill.
10,000—Ellison Goodall, Duke.
5,000 Walk—Susan Liers, Island TC.
10,000 Walk—Sue Brodock, S.C. Road Runners.
100 Hurdles—Deby LaPlante, Englewood, N.J.
400 Hurdles—Debbie Esser, Iowa State.
440-Yd. Relay—Texas Woman's U.
Mile Relay—Prairie View A & M.
2-Mile Relay—San Jose Cindergals.
Sprint Medley Relay—Tennessee State.
High Jump—Louise Ritter, Texas Woman's U.
Long Jump—Jodi Anderson, Los Angeles.
Shot-Put—Maren Seidler, San Jose, Calif.
Discus—Lynne Winbigler, Oregon TC.
Javelin—Sherry Calvert, Lakewood, Calif.

NCAA Outdoor Champions
DIVISION I

100 M.—Clancy Edwards, So. California.

100—Clancy Edwards.
400—Billy Mullins, So. California.
800—Peter Lemashon, Texas-El Paso.
1,500—Steve Scott, California-Irvine.
3,000-Steeplechase—Henry Rono, Wash. State.
5,000—Rudy Chapa, Oregon.
10,000—Mike Musyoki, Texas-El Paso.
110 Hurdles—Greg Foster, UCLA.
400 Hurdles—James Walker, Auburn.
400 Relay—Southern California.
Mile Relay—Villanova.
High Jump—Franklin Jacobs, F. Dickinson.
Pole Vault—Mike Tully, UCLA.
Long Jump—James Lofton, Stanford.
Triple Jump—Ron Livers, San Jose State.
Shot-Put—Dave Laut, UCLA.
Discus—Kenth Gardenkrans, Brigham Young.
Javelin—Bob Roggy, Southern Illinois.
Hammer—Scott Neilson, Washington.
Team—Southern California.

Other Champions

AAU Decathlon—Mike Hill, Boulder, Colo.
AAU Women's Pentathlon—Modupe Oshikoya, Nigeria.
Boston Marathon—Bill Rodgers, Melrose, Mass.; women, Gayle Barron, Atlanta.
New York City Marathon—Bill Rodgers; women, Grete Waitz, Norway.

VOLLEYBALL

World Champions

Men—Soviet Union.
Women—Cuba.

United States Champions

USVA Open—Chuck's Steak House, L.A.
USVA Women's Open—Nick's Fish Market, Beverly Hills, Calif.
AAU—Chuck's Steak House.
AAU Women—Nick's Fish Market.
NCAA—Pepperdine.
NAIA—George Williams.
AIAW—Utah State.
Pro—Santa Barbara Spikers.

WATER POLO

World—Italy.
AAU Outdoor—Concord, Calif.
AAU Women's Outdoor—Commerce, Calif.
AAU Indoor—New York AC.
AAU Women's Indoor—Long Beach, Calif.
NCAA—Stanford.

WEIGHTLIFTING

World Champions

114 lb.—Kanybok Osmanaliev, Soviet Union.
123—Daniel Nunez, Cuba.
132—Nikolai Kolesnikov, Soviet Union.
148—Yanko Russev, Bulgaria.
165—Roberto Urrutia, Cuba.
181—Yuri Vardanyan, Soviet Union.
198—Rolf Milser, West Germany.
220—David Rigert, Soviet Union.
242—Yuri Zaitsev, Soviet Union.
Super Heavy—Jurgen Heuser, E. Germany.

National AAU Champions

114 lb.—Ronald Crawley, Washington.
123—Stewart Thornburgh, Charleston, Ill.
132—Don Warner, York, Pa.
148—Don Abrahamson, Maitland, Fla.
165—David Jones, Eastman, Ga.
181—Mike Karchut, Chicago.
198—Lee James, York, Pa.
220—Kurt Setterberg, Warren, Ohio.
242—Mark Cameron, York, Pa.
Super Heavy—Tom Stock, Belleville, N.J.

WRESTLING

World Freestyle Champions

105 lbs.—Serge Kornilaev, Soviet Union.
114—Anatol Belogazo, Soviet Union.
125—Tomiyama Hideari, Japan.
132—Vladimir Junine, Soviet Union.
149—Pavel Pinguin, Soviet Union.
163—Leroy Kemp, Madison, Wis.
180—Magomedkhan Arazilov, Soviet Union.
198—Une Neipert, East Germany.
220—Harald Buttner, East Germany.
Over 220—Sosian Andiev, Soviet Union.

NCAA Champions

118—Andy Daniels, Ohio U.
126—Mike Land, Iowa State.
134—Ken Mallory, Montclair State.
142—Dan Hicks, Oregon State.
150—Mark Churella, Michigan.
158—Leroy Kemp, Wisconsin.
167—Keith Stearns, Oklahoma.
177—Mark Lieberman, Lehigh.
190—Ron Jeidy, Wisconsin.
Heavy—Jimmy Jackson, Okla. State.
Team—Iowa.

YACHTING

U.S. Yacht Racing Union

Mallory Cup (Men)—Glenn Darden, Fort Worth.
Adams Trophy (Women)—Bonnie Shore, Newport, R.I.
Sears (Junior)—Mark Thompson, Jamestown, Pa.

WHO'S WHO IN BEST SPORTS STORIES—1979

WRITERS IN BEST SPORTS STORIES—1979

PAUL ATTNER (The End of a 10-Year Quest) has been a member of *The Washington Post* staff for nine years, joining the newspaper immediately after graduating with honors from California State University, Fullerton, in 1969. He has written two books, *The Terrapins: A History of Football at the University of Maryland* and *The Fat Lady Sings for the Bullets*, and his articles have appeared in numerous national publications. His *Post* chores have included NBA championships, baseball all-star games, and major football games. This is his first appearance in this sports anthology series.

PETER AXTHELM (Courting the Stars) joined *Newsweek* in 1968 as sports editor and has covered the sports beat extensively. In 1970 he became a general editor of *Newsweek* and he has written about 30 cover stories. Honors include an Eclipse Award from the Thoroughbred Racing Association, Page One Awards from the Newspaper Guild, a National Headliner's award for consistently outstanding columns, and a Shick Award for professional football writing. He has contributed to most of the better magazines, such as *Esquire, Harper's,* and *Sport*. His writing also includes many books on sports, a work on literary criticism, and the definitive book on basketball, *The Inner City*. He was graduated from Yale in 1965 and worked for the *Herald Tribune*, later for *Sports Illustrated*, and then went to *Newsweek*. He has appeared in *Best Sports Stories* frequently.

AMANDA BENNETT (Ladies in Weighting) was born in Cambridge, Mass. She is a graduate of Boonton High School in Boonton, N.J., and is a 1975 graduate of Harvard, where she majored in English. She joined *The Wall Street Journal* in November 1975 as a reporter in the Toronto bureau. In November 1978 she was transferred to the *Journal*'s Detroit bureau, where she now is. This is her first appearance in *Best Sports Stories*.

PHIL BERGER (Spinks) has been a free-lance writer for 12 years. He is a former associate editor of *Sport Magazine* and has been published in *Playboy* (where this story appeared), *Penthouse, New York, Look, TV Guide,* and *Village Voice,* among others. He is the author of many books, including *The New York Knickerbocker's Championship Season* and *The Last Laugh: The World of Stand-up Comics*. This is his first appearance in *Best Sports Stories*.

HAL BODLEY (The Incredible Graig Nettles) has been sports editor of the *News-Journal* papers in Wilmington, Del., since 1971. He joined the papers in 1960 and has served as sports writer, night sports editor, and assistant sports editor. He presently is Philadelphia chapter chairman of the Baseball Writers Association of America and a member of its national board of directors and national treasurer for the Associated Press Sports Editors Association. Since February 1978 his column "Once Over Lightly" has been syndicated by the Gannett News Service. He has been in *Best Sports Stories* three previous times.

JIM BOLUS (Diary of a Triple Crown Winner), a sports writer for the *Louisville Courier-Journal* and *Louisville Times*, has won four national writing awards. With colleague Billy Reed he won the National Headliners Award and the Sigma Delta Chi Distinguished Service Award. Bolus is also a two-time winner of the annual turf-writing contest sponsored by the Ocala-Marion County Chamber of Commerce and the Florida Chamber of Commerce. In 1970 he won the Florida Breeder's Association award for his feature story about Florida breeds that have run in the Kentucky Derby. This makes his first appearance in *Best Sports Stories*. It appeared in *The Florida Horse Magazine*.

PETER BONVENTRE (Mighty Like a Rose) has been a general editor of *Newsweek* since 1976. He has covered such variegated events as the Olympic tragedy in Munich, Bobby Fischer's chess playoff in Iceland, and the Ali-Frazier fight in Manila. He joined *Newsweek* in 1969 and two years later became the associate editor of his department. His fine work has been selected three times for *Best Sports Stories*. Previously, he worked as an assistant sports editor at the *New York Times*. He is a graduate of the University of Pennsylvania, where he majored in journalism.

THOMAS BOSWELL, winner of the 1978 news-coverage award with "The Right-Field Sign Says 'Reg-gie, Reg-gie, Reg-gie,' " is the only roving national baseball writer on any paper, covering the game for *The Washington Post* from coast to coast and from sandlot to World Series. At other times, the Amherst College graduate (1969) writes features and columns on almost every sport. He has appeared in *Best Sports Stories* for the last three years and has won national Associated Press awards in both news and column categories.

SI BURICK's story, The Least Plausible Dateline, was actually inspired by Si Burick's own career with the *Dayton Daily News*, of which he is sports editor. He has appeared in *Best Sports Stories* many times.

COLIN CAMPBELL (The Sharkers) was born in Boston and was graduated from the University of California at Berkeley, studying there during its time of trouble. He was associate editor of *Psychology Today* for three and a half years and at present is the managing editor of *Human Nature*. Campbell is now writing a book on Kuwait. The sea has always fascinated him. His great-grandfather was a commercial fisherman out of Provincetown, Mass., who scrimped and saved for years to buy a boat and was lost at sea on his first voyage out. His article, "The Sharkers," is from the magazine *Sports Afield*. This is his first appearance in *Best Sports Stories*.

PAUL CHANDLER ("Thriller on the River") is an inmate of Bossier Parish, Louisiana State Penitentiary, serving a life sentence for murder. An outstanding athlete prior to his imprisonment, Chandler played basketball for Baptist Christian College of Shreveport and Louisiana Tech University. He is a sports writer for the prison magazine, *The Angolite*, located in Angola, La. This is his first article in *Best Sports Stories*.

BUD COLLINS (Ali's Last Hurrah) is one of America's best-known tennis writers and television broadcasters and one of the most respected reporters of all sports. He is a columnist for *The Boston Globe*, has received warm critical acclaim for his books on Rod Laver and Evonne Goolagong, and has been a regular contributor to *World Tennis* magazine. He has made many appearances in *Best Sports Stories*.

BETTY CUNIBERTI (Her Hands Were Meant for Golf) was born and raised in San Francisco, graduated from Southern California, worked as a sports reporter for the *San Bernardino Sun-Telegram* for three years and for the *San Francisco Chronicle* for one year, and has been at *The Washington Post* since July 1977. Her story on the NCAA championship basketball game between Indiana and Michigan appeared in *Best Sports Stories—1976*. She is currently a member of the All-America Team Selection Committee of the United States Basketball Writers Association.

JOE GERGEN (Raggedy Andy's Closing Charge) who is making his sixth appearance in *Best Sports Stories*, is a sports columnist at *Newsday* after serving the Long Island paper as baseball and pro football writer for seven years. He is a graduate of Boston College and did five years of postgraduate work at United Press International in New York. He thought he never would live to see a repeat of the excitement attendant to the Dodgers-Giants playoff game of 1951 when he was nine years old. And then there was last season, Fenway Park, Yankees against the Red Sox in the most marvelous of baseball confrontations. He thought it was wonderful to feel nine years old again.

RANDY HARVEY (The Stakes Race) was born, raised, and educated in Texas, but moved in July of 1976 to Chicago to work in the sports department of the *Sun-Times*. He had previously served in the sports departments of the *Tyler Morning Telegraph*, *Austin American-Statesman*, and *Dallas Times Herald*. He is 27 years old and has a bachelor's degree in journalism from the University of Texas in Austin. This is his first appearance in *Best Sports Stories*.

DAVID HIRSHEY (The World's Finest Soccer Player Finds Peace in America) has worked at the New York *Daily News* for the past seven years as a sports reporter, columnist, and feature writer for the Sunday magazine, where he has profiled everyone from Woody Allen to Candy Hernandez, a 260-pound stickball player. His stories have appeared in *Sports Illustrated, Sport* (where this story appeared), and the *New York Times* and he is co-author of two books, including *The Education of an American Soccer Player* selected by *The Boston Globe* as "the best sports book of 1978." This is his fourth appearance in *Best Sports Stories*.

STEVE JACOBSON (The Yankees Can Finally Say It) has been covering a wide variety of sports at *Newsday* since 1960. That was the year Mazeroski's home run beat the Yankees in the World Series. He now feels he has gone the full circle with the Yankees from the years of the arrogant dynasty to the new era of wealth and arrogance. This year he joined the transatlantic set by covering Wimbledon for the first time and finding that the work tables in the press room were claimed in perpetuity by reporters who had been there since 1952. He is the author of *The Best Thing Money Could Buy*, the story of the 1977 Yankees. This is his third appearance in *Best Sports Stories*.

DAVE KINDRED (On a Cold Day 15 Years Ago) is sports columnist for *The Washington Post*, where this story appeared. He was sports editor of the *Louisville Times* and then *The Louisville Courier-Journal* before joining the *Post* staff. He won a National Headliner Award in 1970 for general interest columns and five times was Kentucky Sports Writer of the Year. He is the author of two books on basketball in Kentucky. A native of Atlanta, Ill., he is a graduate of Illinois Wesleyan. This is his fifth appearance in *Best Sports Stories*.

DAVE KLEIN (The Boxer Unseats the Puncher) has captured first prize in this sports anthology twice before. The first winner was his humorous piece on the Billie Jean King-Bobbie Riggs match in 1974; then in 1978 he took top honors with his elegiac piece on the premature death of Wells Twombley. In addition he is the author of 15 books, including *The New York Giants: Yesterday, Today and Tomorrow*. He contributes to most of the national periodicals. He attended the University of Oklahoma and Fairleigh Dickinson University in New Jersey and is a columnist and editor for the *Newark Star-Ledger*. He has merited many inclusions in *Best Sports Stories*.

TONY KORNHEISER (Reggie Jackson's Lonely World) is a reporter for the *New York Times*. In 1977 he won the Associated Press Sports Editors award for the best feature story of the year. His work has appeared in such magazines as *The New York Times Sunday Magazine*, *New Times*, *Rolling Stone*, *New York Magazine*, and *Sport*. He and his wife, Karril, live in Long Beach, N.Y., where they spend their free time thinking of schemes to get rich quick. This is his seventh straight appearance in *Best Sports Stories*.

JOE LAPOINTE (Love Him or Hate Him) has been a sports writer with the *Detroit Free Press*, where this story appeared, since June of 1978. Prior to that he worked for three years for the *Chicago Sun-Times*. He was a winner of the 1976 UPI award for sports writing in Illinois, and in 1974 won the Barney Kilgore award of Sigma Delta Chi Society of Professional Journalists for college journalism. Twenty-eight years old, he is a graduate of Wayne State University in Detroit. This is his first appearance in *Best Sports Stories*.

JILL LIEBER (Noah Jackson Was Not Inhibited) was graduated from Stanford University in March 1978 with a B.A. in communications and a minor in violin performance. She is twenty-two and began writing sports for the *Milwaukee Sentinel* in April 1978. While at Stanford, she was the first woman sports editor for the *Stanford Daily* and also worked at the *San Francisco Chronicle*. She was an intern at the *Milwaukee Journal* in the summer of 1977. She is now a sports columnist and major feature writer for the *Sentinel* and has covered all sports, including small college football, the greater Milwaukee Open golf tourney, and NCAA cross country meet, and has written sidebars on pro football, basketball, and baseball. This is her first appearance in *Best Sports Stories*.

BARRY LORGE (Martina Is Proud) joined the staff of *The Washington Post* in 1977 after five years as a free-lancer. He started writing sports for the Worcester (Mass.) *Telegram & Gazette* while an undergraduate at Harvard, from which he was graduated cum laude in 1970. His specialty is tennis, which he has covered on five continents. He is a contributing editor of *World Tennis* magazine and president of the U.S. Tennis Writers Association. He writes features on all sports for the *Post*, his assignments ranging from the Boston Marathon to the British Open and from the Sugar Bowl to Wimbledon. He has appeared in *Best Sports Stories* on numerous occasions.

JACK MANN (The Puck Stops Here) is a mostly racing columnist of *The Washington Star* who broke into *Best Sports Stories* with the 1958 Giants-Colt game, the occasion of the first NFL sudden-death overtime. His newspaper background is fairly extensive: he has been sports editor of *Newsday* (Long Island), racing writer for the *New York Herald Tribune*, staff writer for *Sports Illustrated*, and sports columnist for *Washington Daily News*. Then he left the sports desks and free-lanced for seven years. In 1978 he returned to *The Washington Star* to become its racing columnist. He has merited seven appearances in *Best Sports Stories*. This story ran in *The Washington Post* (sic) *Sunday Magazine*.

JEFF MEYERS ("Swivel Those Hips!") has been sports columnist of the *St. Louis Post-Dispatch* (where this story appeared) since 1972, and this is his second appearance in *Best Sports Stories*. He grew up in New York and went to Miami of Ohio, where, he says, he was the only male on the campus who did not want to become a football coach. He covered the St. Louis Football Cardinals from 1970 through 1974 and won the Sigma Delta Chi Award in 1977 for outstanding reporting. His wife is a well-known St. Louis actress and he is proud of the fact that he once beat Marty Hogan in racquet ball.

LEIGH MONTVILLE (They'd Win in Any Game) is a sports columnist for *The Boston Globe* and has been for five years. Prior to that he covered the misfortunes, he says, of the New England Patriots football team. He once worked for the *New Haven Journal-Courier*, where everyone, again quoting, asked him if he had gone to Yale. He never went to Yale or even came close, he avers. This is his first appearance in *Best Sports Stories*.

JIM MURRAY (The Irish Haberdasher's Dream) writes a daily syndicated column that is distributed by the *Los Angeles Times*. His perceptive and humorous thrusts have caused him to be named America's Sportswriter of the year for eight consecutive years by the National Association of Sportscasters and Sportswriters. He was born in Hartford, Conn., graduated from Trinity College, and started his writing career with the *New Haven* (Conn.) *Register*. In 1944 he went to work for the *Los Angeles Examiner* and in 1953 was one of the founders of *Sports Illustrated*. In 1961 he returned to the *Los Angeles Times* as its premier sports columnist. He won the National Headliners Award in 1965 and is also the author of two books, both anthologies of his own writing. This marks his third appearance in *Best Sports Stories*.

MICHAEL NELSON (Behind the Scenes at Baltimore's Big Bowl) is a contributing editor of *The Washington Monthly* and a professor of political science at Vanderbilt University. This, his first story in the *Best Sports Stories* annuals, appeared in the *Baltimore Magazine*. He has also written extensively for *The Washington Post Sunday Magazine, Virginia Quarterly Review, Newsweek,* and *The Nation,* among others. This is his first article about baseball, but it probably will not be his last: He is planning a piece on the Nashville Sounds for *National Magazine*.

TIM NOONAN (Big-Time College Tennis: The Inside Story) was graduated with honors from Stanford University, where he earned four letters in tennis and also played on the 1974 championship team of that school. He later became a tennis pro and won the title in the New Zealand Hardcourt Open in 1973. He was ranked fifty-first out of the top 200 players in the United States. In 1977 he left the full-time tour to devote more time to free-lancing, which includes magazine and newspaper work plus collaboration on books devoted to tennis. He is a New Englander and this marks his debut in *Best Sports Stories*. This story appeared in *Tennis Magazine*.

MURRAY OLDERMAN (The Importance of Being Howard) has appeared frequently in *Best Sports Stories*. He is a contributing editor for Newspaper Enterprise Association, and his columns and cartoons are syndicated in 700 newspapers. He has degrees from Missouri, Stanford, and Northwestern and is the author of seven books on sports. He is a recipient of the Dick McCann Award for outstanding writing in professional football, and he has done 12 murals for the Pro Football Hall of Fame.

EDWIN POPE (The 500 Seems to Last Forever) is a most prolific and provocative writer from the East Coast. He is with the *Miami Herald,* and in 1957 became the editor of its fine sports page. He has acquired a large reading audience with columns and coverage of sports events in the Southeast. He was formerly with the *Atlanta Journal Constitution* and the United Press International. He is the author of four books: *Football's Greatest Coaches, Baseball's Greatest Managers, Encyclopedia of Greyhound Racing,* and *Ted Williams: The Golden Years*. He has merited many appearances in *Best Sports Stories*.

SHIRLEY POVICH (Gene Tunney: A Man in Search of Oblivion) won the *Best Sports Stories* news-coverage award in 1957 and again in 1977. He attended Georgetown University, chose journalism as his profession, and at the age of 20 became sports editor of *The Washington Post,* perhaps the youngest sports editor of any metropolitan daily. This story appeared in the *Post*. His other prizes for fine writing have included the National Headliners Award and the Grantland Rice Award. A book, *All These Mornings,* was published by Prentice-Hall. He has appeared in *Best Sports Stories* on many occasions.

BILLY REED (Jack's the Ripper), a graduate of Transylvania College, began his journalism career with the *Lexington Herald* in 1959. There he served as assistant sports editor for both the *Herald* and the *Leader*. In 1966 he joined the sports staff of *The Louisville Courier-Journal* and *The Louisville Times*. He later spent four years as a writer for *Sports Illustrated* before returning to these newspapers in 1972. In 1974 he became a general columnist for *The Courier-Journal*, and appears four times a week, and then in 1977 he was named sports editor of the paper. In 1973, Reed, with reporter Jim Bolus, won national journalism awards from Sigma Delta Chi and the Headliner Club for a series of investigative stories on thoroughbred horse racing. In 1978 he was named Sportswriter of the Year by the National Association of Sports-writers and Sportscasters. This marks his second appearance in this sports anthology.

JON ROE (Man on a Crusade), 39, attended the University of Minnesota and was graduated from St. Cloud (Minn.) State University. He is a staff writer for the *Minneapolis Tribune* and has covered University of Minnesota sports since 1968. He has also covered the Masters tournament for two years. This is his first appearance in *Best Sports Stories*.

JACK SAMSON (Salmon of the Tundra) is the editor of *Field & Stream*, where this story appeared. He was a staff writer and foreign correspondent for United Press Interna-tional and The Associated Press, covering the Korean War and the Far East. He wrote an outdoor column for The Associated Press for nine years and his stories have appeared in all the major outdoor magazines. He won a Nieman Fellowship at Harvard University in 1960 and is the author of numerous books on subjects ranging from trap and skeet shooting to big game fishing. This is his third appearance in *Best Sports Stories*.

LOEL SCHRADER ("How Are You Going to Do in the Big Game?") has been a sports writer and columnist for 37 years, all in the Ridder (now Knight-Ridder) chain. At the *Long Beach* (Calif.) *Independent Press-Telegram*, where this story appeared, he has covered college football, professional baseball, college basketball, and college hockey. He is a bachelor of philosophy with a major in journalism, and also a J.D. from Western State University and its College of Law. This is his second appearance in *Best Sports Stories*.

JOHN SCHULIAN (And Still Champion) took his sports column to *The Chicago Sun-Times* after the *Chicago Daily News* went under in March 1978. Moving was hardly a new experience for him. He had spent the previous decade going to school at the University of Utah and Northwestern and newspapering in Salt Lake City, Baltimore, and Washington. In his travels, he has earned a Phi Beta Kappa key, assorted Associated Press writing awards, and two nominations for the Pulitzer Prize.

NICK SEITZ (The Enigma of Johnny Miller) probes into golfers' lives and his findings are interesting and helpful. He majored at the University of Oklahoma in philosophy, a discipline interested in "cause and effect sequences," which probably led to his concern with the techniques of the game. His major contribution to the game, besides being the editor of *Golf Magazine*, is his analysis of the bewildered golf pro who suddenly finds he can hack it no longer and resigns himself to the fact that he must now become a country club pro. It is then "Dr. Seitz" steps in for consultation and restores athletes like Miller, Beard, and Weismiller to the tube. His articles have appeared in *Best Sports Stories* 11 times.

BLACKIE SHERROD (Grant Teaff and His Amazing Worm Act), executive sports editor of the *Dallas Times Herald*, has been included in *Best Sports Stories* more than a dozen times. He has garnered just about every important sports-writing prize in the country. To name a few: the National Headliners Award, seven citations as the outstanding sports writer by newspaper, radio, and TV colleagues. As a master of ceremonies and banquet speaker he has made a reputation almost equal to his reputation for writing. He also has his own radio and TV programs.

RANDY SMITH (Toughness) is sports editor of the *Journal Inquirer* of Manchester, Conn. He assumed that post in June 1972 after working as an assistant for a year and a half. He has won awards in the last four UPI New England writing contests, one first, two seconds, and one third. He served as president of the Connecticut Sports Writers Alliance in 1975–76. This is his first appearance in *Best Sports Stories*.

JOE SOUCHERAY (The Real Boston Marathon) is a featured sports columnist on the *Minneapolis Tribune*. He is twenty-nine and was graduated from the College of St. Thomas in St. Paul, Minn. He joined the *Tribune* in 1973, and has covered a variety of sporting events—from a cross-country snowmobile race to Muhammad Ali's various title defenses. He has appeared on numerous occasions in *Best Sports Stories*.

HARRY STEIN (Sports Writing's Poet Laureate). In addition to *Sport Magazine* where the story on Red Smith originally appeared, Stein writes regularly for *The New York Times Sunday Magazine* and *Esquire*, which he serves as a contributing editor. He was co-founder and editor of the *Paris Metro*, an English-language city magazine for Paris, and also worked as an editor at *New Times*. He is currently writing his second book, a novel dealing with turn-of-the-century sports. This is his first appearance in this sports anthology.

D. L. STEWART (Why Horses Don't Bet on People) is a syndicated columnist of *The Dayton Journal Herald* and he says he is that paper's answer to the *Gong Show*. After 10 years as a sports writer, he took over the *Journal Herald*'s "Off the Beat" column in 1975 and plans to keep writing it until the editors wise up. Other editors, however, thought highly enough of these columns to reprint them in a book entitled *The Man in the Blue Flannel Pajamas*. He has appeared in two previous *Best Sports Stories* anthologies, those of 1974 and 1978.

PHIL TAYLOR (Moon, Stars, and Roses) is a veteran newspaper man in the great Northwestern section of the United States. He has covered every major sport as a member of the sports staffs of the *Tacoma News-Tribune, Seattle Star, Seattle Times,* and *Seattle Post-Intelligencer*, which he joined in 1951 and where he serves as the editor of the golf section and chief football scribe. He also writes a column. He also served as a sports editor earlier with the *Stars and Stripes*, when he first broke in four decades ago. He has garnered many honors, including two firsts in the National Golf Writers competition. This is his fourth appearance in *Best Sports Stories*.

VIC ZIEGEL (The Craziness of the Long-Distance Runner) is a former *New York Post* sports writer and co-author with Lewis Grossberger of *The Non-Runners Book*. He lives in the metropolitan area and is mostly a free-lance writer. His work has appeared in *Sport, The Soho Weekly News, Look, The Village Voice,* and *New York Magazine*. This is his first appearance in *Best Sports Stories*.

PHOTOGRAPHERS IN BEST
SPORTS STORIES—1979

MICHAEL A. ANDERSEN (Three Down and Goal to Go) is making his tenth appearance in *Best Sports Stories*. He has won more than 150 other awards in his distinguished career with *The Boston Herald American*, where he has worked since 1960. Twice he has been named New England Photographer of the Year. He has also garnered a first place in *Best Sports Stories—1977*, in the feature section.

JOHN E. BIEVER (Three in One) is one of the fine young photographers employed by *The Milwaukee Journal*. He was graduated from the University of Wisconsin with a B.A. in business administration. He has won a number of prizes both state and local, including a first in this sports anthology.

JOSEPH CANNATA, Jr. (Twin Tackles) has been a staff photographer for five years with *The Hartford (Conn.) Courant*. This is his second appearance in *Best Sports Stories*. He is the editor of NPPA's News Photographers Association. His wife and he reside in New Britain, Conn.

J. DON COOK (A Novel Student), the feature photo winner in his *Best Sports Stories* debut, is a photographer for the *Daily Oklahoman and City Times*. Cook has already had a number of one-man shows, has been published by the nation's better magazines, and has done a number of book jackets. His many honors include Oklahoma Press Association citations as Photographer of the Year from 1970 to 1977 and the award for the best AP Press Photo for 1977. His work has been the subject of a 30-minute documentary, which was purchased by Kodak for an educational series.

ROBERT DICKERSON (The Santa Marie Lands) came to *The Cincinnati Post* about two years ago from the University of Missouri, where he earned a degree in photojournalism. Previous to that he had taught grade school in Cincinnati for nine years. He also has a degree in education from Miami University of Ohio. He is a native of Cincinnati.

DAN DRY (The Agony and the Ecstasy) has been working for *The Courier-Journal*, and *The Louisville Times* for three years. As a senior at Ohio University, he was awarded the Hearst Photojournalism Prize. He has also merited several awards in their yearly contests. His hobbies are running and listening to fine music. This is his first appearance in *Best Sports Stories*.

MELISSA FARLOW (Uneasy Rider's Nightmare) has been with *The Courier-Journal* and *Louisville Times* for five years since her graduation from Indiana University, where she obtained a B.A. in journalism. Her first experiences with the camera were on the school paper and the yearbook. Her hometown is Paoli, Ind., and she is a member of NPPA. She already has won several awards.

CARMINE FILLORAMO, Jr. (Net Break-in Nets Nothing) has been with the *Manchester (Conn.) Journal Inquirer* for four years. He is a graduate of Temple University with a B.A. in general communications and television production. He began working for the *Journal* as a student and as a summer intern served as a member of the staff. He is a self-taught photographer and is making his first appearance in *Best Sports Stories*.

JOHN P. FOSTER (Lifting a Horse?) is our erudite associate professor and moonlights as a stringer for the *Seattle Times*. He has taught photojournalism for 11 years at Central State University. Most of his shots are exceptional rodeo pictures that capture the excitement and drama of rugged cowboys extricating themselves from precarious situations. He has merited a number of appearances in *Best Sports Stories*.

JOHN FREEMAN (The Loneliness of a Long-Distance Shooter) was graduated in 1975 from the University of Missouri School of Journalism. At present he is the editor of *Darkslide*, Region 7 publication of the NPPA. He is now working at *The Wichita Eagle and Beacon*, where he has served for three years. This is his first appearance in this sports anthology.

CLETUS ''PETE'' HOHN (Ring Around the Rosie) has been a photojournalist for over 25 years. A graduate of the University of Minnesota in 1953, he has been with the *Minneapolis Tribune* since 1955. He has won many state, regional, and national awards, including the Action Photo Award that *Best Sports Stories* bestows.

JEFF JACOBSEN (Unwelcome Homecoming) was born in Lincoln, Neb., and moved to Topeka in 1954. He began his work in photography as a lab boy for the *Topeka Capital-Journal* in 1969, shooting sports assignments on weekends with the director of photography, Rich Clarkson. Jacobsen became a full-time staff photographer in 1973. This is his freshman year in *Best Sports Stories*.

GEORGE KOCHANIEC, Jr. (At the End of His Rope), was born in Mt. Clemens, Mich., and moved to Florida in 1971. With the help of his dad, also a professional photographer, he shot his first picture at the age of seven. He majored in photo-journalism at the University of Florida and after graduation he went to work for the *Tallahassee Democrat*. He appears in *Best Sports Stories* for the first time.

GEORGE T. KRUSE (Not a Prayer of a Chance) has been a free-lancer in San Francisco since 1971. He graduated from the University of Iowa with a degree in history in 1964, and went over to the *Newton Daily News* in Iowa as a photojournalist. From there he started working for the *Cedar Rapids Gazette* in the same state. In 1969 he moved West. He specializes in political antics and tennis. This is his first appearance in *Best Sports Stories*.

RICHARD LEE (Reporters See New Type of Press Game) is currently a staff member of the *New York Post*. Previously he had been a member of the *Long Island Press*. He started his career as a free-lancer and was a regular contributor to the *New York Times* and to many of the nation's better magazines. He also had his work displayed on national television. This marks his debut with *Best Sports Stories*.

JOHN LONG (A Shot in the Dark) has been a staff photojournalist with the *Hartford (Conn.) Courant* for seven years. Previously he taught high school English. This marks his fourth appearance in *Best Sports Stories*. At present he is serving his second term as president of the Connecticut News Photographers Association. He lives in a suburb of Hartford with his wife and three daughters.

NANCY MANGIAFICO (Meditation) has been employed at the *Atlanta Journal-Constitution* for almost three years. She attended Georgia State University, where she received her degree in journalism. She has been interested in photography for the past 10 years and has won several Georgia regional awards. In 1978 she placed second in the *Atlanta* Press Photographers contest. This is her first appearance in this anthology.

FRED MATTHES (His Breath Also Comes in Short Pants) is one of the fine veteran photographers on the West Coast. He has been with the *San Jose Mercury-News* as a staff photographer for 17 years. He is a member of the following organizations: National Press Photographers, California Press Photographers, and the Bay Area Press Photographers. His talents have merited many distinguished awards, including a number of firsts with the California Newspapers Publishers Association; Pro Football Hall of Fame with a permanent display of his work; first place award in 1978 from the California Press Photographers Association; and best photo award for 1979 from the San Francisco Press Club. He has appeared in this anthology yearly since 1973.

JOHN H. McIVOR (Coming in for a Landing and Six Points) was born in Cedar Rapids, Iowa, and after high school joined the Marine Corps. Returning home, he took a night position in the darkroom of *The Cedar Rapids Gazette* and got training there in photojournalism. After a short stint in the Korean conflict he returned to the *Gazette*. Here he developed ability at using cameras from the 4 × 5 Graphic to the present 35mm format, retouching, diagramming football sequences, and now processing E6 color transparencies for four-color separations. His photos have won many state and national awards. This is his first time in *Best Sports Stories*.

WILLIAM MEYER (Don't Shoot! Count One, Two, Three, Go!) is a staff photographer for the Journal Company, publisher of *The Milwaukee Journal* and *Sentinel*. He was graduated from the University of Wisconsin and has merited five inclusions of his pictures in this series.

WALTER NEAL (Model for a Gargoyle?) has been with the *Chicago Tribune* for 12 years, shooting news and features. This year he's doing sports, but does not mind. However, talent will assert itself, and Mr. Neal has come away with a beauty of a sports picture that will leave his viewers slightly stunned.

JAMES ROARK (Watch Out NBA, Here They Come!) is now the Director of Photography and in charge of the Photo Department of the *Los Angeles Herald Examiner*. He was a staff member there for many years and his talented work has been part of this sports anthology for the last five years. He has captured many prizes, including the awards of the Los Angeles Press Photographers Association, the Los Angeles Press Club, the California Photographers Association, and the California State Fair.

BARNEY SELLERS (''The Coach'') is a journalism graduate of Arkansas State University. He has been a staff photographer with *The Commercial Appeal*, Memphis, Tenn., since July 1952. His unusual work has garnered for this veteran many regional and local honors. He is at home in all types of assignments for his newspaper. Sellers spends his off-time camping and photographing barns and rural scenes in color, for which he has received national recognition.

NORMAN SYLVIA (This Cheer Is for Themselves) is a newcomer to the photo section of *Best Sports Stories*. He is a staff photographer at the *Providence Journal-Bulletin* and his assignment for the past two years has been to shoot pix for the *Bulletin's* Massachusetts edition. This suburban section is made up at two offices, one in Fall River and the other in Attleboro. This is Sylvia's first appearance in *Best Sports Stories*.

THE YEAR'S BEST SPORTS PHOTOS

UNEASY RIDER'S NIGHTMARE

by Melissa Farlow, *The Courier-Journal* (Louisville, Ky.) captures an American rider who has lost control of his horse while taking a jump at the Three-Day Championships, a world equestrian meet at Horse Park in Lexington, Ky. Miraculously neither the horse nor the rider was injured. Copyright, ©, 1978, *The Courier-Journal* (Louisville, Ky.).

A NOVEL STUDENT

by J. Don Cook, *Daily Oklahoman*. It's difficult to imagine a 7-foot 3 basketball player not practicing dunk shots in the gym rather than reading a book in the library. However he hated being tall and disliked the pressures being put upon him; or perhaps he even had a date with his dream girl. That could be she down near his feet. Copyright, ©, 1978, *Daily Oklahoman*.

"THE COACH"

by Barney Sellers, *The Memphis Commercial Appeal*. Coach Bill Garnett is getting his team up mentally for the game, and himself too. It's the County High (Paris, Tenn.) team against a city team. But Coach Garnett's team lost. Copyright, ©, 1978, *The Memphis Commercial Appeal*.

MODEL FOR A GARGOYLE?

by Walter Neal, *Chicago Tribune*. This grotesque position of high school catcher Anthony Antobelli was created by his superhuman attempt to grab a pop-up fly that fell just beyond his frantic reach. The incredible angle of his feet, the crablike position of his arms, added to the turbulence of the scene and his openmouthed dismay, make for an unusual geometric pattern that would do justice to a Gothic church gargoyle. Copyright, ©, 1978, *Chicago Tribune*.

THE AGONY AND THE ECSTASY

by Dan Dry, *The Courier-Journal*, has caught the ultimate essence of any important contest. The winners are elated, the losers miserable. The picture's action occurred seconds after a final touchdown decided the winner. Copyright, ©, 1978, *The Courier-Journal* (Louisville, Ky.).

NOT A PRAYER
OF A CHANCE

by **George T. Kruse,**
City Sports Monthly, San
Francisco. British tennis star Virginia Wade
pleads with a linesman
to change his call in a
crucial match with
Evonne Goolagong.
Wade lost the plea and
the match. Copyright, ©,
1978, George T. Kruse.

COMING IN FOR A LANDING AND SIX POINTS

by John McIvor, *The Cedar Rapids Gazette*. Wide receiver Brad Reid of Iowa used a high-dive finale to finish a 10-yard sprint for Iowa's third and final score against Northwestern in their opening game. Iowa won, 20–3. Copyright, ©, 1978, *The Cedar Rapids Gazette*.

UNWELCOME HOME COMING

by Jeff Jacobsen, *Topeka Sunday Capital-Journal*. Yankee catcher Thurman Munson rudely prevents Kansas player Willie Wilson from crossing the plate. The play cost Munson five stitches when he lost his mask. Yanks won the game. Copyright, ©, 1978, *Topeka Sunday Capital-Journal*.

REPORTERS SEE NEW TYPE OF PRESS GAME

by Richard Lee, *New York Post.* New York Knick basketball player Glen Gondrezick lands upside down at the press table after chasing a loose ball in a game with the Atlanta Hawks in Madison Square Garden in New York City. Copyright, ©, 1978, *New York Post Corp.*

TWIN TACKLES

by Joseph Cannata, Jr., *The Hartford Courant*. Newington's fullback (47) tries to get away from a tackle by airborne Glastonbury defender John Preli while teammate Tony DePaolis puts a flying block on Glastonbury's Keith Congdon (30). Newington won the game, 34–7, and the Central Valley (Conn.) Conference. Copyright, ©, 1978, *The Hartford Courant Co.*

NET BREAK-IN NETS NOTHING

by Carmine Fillorami, Jr., *Journal Inquirer*. Warren Miller of the New England Whalers smashes into goaltender John Garret as Edmonton's Dave Semenko looks for the puck. It actually hit Miller's skate and went into the net, but referee Ron Harris ruled "no goal" since Semenko was in the crease. Whalers won 5–3. Copyright, © 1978, *Journal Publishing Co., Inc.* (Manchester, Conn.)

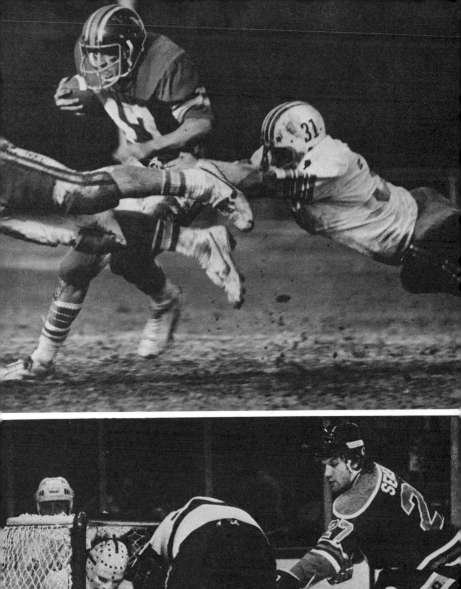

AT THE END OF HIS ROPE

by George Kochaniec, Jr., *Tallahassee Democrat*. Terry Town's first attempt at ski jumping ended on a backward note as the ski rope slipped from his grasp. The shot was taken at the Seminole Reservation in Tallahassee, Fla. Copyright, ©, 1978, *Tallahassee Democrat*.

LIFTING A HORSE?

by John P. Foster, *Seattle Times*. Actually it does appear that Jerry Bruhn of Puyallup, Wash., is lifting his saddle bronc for applause to an appreciative audience at the Ellensburg (Wash.) Rodeo. In reality Bruhn failed to ride the required eight seconds to record a judge's score. As he left the saddle the illusion appeared of a very strong man able to lift a horse on his left shoulder. Copyright, ©, 1978, John P. Foster.

THIS CHEER IS FOR THEMSELVES

by Norman Sylvia, *Providence Journal-Bulletin*. The governor of Massachusetts with his Road Safety Program and the New England Patriots devised a program where all the state's high school cheerleaders would make up a safety cheer. After a series of eliminations, these cheerleaders from Fall River Durfee High won. The photographer was on hand when the news broke. Copyright, ©, 1978, *Providence Journal Company*.

A SHOT IN THE DARK

by John Long, *The Hartford Courant*. Pro golfer Douglas Pines chips onto the seventeenth green from under a pine tree. He did find the ball, swung blindly, and wound up in second place in the Hartford Open Tournament in Connecticut. Copyright, ©, 1978, *The Hartford Courant Co.*

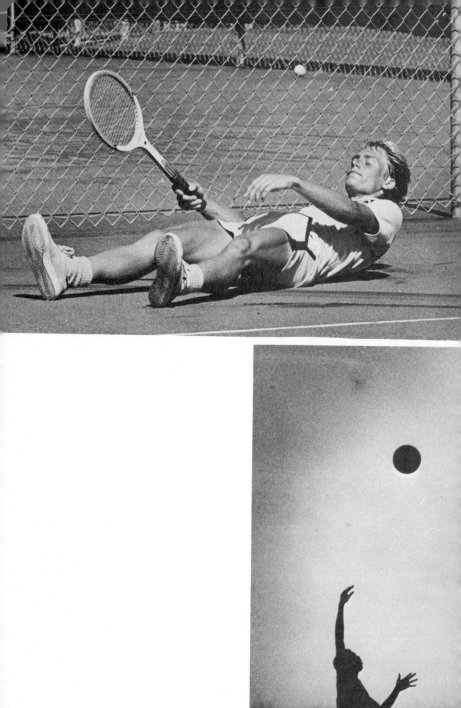

MEDITATION

by Nancy Mangiafico, *Atlanta Journal Constitution*. It really does look like Brad Langevad has chosen the wrong moment for silent meditation. He lost the point and the match at the Georgia State Open Championship tournament at South Fulton Tennis Center. Copyright, ©, 1978, *Atlanta Newspapers*.

THE LONELINESS OF THE LONG-DISTANCE SHOOTER

by John Freeman, *The Wichita Eagle* and *The Wichita Beacon*. The ball mirrored against the stark background, the graceful movement of the shooter, the silhouette of the basket and its stanchions combine to give this picture a sense of isolation and remoteness that the photographer's eye was sensitive enough to catch. Copyright, ©, 1978, *Wichita Eagle & Beacon Pub. Co.*, John Freeman.

THE SANTA MARIE LANDS

by Robert Dickerson, *The Cincinnati Post*. Linda Rumsie takes a punch in
the face from Santa Marie during the U.S. Karate Assocation National
Championships. Marie won this match and later placed in the finals.

RING AROUND THE ROSIE

by Cletus "Pete" Hohn, *Minneapolis Tribune.* Minnesota Kicks' Ace
Ntsoelengo beat Allen Wiley to the ball and drilled the Kicks' second goal
past Houston's John Stremlau, Radmir Stefonovic, and diving goalie Keith
Van Eron. Copyright, ©, 1978, *Minneapolis Tribune.*

WATCH OUT, NBA, HERE THEY COME!

by James Roark, *Los Angeles Herald Examiner.* The ebullient outburst of this group of pretty basketeers from Maryland University was evoked when they won the NCAA women's basketball semifinals. Now the men who constitute the National Basketball Association have something else to worry about. Copyright, ©, 1978, *Los Angeles Herald Examiner.*

HIS BREATH ALSO COMES IN SHORT PANTS

by Fred Matthes, *San Jose Mercury-News*. At the Holiday Bowl game in San Jose, Calif., the two top semipro teams got together. All things did not go as planned, as in the National Football League. For instance, San Jose Tiger defensive end Bob Alexander, 6-feet-7, 333-pounder, finds it very difficult to get pants that fit him properly. Still, the Tigers defeated the Pierce County Bengals, 43–13. Copyright, ©, 1978, *San Jose Mercury-News*.

THREE IN ONE

by John Biever, *The Milwaukee Journal*. The photographer caught this triple exposure of Ron Guidry, who is generally conceded to be the best pitcher in baseball today. Biever must have believed that Guidry is three pitchers in one. Copyright, ©, 1978, *The Milwaukee Journal*.

THREE DOWN AND GOAL TO GO

by Mike Andersen, *The Boston Herald American*. Peter McNab of the Boston Bruins leaves three black-shirted Chicago Black Hawks and even two of his own teammates in his wake as he tries to score during the early round game of the Stanley Cup playoffs. Copyright, ©, 1978, *The Boston Herald American*.

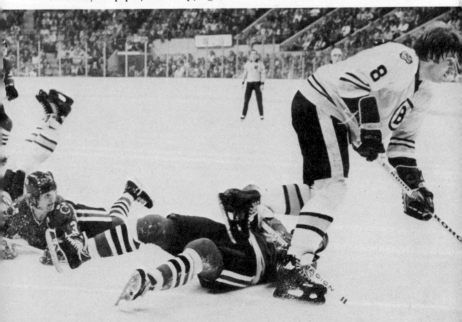

DON'T SHOOT! PLEASE COUNT ONE, TWO, THREE, GO!

by William Meyer, *The Milwaukee Journal.* Sheri Zore, an eight-year-old from Milwaukee, clapped her hands over her ears as the starter's gun went off to begin the 50-yard dash at the Wisconsin Special Olympic Track and Field Meet. More than 500 retarded people participated in the event.

ABOUT THE EDITORS

IRVING T. MARSH and EDWARD EHRE are both well known in the world of sports. This is the thirty-fifth annual anthology in the *Best Sport Stories* series, which they have edited jointly since its inception.

Formerly Assistant Sports Editor of the *New York Herald Tribune*, IRVING T. MARSH served until recently as an executive of the Eastern College Athletic Conference. He was honored with the Joe Lapchick Award of the Metropolitan Basketball Writers Association for his outstanding contributions to college basketball. He is a native of Brooklyn.

Besides editing *Best Sports Stories*, EDWARD EHRE served more than 30 years on the faculty of Port Washington, N.Y., High School, a post from which he is now retired. Born in Rochester, N.Y., he studied at the University of Rochester and did graduate work at Columbia. Both editors spend winters in Florida and summers at Canaan, Conn.